SHARPSHOOTER

SHARPSHOOTER

LESLIE MURRAY

SAPPHIRE BOOKS

SALINAS, CALIFORNIA

Editor - Kaycee Hawn
Book Design - LJ Reynolds
Cover Design - Leslie Murray

Sapphire Books
Salinas, CA 93912
www.sapphirebooks.com

Printed in the United States of America
First Edition – October 2014

This and other Sapphire Books titles can be found at
www.sapphirebooks.com

Dedication

To My Spouse, Cindy

For always making me laugh.
For your never-ending support and encouragement.
For being my rock, and my rock star.
The next 25 years will be even better than the last.

To My Mother, Marion

Who taught me to see the humor in life's little hiccups by turning everyday anecdotes into hilarious adventures. No one can tell a story like you. Oh yeah, and for all the extra hugs.

Acknowledgements

I would to thank the following women for their help and support in making this book happen. To my beta reader, Erin Saluta, whose assistance and persistent encouragement was invaluable and very much appreciated. To my publisher, Chris Svendsen, for saying the words I longed to hear, "I want to publish this book." To my editor, Kaycee Hawn, for your patience and guidance. It was a pleasure working with you.

Prologue

1987

Today, she would push herself higher than she ever had before. The young girl of eight squinted her emerald colored eyes in determination as she backed the swing up and held herself on the tips of her toes, preparing to release. She was absolutely certain that one day, she would swing with such force, her momentum would take her up, over, and completely around the metal pole that held the swinging chains.

She turned her freckled face into the early fall breeze and took note of her surroundings for the record books. *Guinness* would want to know every detail when they called.

Jenny MacKenzie was in Chinquapin Park a couple blocks from where she lived. The leaves on the big oak trees were just beginning to turn and the grass surrounding her had long lost the bright green hue of spring, well on its way to the dried brown of fall. To her right, her babysitter and best friend, Seven Michelis, pushed her little brother Philip in a diaper-style swing seat.

"Higher Sev, higher!" Philip squealed with glee, as Seven pushed him as hard as she felt was safe for the five-year-old. Jenny certainly understood the need to swing higher, but she was convinced, due to past actions, that her little brother had a death wish.

She lowered herself back down to a still position, deciding to delay launch for a little longer as she looked over at her friend. Although Seven was a much older girl of fifteen, they hung around each other often, even when babysitting wasn't a factor. Jenny wasn't exactly sure why she felt compelled to hang around Seven all the time, but when she got a crooked smile and a flash of those electric blue eyes meant just for her, it made her so very happy. Seven made her feel like an equal. She liked that.

Seven tucked her vibrant ebony hair behind her ears with both hands and smiled at Jenny as Philip happily twisted in his swing. "What's up, Pumpkin Head?" The older girl asked the young redhead. Even with a mouthful of new braces, Seven still had a captivating smile. Jenny hoped she never had to get braces, but it wasn't looking good.

"What are you doing later, Sev? You wanna play Nintendo or something?"

"Can't today, P.H." Seven replied with the abbreviated version of her nickname. "I'm going to the mall with a girl from school and then we're going to see *Full Metal Jacket*. My friend's brother works at the theater and will sneak us in the fire exit door for a few bucks."

"I thoughta' somethin' I wanted to ask you last night," Jenny said.

"Yeah?"

"I was wondering how you got your nickname. I guess I just always called you that 'cause everybody else did."

"What nickname?"

"Seven."

The older girl laughed. "That's not a nickname, Pumpkin Head. That's my real name, birth certificate 'n' all."

"I just thought it must be a nickname since it's different."

"Nah. My dad named me. He said every good thing that ever happened to him, happened on a day with seven in the number."

"Oh."

"He and my mom met on the seventeenth day of the month, got married on a seven, his birthday fell on a seven. Mom found she was pregnant on a twenty-seventh. When I was born on January seventeenth, he said that was it, a sign of some kind. He would have named me that even if I had turned out to be a boy. Sometimes he calls me his Lucky Number."

Seven gave Philip another push. "So what will you do today since I won't be around to entertain you?"

"I don't know," Jenny said dejectedly. "Maybe I'll make up another story to tell you. You like my stories, don't you?"

"You know I do. I think you're very creative."

Jenny backed herself up and prepared for liftoff. She let loose, kicking her legs forward then pulling herself back to build momentum.

"You want me to give you a push?" Seven asked.

"Nah. Gotta do it myself if I want to get into *Guinness Book of World Records*." The young girl pumped her legs, pushing herself higher and higher. She grinned maniacally, enjoying the split second of free-fall before the chain jerked back into a straight line.

"What are you getting at the mall?" Jenny asked

as she whooshed by her tall friend on a skyward trajectory. Her long strawberry blonde hair flew wildly in the wind.

"Nothing really. We usually just hang around the food court with other kids from school. There's a killer leather jacket in this little boutique I like to try on whenever I'm there. It looks just like the one Joe Strummer from the Clash wears. I'll never afford it, but it sure is fun to wear for a couple of minutes."

Jenny enjoyed the feel of flying and the desire to jump out of the seat when it reached its apex was overwhelming. Finally she let go, catching Seven by surprise. "Wheeeee." Thump. Jenny hit the ground and rolled laughing onto the browning grass.

"Jen, are you crazy? You could have broken and ankle or something. God, you must have flown eight feet in the air." Seven was astounded. She laughed at her small friend.

"Ha! It was fun. I was scared to do it at first, but then I just let go."

"Yeah, Jenny!" Philip squealed, laughing.

"You are the most fearless kid I have ever seen. You're going to give your parents fits when you get older."

"I'm givin' 'em fits now. That's fun too."

"Come on. Your mom's probably home by now. We should head back."

As the trio walked through their neighborhood, Jenny noticed several cars parked in Seven's driveway and on the street around her home. "What's with all the cars at your house, Sev? Your mom having a party or something?"

"Not that I know of," Seven said, then sucked in a lungful of air. "Oh my god! Maybe my dad got his leave early!" She exclaimed happily. "Come on, you guys. Come on, let's go!" She ran toward home with her charges in tow.

≈≈≈≈≈

After dropping Jenny and Philip off, Seven ran full tilt into her house but the mood in the room slammed her excitement to a screeching halt. The first thing she noticed as she scanned the conservatively furnished living room was her Aunt Margaret crying quietly on the loveseat. Three somber people she didn't recognize stood near; one very serious looking man to Margaret's right was wearing a tightly pressed Marine uniform. Her gaze darted around the room, searching for her mother to no avail, when she heard a voice in the kitchen. It was her mother's voice. She walked slowly over the rust colored carpet toward the brightly lit room with a deep sense of foreboding building in her gut. She felt like throwing up. Everything seemed to move in slow motion. Stopping at the kitchen entrance, she stood for a moment and watched her mother sobbing uncontrollably onto the shoulder of her Uncle Nick, her knees barely able to keep her standing.

Seven knew in her heart what she was witnessing. She debated for an instant whether she should announce herself, or just run back out the door before anybody could tell her for sure what was happening. Maybe if she didn't hear it, it wouldn't be true.

Her father was killed in action. She didn't need to be told. It was the only thing on earth that could possibly explain her mother's hysterical behavior. She felt like throwing up again. *I have to take care of mom. Dad would want me to take care of her. I have to suck it up. Oh God, please don't make it be true. Get a hold of yourself.* A cold veil dropped over her mind, a protective shroud meant to keep her from feeling. It was a strange sensation. A nothingness. Seven stood up straight, threw her shoulders back, and entered the kitchen with a stoic expression on her face.

"Mom."

"Oh god, Seven," Catherine cried and lurched from Uncle Nick's arms toward her daughter, embracing her in a crushing hug.

"What's going on, mom?"

"Oh baby, I'm so sorry. I'm so sorry," Catherine wailed. "It's dad, Sev. He didn't make it out. He... he...didn't. He..." She stuttered and sobbed through copious tears.

Seven locked her shaking arms tightly around her mother and glanced over to her uncle's stoic but tear streaked face. He walked over and embraced both mother and daughter. "What happened, Uncle Nick?" She asked, looking into his red, puffy eyes.

Nick Michelis was, like her father, an officer in the Marine Corps. Though they chose different career paths within the service, the brothers remained very close and in constant contact. Nick was a Major and worked at a recruiting base in South Carolina. Seven's father, Dean, chose to remain in the field doing what he loved. "We don't know all the details yet, but it looks like his crew was working on diffusing a hostage situation somewhere near Karaj, outside of Tehran." Nick took a frustrated swipe at his tears and drew in a quivering breath. "The mission was off the charts, so we may never fully understand what went wrong, but suffice it to say, it went bad."

Seven held tightly to her mother while she picked a speck on the popcorn ceiling to focus on. Her chin quivered, her knees grew weak, and a single tear tracked down her young face as she digested this heartbreaking information. *Hold it together, Seven. You've got to hold it together. Oh, Daddy. I'll miss you so much.*

"It's okay, Seven. We're all going to cry for a long time over this. Let it out, sweetheart," Uncle Nick said sadly, as he placed a comforting hand on her shoulder and pulled the hug tighter.

Seven sniffed, straightened her shoulders once again, and said, "I can't, Uncle Nick. I'm afraid if I start, I may never stop."

≈≈≈≈

Three weeks had passed since Seven's life changed forever. She lost a happiness in herself she doubted would ever return. It felt strange to feel numb all the time. School didn't matter. Eating and sleeping didn't matter. She was giving everything she had just trying to keep herself from breaking down, convinced that to be strong would help her mother better cope with their loss. Things that seemed so important before now felt childish and silly. She couldn't believe she ever worried about not getting to the video store before all the good stuff was gone, or hanging out with Rachel, or what tennis shoes went best with what jeans. Whatever.

Her father's funeral was held at Arlington National Cemetery not too far from the Alexandria, Virginia home that Seven and her mother were currently packing up to leave. The local foliage seemed to be fading from green to yellow a little early this year, which could indicate a colder than normal winter to come. She had gone back to school a few days after the funeral, but hadn't bothered to continue with it after her mother decided to relocate to South Carolina. Her Uncle Nicky was stationed at the Marine Corps base in Beaufort, and Catherine thought it would be a good idea to be close to family.

Seven was not looking forward to the move. A kid she met in school once told her that Yankees don't do well in the deep south. *Great,* the young girl thought sarcastically. Seven supposed she would miss this place, though it was hard to think of anything in a positive light at the moment.

She would miss Jenny. The kid seemed to be able to read her ever-evolving moods with the patience of a saint. The younger girl seemed to know when to leave her alone, and when to step in with a funny little story or some mindless entertainment. Seven had no idea how a kid so young could be so mature. *I sure as heck wasn't like that when I was eight.* "My grandma calls me an 'old soul,'" Jenny had said to her once while they were talking. Her grandma was right. That's exactly what it seemed like. *When she looks at me, she seems to know things.*

The best friends were sitting on the swings in Chinquapin Park, the same place they'd been the day Seven found out her father had died. Both of them were quiet, as they knew this would be their last opportunity to 'hang' with each other before Seven moved to South Carolina tomorrow.

It was downright chilly this morning. Jenny was wrapped in a corduroy jacket and her favorite purple scarf, which she was wearing for the first time since last winter. Seven wrapped her arms around the chains and rocked back and forth. Jenny glanced over and noticed Seven's demeanor had changed from silence to sadness. "Are you still sad all the time, Sev?"

She sighed deeply, and slumped deeper into the swing. "I can't laugh anymore. I can't cry. I can't seem to feel anything but numb," Seven said as she ground her heel into loose rock with an angry thump. "I just can't believe he's gone. He can't be gone!" Seven hung her head and stared at the empty space between her feet.

A long silence rested between them as they rocked quietly back and forth. "I wrote you a story," Jenny said after a while. "It's kind of a going away present. I wrote it down and everything, so you could take it with you if you wanna. It's about your dad." Jenny glanced over to see Seven staring at her with a quizzical look on her face. "You wanna hear it?"

Seven answered with a nod and a small smile that didn't reach her eyes. She was able to appreciate the effort her caring friend was making to help her cope.

Jenny proceeded to weave a tale about Seven's father, Dean. In the happy story, Dean had been summoned before God with a request to become the guardian of Puppy Heaven. Her story made Seven laugh at the thought of her father rolling around in green grassy fields covered with puppies, and fighting the good fight against evil cats.

As Jenny read the story, Seven began to feel something opening within herself. For the first time since her father died, she felt that all was not lost.

Seven glanced over at her small friend who was reading aloud with such earnestness, and knew for certain she would somehow survive the tragedy of her father's death. She wondered for the hundredth time how this young girl of eight could possibly make her feel, when nothing and no one else could.

By the time the story ended, Seven was smiling. She got out of the swing and knelt before Jenny, taking her friend into a bone-crushing hug. "Thank you," she said. "That was fantastic." She folded the proffered story and tucked it carefully in the back pocket of her jeans. Then, patting the young girl on the head, she put her arm around her shoulder to lead her back home.

"I gotta get home now. I still have a bit of packing to do and I need to see mom about a couple of things. Walk with me?" They ambled back toward home, each thinking they would miss this friendship.

Not long after, Seven sat alone in her room with the door closed. Boxes and clothes were strewn about in a festival of disarray. Her Clash, Queen, and the Smiths rock posters looked down at her from on high. She read through Jenny's story one more time, running a fingertip over the little drawings of grass and flowers in the margins of the pages. Before she was quite finished, she began to cry. And cry she did. It was sad, but felt good to finally let it out after all this time.

❧❧❧❧

An eight-year-old girl, soon to be nine, sat quietly on the front porch steps of the empty house three doors down from her own. The wind had definitely changed as the smell of summer was no longer in the air and a chill breeze blew the brown leaves off the oak in front of Seven's old house. A loose rain gutter somewhere behind her made a squeaking noise that served to remind that trick-or-treating was right around the corner. She spent a few minutes pondering what she would like to be for Halloween when her melancholy thoughts returned.

Once upon a time, she would sit here and wait for her friend Seven. Today she waited for no one.

Jenny MacKenzie folded her arms across her knees and rested her head upon them, looking down at her beat up navy blue Adidas. She idly reached down and tugged on a loose thread at the hem of her jeans. She was saddened by her friend's loss. She was saddened by the loss of her friend.

Chapter One

2003

A ll right, now listen up!" The Team Leader yelled over the roar of the C-130 plane engine flying a high altitude route over the small South American country of Bolivia. "I want you to check yourselves one more time for any identifiable information. No wallets. No jewelry. No passports. No identifiable U.S. made military gear. Nothing! Do you understand me?"

"Yes, T.L." Both men agreed with proper military enthusiasm, born from years of distinguished service. They began going over their gear one more time. The adrenaline and anticipation of a high altitude stealth drop was thick in the air.

"T.L.?" Marcus Johnson, the senior of two Delegates from Black Flag Company yelled to the Team Leader. "What's the E.T.A. to drop? Do we need to make any adjustments for wind speed?"

"About fifteen minutes, and negative. Drop is according to plan. Conditions are holding. Did you both remember to put fresh batteries in your GPS devices?"

"Affirmative, T.L."

"Get on your oxygen, boys, I don't want any shit goin' down. One hundred percent success, one hundred percent return. You know the motto. We jump together and stay together until we reach 2,500 feet. We need to come down as close to each other as possible in the drop zone. Once you touchdown, make your way immediately to the rally point. Do not play grab ass. Do not pass go. Get there as soon as you can; we have little time to waste and much ground to cover on this mission. Am I comin' in loud and clear, Delegates?"

"Yes, T.L.!"

Team Leader Seven Michelis could feel herself starting to get hoarse from all the yelling. She normally talked as little as possible, but sometimes in her job, this kind of assault on the vocal cords was inevitable. She tightened the lace on her nondescript black combat boot, and checked the buckles and clips on her chute, oxygen bottle, helmet, and gear bag one more time. She lowered her night vision goggles and yelled, "All right, let's move out! Two minutes!"

The adrenaline was really pumping now as the team did last minute mental preparations for their 40,000-foot HALO jump. High Altitude-Low Opening parachute jumps were dangerous, but an optimal method of stealth personnel insertion. No country on earth had the capability to track a human body flying at terminal velocity into their airspace. One thing the Delegates all knew for certain, when freefalling at terminal velocity there was no room for error.

Seven moved into position between her two teammates and grabbed a wrist on either side as they did the same. A slow, wicked smile crept across her serious face. *Yeah, baby. Bring it on!* "Three! Two! One! Go!" She yelled to be heard over din of the massive engines. The team stepped as one, first right foot, then left foot, then a leap into space off the back gate of the C-130. The wind was screaming at a deafening volume as they fell blindly through the damp cloud layer. Outside, Seven was a mask of professionalism; the only thing hinting at her true feeling was a slight crinkle in the corners of her eyes and a small smile she was trying hard to eliminate. She glanced over to her friend Marcus, who never bothered to hide his true feelings.

"Woohoooo this is awesome!" Marcus screamed to the night sky.

Several minutes later the team was making their way separately to the rally point, bunching their chutes up as they walked stealthily toward the cover of forest. The Team Leader was the first to arrive and quickly shucked her packs, helmet, and flight suit, revealing a tall, elegant, athletic figure in full tactical gear. Her long black hair was tied neatly into tight braids and tucked away under a black mesh skullcap.

In civilian clothes, Seven was considered a truly beautiful woman. Her high cheekbones, lovely, expressive eyebrows, brilliant blue eyes, and crooked, devil-may-care smile could break hearts wherever she went. She left a long and distinguished line of disappointed suitors in her wake after eleven years of working mostly with men in the United States Marine Corps.

Seven found it useful at a very young age to bury that part of her as deeply as possible while on duty. She donned a permanently serious expression that projected the focus and determination within. To be taken seriously in her line of work, she personified a sexless, emotionless warrior who was nothing more, or less, than 'one of the guys.' There was no doubt that to be a Scout Sniper was to be living in a man's world.

After some time, the men in Seven's platoon stopped looking at her as an outsider, and began to respect her as a consummate professional. She didn't have the most kills on record, but her patience in stalking and scouting was well known and respected, and her accuracy record of one-hundred percent confirmed kills had gained her notoriety in the 3rd Battalion. She was known to be a fearless stalker, getting closer and better recon than any other surveillance specialist. Extremely patient, level headed, brave, and skilled to the point of being neurotic, she had the perfect combination of characteristics that made an exceptional sniper.

In 2002, Seven left the Marine Corps to join the Black Flag Company, a little known branch of the newly formed Department of Homeland Security. The BFC, as it was known in the Department, was a test division of sorts, trying out a different kind of special operations force. The primary goal of this new company was to weaken the hold that terrorism had over the world.

The BFC was made up of several different teams, each with specialties ranging from humanitarian efforts to black ops. Seven was recruited to lead a black ops team. Their assignments would involve researching individuals around the world deemed of interest to the U.S. government, and determining the level of threat, if any, to national security. Once the level of threat was determined, immediate and decisive action was taken. No red tape. No politicking. Unlimited budget. The level of action ranged in severity depending on what the individual being investigated was doing, inconsequential being at one end of the spectrum, and kill-worthy being at the other.

A nightcrawler recruited Seven, a man by the name of Mitchell Lebo, whose sole function was to prowl the various branches of military, government, and law enforcement agencies looking for appropriate candidates with special skills. Her years of experience, flawless record as a skilled sniper, and high intelligence aptitude caught the nightcrawler's attention right away. The fact that she was from a long serving military family and a Medal of Honor recipient didn't hurt either. But the icing on the cake was that she was a woman. It was so very rare to find a woman who could do what Michelis did with a rifle. Her skill combined with her appearance and smarts could prove to be of immeasurable value to the Chairman's new department. A woman like Michelis could travel in most circles around the world beyond suspicion, which made her an ideal candidate for covert operations.

After much thought, Seven decided to take this career path and see where it led. She was ready to move on. Ready to settle down in one place, and was looking forward to finally letting herself have a real relationship with somebody she didn't have to hide in order to keep her job. This seemed like a good opportunity to continue doing what she was good at, and free herself from the constraints of military service. Plus, it was a new and exciting challenge. Her father would say, undoubtedly quoting either Greek philosophy or classic rock music, "Change in all things is sweet."

A man simply referred to as "the Chairman" headed up the Black Flag Company. It was explained to Seven that members of the BFC were referred to as "Delegates," and the organization consisted of several small four-person teams of specialists. The Chairman created each team to execute a very specific function within the BFC. The team's specialties were extremely diverse but designed to achieve the overall goal of eradicating terrorism. Seven understood that her team would function as black ops, but that only a few held such dark responsibility.

Another unique characteristic of BFC was that each team of four operatives worked completely independent of the other teams. They didn't share office space or interact in any way. Their only common denominator was the Chairman himself. Seven suspected that some of the men and women she occasionally passed in the hall were also BFC, but they never mingled. They did not communicate with each other, and their missions were never the same. To them, it was as if the others didn't even exist. Each team of Delegates had its own missions, responsibilities, and specialties. Each team was designed to function with no external influences to color their judgment and actions.

The Chairman would assign a "mission," which in Seven's case would be the name of an individual he deemed worthy of investigation and possible elimination. Seven's team would investigate their targeted individual, determine the level of threat, decide on the appropriate action, and execute that action completely on their own with no outside interference.

Once the mission was complete, a report would be filed with the Chairman of the findings and final result. Only then did the Chairman know fully how the team had spent their time and resources. This allowed the Chairman and individual teams plausible deniability should something go awry. Only the team executing the mission would voluntarily take full responsibility for their actions. Seven's team was specially trained by the BFC to be judge, jury, and if deemed necessary, executioner.

This was an awesome responsibility. One the entire team took very seriously and with very little glory. The Delegates understood it was up to them, and them alone to make the right decisions to the best of their ability, and follow through with them. The consequences of a bad call were that they, alone, would take the fall and share the guilt. An extreme measure, like assassination, was only carried out if it was determined the target in question was an immediate, direct or indirect threat to the people or foundation of the United States. Anything that could be done to disrupt terrorism or other such threats toward the nation would be done. It was hard and fast and decisive.

Because of the level of this responsibility, each Delegate of the BFC was chosen with the utmost care. It wasn't enough to be good at what they did. They also had to display the intelligence, demeanor, and decision-making skills necessary to carry out the requirements of their positions fairly.

Seven looked around at the local flora and fauna while she waited for her teammates. *Damn it, they should be here by now.* She laid out her gear and rechecked it one more time before separating what would be left behind. Her DSR-1 sniper rifle was disassembled and stored in the large pack she carried along with her other essential equipment. She looked up as she heard rustling in the undergrowth to see both her teammates coming through the woods. "Everyone good?"

"All is well, T.L." Marcus said with a grin.

"Okay, let's get everything we're leaving behind buried and move out. There's a good spot over there for it." Both men worked to conceal the chutes, suits, and other various equipment they needed for the jump, then returned to double check and adjust their gear and weapons before heading out.

Seven knelt and placed a small laminated map on the ground, lighting it with her tiny Maglite. "Okay. We're here." She pointed to the map. "I know we've been over this a hundred times, but listen up anyway. We'll travel fast for about twenty klicks, south-southwest before we have to get serious." She trailed her ungloved fingertip along the map toward their destination. "We'll take a quick break before we get all gussied up and move the last five klicks toward the Reyes Hacienda. We are completely out of contact and on our own until mission is complete and we get to our exit coordinates. We have exactly"—she checked her watch—"forty-five hours and thirty-eight minutes to get this mission accomplished and get there or it's gonna be a bad day at Black Rock."

Delegate Marcus Johnson smiled at the old military term he'd heard Seven use many times before. She had told him years ago that she had picked it up from her father.

"Stay tight to me. It's lightly populated between us and them, but keep your eyes open anyway. We cannot be seen. And remember…one hundred percent success, one hundred percent return." They spoke their team motto with her.

"Marcus, take the lead. Cooper, you're flank. Let's go."

❧.❧.❧.❧.❧

Three members of Seven's team, including herself, were field experienced ex-military professionals. The fourth member, Takeo Takashi, was a self-proclaimed computer geek and all around horn-dog. An honored graduate of the much-lauded UC Berkeley computer science program, he was generally considered one of the most creative and effective hackers and programmers in the Black Flag program. Each Delegate had multiple responsibilities categorized by "field" specialties and "office" specialties. Only Tak, as he preferred to be called, would remain in the office while the others were in the field.

Marcus Johnson was the lead Delegate under Seven. She and Marcus had known each other since they went through boot camp together in 1990. He was a good-hearted man who lacked the height and looks that made a pin-up Marine, but compensated with his larger than life personality. In high school, Marcus was the guy least likely to get a date, but also the most popular kid in his class.

Always conscientious of others, Marcus took a brotherly liking to Seven the first time they met. He was the youngest of seven kids and the only boy in his large and loving family. At five-foot, five-inches, Marcus was the jovial winner of the unofficial "shortest African American male" in the platoon award. He found this a convenient segue to use while introducing himself to Seven, offering jokingly to protect her from other vertically challenged jarheads who would naturally want to take her six foot frame down a peg or two. They hit it off immediately, though over the years Seven often teased him that the real reason he befriended her was to garner protection for himself.

They joined the Scout Sniper program at Camp Lejeune and quickly became the duo to beat. Michelis and Johnson worked so well together, the other teams realized they needed to stop teasing them and put up or shut up, being reminded frequently by their sergeant that the odd couple were kicking all their asses. They were a strange pair, but well suited to each other. Seven was the only woman in the Scout Sniper program, and Marcus...well...he was just Marcus, a sociable man with a never-ending supply of short jokes, juvenile pranks, and homemade cookies constantly sent to him by his mother and six sisters.

Seven was the better shooter of the two, and though Marcus also showed talent, they agreed he would be the Spotter and she the shooter in most circumstances. When the nightcrawler came after Seven, she agreed to make the move if Marcus came too as he was her trusted, career long partner. The decision was easy for the nightcrawler. Marcus shared many of Seven's professional traits, including intelligence and level-headedness, so he was as good a candidate as she. The decision was easy for Marcus also. He had recently met a young woman named Alicia that he thought could be "the one." A lovely, petite young woman, Alicia worried constantly about him being on the front lines somewhere. This was Marcus' golden opportunity to settle down and get out of the line of fire.

Marcus' field jobs for the team were Spotter and Navigator. As Spotter, he would assist Seven in calculating distance, wind speed, and all other factors effecting the accuracy of her shot. In reality though, most of the time together they would just dig in and watch. They would camouflage themselves thoroughly, sometimes for days at a time, then watch and wait for the shot or intelligence they were there for. Whatever the situation called for. In this job, patience definitely paid.

As Navigator, his job was to get them from the drop site to their target, then out in one piece. Marcus' office jobs for the team included a specialty in national and international law and extradition, as well as linguistics in French and various dialects of Arabic. He was invaluable to the team, but more importantly to Seven, he was the friend and operator she could trust without question. She was a perfectionist, and demanded the same from her team. Seven knew from years working closely with Marcus that he was a man who shared her need for tight corners.

Ty Cooper was the newest addition, having only joined while the others were already fully entrenched in their new job and training regimen. Ty was recruited from the Army Special Forces. As a Green Beret, he specialized in weapons and also excelled in engineering when needed. His outstanding service record was a card he played to get himself out of trouble caused by his roguish behavior on more than one occasion. A tall and handsome man with dusty blonde hair and gray eyes, it was the endearing dimple in his right cheek the ladies seemed to find irresistible. In the field, he was a professional machine. But in the real world, he proudly displayed character flaws too numerous to count. A self-proclaimed narcissist, social snob, and sexist pig, he seemed to get a thrill out of stirring up hornet's nests.

His biggest benefit to the team was his social connections. Born into a prominent and old banking family in Manhattan, Ty chose during a particularly rebellious period of his young life to reject acceptance into Yale and join the Army against his father's wishes. His father was so sure of his eminent failure in the regimented military, he began to arrange his release before he had a chance to get fully started. This pissed the young man off so badly, he signed up for special forces and vowed to be the baddest commando known to man, rejecting every maneuver his parents tried to get him out. And he was good at it. It didn't take long for his superiors to recognize his outstanding work ethic and ability to think his way out of most situations. He got an undergraduate degree and an MBA while still in the service. Ty had something to prove to his father, and he was going to do it with a grenade if he had to.

Ty agreed to join the newly formed Department of Homeland Security because he felt it would be an excellent career move. It seemed to him that a brand new government department of this size and caliber would be a huge opportunity to make something of himself outside his father's banking world, especially if he got in on the ground floor. A couple years at BFC and he could shift and groove his way up the ladder. The sky's the limit.

Ty's field job for the BFC was to serve as Flanker for the sniper team. Basically, that meant he would watch their perimeter while they watched for their target. In addition, he specialized in weapons, explosives, and hardware engineering, should the need arise for a little more personal covert surveillance or action. In other words, he could construct and deploy devices that Takeo came up with to get information on their targets if the job was proving difficult through normal hacking channels, or, go in guns blazing.

In the office, the ambitious young man specialized in trade and banking practice, and international communication. His connections opened doors, providing the kind of information not readily available through standard channels. His banking and business knowledge often led to critical information on targets, since financial transactions were usually good indicators of what a person was really up to. Being able to spot trends in how, when, and why money was moving was critical in most cases, especially the one they were currently on in Bolivia. He was also trained to communicate fluently in Russian and Mandarin.

The ironic punch line to Ty's career path was now that he was working for the DHS, his father was acting proud and taking credit for directing his son's wise decisions. Ty loved to complain about the hypocrisy of the upper class, while buttoning the jacket of his Dolce & Gabbana suits.

Seven only had an opportunity to get to know and work with her two new teammates for a few months. They had gotten together off the clock a few evenings to spend time finding common ground. A trip to a nearby pool hall for drinks led to Seven's first opportunity to prove she did indeed have many skills. She collected her winnings, and ordered the next round of drinks on her. At times she wondered if their personalities were suited to each other, but she gained a good deal of respect for their various talents and work ethic.

Her responsibilities within the group as Team Leader included Scout Sniper when in the field, along with being her team's tactical planner. In the office, she handled the coordination of all efforts as well as spoke and translated the languages of Spanish, German, and Greek. All the team members were trained in multiple languages to assist in their travels and investigations around the globe. The final decision regarding appropriate action against a target was also Seven's responsibility, though to date she preferred, and had been successful with a more democratic method of decision-making. She would put the fate of their targets to a vote. It was a way to test the temperature of the team to see if they were all thinking as one. So far, they all were.

When it came to work, they were on the same page. Personally, however, she was still getting used to Takeo and Ty's personalities. Tak always seemed kind of intimidated by her, but she often caught him peeking around various monitors and paperwork as she walked by. She couldn't decide if he had a crush on her, or if he was just voyeuristic. She would withhold judgment. Ty, on the other hand, hadn't wasted any time hitting on her, but figured out early she batted for the other team.

Seven was sorting paper in a cubicle when she overheard a conversation between them that made her stifle a grin and shake her head.

"No way. How the hell do you know? Did Marcus say something?" Takeo asked Ty incredulously, glancing over his shoulder to make sure he wasn't overheard.

"He didn't have to. I know because there are two kinds of women in this world, Tak," Ty paused for effect, "those that want me, and those that are dykes." He smirked confidently as Tak rolled his eyes.

"You're such a dick," Tak said. "She is way too fine. There is no way she's a Friend of Dorothy."

"Yes, there is," Seven deadpanned as she walked past the gossiping men.

Two sets of wide eyes watched long legs make their way across the room. "Cold busted talkin' shit about the boss. Thanks, Ty. I really appreciate you helping to get my day started off right."

"Look at the bright side, Buddha." Ty patted the rotund belly of his co-worker. "At least that explains about us getting taken to the cleaners in the pool hall the other night."

❧❧❧❧

The Team Leader swept her gaze from side to side, admiring the lush beauty of the Andes foothills and the terrain they were hiking through. She inhaled the cool mountain air deeply through her nose and thought briefly of the peaceful feeling she always got when in the woods. Seven compared that feeling to the one she associated with the act of extreme violence she was about to undertake, and shook her head in wonder.

It had been a quiet hike so far, but as they closed in on their target's home, she knew peace wouldn't last long. Their positions had been casual and she now walked the lead, with Marcus and Ty following closely together as they chatted quietly and scanned the area. Ty had his Shrike 5.56 automatic rifle slung casually over his shoulder as the sunlight through the forest canopy offered an interesting play of light over their woodland camo tactical gear. She couldn't hear what they were talking about, but occasional words drifted her way on the breeze.

Seven used the hike time to review their objective,

thinking back to their last team meeting. Armando Miguel Reyes was deemed a kill-worthy target. They were assigned to investigate him a little over a month ago, and it didn't take long with Tak's talent to find a considerable amount of damning information. The team discussed the possibility Reyes may not have originally realized the scope of what he was involved in, but after 9/11, Reyes knew for sure what his associates had done, yet he continued.

A wealthy Bolivian businessman, Reyes was ivy league educated, and thought himself the closest thing to Bolivian royalty in the country. In his opinion, he was above the law, and on more than one occasion was heard to say so in public. The only son of an old and wealthy family of high political standing, he turned his personal family fortune into some serious money when he started investing heavily in the mid-1980s.

His ancestors began mining metals and using the money to invest in farmland and coca production several generations earlier. The coca became the family's primary source of income in the 1930s when the Coca Cola Company in the United States heavily purchased the export. In the late '70s, the profit turned more to cocaine production, which skyrocketed soon after. The cocaine production quickly slowed after the boom and it went underground with heavy government pressure. Many millions were made, however, which gave Reyes the capital to make his real fortune investing.

Reyes traveled the world on his successes, seeing himself as equal company to princes and presidents. He laughed loudly, drank deeply, and never hesitated to laud his expertise in manipulating the market to his favor. Being an acquaintance, and sometimes business ally to the outspoken Hugo Chávez opened some interesting new doors for the Bolivian, as he let his displeasure with the U.S. be known more and more frequently, as did the Argentinean. He felt the Americans were the world's worst hypocrites when it came to the pressure they brought to bear on South American coca growers. They wanted what they wanted, and didn't want anybody else to have what they didn't want, like bullies in a schoolyard.

Takashi was able to piece together bits of information collected from the CIA, Mossad, MI6, and several other security organizations around the world to draw a cohesive picture of Reyes' introduction and involvement with his terrorist partners.

In late 1995, Armando Reyes attended a small but exclusive dinner party in a lovely chateau outside Bordeaux, France. His host, a Frenchman named Jean Durand, introduced him to a very serious looking Saudi named Yeslam Aziz. The gentleman's conversation eventually turned to money and investing, when Yeslam asked politely for Reyes' assistance in a matter of some importance. Reyes' ego could not refuse the complement, made easier by the free flowing supply of outstanding wine. He agreed to assist in the investment of a large sum of money as a "favor," with a fair commission, of course. The chance to test his might using someone else's money was an opportunity he couldn't resist.

The two gentlemen agreed to a mutually beneficial and private arrangement of financial assistance in future years. Reyes enjoyed the challenge, and enjoyed even more the lavish treatment bestowed upon him by his new Arab associates. He was treated like a king in every way. A fitting tribute, he thought.

After 9/11, he stepped back and realized for the first time the deep truth of what he was involved in, having recognized some names making it regularly into the news associated with Al-Qaeda. At first, he was terrified, but calmed himself after a while, realizing that his trail was well covered. Or so he convinced himself. He toyed with the idea of getting out of his involvement with the Arabs immediately, but dismissed it partly out of fear. His associate Yeslam Aziz contacted him a few months after 9/11 and hinted there would be no separation and requested, politely, that another "favor" was needed.

Seven's team determined that the immediate loss of this connection would be a devastating financial blow to the terrorist organizations Aziz represented. In addition, they felt a disruption at this level would stir the pot, causing a ripple effect and allowing them to see whom else may be involved, getting more names, unknown organizations, and the like. In addition to his investing, it was also discovered that Reyes was indirectly involved with the financial support of the men who hijacked the 9/11 flights, whether he knew it or not. The team agreed unanimously that Reyes was a kill-worthy target.

The team's mission objective was to approach the Reyes compound from the foothills, by stealth. Observe security and any other concerns that may affect a successful completion, then take out the target. They knew Reyes was in the compound, but he was the unknown factor. They didn't know when and where he would show himself, so Seven built a time cushion into the plan to allow for waiting. If the target showed his face early, they would take the shot then get to the exit point, dig in and wait. If the shot proved impossible, they would wait until the last minute, then send Cooper and Johnson in to search and destroy while Seven sniped from the hills. This was Cooper's favorite way to work, but the original plan provided total anonymity, which was always preferable. One hundred percent success, one hundred percent return…as in, everybody gets out unseen and unharmed, mission accomplished.

After the shot, it would take them precisely two to two and a quarter hours to reach their exit site at a good clip. A helo would fly in low, pick them up at a prearranged time, then get the hell out of Dodge. They were completely without communication, so everything had been planned down to the minute. Even if the mission failed, they had to make the helicopter or be stuck with no I.D., no money, and a much greater chance of local authorities picking them up. So far, everything was on schedule and looking good. *This feels funny, like it's too easy.* Seven thought and then chastised herself for her negativity. *Never ever look a gift horse in the mouth.*

❧ ❧ ❧ ❧

Bolivia was an interesting, and surprisingly untouched country. With the Andes mountain range on the western side, and the Amazon River basin to the east, it had everything from wild untamed jungles to snowcapped peaks. Seven did quite a bit of research on the small South American country when she was working on her tactical plan, and was impressed with what she learned of the local peoples and their history and culture.

Landlocked by five other countries, Bolivia

was once part of the Incan Empire, and to this day, Amerindian people heavily populated it. The primary language was Spanish, but the native languages of Aymaran and Quechuan were still spoken widely across the Andes region. A culture rich in tradition, the native people still wore the brightly colored ponchos and bowler hats similar to the dress of native North American Indians two hundred years ago.

Having a relatively small population of about a million more people nationwide than New York City, Bolivia was a relatively unknown country. The third largest producer of coca, it had a history of strife with countries trying to stem the illegal production of cocaine like the United States. Though far from enemies, there was little love lost between these two nations. Bolivia felt it had a historical right to grow coca, a plant used for medicinal purposes by indigenous people for centuries. The U.S. and the U.N. felt it had a right to do whatever it could to stop coca from being turned to cocaine and distributed around the world. As it stood, the growing of coca was legal in Bolivia, but the production of cocaine was not. The problem was trying to keep track of who was doing what.

Seven didn't really care much about the Bolivian cocaine issue, as her mission had nothing to do with that. Another time, another agency, maybe. But right now, the world was focused on doing what they could to stem the growth of terrorism around the world. One thing she was definitely glad for was a small population. If she could traipse through the countryside without running into other people, she could get in and out, fast and easy. Fast and easy was good.

She adjusted the heavy pack on her back and began to climb up the next incline. Still, something about this mission was nagging at her. She could not, for the life of her, put her finger on what it was. It's almost as if the whole thing was rushed for some reason. *Probably just working the kinks out of a new team.* She thought. *I should have designed a more thorough contingency plan. Just in case.*

Chapter Two

The morning fog lifted slowly as a young woman of twenty-four jogged energetically up the dirt road near the Peace Corps camp where she was living. She wore only a dark blue pair of nylon running shorts and matching cropped bra top, exposing almost all of her well-toned body. There was a definite mountain chill in the air, but she was sweating from head to toe after a vigorous workout, her short cropped blonde hair stuck to her head with a combination of sweat and early morning humidity.

She held a Nikon digital camera with the strap firmly wrapped around her right hand and wrist. Arriving near the camp, she paused, jogging in place for a moment as she scanned her surroundings for a potentially good picture. She spotted one, stopped her motion, and brought the viewfinder to her eye. *Focus. Click.*

"Dr. MacKenzie?" The voice of Grace Richards called out from the silent fog, startling the young woman. Grace was the Peace Corps satellite camp coordinator and environmental conservation specialist.

"Yes, Grace. Please...call me Jenny, and what are you doing out here so early in the a.m.?" She breathed heavily, thinking she'd never get used to running at this high altitude.

"Looking for you. I checked your hut, but since you weren't there, I thought maybe you were running again. I spoke with Daniel before he left his shift at the clinic. He wanted me to tell you the Aymara boy passed in the night."

"Damn." The young doctor looked sadly to the ground. "Is his mother still here?"

"Yes. I think she's in the clinic."

Jenny sighed heavily, melancholy evident in her normally sparkling green eyes. "Okay. I'll get cleaned up and go talk to her. Seems like these rural folks always get hit the hardest, doesn't it?"

A chill settled over her as she made way toward her hut for a shower and a warm change of clothes. She wanted to make a difference in the world and set out to do so after medical school by volunteering for a two-year stint in the Peace Corps. But it was so disheartening sometimes. It seemed such a great loss to lose children to nothing more than ignorance and improper care. She was determined to do what she could to educate these impoverished people on how to avoid this type of loss, and with luck, they would do the same and pass the word.

Most of the cases she treated here in Bolivia were suffering from Chagas disease, a parasitic infection of the blood that had gone seemingly unchecked for a century. But Jenny noted after several months working this rural site an unusually large number of infant and child deaths due to plain, old fashioned neglect. They normally operated out of a facility in one of the larger cities, but a small group of visiting and local volunteers determined it a good idea to set up a small satellite camp in a remote area to attract people without the means or desire to travel to the city. It was working out well, so far, and all the volunteers felt they were making headway.

Grace Louanne Richards was the driving force behind the creation of their small camp, but the other volunteers quickly realized her vision was well worth the effort. The older woman had a master's degree in Agronomy from Texas A&M University, but her twenty years of experience with the Peace Corps made her the unequivocal leader of this small troupe of volunteers.

A tall, thin woman with graying brown hair, the Texan was a study in quiet strength. Grace was from Fort Worth, Texas, the youngest daughter of a successful businessman in the oil industry. She inherited a good deal of money when she turned eighteen and decided to pay the earth back for her father's intrusion by dedicating her life to helping others. She had done little else in twenty years. Her father was not pleased.

Jenny thought about Grace's gentle soul as she sat on the edge of her bed and bent to untie the laces of her running shoes. Her hut was small and extremely rustic, but comfortable. The floors were wood plank, a luxury in this part of the world, with some grass mats thrown here and there to keep the chill off her feet. There was a single window near the bed, closed to the cool air, and a tiny semi enclosed space in the corner with a shower and drain, a freestanding sink and a small space heater in the corner. She pondered the empty wall over the bed and thought again how she needed to paint something to hang there. *Maybe I could use one of these grass mats as a canvas. That would look interesting.*

After a quick and unfortunately lukewarm shower, she donned her white lab coat over a pair of button down Levis and a warm v-neck sweater that hugged her five-foot, four-inch frame nicely. She ruffled her fingers through still damp hair to air it out, as her energetic and happy disposition slowly returned. The young doctor psyched herself up for the inevitable chat with the grieving mother. *Come on, Jen. You knew this was going to be a tough job, but you wanted the challenge. Do your best to make some good come out of this bad situation.* Nodding to herself, she tied the laces of her hiking boots and headed over to the sink, brushing her teeth with bottled water before leaving for the clinic.

The clinic...*her* clinic as Jenny preferred to think of it, was a small, one story building with metal and wooden walls. Peeling paint and some rust on the outside did little to indicate the immaculately kept interior. One side of the building had large double barn doors to ease a patient's passage into a sterile room with a half dozen clean cots ready and waiting. Five of the six were currently occupied. There was an open space near the doors with a small desk and a couple chairs where people could come for checkups and vaccinations if they chose. The inside was painted a cheerful color of blue with polished concrete floors and windows spaced evenly across the walls to let in as much light as possible.

On the other side of the building was one of the most coveted rooms in all the camp, the only fully equipped bathroom with indoor toilet, sink, bathtub, and an enclosed shower with a decent water heater. Most of the camp staff would only deem to use it on special occasions, preferring to leave it to the patients, but it sure was nice to have when you felt the need. Down a narrow hall to the left of the bathroom was Jenny's small office and storage for the clinic medical supplies. The office was white and spotlessly clean with a metal desk in one corner, locking cabinets and a small refrigeration unit in the other. She kept the fridge stocked with medications, blood bags and if there was room, the occasional six-pack of Bolivian beer.

Jenny sat there now, having just offered condolences to the mother of the deceased child. She listened to the hum of the generators just outside the building, hoping she was successful in imparting some pearls of wisdom so the mother would not make the same mistakes again. Her Aymaran was spotty at best, only slightly worse than her Spanish, so she never went far without a translator. Miyera, her regular translator, was a local volunteer and nursing student who was with the mother now, making sure she had the proper information and helping to arrange transport of the child back to her village for burial.

The generators hummed.

✿ ✿ ✿ ✿

After a full day of attending her bedridden patients, vaccinations, and the occasional emergency, Jenny was more than ready to call it day. She hiked through the bustling camp toward the mess hall to grab a bite before heading back to her hut. She was looking forward to reviewing her new photos taken that morning to see if she'd gotten any keepers. The camp was an efficiently run operation consisting of her clinic, a mess hall, a covered school house of sorts, a dormitory for the volunteers, and a couple huts, one of which was Jenny's; the other belonged to Grace. The rest of the volunteers, eight total, shared space in the dorm. There was one room for the chicas, and one room for the caballeros.

The camp was surrounded on three sides by woods with a nice view of the valley out the open side and a dusty road going through the middle. It was normally dry and rocky in this area, the wind wreaking havoc certain times of the year. There was a river nearby, a far tributary from the Amazon basin that the volunteers would swim in from time to time, weather permitting. The camp was centrally located to several small farming villages in the region, and a couple hours' drive to the nearest city where they could pick up supplies and venture out for the occasional night on the town.

The volunteers were a good-hearted bunch of people, each with their specialties and personal missions to achieve. The group of ten included agriculturalists, multi-lingual teachers, and health care professionals who were committed to making a difference. They all worked hard and enjoyed the fraternity they had created out here in the Bolivian boondocks. The teachers had a classroom where they would give basic reading, writing, and arithmetic skills to the surrounding village children, adults too if interested. The agricultural specialists, like Grace, would travel into the field and show farmers and other village folks soil conservation, alternative crops, and smart forestry practices. The health care pros were doing their best to inoculate and treat the common ailments of the area and educate the indigenous people as best they could toward good health practices. It was an uphill battle, but each and every one earned their sleep at night.

Of the ten volunteers, only four were Americans.

The rest were Bolivian locals, most from the La Paz area. Their day-to-day activities around camp were usually filled with a range of successes, failures, triumphs, and revelations. They were a team, and each felt his or her mission was helping to make the world a better place.

Jenny popped open a beer and put her feet up on her bed, reviewing the photos she had taken that morning. She was hoping for dramatic lighting and effect from the fog combined with the sunrise, but didn't seem to get a single good shot. *Oh well. There's always tomorrow.* She thought. *Maybe I'll hike into the woods again and see if I can find a three-toed sloth. If I run really fast, I'm bound to come across one sometime since they never move.* She smirked at her own stupid joke.

⚜⚜⚜⚜

Daniel Jarvis approached Jenny in the mess tent while she studied her third cup of coffee intently. Daniel was a nurse and Jenny's right hand man. He was born in Sacramento, but came to Bolivia from San Francisco after a messy breakup with his live-in boyfriend of three years. His parents were alive and well, and still lived in the same house he was born in, in 1974. They were simple people, but loved their only son and supported his lifestyle and career choices without question.

"Hi, Sunshine. What's a D-Mac like you doing in a place like this? May I sit, oh unusually silent one?" He asked.

Jenny nodded her assent sleepily, never having been a morning person.

A prematurely balding man with a crown of reddish brown hair, Daniel focused his narrowing hazel eyes on his prey. With dark bushy eyebrows, a ready smile, and a stocky six-foot, one-inch build, he was often told he looked like a pudgy George Clooney on a bad hair day. "D-Mac, earth to D-Mac, anybody home? Come in D-Mac."

Jenny finally looked up and offered a weak hello. "Sorry. Can't seem to wake up today."

"Did you skip your ungodly exercise this morning?"

"Yeah. I decided yesterday that I wanted to go out this afternoon instead. Different light. See if I could find some wildlife to snap, maybe." She refocused on her coffee.

"Wildlife. Sheesh!" He said exasperatedly. "What the hell are you gonna do if one of these days you come across a panther or something?"

"Shoot it."

"You don't carry a gun, or have I totally misjudged you?"

"With my camera," she said with a slight twinkle in her eye. "Then run like I stole something." Jenny chuckled as the edge of her mouth twitched into the first smile of the day. She pushed the joke home. "Why do you think I always wear my running clothes out there? So I can be super fast in case a rapid get-away is required."

"Well, I feel *so* much better about it now that I know you have a plan." Daniel was usually too cheerful to bring off sarcasm, lacking the snide demeanor required to be good at it, but this time it worked. They looked each other and laughed again.

"Wanna come with?" Jenny asked hopefully.

"Why? You evil, evil, woman. What are you plotting at my expense?"

"Nothing." She smiled innocently. "I just thought if I spot any big cats out there, I wouldn't have to run that fast to get away...I'd just have to run faster than you."

"Mm mmm, D-Mac, sweetheart." Dan shook his head no. "Pussy don't like me, remember?"

"Ohhh *god*! It's *way* too early in the day for *that* kind of humor." Her head fell to the table, shoulders shaking in silent laughter.

"You started it. And besides, I got you to wake up didn't I?"

"You did." She flashed a bright white smile at her friend. "I don't know what I'd do without you, Dannyboy. You're always looking out for me."

"Speakin' of looking out for you...Rico Suavé, the Latin lover, is heading over here." He refrained from further comment, not quite sure how Jenny was feeling about JC these days.

Juan Carlos Alveda, or JC as he was known, was a Cuban born expatriate raised in Miami, Florida. He literally floated to Key Biscayne on a boat with his cousin at the age of ten, and was raised by an aunt and uncle in Miami, having lost his parents to Castro for reasons unknown. JC lived in La Paz for ten years working as an English teacher to Bolivian businessmen before he decided on a higher calling and joined the Peace Corps.

"Hi, Jenny. Dan. Can I join you?" JC slid onto the picnic table bench without waiting for a response. "How are you today, Jen? You look a little tired. Are you getting enough sleep?"

Jenny rolled her eyes so only Dan could see.

She smiled at JC, thinking he was rapidly becoming the biggest mistake she had made in her young life. Juan Carlos was a handsome guy with jet-black hair and a confident stature. He was fun at a party, and very personable. She really liked him a lot, as a friend. Unfortunately, she only figured that out after she had already gotten involved with him.

It seemed like a good idea at the time.

They were all taking a rare night off in town, drinking at a local club. The group had become real friends over the last few months, and everyone was having a blast. The smoky, seedy bar was a welcome respite from their wholesome country living. Refreshing and potent Caipirinha cocktails were flowing unchecked, and after many drinks and a lot of dancing, one thing led to another.

Almost the next day JC started acting very possessive of her. He tried to joke it away, claiming it was a 'Latin' thing, but he never attempted to curb it. She didn't know what to think at first, preferring to just go with the flow, but after a few weeks it really started to annoy.

The worst part of the situation was that she really liked JC and was afraid to be honest with him about wanting to end it. She didn't want to hurt him, and more importantly didn't want to be the cause of any dissention in their great working relationship. The team would suffer, and it would be her fault. *Stupid!* She thought. *Don't ever get involved with someone you work with again.* The day was rapidly approaching when she would have to have 'the talk' with him. She only hoped it could be done in a way that wouldn't lose him as a friend.

"What are you doing tonight, Jen? Maybe I

could come over for a while. I still have a bottle of wine I picked up last time we were in town." He smiled charmingly.

"Not tonight, JC. As you said, I'm tired. I think I need to turn in early and I still have a long day ahead of me." She caught Dan smirking.

"Okay, maybe tomorrow then. How are things going for you, Dan? Everything work out with that crazy man in the clinic yesterday? *Coño.* That guy was a *culo.* I expect that kind of behavior in the city sometimes, but not out here. These Indian people are too friendly to act like that."

"Yeah, he wasn't local people. I think he works for that Argulla guy up the river. He was fine once D-Mac stitched him up. He was just panicking at the sight of his own blood or something. Big, tough-guy like that going ballistic over a cut on his finger. What a poser."

"Took eight sutures. Lot'a blood," Jenny said matter-of-factly.

"Still. P...O...S...E...R." Dan spelled out for effect.

"Jen, I hope you don't ever leave yourself alone in the clinic with guys like that. He could've been dangerous." JC put a condescending hand on Jenny's shoulder and looked at her with concern.

"Look. JC. I know you mean well, but please stop hanging over me like a mother hen. You know I don't like it. I can take care of myself, you know."

"Oh yeah, how? A little thing like you? That guy could have done some damage if he wanted to."

"I took a Tai-Bo class once," she said defensively with a straight face, as if that explained everything. She glanced over at Dan to catch his reaction to her deadpan joke.

Dan choked on a sip of coffee and quickly stood and walked away to cover up his laughter at Jenny getting the better of JC. He wasn't going to get in the middle of their tiff.

Jenny stood to make her exit as well. "JC, I'm not going to go rounds with you on this right now. I've got to get to the clinic. I have asked you repeatedly not to hover, but you continue as if my feelings about it don't matter to you at all."

"I just worry about you, Jen. Is that so wrong?" Jenny turned and walked away with a sigh.

๑๑๑๑๑

The woods behind the clinic were still with the exception of a young blonde woman in running clothes, creeping along with camera in hand. "Stop flitting around, you little bugger," she whispered to an uncaring Scarlet-Bellied Mountain Tanager. "I don't care how cute you are, if you don't stop hopping from branch to branch your revered position in the Jenny MacKenzie photo Hall of Fame is a goner." Jenny stepped on a dry twig, the resulting noise sending the little bird to the air once more. "Damn," she whispered as her target swooped around and chose a new position even better than the last. A ray of sunlight shone across his bright red belly. *Focus. Click. Gotcha!*

The underbrush rustled behind her. She spun around, willing herself to see deep into the green filtered sunlight, the shadows playing tricks on her imagination. Her breath held, she waited for either a great photo op or a dangerous animal to come barreling out of the bushes.

It was Dan.

"Shit! You scared the crap out of me!" She laughed nervously.

"Hey, gorgeous. I can see by your shiny exterior coat you've been running already."

"Yep. Just winding down. What brings you out here?"

"Looking for you. Sorry to cut your break short, but we've got a situation back at the clinic. Time is of the essence." He nodded in the direction of the camp, willing her to go.

"After you, dahhhling." She bowed dramatically, swooshing her hand in the direction of camp. "Do I have time to get cleaned up, or should we head straight there?"

"Straight there, I'm thinkin'."

"Okay. Fill me in while we walk," Jenny said, suddenly all business.

"A couple of locals brought in a Quechuan girl, estimated age around fourteen, and her father, estimated age around thirty-eight. Car accident. Looks like her father may have had a blow out or something and the car went off a cliff. Girl was thrown but her left arm and hand are totally mangled. It may have been caught under the car as it went. Hard to tell. She's lost a lot of blood. Unconscious. Heart rate weak and getting weaker. Father has a piece of jagged metal the size and length of a coffee thermos sticking out of his gut. Also lost a lot of blood. He's conscious but appears to be in shock."

"Jesus, is it my imagination or does this place seem more like an E.R. this week than an immunization clinic? All right. What's been done so far?"

"Arm has a tourniquet. She's on a drip. Father's

been sedated and IV'd also. Old Miguel was bumped to a chair and the back corner beds have been cordoned off and prepped for surgery. I raided your office and got together as much of the emergency gear as I thought you'd need. Neither one will last to make it to the city hospital, so it's you or nothing."

"Blood's going to be a problem," Jenny worried. Her pace picked up speed as she neared the clinic. "I don't keep much around and I'm probably going to need it all for this. As soon as we get back, fill out a req and bring it to me to sign. Get JC or one of his guys to drive to the city and get as much as they'll part with. Make sure they talk directly to Silva and get the imported blood. I don't want any of that Chagas contaminated Bolivian stuff. And make sure they take the cooler and keep it well iced. We may not need it, but if we do, we do. Tell 'em to get back here with it tonight. Don't take no for an answer."

She charged into the clinic and headed straight for the bathroom, Dan following quickly behind with a towel and a fresh pair of scrubs. Nala, a volunteer nurse from La Paz, and Miyera, the student nurse and sometimes translator, watched over the newcomers and existing patients. Two minutes later Jenny bumped out of the bathroom and headed to the makeshift operating room. "Get scrubbed and meet me," she said to Dan in a no-nonsense tone.

Jenny quickly assessed the situation, nodding approvingly at Dan's hurried attempt at an instant O.R. "Okay, girl first," she said to Dan as he entered the area. "That arm's gotta go. Let's get some ligatures around those arteries to stop the bleeding. Where's the thread?" Dan pointed to the tray between the beds. "We'll disarticulate at the elbow. Won't have to transect any muscle, the damage is all in the forearm and hand. Have Nala grab some O negative from the fridge. And stay out of my beer." She winked at the nervous looking nurse. Miyera tied a mask over the doctor's face and slipped some clear glasses over her eyes, then moved behind Dan to do the same.

Jenny was in her element. She wondered, once upon a time, if she would have what it took to rise to an occasion such as this. The young woman found out in med school that not only could she hang, she thrived on it. Dealing with a life or death emergency took a cool head and a clear mind. Jenny found that the world seemed to fade away during those times and her focus was absolute. She liked the feeling. It seemed like a combination of adrenaline and her synapses all firing in harmony.

Six hours after both father and daughter had been treated and stabilized, Jenny sat in a chair between them with her elbows resting on her knees, head hung low, staring at her hiking boots. *Why isn't this enough?* She asked herself. Jenny thought back to the conversation she had with Daniel just two hours earlier. "I don't know, Dan. I love what I do, but why isn't it enough? I should be totally satisfied after a day like today. I should be feeling great about what I've accomplished, but it's just not enough. It's like there's a part of me that's not there." She sighed heavily. "Maybe there's something wrong with me. I can't even make a relationship last for more than a few months, and how hard can that be? I mean, I run around taking pictures. I keep in shape. I love my work. I bust my ass trying to be better than good at what I do, but I just can't feel content. *Why?* I thought for sure when I got out of school and finally started working it would all come together, you know?"

Dan shook his head in sympathy. "I don't have the answers for you, sweetheart."

Jenny thought Dan was holding an opinion about her feelings back, but she was too tired to press him about it.

"You did fantastic today. You should toddle off and get some rest now. I'm sure you're exhausted." He proceeded to rub a few kinks out of her shoulders.

"Ha." She laughed tiredly. "No more than you. Nah. I'm going to stay here with them tonight. Just wanna be sure there aren't any complications in the night. The girl is still a little unstable. You can tell Nala to take the night off. Any word from the mother?"

"Not yet. The two guys that brought them in went back over the pass to get her from their village. Probably won't get back till morning, though, since that's some seriously dangerous night driving."

"Do one more thing for me before you go?" Jenny asked as Dan nodded his assent. "Check the cabinet to see how much more Benznidazole we have stocked. We've had so many in for it the last few days, we must be running low." Jenny was referring to the anti-parasitic medication they used to treat Chagas disease.

"Sure thing, D-Mac. See you in the a.m." Dan went to leave but paused and turned with his hand on the door. "You know...you impressed the shit out of young Miyera today. She was over in the mess talkin' you up like you were some kinda god or something." He smiled and rubbed it in a little further. "Said her parents encouraged her to be a nurse, but after watching you today she's going to try for medical school instead. The whole team is really proud of you."

Jenny blushed and sighed. "Thanks, Dannyboy. It was a group effort."

Her thoughts returned to the present as she looked over at the young girl whose life she'd saved earlier in the day. Jenny sighed deeply and hunkered down into her chair, trying to get more comfortable. She closed her eyes and willed herself to empty the questions from her mind so she could rest.

Chapter Three

The pace through the forest was steady, but in the last hour had slowed considerably on the inclines. This was to be expected. They would be taking a break soon, stopping long enough to rest, eat something, and get their gear put together for the short haul to their destination. All three Delegates were well used to this level of physical activity, but long distances at altitude, mixed with hilly terrain and heavy packs were enough to tire anybody out. Marcus gulped a swig of water as he waited for Ty to catch up. He would never admit it to Seven, but he couldn't wait to shed his hundred-pound pack.

He mopped perspiration from his brow as Ty finally got there. "Man, that bitch is a slave driver," Ty wheezed to unsympathetic ears.

"Shut it, Toolbag. I'm gettin' sick of you trash talking the T.L." Marcus came to Seven's rescue. "A day may come when you will thank your lucky stars she's on your side."

"Doubt it," Ty replied, eyeing Seven in the distance, trying to catch his breath. "I've told you before, and I'll tell you again. Conquest is a man's game. It's ingrained in our psyche from birth. We conquer our enemies. We conquer the land. We conquer women. We conquer, period. It's who we are. I can't take answering to a woman. If she's in the lead, it implies that she is the conqueror, and that's not my song and dance. Know what I mean?"

"Shit no. I'd go to war any day of the week with her before you, Toolbag. You have no idea what she's capable of. I've seen her do shit that makes Schwarzenegger movies look boring. There's a reason they call our team elite operators, you know? And there's a reason she's the leader, get it? Because *she* is the best. You need to stop seeing her as woman and start seeing her as a soldier. Just like you. When you're in the field guns blazing, are you telling me you actually give a shit that the person guarding your six is a female? 'Cause that's just stupid."

"Why the hell do you keep calling me Toolbag?"

"'Cause you're a big mouthed asshole without a lick of sense," Marcus said, disgusted by Ty's sexist position. They continued walking uphill, keeping Seven within sight. "Look man, I read the report on you before you joined the team, just like I'm sure you read ours. File said you were a real operator. So are you telling me that you wouldn't give everything if you had to, just like when you were a Green Beret, because she's a she? You took this job knowing that, so what's up?"

Silence was Ty's reply as he struggled against his nature to find the truth.

Marcus continued. "She's a Marine. I've been her partner for thirteen years, and I mean to tell ya, there's nobody better. Michelis would die to protect me, and I know this. I've seen it. And whether you know it or not, she'd do the same for you. She even won a Medal of Honor in '99 for some shit that went down in Kosovo. Threw her ass in front of a bullet to save me and took it right between the shoulder blades. Kevlar did its job that day. In thirteen years, we have never not accomplished what we have set out to do. I am really proud of myself for that, and I have her to thank for it."

"What happened in Kosovo? I was stationed in Africa during that conflict," Ty finally asked, finding his tongue.

Marcus drew the earthy smell of the woods deep into his lungs and scanned the treetops for the bird he heard chirping. He checked his distance from Seven to make sure she was far enough away not to hear him tell this story again. He knew she didn't like it when he talked about what happened. He'd seen her in close combat a couple times before when their situation called for it, but nothing like this. He collected his thoughts for a moment more, wondering if this heroic tale would even be enough to convince Ty of their leader's worth as a warrior. *Toolbag.*

"So we were part of the 26th Marine Expeditionary Unit out of Camp Lejeune in North Carolina. We were shipped to Kosovo in '99 for Operation Joint Guardian, to join forces with some other UN troops as part of KFOR...that's what they were calling the UN Kosovo Force. Anyway..."

Seven sat with a couple of guys from her sniper platoon at a mess hall table, pondering the meal before her. She'd been in Kosovo as part of the UN peacekeeping unit for a few months now, and so far, the food was par for the course. Didn't really matter if it was bad, it sure as hell beat MREs. Hmmm. Something resembling Chicken Cacciatore sat on her tray next to some likely lukewarm kernels of yellow corn, a hopefully not stale roll, and a corner piece of chocolate cake that looked like it had been left in the oven too long. Oh well, at least the frosting looks okay. A tall red plastic glass full of sweet tea stood ready and waiting. She picked up her fork and prepared to tuck in.

"Captain Michelis. May I sit?" Congressman Deets from the great state of South Carolina asked, then did so with an affirmative nod from Seven. He introduced himself. "Your Commanding Officer told me I could find you here. Thanks for the ear. I appreciate it," he said with a smile that didn't reach his eyes.

Seven pinned him with an intimidating stare, willing him to get to the point so she could get to her dinner. "Lieutenant Colonel Moreland said you and your partner were in camp here for the next few days. I wonder if you might do me a favor?" He waited for a response that didn't come, adjusting his collar with a slightly nervous twitch under her intense scrutiny.

With a raised eyebrow and slight tilt of the head, she encouraged him to continue. "A very good friend and important contributor of mine has a son coming in tomorrow. He just graduated from the Academy and got his Hunter of Gunmen certification. This will be his first time in the field, as it were. Second Lieutenant Mark Stephanovich is his name."

"A virgin, huh? Big, bad H.O.G.?" One of Seven's tablemates snickered toward the pandering politician.

"Well...yes...I guess you could say that. Anyway, I promised his father I'd do what I could for him, if anything. Lieutenant Colonel Moreland suggested I talk to you and see if maybe you could take him under your wing for a couple days until the platoon he's assigned to gets back. Show him the ropes. Maybe give him some pointers on how to stay alive out here. You get the picture."

"Sure, why not." Seven sighed. She was a rookie once. Probably would have done her a world of good to

have had a friend the first few days in Desert Storm.
Damn, that was a long time ago.

Second Lieutenant Stephanovich and his partner
Second Lieutenant Darnell Vargas reported the next
afternoon while Marcus and Seven were half way through
a game of Cribbage. Seven knew Marcus was relieved at
the interruption because she was about to skunk him,
then tease him mercilessly about her superior card-
playing skill. She squinted at him deviously, knowing
as well as he did that he'd just dodged a bullet.

"At ease, fellas. This is just a casual favor for
my Congressman, no need for formalities." *Seven*
addressed the two young marines as she strode from her
tent. Damn, it's hot today. "This is my partner Platoon
Sergeant Marcus Johnson. I'm Platoon Commander
Captain Seven Michelis." *They shook hands all around.*
"You guys get settled in okay?"

"Yes, Captain. Thank you. Please call me Mark,
and Darnell goes by D. I'm sorry about this intrusion,"
he said somewhat sheepishly. "My dad can be kind
of a bully. When Congressman Deets met us at the
transport, I knew he had a hand in this somehow. I
hope it's not too much of an imposition, but we really
do appreciate it, and it's an honor to meet you both.
You know, several of your team records still stand, back
at Lejeune," *he said, smiling, as Seven and Marcus eyed*
each other shrewdly.

"Told ya." *Marcus nudged his friend.*

"All right, well, welcome to Kosovo. We'll give
you a little tour around camp and a rundown on how
things tend to go around here. Afterward, Sergeant
Johnson and I are going to run a little errand off base.
You guys are welcome to tag along if you want. There's
no fighting in this area at the moment, according to the*

latest reports, but you'll still need to gear up. We never leave the base without being prepared for anything. We'll show you the countryside while we're out and about."

Some hours later, Seven and Marcus waited next to a Humvee for the two rookies to show up. He teased her constantly when they were alone about anything and everything he could get away with, determined to break through the serious mask that only he knew was just a front. He gave himself one point for a hint of a smile, two points for a hint of a smile plus eye crinkle, three points for a full smile showing teeth, and five points for a full out laugh. If she laughed and took a swing at him, it was an automatic win. She was very good at this game. He rarely won.

"Hey. Here we are. You guys ready to go?" Young Mark asked enthusiastically. Seven noted it was D holding the sniper rifle. "Where are we headed, anyway?"

Marcus got behind the wheel with Seven in the passenger seat as the new guys climbed in back. "We're headed to this little no-name village near the Albanian border. There's an artist living there that makes these really nice embroidered and beaded coats and jackets. Very colorful. A real local flair. Anyway, the Lieutenant Colonel wanted to get one for his wife so I volunteered to drive over and get one for my mom at the same time. Her birthday's coming up. Should be a few hours round trip, shopping included."

"Not going to get one for yourself, Captain?"

Seven snorted. "No. I don't do beads. I'm more of a leather jacket kinda girl." Marcus glanced at her sideways and hid a smile.

The little village was a bit run down looking,

but the people seemed happy with their home. Many friendly smiles were freely given. There were several coats to choose from in the tiny shop and Seven bought a knee-length duster for Colonel Moreland's wife, and a short, brightly colored one for her mother. Even Darnell was impressed enough to pick one out for his girlfriend back home.

On the way back to camp, Marcus pulled the Humvee off the road and killed the engine. "Nature calls," he said and hopped out of the vehicle, trotting to a nearby copse of trees. Seven took the opportunity to walk around back for a bottle of water. In the silence of the late afternoon countryside, she heard a gunshot on the breeze. Then another. She quickly scanned the area to get a feel for their location, trying to ascertain where they were in relation to camp. Far. Damn.

Marcus trotted from the trees as she waved him over to the truck. "Did you hear that?" He nodded his assent. "Let's check it out. Sounds like it came from over that hill to the northwest. Mark, D, get your gear and follow us. We gotta check out some gunshots over that hill. What's over there, Sergeant?" She said as Marcus pulled out a map of the area.

"If we are where I think we are, Captain, it looks like there's a town just over that ridge." The four marines made quick work of climbing the hill and crawled the last ten yards to the crest, looking down into the small village. All four put their scopes to their eyes and assessed the situation. The Captain swore under her breath as she saw what she feared she might. Fuck! "Those people are in some serious shit," she stated emphatically. "How many do you count, Sergeant?" She said to Marcus, all pretense of casual out the window.

"I count forty-five to fifty civilians, one down that

I can see, half or more women and kids, twenty to thirty Serbian military, a little scruffy but most of 'em have weapons. Don't see any other activity in the village. The entire party appears to be happening in the clearing we're looking at to the west of the last building. Looks like they're lining the civs up for execution. SHIT!" Another gunshot reached their ears just after they saw another civilian hit the ground.

"Shit is right, as in, we're in it. Okay, listen up. Hope you boys can suck it up 'cause you're about to get your first lesson in real combat. And that lesson is... don't get your asses dead. Stephanovich, take my rifle. Here...ammo too. Give me your 9mm and your ammo." She handed her precious rifle to the new kid, taking his sidearm in return. "Get your ass over to that next hill and take position. Vargas, you stay here and focus on the leaders. Figure out who they are and be ready to take them." She paused to give an encouraging smile and shoulder pat to the terrified and excited looking rookies.

"Sergeant Johnson, run back to the truck and radio the camp what's going on. Then, drive it over between those two hills." She pointed toward another rise to their left. "I'm going to run around and come up from the other side of that little white building on the right over there. When you see me coming up, drive like a bat-out-of-hell cross-country right toward them. When they're distracted by you, I'll charge from behind, and you guys"—she nodded at Mark and D— "start picking off the leaders. Marcus, cause as much trouble as you can. See if you can get between them and the hostages."

"Trouble is my last name. Big Fuckin' is my first and middle." Marcus darted off at a run.

She turned to the young men. "Neither one of you guys start shooting until you see me go in, okay? I don't want them to scatter until I'm in the middle of it. Got it?"

"Yes, Ma'am," they said in unison.

"And for God's sake, don't shoot me or Marcus. That would look really bad on your record." Seven smiled to reassure them, looking them over coolly to determine if they were going to be heroes or heels. She decided they were both hero material. "One last thing. We are severely outnumbered. If Sergeant Johnson and I are killed or captured, you two get the hell out of here. Drop the heavy shit and make way toward camp. Reinforcements will get here probably not long after the Sergeant can make the call, so hide out and wait for them. Got it?"

"Yes, Ma'am." Mark and D glanced at each other, then back at their leader.

Seven backed down the hill a short distance then ran full out around the hill Mark would soon be perched on with her rifle at the ready.

The rookies watched from afar as the Captain ran toward the other side of the small village. "Jesus, look at her go," Darnell commented. "You thinking what I'm thinking?"

"Yeah. Suicide mission. How the hell does she think she's going take all those guys on her own?"

"She's not on her own. Come on...get to your position. One shot, one kill. Take as many as you can, partner, and don't forget to duck." They shook hands as Mark turned toward his hilltop and took off, crouching as he ran. Dear Lord, if you can hear me, please make this go our way...and give that crazy woman wings.

Seven checked that both of her 9mm handguns

had full clips and rounds chambered while she was squat running toward the village out of the enemy's line of sight. What the hell are you doing? You must be out of your mind. Daddy, does this make me crazier than you? Nah. Not from the stories your old war buddies told me. Wish me luck.

She reached the back of the old white building, and peeked around the corner. She was close enough now that she could hear the soldiers yelling at their hostages, women and children crying, and what sounded like a sobbing man pleading for his life. She estimated more than twenty-five soldiers. "Shit," she whispered to herself, coming up with a plan of action as she unsnapped her knife sheath.

She saw Marcus gunning the Humvee between the hills, effectively drawing the soldiers' attention away from their hostages and her position. The momentary confusion was her signal. The temperature was oppressive. Heat radiated from the parched earth. She took a breath deep into her lungs and slowly released it, as the adrenaline washed over her in a flood of pure energy. The captain smiled a little, enjoying the high she always got before a good fight. Here I come, assholes, *she thought and bolted from her hiding place at a dead run, a 9mm in each hand.*

Seven made for her first target, the closest soldier to her, who was standing near a wall looking disinterested in the proceedings. He turned as he heard someone approach. In an instant, he sensed something primal in his attacker and knew he was in for it. She leapt through the air with a maniacal gleam in her fierce eyes. Her target reared back in shock as she landed a powerful kick to the center of his chest with such force he flailed through the air and hit the wall behind him, crumpling to the dirt.

She hit the ground at a run and raised her weapons, quickly putting two bullets each into the next two guys standing by. The confusion of the soldiers was just beginning to set them into motion. Several of the Serbians turned toward the gunfire at their backs as Seven ran into the fray of loosely scattered soldiers. She shot another man directly in front of her as she heard the first sniper report echoing from the hillside and saw the Humvee getting closer.

The yelling of panicked soldiers began in earnest as Seven caught sight of a man to her right raising his gun toward her. She dove into a roll, taking the legs out from another man, cracking him on the skull with the butt of her weapon as he fell. The soldier to her right shot one of his own people who had the misfortune to be standing behind the fast moving Marine before she rolled. Seven quickly righted herself and aimed for the man pointing the gun, popping him twice before taking quick steps toward her new target. She felt her pant leg jerk and glanced down to see a bullet hole as she heard another whiz past her head. Shit. Keep movin', keep movin'.

On the grassy hilltop, Mark looked through his scope, stunned motionless by what he was witnessing. The Captain had downed four enemies single-handedly before he even got off his first shot. The bullets were really flying now as he lined up his second. The late afternoon sun was beating down on his back and legs as he made a distance adjustment and squeezed off another round closer to where Marcus was driving up. He looked to where Michelis was fighting to help her out if he could, just in time to see the most amazing thing.

A tremendous surge of adrenaline seemed to shoot through the focused warrior as she pierced the air with a reverberating cry. She took three quick steps, jumping into the air, and delivered a spinning roundhouse kick that broke a soldier's neck. Before her feet hit the ground, she spun her upper body a bit further and shot the man behind him between the eyes.

It was as if she was bulletproof.

Mark was mesmerized. Snap out of it! You're supposed to be shooting. *He could see from his position, as he took another shot, that at least three different soldiers were firing at her. Some were taking aim at the Humvee, the captives forgotten, as Sergeant Johnson was firing out the vehicle while he drove. Some were firing in the direction of D and himself, and some were just standing there in apparent shock.*

Back in the village, Seven moved so quickly it seemed they were more likely to shoot each other than her as she continued to fight her way through toward Marcus' position. One weapon empty, she dropped it and popped a clip in the remaining one, and pulled her knife into her free hand. She spun around just in time to escape a bullet that grazed her collar, dropped down and drove the blade deep into the chest of an oncoming soldier.

Marcus was out of the truck now, using it as a shield while encouraging the civilians to run for the cover of nearby houses. The scene was complete chaos. Just what Seven was hoping for. She spun to her left just in time to see the head of a nearby Serbian disintegrate into the pink mist left by a 7.62mm caliber sniper round. The Captain didn't think her luck would hold for much longer. It's time to end this, *she thought as she kicked the gun from the hand of the closest guy, grabbed his wrist, and spun him around, forcing her knife to his throat. She backed quickly behind the vehicle, using the hapless Serbian as a human shield.*

"Stop! Ndalu!" The fierce woman yelled at the top of her lungs. She raised a hand to pause the snipers she knew were watching. "Drop your weapons! You are completely surrounded!" She bluffed. "Drop them now or the rest of you will join your friends. Look around!" She studied their eyes as they looked over their fallen comrades. Most looked fearful, some furtive, some angry. "Surrender! Drop your weapons!" She yelled once more for good measure.

And much to her surprise...they did.

Slowly at first, but after the first few guys started, the rest quickly followed. Seven shoved the man she was holding forward to join his mates, pointing her 9mm at the rest of them. "Hands on your heads...everyone move to the wall, now! Sada!" They complied grudgingly, but soon Seven and her tiny crew had ten prisoners to their credit. The rest of the twenty-eight were either dead or injured, she assessed.

What happened next seemed to move in slow motion. Seven would later replay the moment over in her head, wondering at the exact order of things, since so much seemed to happen at once.

She was standing behind the front of the bullet-riddled Humvee when she caught a subtle movement from the clearing where the downed Serbians lay. One of the soldiers had come to, and was lying silently like a snake in the grass. His rifle was aimed directly at Marcus, who was squatting with his back turned, consoling a little girl crying over her dead father. Seven's instincts screamed and her feet were in motion before any thought entered her brain. Two running steps and she was airborne, flying toward her friend when she heard the crack of a rifle and another immediately following.

She felt the violent impact between her shoulders and could not draw breath as her body was flung crashing into Marcus and the little girl. They rolled in a heap over the body of the girl's father before Seven fell unconscious. For the first time since she charged around the corner building, there was silence.

The unconscious Marine became aware of someone shaking her and slid lethargic eyes open to see a smiling Marcus right in her face. "Ow," she said, a slight grin twitching at the edge of her lips.

"You are one crazy son-of-a-bitch, Captain Michelis, you know that? I thought I was supposed to be protecting you." Marcus smiled, bringing up their age-old joke.

"Thank God for Kevlar," she replied weakly, rolling onto her side in an attempt to stand. "What happened to the shooter?"

"Boys pegged him the instant he pulled the trigger. If they'd spotted him a half second sooner he never would've got the shot off. Reinforcements are coming up the road now."

"Hmpf. Better late than never. Son-of-a-bitch that hurt like hell. This is what my dad would call a bad day at Black Rock." A painful grunt escaped her throat as she found her feet.

Darnell was standing guard over the prisoners while Mark sorted the dead from the wounded. A low rumble of approaching trucks could be heard as the sun was beginning to set, turning the cloudless sky to a deeper shade of blue.

The trucks pulled to a stop at the edge of the

clearing and military personnel poured out from both sides and ran to surround their fellow Marines in a ring of protection. Seven's Commanding Officer Lieutenant Colonel Moreland, a tall, pockmarked man with a jet-black crew cut, hopped out of the second truck and walked her way. "I said show the new guys the ropes, Michelis, but Jesus!" He said, chuckling and looking around at the carnage. "You look like Satan, himself," he commented on Seven's blood and gore covered body. "Any of that yours?"

"Not sure, sir. Too much to tell."

"You and your crew ride with me back to camp. Fill me in on the way. We'll get you looked at." Moreland spoke quietly in the ear of his second, who darted off with new orders. Seven grabbed the packages out of the Humvee; the shopping excursion seeming ages ago. Marcus and the two rookies fell in with the Colonel as they headed for the trucks.

"You guys okay?" She asked Mark and D as they walked. Both young men nodded mutely as if suddenly intimidated, each sneaking furtive glances in her direction. "Good. Like I said, welcome to Kosovo. You both did great." She smiled at them and kept walking, unaware of the wide-eyed stares the young men were throwing at her. The Colonel noticed but said nothing. He would get the real story from them later.

Lieutenant Colonel Moreland hopped out of his truck back at base camp. "Boys, get cleaned up and be in my tent in an hour for debriefing. Michelis, come with me. We have a date."

"Buh..." Seven quickly followed the speedy pace set by her Commanding Officer as he headed directly for the Battalion Commander's tent.

"Colonel Lemsky, this is Captain Michelis." He

introduced her, walking boldly into their leader's private quarters. Seven was suddenly aware of her repulsive appearance, wishing she'd at least had the foresight to clean the battle grime off her face. She saluted and stood at attention. Moreland briefed Colonel Lemsky, giving him a short and succinct account of the events that took place. For a moment, Seven doubted her actions under his intense scrutiny and wondered if she'd be reprimanded in some way.

Lieutenant Colonel Moreland finished his report as the short, barrel-chested Colonel continued to stalk silently around Seven, eyeing her up and down, taking in every detail of her appearance. Finally, the wily looking Battalion Commander stopped directly in front of his Captain, who was several inches taller, and stared into her eyes as she looked straight ahead. Lemsky reset himself, spreading his legs slightly in a more comfortable stance and locked his hands behind his back. He barked suddenly, startling Seven a little.

"Out...fucking...standing!

"Holy Mary Mother of God, Michelis, you are my god-damned hero!" He yelled in her face then slapped her on the back. "Bill!" The Colonel barked at his assistant. "Break out the Wild Turkey! This Marine needs a drink. Moreland! How many civilian lives did you say this Marine saved today?"

"Forty-four, Sir," the Lieutenant Colonel replied, beaming with pride as he handed her a double. "At ease, Michelis. Bottoms up."

Seven pounded the double, relieved beyond measure her commanders found their efforts heroic and not stupid. Could've gone either way. "Thank you, sir." She took a deep relaxing breath, letting the adrenaline and stress of the day begin to drain. She noticed for the first time an ache in her shoulder and glanced over to see she'd been nicked. "I'm sorry, sir, but I seem to be bleeding on your floor. I guess I should get over to medical and get this looked at."

"You're a walking god damned miracle, Michelis," Lemsky barked again. *"I can tell by your uniform you were shot four damn times, yet here you stand before me. You get over there to medical. Get stitched up. Grab a shower. Get the gore washed off that uniform, then I want you to bring that uniform back here to me. I'll be god damned if that isn't goin' in my all-time Marine hero hall 'o fame. Shot four times and lived to tell the tale. Dismissed."*

The Captain saluted then turned to leave with Lieutenant Colonel Moreland on her tail. "Get cleaned up, Michelis, and get some rest. I'll get your official report in the morning."

"The funny thing was, before T.L. even got to sleep that night the stories about what happened were already flying around camp like wildfire." Marcus finished up his tale as Ty dropped back, slack-jawed. He continued talking, oblivious. "I overheard one guy telling another she took out all twenty-eight guys by herself. I think those two newbies we were showing around were making her out to be superhuman or something. The truth was good enough though. All told, she took out twelve guys by her own hand. Me and the other two got seven together, the rest surrendered and were taken into custody. Anyway..." Marcus finally noticed Ty was no longer walking with him, and turned to see the younger man standing some distance back, deep in thought. "What?" He yelled back.

Ty shook his head. "I don't believe it," he said

more to himself than anyone. He caught back up. "I was having a couple beers with this guy I went through basic with a while ago. We got to telling war stories, and I shit you not, he told me that exact story. I was absolutely convinced he made that shit up." He looked ahead to where Seven was walking. "Are you telling me that story was for real, and the T.L. up there was *the* Marine?"

"Yep." Marcus smirked with pride. "I was there. Gave her the Medal of Honor for it."

࿏ ࿏ ࿏ ࿏

Seven had to admit to herself, she was no spring chicken anymore. She felt the strain in her lower back from the heavy gear and the long hours hiking over uneven terrain. When she was nineteen in Desert Storm, she could have gone all day long, even in that insufferable desert heat. She was looking forward to their little lunch break coming up, though she would never admit that to Marcus in a million years.

Walking steadily at a good clip down the next hill, the Team Leader glanced back over her shoulder to see how far ahead of the others she had gotten. *Not far. Good.* The word "Lemsky" drifted on the breeze toward her and she rolled her eyes. "Tch. Marcus, I can't believe you're still rehashing that old tale," she said quietly to herself, shaking her head. She adjusted the pack straps at her waist and continued on.

Seven checked their course again on the GPS device, satisfied they were on track and on schedule. There seemed to be a chill in the air now that wasn't there before, making her wonder if they were in for some inclement weather. Their pre-mission weather report didn't say anything about that, but weather was weather. Her mind drifted back to her father for the umpteenth time that day.

I wonder if he would be proud of me. My decisions. My accomplishments. I wonder if he would be happy with how I turned out as a person. A sad smile graced her lovely face. *Something about being in the woods always makes me think of you, Dad. Remember that time when I was about fourteen when you took mom and me camping in the Smokies? Damn, I didn't want to go. I was feeling resentful of you being gone all the time, and being around you and mom was the last thing I wanted to do.*

You made me go, though. What a little shit I was. Heh. At first, it was such a drag being forced into amicable conversation, but somehow you turned me around. By the end of the week, I didn't want to go home.

That first night in the tent...good god. It was raining and cold and we couldn't get a fire going because everything was wet. You and mom thought it was a funny predicament to be in, laughing at our bad luck. Making the most of just being together. I sat in the corner like a spoiled baby, feeling sorry for myself. Convinced you guys were out of your minds.

You said, "Just remember this, Seven. In the words of our ancient Greek forefathers, 'She conquers who endures.'" I looked at you with contempt, a sarcastic reply already forming in mind. Then you said, "I think it actually says 'He' but in this case, I'm sure Perseus would be okay with the slight alteration." You looked into my eyes that so closely resembled yours, to make sure I'd heard, then proceeded to tickle me mercilessly. I was quickly reduced to tears of squealing tickle pain.

I pleaded with mom for assistance, but she just shook her head as if to say, "Oh no, you had this comin'."

The next day during some very muddy hiking, we spied a deer in the woods, and you showed me how to stalk it so she'd never know we were there. It seemed a peaceful adventure at the time, but I look back on it now and realize that week was probably the closest we'd ever been. You taught me all those cool survival skills, like how to start a one-match fire, how to catch fish without a pole, how to stay warm, how to love nature, and of course, the all-important how to play Cribbage.

We laughed a lot.

I think I grew up a lot that week, also.

You taught me I had to be responsible for my own actions, and to always take pride in what I do. To be above reproach by always being honest with myself and those around me. To work hard. To have patience. God, I wanted so much to be like you. You seemed to embody all those things. I wish I'd known you as an adult. I wish I'd known then what I know now. Would you respect me? Would you think the sacrifices I've made to follow in your footsteps were foolish? Or would you be proud?

I feel a little lost sometimes, Dad. You're gone. Mom's off in her new life. Sometimes I feel like a leaf swinging in the wind, just a tiny gust away from falling off the tree. I wish I could remember if you'd ever imparted any words of wisdom to me on how to deal with that feeling.

Seven snapped out of her mental wanderings, having heard a rustling in the bushes to her left. She paused to look as a beautiful black bird with a brilliant red belly hopped up onto a nearby branch and chirped cheekily at her. A quick laugh escaped her throat before she could firmly reestablish her no-nonsense warrior mask. For the briefest instant, she forgot where she was and the seriousness of what she was there to do. It felt good to laugh. She hadn't done much of that lately.

❧ ❧ ❧ ❧ ❧

The crew of three Delegates reached their predetermined stopping point, having made fairly good time. The spot Seven had chosen while designing their tactical plan was next to a small stream where they could refresh and refill their water containers, have something to eat, and get prepped for their push to the Reyes Hacienda. It was late afternoon now. The plan was to move the final five klicks to the Hacienda perimeter, dig in for the night, and watch. With any luck, they would acquire the target before long, take the shot, and move out to their pickup site.

Seven sat on the ground against a fallen log and glanced around at her teammates. She focused on the ghillie suit in her lap, attaching some twigs and leaves from the local fauna to the headpiece. Marcus had purified some fresh drinking water from the stream and was now splashing cool water on his face. Ty was digging in his pack for something, having already applied an interesting pattern of camouflage paint to his face.

Marcus strolled over at a leisurely pace and plopped down next to Seven, grabbing her container of face paint and beginning an energetic application on his forehead. "This makeup does nothing for my sexy complexion," he joked to his friend, doing his best gay guy impersonation. "I don't know, maybe we should petition the government for face paint by Lancome or Clinique. Somebody has to take the importance of our healthy, gorgeous skin into account for a change. At the very least, they should come up with some more interesting colors. This dark green does absolutely nothing to bring out the highlights in my eyes."

Seven raised an eyebrow and looked wryly at her friend, taking back the face paint and beginning her own application. "What's up with Cooper? He seems unusually quiet for a change," she asked her friend.

"Oh nothing," he replied innocently. "Just gave him a little something to think about is all."

"Hmm. And does that little something have anything to do with me, by chance?"

"Who else? You know I'm your number one fan, Sev. Can't tolerate that guy talkin' shit all the time. Just had to set him straight about who's in charge, and why." Marcus glanced over at her ghillie suit and started to remove his from the pack.

"Listen, Seven. There's something I've wanted to show you." He fished around in one of his many pant pockets and pulled out a shining engagement ring.

"Oh, Marcus. You shouldn't have! For me?" Seven said, feigning a damsel being wooed.

"Look. I know you said we shouldn't bring anything personal, but I've been carrying this around with me for weeks now. It's not engraved yet or anything. Anyway, I've been trying to work up the nerve to ask Alicia if she'll marry me. I think I finally have. I'm gonna do it when we get back. She's the one, Sev. I just know it. I love her." He finished quietly with an adorably bashful look on his face.

"That's great, Marcus," Seven said, grabbing hold of his shoulder and giving it a little shake. "I'm really happy for you. I think Alicia is a beautiful person and you'll make each other very happy. God! That is fantastic." She beamed at him, grinning from ear to ear.

"Wow. Guess that was a five-pointer."

She laughed and punched him in the arm, then grabbed the ring to give it a closer look. "Hell no, buddy. That was an automatic win."

"Now that's what I call a Hallmark moment," Ty said as he came trotting out of the woods. "Well, are you just gonna sit there Johnson, or will you be accepting the T.L.'s proposal?"

"Tch." Both friends rolled their eyes in unison.

Marcus accepted the ring back from his friend and tucked it safely away in a zippered pocket. "One more thing, Sev. Um...ah..." The love struck Marine was suddenly at a loss for words. "If you wouldn't mind...um...I would really appreciate it if you would maybe consider being my Best Man?"

This earned him a rare Seven Michelis bear hug. There weren't enough points on his scoreboard to assign value to that. "Of course. It would be an honor, my friend."

"Can you two knock off the grab ass? I'd really like to get on with this mission." Ty, ever the gentleman, strikes again.

The Team Leader and her friend stood and donned their ghillie suits, making the last preparations for the next leg of their hike. She slid a clip of 7.62mm caliber ammo into her now fully assembled rifle, deciding to save the long distance .300 caliber Magnum clip until after she'd seen the Hacienda for herself. She'd make the final decision on what to use once she'd seen the terrain up close and personal. The powerful German-made rifle was attached securely to her back in readiness for the slow and tedious haul before them.

"Okay, we're in total stealth mode from here on out. No more chit chat. When we get to the Hacienda perimeter, we'll fan out, find the best spot for reconnaissance and surveillance, and dig our hides for the night. Cooper, I want you scouting our flank at all times, never outside of voice range. I don't want to see you unless the hounds of hell themselves are on your ass. Got it?"

"Affirmative, T.L."

"We'll get as close as we can today, and if we have to get super-sneaky, we'll move the rest of the way in tomorrow, and then stick until we acquire the target. Take your position, Cooper. We'll catch up with you after I take the shot and we head for the exit point. If the target doesn't show himself in"—she checked her watch again—"thirty-two hours, we go to Plan B. Get going." Ty took off into the woods, separating himself from the pair.

The shooter and her spotter headed for the trees in the direction of their final goal. "So what do you think, Sev? Will she be a traditional, white wedding kinda girl? Or maybe flip flops and Hawaiian shirts on the beach? Or may..."

Marcus never finished his sentence.

The Delegate's head jerked sideways with the impact of a fatal bullet just before the sound of the shot reached their location.

Chapter Four

They never saw it coming.

Seven stood riveted to the spot as she watched her best friend's body drop lifelessly to the ground just two feet from where she stood. Stunned. Immoveable. In complete denial. For the briefest instant she could not comprehend why he would just fall over like that.

Something painful stung her neck, snapping her back into the moment where sound filtered back into her reality. She heard yelling and gunshots, all apparently coming her way. Seven's world seemed to come crashing down as she grabbed her sidearm from her hip and took aim in the direction of the gunfight, moving into a defensive position. She could feel warm blood flowing freely down her neck, into her shirt, just now realizing on some other plane she'd been shot. Her senses flared as the smell of gun smoke reached her, the taste of it acrid in her mouth.

Ty raced out of the woods, running at breakneck speed toward Seven, hurtling downed logs and rocks along the way. He was panic stricken, waving one arm, signaling her to run and firing behind himself with his automatic as he careened through the clearing. She took aim over his shoulder and fired at unseen enemies, still numb with shock about Marcus. "Run, T.L., run!" He screamed. "Can't hold 'em! We're fucked!"

At that moment, one of the gunmen came barreling from the underbrush, aiming a rifle in Seven's direction. Her attention was focused on several slippery shadows coming up behind Ty as he closed the gap between them. "Get the hell out of here!" He screamed...one last ditch effort to convince her to run for it. Ty launched himself between Seven and the rifleman as the crack of the enemy's weapon erupted. Caught in mid-air, feet ungrounded, his body jerked with the impact of the bullet as he was thrown to the ground in a bleeding heap.

"Nooo!" Every one of Seven's natural instincts to fight over flight was screaming in her ear to kill them all. The only instinct that didn't appear to be cooperating was that of survival. On some level, she knew there was no chance if she didn't try to save herself. Before Ty's body hit the ground, her feet took charge over her mind and she sped headlong through the trees toward anywhere but there. "No, no, no, fucking noooo!" She screamed at herself as she fled for her life.

Seven's adrenaline was pumping on maximum overdrive. The sound of bullets following her through the woods, ripping leaves and pinging off tree trunks around her was unnerving. She felt something harsh bite her arm, the impact sending her into a half spin, which almost sent her crashing to the ground. She was running for her life and she knew it. Dodging trees and bushes, her head was filled with the sound of her own labored breathing, her heartbeat pounding in her ears, feet crushing the unsuspecting leaves and branches of the forest floor as she barreled over them. Duck and weave.

The sound of bullets began to fade, but voices

calling to each other in the distance were distinct enough for Seven to understand she was still too close for comfort. Pausing for a moment to catch her breath, she realized she couldn't move her left arm. She glanced down to see a considerable amount of blood dripping off her hand, her sleeve soaked with it. Seven put her free hand to her neck, attempting to stay the flow of blood there, thinking it wouldn't do to bleed to death out here in the middle of nowhere. A wave of nausea and dizziness suddenly overcame her, an effect of the blood loss. *Gotta stop the bleeding.* She kept from falling to her knees by sheer will alone.

The wounded woman pulled a handkerchief from her coat breast pocket and wrapped it securely around her upper arm where a bullet was undoubtedly lodged. She tied it as best she could with her shaking right hand, and bit the inside of her lip from pain and to hold back the nausea. *Oh my god,* she wailed silently in her head. *What did I do wrong? How could I have so completely fucked this up? God, Cooper, Marcus. Dear Marcus, I'm so sorry.*

Her momentary need to wallow in self-pity was cut short as her pursuers suddenly appeared and yelled to their hombres that they had found *la puta*. She was able to shoot one of the men, and was off and running again, praying to herself that she wouldn't faint from blood loss and exertion. The sound of rushing water suddenly caught her ear. She headed for it, not knowing what to expect but hoping for a way to lose herself.

Pounding head. Quickness of breath. Her pulse jumped out of her skin. Her mind was racing and foggy. Seven was finding it increasingly difficult to focus on keeping up a good pace, and felt the presence of men closing in from behind. *Dizzy. Damn it. Focus or die, Marine.* She pressed two fingers to her neck to slow the bleeding. The sound of raging water up ahead became louder as the distance to it closed. She thought the water would be either her savior or her death, not sure which, and at this point, not really caring much. If she didn't go in the river, she was dead. If she did go in, she'd probably also end up dead, but at least it would be on her terms. All she knew for sure was her mission was FUBAR, and she was to blame.

Seven charged to the edge of an overhanging cliff, getting her first look at the raging waters below. In another life, in another time, it would be a breathtaking sight. Absolutely beautiful. It was about twenty-five feet down to the water's surface, and appeared deep where the waterfall relentlessly pounded the earth below. Pausing only a heartbeat, the determined woman launched herself into a suicidal leap to the foamy depths below, holding her useless arm to her body to protect it from further damage.

She closed her eyes, sucking in a deep lung full of air, and prepared for impact.

❧❧❧❧

The shock of cold water momentarily clarified Seven's thoughts. *Dear God, I'm in trouble.* She tumbled under the frothy white madness, trying to right herself and protect her head from hitting any boulders at the same time. The need for air became paramount as she fought to the surface, the strong rapids sweeping her away from the falls perilously close to dangerous rocks and tangled foliage. *Feet first, feet first,* she chanted in a semi-panic, attempting to maneuver her body into a safer position, just barely avoiding a head-on collision with a sedentary boulder downstream.

The injured woman let the current take her. At this point, she didn't have much choice anyway. She glanced back toward the falls as the water swooped her around a bend, seeing her pursuers standing on the overhang gazing at the raging foam below. *They didn't get there in time to see me come out of the jump. Heh. Assholes.* She was swept out of sight just as the man standing at the edge of the cliff looked downstream.

"Whoa!" Seven yelped at a near miss with a jagged boulder, just before she dropped several feet into a fresh swirl of raging foam. She was relieved that at least the cold water had eased her throbbing arm somewhat. *Gotta get as far away from here as I can, then come up with a plan.* A wave of dizziness hit her again and she grappled for clarity.

Fighting for breath, she was sucked under the water again, coming up winded after another struggle with the weight of her heavy clothes and weapons. Somehow, she had gotten turned around and was now in the dangerous position of going backward down the rapids. *Must...get...turned...Ow!* Her shoulder slammed into a rock. *Damn it. I've got to get out of this before I drown.* She glimpsed movement on the bank of the fast flowing river. *Sonofabitch! Please, God, tell me I didn't just see a freakin' crocodile on the riverbank. Like I don't have enough problems.*

A wave of utter loneliness washed over her. *Okay. Think. Try to stay focused. No time to feel sorry for yourself.* Seven took a deep breath and looked around, getting a momentary reprieve from the boulders. The water was still fast flowing, whipping the lone Delegate through the dense forest at a good clip. She was relieved because the faster she moved, the further away she got from her hunters.

Seven felt her lightheadedness getting worse. *I've got to get out of the water before I get too spacey to know what's what. Should be safe from the crocs as long as I'm in the rapids, but once the river slows, got to get out fast. I sooo do not want to be something's snack. Bleeding in a river with god only knows what. Okay. Priority One: Get out of river.* She reached up to her neck, still feeling the warm ooze of blood running over her fingers. *Priority Two: Stop the bleeding. Priority Three: Find some shelter and hide. Got to rest and recoup as much as possible before I can move forward. Got to get my head on straight and come up with a plan. Got to figure out what the hell went wrong. Oh, Marcus...what have I done?*

Seven grabbed onto a floating branch as her rifle butt bottomed out on something below her. She was relieved she hadn't somehow lost the weapon in the melee of the last hour. Her teeth were chattering now, an unwelcome distraction that made focus even more difficult. The sun was setting, providing a change in the sky's hue peeking through an overhanging canopy of thick trees. The drifting woman became aware of the river's flow slowing. The welcome support of the floating branch was set free as she made her way foggily to the shore, knowing only that she must get out now, not really remembering why it was so important.

The shoreline was slick with dead leaves, forest debris, and mossy rocks. After several attempts to stand, Seven decided, given her condition, that crawling out would be better. Her left arm was definitely no longer cooperating, so she scooted slowly along on three appendages. The weight of the soaked gear and equipment she was wearing seemed unbearable in her weakened state.

Finally free of the chilling water, the exhausted warrior used a tree trunk to help right herself. Her knees gave out and she fell again to the forest floor. *Maybe I'll rest here for a minute.* She shifted to a sitting position and looked around for the first time, idly placing two fingers back on her neck. *Cold. Come... on...Sev.* She shivered. *S...snap...out...of...it.*

In the waning light of sunset, Seven spied a small dock sticking into the river about thirty yards downstream. *Yes! D...Dock means p...path. Path means people. People means help if I can s...steal it.* She pulled herself up to a standing position and better gained her balance before heading once more into the woods.

❧.❧❦.❦

"What the hell do you mean, she got away?" Armando Reyes yelled, then backhanded his armed security guard across the face, bloodying his nose. A tall, thin man of fifty-three, the Bolivian businessman ranted around the covered patio of his palatial hacienda, boot heels clicking on the posh ceramic tile. He removed the no-longer-needed reading glasses from his long, regal nose and ran the fingers of one hand through his thick, disheveled salt and pepper hair. "You think she may have drowned? You god-damned idiot!" He screamed once more before storming into the dwelling, leaving an embarrassed security force standing wide-eyed on the patio.

His anger was boiling over as he stomped into his den, closely followed by his son, and slammed the door. Armando Jr., or Manny as he was known, poured his father a stiff shot of decanted scotch and crossed the luxuriously appointed room to hand it over. The pungent aroma of the scotch made him turn his head away.

"Imbeciles!" The older man bellowed. "Manny, do you know what this could mean to me?" He whined to his son.

Manny shook his head, encouraging his father to elaborate. Armando's only true confidant, Manny played along willingly encouraging the older man to continue. His position as his father's advisor was a farce. The older man never sought advice from anyone, so confident was he in his own decision-making. He merely used his son as a sounding board.

Armando never bothered to notice if his son was paying attention, or even if he understood him, for that matter. He made an assumption from the day of his birth that Manny would follow in his exact footsteps and eventually take over the reins of the Reyes family estate. He would inherit his ancestor's good looks, smarts, work ethic, and premium societal standing in Bolivia, and in the world. At the age of twenty-five, it appeared to everyone *but* Armando that the only thing actually passed down from the Reyes ancestors to Manny was his good looks. The elder Reyes had no idea his son's only interest was his inheritance. If Armando had ever taken the chance to talk with his son, instead of just at him, he would have undoubtedly received an unpleasant surprise.

"Manny! Did you even hear what I said?"

"Yes, Father. No need to shout. You said the assassin jumped in the river," Manny replied, feigning interest.

"That means the *puta* will have washed downstream into that son-of-a-*whore* Argulla's lands. Do you have any idea how humiliating it will be that I, Armando Reyes, will have to travel to the home of that filthy, repulsive, street trash and beg a favor of *him*? Ahhhh!" He kicked the leg out from under an antique side table, sending the fresh flowers and vase crashing to the floor.

"Why can't you just send the men down the river to find her?"

"Because!" He yelled in utter frustration. "I've told you before. Many years ago, I had some of his men that were caught on my lands shot for trespassing. One of them, he claimed, was a cousin of his. He was livid! I never found out for sure what that rat bastard was up to, but I know he was up to something. He has been trying to get his whoring hands on our estate for a decade. Argulla wants our coca production under his control and figured I would move on without a fight since my interests no longer lie in our farming. I will *never* give up our estate. It is our birthright. But, we came to an agreement that we would forever stay away from each other's lands or else there would be very serious trouble." He paced over to the bar and refilled his empty glass of scotch. "If my men go over there and are seen, it will mean the all-out war he has been wanting for years. A blood bath. Too big for me to erase even with my connections, and I can't afford any publicity right now of any kind."

Manny turned from the window where he had been gazing out at the men still milling around on the patio, awaiting their new orders. He strolled to the settee at a leisurely pace, hiked up his gray Prada slacks, and sat, crossing his legs and flicking a speck of dust from his custom-made Italian leather shoes. "Father, what is so important about this assassin? Surely you don't fear her return. Her mission has been squashed. The men said she was shot. Your men were successful in accomplishing that, and if she comes anywhere near here, they will kill her on sight. How do you know you hunt a woman, anyway? Hardly seems likely."

"It's a woman. My source in Washington told me everything I needed to know about the team, why they came, where they would be, etc. American pigs! They have to stick their arrogant noses in everything! We got the two men, so that leaves this Michelis person out there somewhere." He swirled the scotch in his glass and walked to the window, looking out. "He said she's very good at what she does and I would be foolish not to take this threat seriously."

"Perhaps you should stand away from the window, then," the young man said with a smirk.

Realization sat uncomfortably on the elder man's face as he moved swiftly from the glass. "We must get her, Manny. My life, everything our ancestors and I have built here depends on it. She must be stopped before she can contact her people in Washington or get out of the country. I have paid my source dearly and have been assured that with the destruction of this team, it would be possible to have my name removed from investigation by this Black Flag organization. The only way that can happen is if she never makes it out alive. Those incompetent morons outside have blown their simple task and put two hundred years of Reyes legacy in danger."

"It's chilly tonight. Should I call Mariana to start a fire?"

"No," Armando dismissed him. "I'm not done

talking to you yet, and I don't want any disruptions."

Taking a seat in a luxurious puffy chair, the older man crossed his legs and pondered the golden liquid in his glass. "It's not really the Americans I'm so concerned with. Most of them can be bought for the right price. Greedy hypocrites. What concerns me is my old friend and business associate Yeslam Aziz and the organizations he represents. You see, they can't be bought. A true zealot can never be bought. If they find out I've made it onto the American's radar... well...they'll kill me themselves, just in case. We're in a dangerous business, and one thing they can't afford to jeopardize is their funding. They will do anything to protect it, including kill their allies.

"So you see, I must get her. I must kill her, even if I have to do it myself. If she is allowed to survive, everything I've built will come crashing down. And perhaps, just to be on the safe side, I will attempt to temper my relationship with Aziz. Maybe now that the climate is so hot, he will understand if I make moves to back away. Perhaps if I am no longer involved, I will cease to be of interest to those post 9/11 witch hunters. If I can get her, and our plan works out, I will be off the U.S.'s radar long enough to disentangle myself and therefore no longer be of interest.

"So I must begin by biting the bullet and going to that pig, Raul...whoreson...Argulla and asking for permission to search his lands for this woman. But first I must figure out a tale to tell him that is worthy, because he is not to know my business.

"Manny. Go down to the wine cellar and bring me a bottle of the Rémy Martin Louis XIII Cognac. I will see if I can ply this bastard with a gift."

"The Black Pearl?"

"No. He is not worthy of a $10,000 bottle. Get the regular kind. He's such an ignorant street rat, he'll probably mix it with a Coca-Cola anyway. Then, I want you to get dressed. You're coming with me and we are going over there tonight. We have no time to waste. The longer she's gone, the more dangerous this situation becomes."

"Maybe she's dead already." Manny sounded less than enthusiastic.

"I will not rest until I've seen the body for myself. Even if all I see is the remains of a crocodile's meal, I must see it myself to feel safe. Round up all the men and make sure they're armed. Tell them just concealed handguns this time, no rifles. I don't want Argulla to think he's being attacked when we drive up. If we're lucky, he'll say yes with little trouble and we'll be on our way to the hunt."

ॐॐॐॐ

The earthy smell of a rotting stump near her feet reached Seven's nose as she made her way slowly up the narrow forest path. *Well, it's nice to know my sniffer's still working, even if everything else seems to be shutting down.* She had no idea what awaited at the end of the path, but at this point, it's find out, or die here in the woods, in a strange land, thousands of miles from home. No one at home would even know what happened. *Maybe that's for the best.*

Seven's passage through the woods was tedious. Her ability to focus on her mission waned and a strange sense of confusion and light-headedness settled over her. It seemed a tremendous effort just to put one foot in front of the other. The blood was still flowing, though not as fast. Still, she feared she'd lost enough to affect her basic motor skills and knew much more would result in unconsciousness. She was being hunted. Now was not a good time to be unconscious.

After some time on the path, Seven began to hear the faint humming of some kind of manmade machinery. *Sounds like a generator. Good. Getting close.* As she walked, she unfastened the rifle sling from her back and hung it loosely over her uninjured arm. The closer she got to the humming, the further off the path she walked, doing her best to conceal herself lest she be seen. The lights of a tiny village, or compound of some kind, shimmered through the leaves.

The sniper dropped to her belly and inched forward through the dense foliage until she could see through the riflescope unobstructed by leaves and branches. Slowly she looked from left to right, getting the lay of the land. Some light emanated from two large structures to her left, but she didn't see any people, and the place was very quiet. *Wish I hadn't lost my night vision goggles.* She inched closer.

Thirty minutes later all was still quiet. Seven decided it was time to move in, see what she could get, and move out. She noticed what looked like a small red cross on the door of the larger structure and was hopeful it was a medical facility of some kind. *That would be some seriously good luck.* Her immediate plan was to sneak in, grab some proper bandages, disinfectants, and whatever else she determined to be useful. Then, get out unseen and undetected. With any luck, no one would even know she'd been there.

Seven stealthily moved to a squatting position at the edge of the clearing and waited several more minutes to see if anything changed. Her heart rate picked up as she mentally prepared for what must be accomplished, and the risk of being captured or killed once more. She placed her rifle on the ground at the edge of the clearing, intent on picking it up on her way out, and unzipped a small pocket in her pants, removing a well-used pocket knife that was a gift from her father. She glanced down at the knife, smiling briefly at the feel of it in her hand. The little thing had come in handy more times than she could count, and it always reminded her of her dad.

Staying in a crouched position, she darted from the darkness of the woods to the rear of the medical building. Safely ensconced in shadow once more, she scanned the area again to determine if she'd been detected. Satisfied, she flicked the pocket knife open to the appropriate tool without looking and headed for the side door at a run.

Seven made quick work of the door, the simple doorknob lock giving way easily. Once inside, the fading woman found herself in a narrow, unlit hallway. She heard faint voices to her right, so quietly scooted in that direction to peek around the corner. A nurse appeared at the far end of the room talking in quiet whispers to an elderly man resting fitfully on a hospital cot. All else was still.

The lone Delegate backed up and tiptoed down the hall to another locked door, praying there was something in there she could use. She watched her trail as she went, careful not to leave any mud or blood traces in her wake. No one must know she was there.

In the tiny, well kept office, there were no windows, so Seven shut the door and risked turning on the light. She went thoroughly through each drawer and cabinet, taking only what she needed. In the last desk drawer, she thanked unseen sources again when she found a box of granola bars and a partially drunk bottle of water. *Yes!* She stuffed her coat pockets with the medical supplies, bars, and water bottle, and glanced around one more time to make sure she'd left things the way she'd found them. She noticed a couple grimy, bloody finger smudges here and there, and grabbed a Kleenex off the desk to wipe them away. Her breathing was coming in shallower gasps now, and somewhere in the back of her mind was a vague thought that she wouldn't last much longer.

Seven made a dash for the safety of the woods, not bothering to stop half way. Her rifle was where she left it, now covered in a slight coating of night dew. She leaned over to pick it up and suddenly her world went upside down.

In her range of vision, she dreamily noticed the night darkened treetops and the black and starless sky beyond. She dreamily wondered why her mom was calling her name.

What the hell?

Seven came to a short time later and froze for an instant, realizing she'd just passed out in the open clearing next to the village. Thankfully, nobody saw her lying there. She shook her head briskly to clear the descending fog settling over her consciousness. *Oh God. Come on, Sev. If ever you needed to dig in, this is it.* She rolled her eyes back up to the heavens and pleaded silently. *If there's such a thing as guardian angels, please send one my way.*

"Okay. Let's get out of here." Grabbing her rifle, she headed back into the dark wood alive with the sound of night creatures. After finding a safe place to clean and dress her wounds, it was time to make a serious assessment of her condition and new goals. She felt she was getting progressively more delirious and decided her next step was to find a safe place to dig in, get warm, and get some rest. She needed to hide and give her body a few hours to recuperate before trusting herself to make a good decision on where to go from here.

She stuck to the trail away from the river for some time before forward motion became impossible. Seven fell to her knees, hardly aware of the new pain caused by impact with the rocky path. Rational thought was gone. It was time to dig in. She crawled into the woods. *Make...go...Marcus...no...got to...need...out... warm...dig.*

Chapter Five

Raul Jozef Argulla took a moment to shift his gaze around the opulent bedroom before settling his deep brown eyes back on the beautiful woman who was currently mounting him, grunting satisfactorily with each thrust. Maria, his chief of security, was like a dangerous animal, and fucking her gave him a thrill his wife could never match. *I am a king. A God. I am the master of all. Life is my playground.*

Raul was sprawled sideways across the large, comfortable four-poster bed adorned with carved golden eagles, wings spread in glory, and deep red velvet bedding. Everything in the room was gold or crimson, the ultimate in luxury for this former petty criminal raised on the streets of La Paz.

At forty-four, he had risen from the bastard son of an impoverished street whore, to a powerful and wealthy man with a deep seeded hatred of the aristocratic class. He was a landholder, who, like so many, made an incredible fortune in the eighties converting his massive coca crop into powdered gold. Short of stature but big on attitude, Raul Argulla never rested as he constantly searched the world around him for ways to increase his fortune.

A loud banging on the door drew Raul's attention from Maria, who was slowly torturing him to climax and getting close to finishing him off. "What? I'm busy!" He grabbed the woman's hips to stop her motion so he could listen to the reply.

"Sir. I am sorry to disturb you, but the forward post says there are two trucks full of men heading up the road." Marcello, one of his many security people, hollered through the thick wooden door.

"Police?"

"No sir. They appear to be from the Reyes estate."

"Well, my dear," he said to Maria, "perhaps you will finally get a chance to meet the man I have told you so much about." He released her hips and encouraged her to continue the motion.

"Shall I send him away, sir?" Marcello yelled from the door.

"No," he grunted. "Make that arrogant bastard wait in the foyer until I am ready to see him. Make sure his..." he grunted again, "men stay outside."

Raul finished with Maria without much fanfare, then lifted her and pushed the woman off to the side. He kicked his legs over the edge of the bed and reached for a cigarette on the bedside table. "Get dressed," he said over his shoulder as he blew his first lungful of smoke in the air. "I want you with me when I see him. Say nothing. Just watch. Later you will tell me your impressions. I don't know what he means by bringing a truckload of men here unannounced, but be ready for action if it comes to that."

The woman acknowledged the instruction then walked to the bathroom, picking up her discarded clothes as she went. Raul saw a rare smile form at the corners of Maria's mouth, knowing that the prospect of potential violence was the only thing that could elicit an emotion of any kind from the crazy bitch.

Cigarette still in hand, Raul fastened his pants

and strolled to the bathroom at a leisurely pace, shaking his parts to a more comfortable position as he walked. He wanted to check his appearance in the bathroom mirror before heading down to meet his recent nemesis. Combing a fresh dose of hair gel into his slicked back black hair, he smiled at his roguish appearance with a mouthful of unnaturally straight, capped white teeth that indicated a considerable amount of dental work. He looked fondly at the ragged scar below his left eye. Gotten in a street fight at the age of fourteen, Raul thought it lent a look of intimidation to his otherwise uninteresting features. The boy that gave it to him died from his injuries.

Argulla straightened the lapels on his jacket and quietly descended the elegant winding marble stairway, hugging the curve of the balustrade as he went, followed some steps behind by the silent Maria. He shrewdly noticed not only was his uninvited guest pacing the floor impatiently, but he looked extremely uncomfortable as well. *Good. Bastard.*

"Señor Reyes. An unexpected surprise. To what do I owe the honor?" Both men regarded each other warily.

"Ah. Señor Argulla. I am sorry to call at this late hour but I need to speak with you about a matter of some importance that affects us both. Please, accept this gift as I am intruding uninvited upon your hospitality."

Argulla accepted the fancy red box of Cognac from Reyes, noting it wasn't the special edition Black Pearl variety of Louis XIII. He inclined his head in thanks and gestured the man toward his den.

"You remember my son, Manny?" Reyes attempted an awkward introduction.

"Yes, of course. And this"—he gestured toward the silent woman standing in the shadows—"is Maria Velasquez, my chief of security." Maria nodded but remained silent. Her eyes never left the man called Armando Reyes. The tension in the air was thick as both parties tried to feel out the other.

Argulla moved to the sidebar and poured four glasses of Louis XIII into ornate crystal snifters. "So what can I do for you, Señor Reyes? I take it this isn't a social call. I can't begin to imagine why you would bring a truckload of men here in the middle of the night. I hope I have nothing to worry about," he said suspiciously, knowing full well that Maria was capable and willing of taking out the entire truckload of armed men if let loose on them.

"Of course not, sir. It is a personal matter that concerns you as well. I wanted to make sure you were aware of what was happening, though I can assure you, we can handle the matter ourselves."

Raul waited patiently for the man to continue, his curiosity now piqued. He noticed the bored expression on the face of the older man's son and smirked to himself. *He is so clueless. That boy would rather be anywhere than here.*

"There is a woman on the loose who we have found to be stealing from us. She admitted under some...persuasion...to have stolen from you too. Bails of harvested coca. She is a foreigner, and has apparently been liberating our product and shuttling it out of the country for her own personal gain. We don't know exactly how much she has taken from us, but we suspect it is a substantial amount." Reyes watched Argulla to see if his fiction was having the desired effect.

He continued. "We captured her raiding a warehouse in our southern fields, but she escaped. Was shot in the attempt. We believe she has come downriver into your lands. We must send a message that this kind of theft is unacceptable, and will incur the harshest punishment." Reyes paused before delivering what he hoped would draw the desired response.

"With your permission, my men are ready to search for her and bring her to justice. We have had our differences in the past regarding our territory, but I assure you, sir, with the utmost respect, we will find this thief and be gone before you even know we were here. It is a matter of pride, Señor Argulla. I must find her and bring her to justice, and I respectfully request my men be allowed to search your lands for this criminal."

Lying pig, Argulla thought to himself. *He must think me a fool.* Raul made eye contact with Maria and could tell instantly she thought the same thing. Nobody stole a thing from him without his knowledge. He ran a very tight ship, and knew every detail of what happened with his crop, right down to each individual bale.

Argulla made the older man sweat for a few minutes before he delivered his response. He refilled his glass as he thought up a reply that would most upset the arrogant man before him. "This is very disturbing news, Señor Reyes. I will, of course, help in any way I can." Raul liked the idea of making the man think he had won for a moment before he pulled out the rug. A visible sigh of relief escaped Reyes at these words.

"But..."—Argulla reveled in the uncomfortable look on his guest's face—"I cannot allow your men to be involved in the search of my lands. I have many...business ventures...in the area that would be dangerous for strangers to come upon. I will have my chief of security take a team of our most skilled personnel out immediately to hunt for your missing woman. I will inform you the moment she is captured, and if you wish, deliver her personally to your door. Or, we can just kill her and give you the body. Your choice."

Argulla silently cheered as he watched Reyes' face drop the moment he realized his hand was not played to success.

"So be it, Señor Argulla. But I do hope that if you have no success in finding her in the next twenty-four hours, you will allow my men to join in the search. It is very important to me she be captured or killed as soon as possible."

Raul acknowledged he heard the man with a nod. "If there is nothing else, Señor Reyes, I shall round up my people and get them to work." He gestured that he was ready for his uninvited guests to leave. "Please give the details of where she was last seen to my man Marcello on your way out." Argulla shut the den door after escorting his guest back to the foyer, then turned to the woman standing beside him.

"What do you think?"

"He is a lying sack of shit," she spit out with no preamble. "I have seen many men like him before. He thinks the world should bow at his precious feet and that everyone else is so stupid they should buy whatever candy-coated bullshit he spews from his superior mouth."

"Hm. So you like him as much as I do?" Raul asked sarcastically. "Don't hold back, just call it like you see it," he joked, once again noting the similarities in their opinions of the aristocratic class. He suspected they had a similar childhood, though she seemed to take a lot more pleasure from inflicting pain than he did.

"Do you want me to round up the men and begin the search?"

"No. Fuck him. You can start in the morning. Chances are if she's been shot and in the river, she's probably dead already anyway."

"What do you think this is really all about? Why would he go to the trouble to create that pathetic lie?"

"I don't know. Yet. But I will find out." Raul poured more Cognac into Maria's glass then refilled his own for the third time. "You know, this could be the opportunity I've been waiting for." He pondered a little longer before continuing. "There seemed to be an undercurrent of panic in his behavior tonight. Perhaps he has finally done something that I can exploit."

Argulla fingered the scar on his cheek, a habit he developed as a young man that indicated he was deep in thought. "Do you still have your contact in the Reyes security camp?"

"Yes. I have worked him for months. I believe he finally trusts me."

"Good. See if you can contact him tonight and get the real information. Or whatever you can. Tomorrow, first thing, take a team out and find that woman. Don't tell anybody anything, just that you're searching for a runaway, or something. Do whatever you have to, but find her, and bring her to me.

"My gut instinct is that she will be the key to my finally getting what I want out of that bastard Reyes. For years, I have wanted to take over his estate and coca production. He has refused every generous offer

I have ever made without so much as a courteous explanation."

Raul did an excited shuffle around the room. "Maria, this is it. I can feel it. Once I get my hands on his estate, I will be the largest cocalero in Bolivia. This would quadruple my legitimate trade and provide me with multiple new transfer routes out of the country for my cocaine. This would be a beautiful thing." He smiled a toothy grin, envisioning himself in this lofty position.

"Now, go," Argulla barked with finality. "I must call my wife and see that she stays in La Paz for a few more days. I don't want her around here if things are about to get interesting."

꧁꧂꧁꧂

Maria Velasquez was a beautiful woman...on the outside.

On the inside, she was an emotionless killer whose only true thrill was watching the life drain like dirty dishwater from the eyes of her victims. Her petite femininity was a convenient disguise covering a psyche that mirrored a cobra coiled to strike.

Slim and elegant looking, at five foot, six inches with long dark hair highlighted with blonde that fell in tight curls down her back, the young woman of twenty-eight had seen things with her golden amber eyes that would make most people choose suicide over continuing with life. Those who had suffered similar crimes normally ended up dying young, mentally deranged, addicts, any number of things that allowed the human mind to cope with a childhood carved from violence and abuse. But occasionally, the victim of horrific crime will themselves turn to acts of extreme violence as a way to exert power over the world that left them behind.

Day to day, Maria felt nothing. If she was lucky, occasionally she could create the illusion of feeling by being the architect of great pain and fear in another. Didn't matter whom, really. She enjoyed killing people who sparked her interest the most, but was perfectly happy with a basic hit job, or messy but effective shoot-em-up. Killing for sport was different from killing for money, but if she could manage it, she would combine the two. Chaos was her numbing drug.

Maria would travel willingly to wherever the potential for violence was most likely.

Her preferred method of death was a skinning knife inserted slowly under the ribcage and into the heart, while she stared into the eyes of the soon to be departed. It was a very personal feeling to hold someone closely the moment their body jerked to lifelessness. In this instant, Maria could almost convince herself that she felt something. It felt good. For a minute. Then it was on to the next one.

In 2002, Maria was working a temporary security job for a prominent member of the Colombian drug cartel when she met Raul. The Bolivian cocalero was visiting Columbia on business when he spied this stunning woman lurking in the shadows like a spider avoiding the burning sun. Her reputation as a hired gun was well known in the drug trade. He was not afraid, even after he found out who she was.

Raul convinced Maria to come to Bolivia when her operation in Columbia was done. He was stimulated at the prospect of having such an infamously dangerous creature all to himself. He knew it was a gamble. Some said she was insane, but it was a risk he was willing to take for the thrill of it. He saw her as exciting. He wanted her expertise to beef up his own security team. He wanted her more specialized advice on possibly ridding him of his pesky nemesis, Armando Reyes. And most of all, he wanted her. He felt she was like him in some ways, and that he could control her occasional bouts of manic violence. With the proper control, she could be a valuable asset to him for as long as she'd stay in his employ.

Maria had been employed by Raul Argulla for five months when Armando Reyes showed up at his door, bottle in hand. So far, their relationship had proved beneficial, but Raul feared Maria was becoming bored with her position. She had a taste for violence, and lately things in his operation had been running unusually smooth. He viewed this latest development as a bonus, something intriguing for her to become involved in, and with any luck, maybe the downfall of Reyes as well.

The rain was falling in washes as Maria pulled her Land Rover up to the front of Raul's hacienda. Mud in massive quantities was unavoidable. She darted from the car up to the patio, kicking the mud off her boots as she climbed the covered stairs. It was three a.m., but Raul pulled open the double front doors as she approached, eager to hear what, if anything, she had learned.

"Did you see him?" The Bolivian asked, referring to Maria's contact within the Reyes estate.

"Yes, I saw him. And he saw me." She smirked. Men were so easy to use.

"He didn't have many details, but the woman Reyes is after is no thief." Maria paused to sip the drink Raul handed her, then set it on the foyer center table and began to remove her muddy boots.

"She is a sniper, sent to kill Reyes." Maria was intrigued. She liked that. A woman.

"An assassin? I don't believe it," he said, chuckling. "I thought I was the only one that wanted that ass dead. Who did he think sent her?"

"He had no idea. They came in a team of three. The other two they got had no identification or markings. But I'll tell you this...he specifically said sniper. Not assassin. Whether it was intentional or not, a sniper with a team smells like government to me. I am an assassin. I work alone. I kill my targets in whatever way I need to, to get the job done. A sniper is a whole different animal."

"Tomorrow you will find her. Then we will get the whole truth for ourselves, and figure a way to use it to our advantage. Now, to bed. Come." Raul turned to the stairs, Maria followed delighted at the prospect of tomorrow's fun and games.

❧ ❧ ❧ ❧

It was sometime in the middle of the night when Seven pulled the last tree branch over herself and collapsed into the hide she made under a large fallen tree trunk. A depression in the ground left by the pulled up root structure was a ready-made hiding place she gratefully crawled into. Near delirium, the injured woman covered herself in forest camouflage before finally surrendering to total exhaustion.

It's raining was the last thought Seven had before slipping into unconsciousness. Lucidity slid into the night as she fell deep into another time.

"Happy New Year, Uncle Nicky." The young teenager kissed her uncle on the cheek and took a sip of her champagne. "I think the Dick Clark countdown was a little boring this year. I didn't really like many of the groups they had playing. I can't believe it's 1989 already, though. Seems like we just moved down here a couple months ago and it's already been over a year."

Nick Michelis noticed his niece seemed melancholy. He thought she'd been that way since Dean was killed, but didn't mention it, assuming she just needed time to get over her father. "We're so happy to have you and your mom nearby, Sev. We never got to see enough of you when you were living in Virginia." The big man hugged his niece affectionately, spinning her around a little while she was still in his clutches. "How are you doing these days? We haven't had much time to talk lately."

"I'm okay. School seems to be the same here as it is everywhere," Seven said to her uncle, not bothering to elaborate with details.

The tall young woman's mother came up from behind and wrapped her arms lovingly around her daughter's waist. "Can you believe how tall she's gotten, Nick? She looks more and more like her father each day."

"She's a real beauty, all right. Probably breaking hearts all over the Carolinas on a daily basis." Seven rolled her eyes.

The girl turned and hugged her mother. "Happy New Year, Mom."

"So what of it, Sev?" Nick poked her playfully in the arm. "You seeing anybody? Got boyfriends lined up around the block?"

"Nah. You know how it is," she played along. "I'm

*not interested in the ones that like me, and the ones
I like aren't interested." In her mind, Seven thought
she wasn't really interested in any of them...the guys,
anyway. And it wasn't for lack of them trying. They all
just seemed so strangely pathetic.*

*"I think she's just a little too mature for the boys
her age," Catherine said. "You'll find a good guy in
college. I have no doubt." She gave her daughter another
squeeze for good measure.*

*"Uncle Nick, do you mind if I go play on your
computer for a while?" She said, not really in the mood
to be interrogated about her lack of a love life. Her
mind was set on a cool war game her uncle showed her
last time she was visiting.*

*"Sure, sweetie. You know where it is. Stay out
of the top-secret files, though. You know the rules," he
kidded her.*

*Seven made her way to Nick's library. She settled
in his comfortable black leather chair and booted up his
machine, taking a moment to look around at the books
and military knickknacks he had decorating the room.
She inhaled deeply, appreciating the smell of leather and
cigar tobacco that permeated the space. She ran a long
finger over the leather spines of a collection of classic
novels,* Treasure Island, War and Peace, Huckleberry
Finn, The Art of War, Of Mice and Men. *Her finger
stopped on the spine of a fine leather photo album and
she pulled it from the shelf.*

*The teen smiled to herself as she opened the book
to the first page and saw a familiar photograph. A
black and white of Uncle Nick and her father as young
Marines fully decked out in their crisp dress uniforms,
with their proud wives on their arms. They all looked
so happy. Her father had a mischievous look in his eyes,*

as though he knew something special that others could only guess at. Her mother had the same photo framed in their house, and once told her it was taken on the day she found out she was pregnant with Seven.

She continued to turn the pages, finding several photos of her father she'd never seen before of his time spent in the military. One in particular caught her attention, and she studied it intently. Her dad was mugging for the camera. His khaki t-shirt sleeves were rolled up to his shoulders, showing off muscular arms. He was flexing his right bicep, pointing to a raw red brand of the letters SS that had been recently burned into his arm.

Seven remembered the brand. Her father once told her it stood for "Super Stud," jokingly referring to what all the ladies he knew before her mother used to say about him. In the photo, his left arm was curled around a long, deadly looking rifle with a huge scope. Seven had never seen a weapon like it, and was immediately drawn to finding out what it was, and what her father was doing with it. She had seen tons of military weaponry photos in the past, but couldn't recall ever having seen anything quite like that.

The computer forgotten, she began to dig through Uncle Nick's library in earnest. She knew she'd seen a title referring to Marine weaponry somewhere. Leaving the photo album open to that image, she pulled a 3-ring binder from the lower shelf, convinced it was the book she was looking for. Yes, here it is.

As she flipped through the binder pages, the teen found what she was looking for on page thirty-eight. An M40 standard marine issue bolt action sniper rifle. Holding her breath, she continued to read. There was little information on the page, but one thing in particular she noticed was the name for the Marines that used this rifle. They were called Scout Snipers. SS, she thought. I can't believe I'm just figuring this out.

Floored by her discovery, Seven sat back in the leather chair and looked again at her father's photograph. He looked so proud of his brand, as though it was something he fought hard to earn. Resting her head in her hands, the young teen tried to decipher what this meant to her and how she felt about it. A sniper. Why didn't he tell me? That's practically the same as being an assassin. How could he be that? How could he have lied to us all those years? *The love and worship she felt for her father was warring with her preconceived notions of what she just learned. She thought for the first time that perhaps she didn't know her dad at all.*

Seven lifted her head from her hands as she felt a draft brush across her hair. Her Uncle Nick was standing in the doorway, silently watching her. She couldn't tell how long he'd been there, but it was surely long enough for him to figure out she was going through his things. The girl was unashamed. Instead, she looked at him steadily with an unspoken question hanging between them.

"It's a tough job, you know...one of the most difficult in the Corps. One of the most elite forces in the military. Not many men have what it takes to do it well, like your dad did. He was one of the best." *The girl listened but said nothing.*

"It's one of the few jobs a Marine can have where a single man can turn the tide of battle. It's unique that way. In the military, we always work together for a common goal. We fight as a group. But a sniper, working alone, can remove the head of the snake with *no assistance, clearing the way for the foot soldiers. One shot, one kill. If done right, it can serve a debilitating blow to the opposition they can't recover from before the battle is over."*

"How could I not know this before? How come he never told us?"

"Your mother knew. He thought you were too young to understand. It's not an easy job to explain to a child. You knew he was a Marine. You knew he fought in wars. Is it just now you're coming to terms with him killing people? All Marines know that potential exists before they join. That is what we do."

Seven rubbed her eyes and tried to explain what she was feeling. "No, it's not that. This just seems different somehow. More...personal. More...wicked. I mean, if you're part of a fighting platoon, you go to battle with your group. You're all fighting the opposition together as a team. There's really nothing personal about it, you know? You're told to go to point A and fight, and that's what you do. That's what it always seemed like to me, anyway, from what I saw in the movies and stuff. But this? It's like... premeditated. Different. Scary. It seems evil, almost."

"Well...it is definitely more premeditated. But that's why it works so efficiently. See, a sniper will dig in and watch, sometimes for days. They can see who is in charge, where the biggest threat is likely to be, all kinds of things that will help the foot soldiers win faster with less casualties. Or if they're after a particular target, they may have intel that says their target goes from village to village killing civilians by the hundreds. To take out this one guy could save hundreds of his future victims. In a battle, they fight from a distance, seeing the whole picture. They can help the ground fighters by *picking off the enemies who are doing the most damage. It's a very important job. Not just anybody can do it. You have to be smart, skilled, patient, and have nerves of steel. Your father was a real hero, Seven. Don't you ever forget that. His actions saved many, many lives."*

"His actions took many lives," she said.

"That's called war, baby girl."

They shared a silent moment together as Seven digested this information from a Marine's perspective. Nick moved to place his books back on the shelf. "Now come on. Your mom wants to get home. It's late and she's looking for you to go."

"Do you think he would have told me eventually?" Seven was still slightly upset she hadn't been privy to this important information.

"Of course, if you wanted to know. He loved you very much, you know. He was incredibly proud to call you his daughter. He would have done anything for you." Nick put his arm around his niece's shoulder and led her to the door. "I want you to know, my door is always open to you. If you ever want to talk about your dad, or anything at all, mom, school, boyfriends… girlfriends…whatever, I'm here for you. Please know that."

Seven threw a quick glance at her uncle, wondering if that last comment meant what she thought it meant. "Thanks, Uncle Nicky. I'm sorry about nosing around in your stuff. I didn't mean to, I just sort of fell into it."

"S'okay, now get going before your mom hunts me down."

Armed with all kinds of new and interesting things to think about, Seven headed to the car, stopping to give her aunt a kiss on the way out the door. "Thanks for everything, Aunt Margaret. Happy New Year. I'll stop by for another visit soon, if that's okay."

"Whenever you'd like, Sev." She took the girl, a full head taller than her already, into her arms for an affectionate hug. "You're always welcome here."

The drive home that night was a quiet one. It was cold and raining, so Catherine was intently focused on driving in less than perfect conditions. This was fine by Seven. She had a lot to think on. She intended to look into what being a Scout Sniper was all about as soon as she could. She wanted to know everything about what her dad did so she could determine for herself what she thought of it. Also that last comment Uncle Nick made about girlfriends. Was that an innocent remark? Or did he somehow sense what she'd been thinking about a lot lately?

It's raining, she thought again, somewhere in the recesses of her mind. How strange I should leave the Marines to attempt a normal life, and look where I am now.

Chapter Six

A s dawn broke over the morning sky, Maria strapped the leather holster over her shoulders, made especially for her custom Nighthawk Heinie 1911 pistol. She relished the cool weight of the finely made weapon in her hand, and ran an appreciative fingertip along the 9mm's shining chrome slide, eager for the chance to use it on a live target.

Anticipation of the day's hunt hung readily in her mind. She knew Argulla wanted the woman alive, but if things got out of hand...well. Whatever. The woman was like her, after all...a killer. Always best to go into these situations prepared. Not sure how messy the day would be, she decided to dress for any possibility. Knee-high boots over trekking pants, and an all-weather shirt, with plenty of pockets for ammo and other such sundries would suffice. *I look like I'm going lion hunting.* She had a special holster in her leg pocket for her favorite skinning knife, just in case things got really, really out of hand. One can dream.

Maria collected her long, thick hair at the back of her neck and quickly threaded it into a tight ponytail, with curls hanging loosely down her back. She thought briefly of pulling it up off her neck, but decided against it, not wanting to spare the time. Raul was still asleep in the next room. She glanced at his slumbering form on the way by, smiling to herself as she had a brief fantasy of sticking her knife in his heart. She didn't do it, but it was fun to think about sometimes. Bad for business, though, so she held herself in check.

Maria collected the half dozen armed men who would accompany her on the front patio, then led the way to a couple of Argulla's Range Rovers, where she hopped lightly into the passenger seat of the first one. They would start their hunt by visiting a few of the villages near the river to see if they could pick up any information or trail. According to Reyes, the woman had been shot. She would be slow and bleeding, more than likely an easy trail to follow. With any luck, they'd have her before lunch.

By late afternoon, Maria was rapidly losing patience. When they reached the third village, she was beginning to doubt she was on the right track. She despised doubt. She refused it. Some of her men were instructed to look around down by the riverbank, while the others were bullying and ransacking the village locals. Apparently, no one had seen nor heard of any stranger in the area seeking medical assistance. She decided to withhold that it was a woman she was searching for, to help her determine if she was hearing the truth when someone finally did give up some information. The unstable part of her began talking in her mind, convincing herself this was some kind of conspiracy. That she would need to punish the liars for protecting this stranger. She put her gun to the head of the village elder's wife and asked him again, but he still denied knowledge. *Liars. Maybe I'll come back later to visit with a different agenda.*

"Miguel." Maria yelled at one of her men, a tall, dark bull of a man. "Are there any other villages in the area? Further away from the river, maybe?"

"Boss. There are some others further out. There

are no other villages on the water around here," Miguel replied, avoiding the crazy eyes of the woman.

Damn it. Maria paced and thought about her next move. *Maybe she died in the river.*

"The only other place near the water is the Peace Corps camp about two kilometers down river. It's not directly on the water, but not far off either," he suggested mildly, thinking to help his boss.

"What did you say?" She whispered dangerously without turning around, barely loud enough for Miguel to hear.

"I said there's a Peace Corp camp, run by Americans, just up the river."

"And what facilities do they have at this camp?" She growled, slowly turning her head to peer at him over her shoulder.

Miguel began to twitch nervously, fearing he must have made a mistake somehow. The sense of danger radiating from the woman grew more palpable by the second. "Um...they have a school where they teach the local Indians Spanish and English. Ah... some people who go around helping farmers learn how to do better for the environment, or something like that, and they have a little medical clini..."

He never finished the sentence. Maria, small by comparison, struck the man with such force his head snapped back as he fell to the ground clutching his nose.

Like a flash, she was on him. The rest of the watching men were instantly sympathetic to their fellow guard. Straddling his chest, pinning his arms to his sides, she sat on the bleeding man, pressing the cool steel of her knife to his throat as she stared unwavering into his fearful brown eyes.

"Do you mean to tell me," she purred into his face, "that we have been chasing shadows in these shit hole villages all god damned day?" She pressed the flat of the knife tighter against his neck, drawing a few drops of blood, "When there is a medical facility in the area?" Miguel whimpered in fear. "And we've been looking for an injured stranger?" She began to trace a thin red line with the point of the knife from his chin to his chest. "I can't even begin to imagine why you wouldn't tell me about that camp this morning. Did it not occur to you that an injured person would, maybe, I don't know...seek *medical* assistance?" A few more drops of blood. Miguel began to hyperventilate.

Maria adjusted her position slightly so he was forced to look in to her eyes. "*You*, for example, may be seeking medical assistance very soon yourself. Is a medical clinic *not* where *you* would go to seek such assistance?" She pushed the blade a little deeper with every emphasis on a single word.

"I...I...I'm sorry, Boss. Y...Y...You said you wanted to visit the river villages." Miguel got out between gasping for air, sure his life would soon be over. "S...So that's where I took you."

And with that, she was off him. Miguel bolted upright and grabbed at his neck, trying to stem the trickling flow of blood she'd left behind.

"Consider yourself lucky to be alive," she sneered. "I'm not usually so forgiving. I guess that means you owe me your *undying* gratitude." The crazy woman barked out a high-pitched laugh at her own play on words. "And, consider yourself demoted, for being such a complete and total moron!"

Maria slowly walked back toward Miguel, as the big man cowered away from her. She got toe to toe with him, never breaking her gaze. Like a flash, she grabbed his shirttail and used it to wipe blood from her knife blade. He breathed a visible sigh of relief. Maria smiled evilly, immensely enjoying his discomfort.

She walked in a slow circle, taking in her men, and the villagers who were milling around a safe distance away. Looking around as if seeing the place for the first time, she took in the pot-holed dirt road, the shabby, run down dwellings and the proud but poor people standing defiantly around the unwanted visitors. *Why would anybody live in a pathetic excuse for a home as this?*

"Ernesto!" She barked.

"Here, Boss."

"Are you more of a man than this pathetic sack?" She nodded toward Miguel, not really caring if Ernesto answered or not.

"Get the keys from Miguel, you're my new driver. Take me to this damn Peace Corps camp. Now! There are still a few hours of daylight left; that should give us enough time to search their camp for the stranger."

As she walked toward the vehicle, she heard the locals speaking in lowered tones to each other about her. She had heard they already had a nickname for her. Not bad for only having been in the region for a short time. She smiled internally, her exercise in intimidation complete, here, for now. *La Loca. Fitting. They're smarter than they look.*

❧❧❧❧

Dr. Jenny MacKenzie stood alone in her small cabin having just decided what she needed was a serious sweat-fest. No camera, this time. She would go for a speed run, and pound the ground until her legs shook with the effort. *A 10k at least.*

It was a good day at the clinic. Her car accident patients were recuperating nicely, and a few others were well enough to vacate their cots. The number of people who showed for vaccinations today had been minimal, so overall it was a pretty laid-back day. *So, why do I feel the need to run myself into the ground?* Something in her psyche had been building for a while now, and though she couldn't put her finger on it, it seemed to take shape into some general discontent with her life. A feeling akin to loneliness seemed to grow exponentially over the last week for some unknown reason. It was as if her body just woke up, and found a part of herself missing. She couldn't explain it. She'd always felt that way a little bit. Different. But it seemed to be magnified now. *Maybe this thing with JC is getting to me more than I thought.*

Jenny stretched into her tight jog top, then bent to put on her running shoes. She would stick to the road this time, not bothering with the woods, so she could concentrate on speed. *Maybe if I force myself into total exhaustion, I'll have an epiphany when my brain is too tired to think of anything else. Yeah. Sure.*

I've worked so hard my whole life to get where I am. Accelerated through school. Studied so hard to finish early. Always worked toward this...finally getting out and going on a grand adventure where I could use my ability to help people who needed it. I always relied on this to be the answer for me. I would finally be doing what I wanted, how I wanted, and that would be the fulfillment I was looking for. So why isn't it? Now that I'm here, and actually doing it, something is still missing. I always thought this was it, but now

that I know it's not, I don't know what else to look to.
She sighed internally. *Work it out, Pumpkin Head, you
can do it.*

Jenny smiled to herself, thinking of her childhood
friend's nickname for her. She hadn't thought of that
name in a long time, especially now that her hair was
more blonde than red, but it always brought a smile
to her face. She shut the door to her cabin and headed
out at a slow jog to warm up her tight muscles. She
would shoot for a forty-five-minute 10k, unless she
was feeling strong at the half-way point, then she
would maybe add another mile or two before she
turned around. It would probably be a little muddy
out there, since it rained last night.

Not quite an hour later, Jenny slowed her pace
to cool down before cresting the final hill into camp.
Her breathing was heavy, but not too labored after
what she considered an exceptional run. She checked
her watch to confirm what felt like a good time for the
distance she'd put in.

As she crested the hill, the first thing she noticed
was two matching Land Rovers parked haphazardly in
the middle of the road. She heard a raised voice on the
air and sensed immediately that something not good
was going down. She moved to the side of the road,
skirting the tree line so she could sneak up a little
closer and get a feel for what was happening. They
weren't in a dangerous area, but everybody knew there
were cocaine cowboys in Bolivia, and the Peace Corps
camp was right in the middle of the Argulla territory,
the biggest fish in the pond. They were there with his
knowledge, and permission of course, but the potential
of being caught in some crossfire always existed.

Jenny knew Grace would pull the plug on their

little outpost in a heartbeat if she felt the volunteers were in any danger whatsoever. A shouting match was taking place somewhere across the way. She couldn't tell who was doing the shouting, but there was definitely some pissed off people in there. She thought it sounded like JC, but couldn't be sure. She glanced to the left in time to see the big man whose finger she had stitched the other day coming out of her cabin. *Shit. Could this have something to do with that? Why? What the hell is going on?*

Just then, on the right side of the road she saw another guy come out from behind Grace's hut holding Dan by the throat. Dan's arm was forced painfully behind his back, an angry grimace on his face. Jenny sprinted into action with no thought required. Whatever was going on, she would find out soon enough, but certainly would not stand by while her friend was being hurt.

࿈ ࿈ ࿈ ࿈

From across the way, a malevolent creature watched intently. Her sharp eyes focused on a brash young woman who darted out from the tree line and ran toward one of her men, who was holding a camp resident by the neck. She turned to the woman she was standing with, but her eyes never left the blonde. "Miss...Richards, was it?" Maria asked Grace, in heavily accented, but fluent and precise English. One of her previous employers, an Englishman living in Colombia, insisted she learn the language. Maria reached across her left breast, running a finger down the strap of her shoulder holster, coming to rest on the grip of her 9mm. "Tell me...who is that foolish blonde over there about to get seriously injured by one of my men?" She seemed amused at the prospect of the pending brawl.

Grace turned quickly to see Jenny running up the road toward Daniel with a determined stride, and a man dressed in black who was holding him forcefully. "Dear Lord," she gasped, taking in the situation. "Please don't hurt her."

"Who...is...she?"

"D...Dr. MacKenzie. She runs the medical clinic. She is very dear to us. A good soul. Please don't."

"As I told you before, I am not here to hurt anyone. I merely require answers to a few simple questions." Maria reeked of insincerity. "I apologize if my men seem a little forceful, but we have a very important task to accomplish, and little time in which to do it. Sometimes, I have found, a touch of fear will help better motivate people into action, even if there really isn't any danger." Maria smiled at Grace, but the statement felt false in every way.

Grace wasn't buying it. She sensed this woman the locals called La Loca, the Crazy, was every bit as dangerous as the villagers seemed to think. She had heard of her from some farmers she worked with, but until now had not seen or met her in person. Now that she had, Grace would have to reevaluate their decision to keep a camp in this area. Regardless of how badly the local indigenous people needed them, the safety of her volunteers was her primary concern.

She watched with trepidation as Jenny reached her target and body checked the man in black with force, sending him to the ground. She grabbed Daniel's arm and put herself between him and his former captor. The man named Miguel, whose hand

Jenny had recently stitched, came running to assist his fellow guard.

"Tenacious, isn't she?" Maria asked, a spark of interest flaring in her hooded eyes.

"You have no idea." Grace nodded, praying Jenny would not be hurt.

Jenny pointed to the oncoming Miguel and said something the two watching women could not hear. Whatever it was stopped the big man in his tracks. Maria noted the failings of her staff at the hands of this petite woman and resolved to teach them more about the proper use of force, even if she had to do it the hard way.

The man on the ground jumped up and made an aggressive move toward the young doctor. Before he knew it, the foolish man was on the ground again. It was obvious to Maria even from a distance, that the blonde was schooled in some type of martial arts. She could tell by the way she held herself, and the imbecile with Miguel didn't seem to notice until he was in the dirt for the second time.

"Miguel! Bring her to me!" Maria finally yelled, growing impatient with the show.

※ ※ ※ ※

"Dan, you okay?" Jenny whispered over her shoulder as she warily checked out the two men standing before her, balancing her weight over the balls of her feet, preparing to strike if necessary.

"Yeah, Hon. Had everything under control, but thanks for stopping by," he said with a touch of humor in his voice. "That Tai-Bo class really did the trick, huh?"

"You know it." Jenny resolved to tell him later she had a black belt in Tae-Kwon-Do. "What the hell is going on here, anyway?"

"Not sure. A bunch of guys and that woman over there just rolled up about a half hour ago and started ransacking the camp. Don't know what they're after. I think they're Argulla's people though."

"Anybody hurt?"

"I don't think so."

The woman across the camp, who Jenny observed was dressed as if she was on a safari hunt, yelled for Miguel to bring her over. He reached for her arm, but Jenny backed away and let him know with her eyes that to grab her would be a big mistake. "Don't even think about it, Miguel. I'm perfectly capable of walking over there on my own."

Miguel indicated with a nod for the two of them to get moving. A silent understanding was struck that no one would get hurt if they went along quietly.

꙰ ꙰ ꙰ ꙰

The camp volunteers were collected and lined up in a row on the muddy road that ran through the camp complex. Even the patients in the clinic were dropped into chairs and carried into the road to be with the others, as Maria strolled casually along the row. She paused from time to time, regarding a particular person from head to toe as if sizing them up for future sport.

She reached the young doctor and took her time walking completely around the woman, eyeing her lean, muscular body with some envy. It was obvious she took good care of herself. The doctor's eyes never left her. She was either fearless, or didn't realize she was looking at someone to be feared, Maria thought. The assassin made an internal bet with herself that the girl would be the first to talk. She could sense an edgy attitude in her that wouldn't cower to fear like so many of the others.

She was dressed in running attire, her body glistening with the sweat of a recent workout. Maria couldn't help but think how delicious it would be to have this young woman bound and at her mercy. She allowed herself a brief fantasy of the thrill she would get watching those defiant green eyes fade to lifeless gray —holding her sweat soaked head in her hands as she struggled to escape. *Mmmm.* Maria licked her lips at the thought, and ran a lone finger down the young woman's sweaty cheek. She hadn't had a challenging one like this in a while, and the thought excited her.

Grace silently prayed the young lady would hold her bold tongue. She didn't think Jenny knew what danger they were all in as long as this woman was around.

Jenny jerked her head to the side as the woman with crazy eyes touched her face. "Who the hell are you, and what do you want here?"

Ha! I win. She was the first to speak. "My name is Maria Velasquez. Have you heard of me?"

"No. Should I have?"

"Not necessarily. But it might have made things go easier for you."

"Oh yeah? How so? And you haven't told me yet why you've rolled in here like a bunch of common thugs, pushing these people around."

Maria let a tiny smile creep up the corner of her mouth. She liked this woman's spunk. The more she showed, the more Maria desired to tear her heart from her chest, and place it still beating before her eyes.

"Do you work for Señor Argulla? Do you know we have permission from him to be here? He even helped pay for us to build this clinic, so I don't think he would appreciate your bullying us and tearing up this place," Jenny said, hoping it would have the desired effect, and make the woman leave. She doubted it though. Something about her said she wasn't easily maneuvered.

"You haven't let me answer the first question yet. Patience, doctor." Maria chuckled low in her throat at the second good play on words she'd managed today. "The answer to how it would be easier for you is, if you'd heard of me, you would know I prefer to do the talking. It usually turns out badly for people who don't listen. Am I making myself clear?" Maria slowly removed the 9mm from her holster, petting the slide in a non-threatening motion intended to intimidate her audience.

"Fine," Jenny said defiantly, seemingly unintimidated. "Get on with answering the next questions then, and I'll leave you to say what you came to say. We have work to do here."

Oh yes. I want this one. "I do, indeed, work for Señor Argulla, and I am here at his behest. It seems there is a stranger in the area who has stolen something very valuable to Señor Argulla. This stranger is injured, and will, no doubt, be seeking medical attention." Maria paused to look at each individual, attempting to detect an uncomfortable shift or sly movement of any kind. "This is a very dangerous and armed criminal that needs to be dealt with immediately. As long as this stranger is on the loose, you are all in danger."

Bullshit. You're the danger. Jenny thought to herself, but what she said was, "How was the person injured?"

"I ask the questions!" Maria barked at Jenny, finally beginning to lose her patience with the younger woman. She circled the doctor again, stopping behind her and leaning dangerously close to whisper in the Jenny's ear. "Have you treated anyone matching this description in the last twenty-four hours, doctor?"

"What description?" Jenny poked, knowing full well she was skating on thin ice.

"Injured strangers," Maria seethed.

"All the people I meet here are strangers. All the people I treat are usually injured. All the people I've treated in the last twenty-four hours are here before you, in these chairs." Jenny was intrigued, wondering who this stranger really was, and what he did.

"Anything missing from the hospital? Any trace of someone rummaging around? Have you seen anybody you don't know lurking in the shadows?"

"No." At that, a thought occurred to Jenny and she silently vowed to check it out later.

Maria walked around to her front where she met the doctor's defiance once again. She stared at her for a long moment, trying to read fear or untruth in her demeanor, but could not determine either. She moved over to Daniel, and asked the same questions. One by one, all the members of the camp were questioned. And one by one, they all denied any knowledge of the injured stranger.

Maria considered torching the camp for a moment. Just out of spite. She paced up and down the line of people once more, looking for any signs of deceit.

"Ernesto, have you completed your search of the buildings and the surrounding area?"

"Yes, Boss. We didn't see anything suspicious in any of the buildings. We searched the wooded area from here to the river and found nothing. There are a few broken branches by the trail, but it appears a commonly used trail, so nothing I would consider out of the ordinary."

Hmmm. Jenny thought to herself. *Add that information to my databank. No one but me has used that trail in weeks, and I don't recall going off trail on those trips at all.*

Maria was livid. She could not believe a whole day was wasted without success. The worst of it was, now Raul would think he could offer suggestions to her method as if she'd done something wrong. She could not tolerate that. This damn sniper was proving to be more of a challenge than she'd anticipated.

Tomorrow she would double her men and start in the woods at the point of river entry. If she couldn't find her alive, then perhaps she died in the river and will have washed up on shore, or been trapped in the whitewater. One way or the other, she would find her. If she couldn't bring Raul back a live person to question, she damn well would bring back the body parts.

"Ernesto, get the car. It's time to go."

Grace Richards breathed an audible sigh of relief.

Maria turned once more to the row of people, but focused her attention on the doctor. "Should any of you see this stranger, I expect you to contact me immediately. Remember...armed and dangerous. I will not tolerate disobedience in this. I will not be held responsible if this stranger should creep in here and kill you all in the middle of the night. You have all been warned of the danger. Be vigilant in keeping watch for your own safety."

Chapter Seven

*T*he U.S.S. Theodore Roosevelt, a Nimitz class aircraft carrier, cruised powerfully through calm seas toward her latest destination, the Persian Gulf. She was so large, the personnel aboard could barely feel her move with the rhythm of the ocean. Her decks fully loaded with tools of modern warfare, she sped with calculated determination toward the latest in what seemed a never-ending series of conflicts for the massive vessel.*

In the large mess hall, surrounded by endless amounts of stainless steel brightwork, sat a young Marine of nineteen, studying the polished surface of a long metal table securely bolted to the floor. To her right by the galley were long shining tables holding a variety of drink machines and cafeteria-style food service equipment. It smelled of a combination of mass-produced cafeteria food over not so subtle cleaning solution. The television mounted in one corner was broadcasting a U.S. News channel loud enough to cover the sound of the screws as they churned through the sea. The room was so functional and industrial, if needed it could be blast cleaned with a fireman's hose and nothing in it would be worse for the wear.

The Marine traveled with her platoon to the Persian Gulf, her first deployment after finishing Scout Sniper training and being awarded Hunter of Gunmen certification. It was early in the year 1991, and she was eager to see some action and try out her new skills, never once doubting in her ability to utilize her training successfully. The young warrior radiated menace. She wore the sleeves of her sand colored, military issue camo jacket rolled high, showing off long, muscular arms in a challenging way. Her hair was dark and cut close to the scalp, her eyes were so noticeably brilliant blue she kept them hooded and focused on the ground. Her sullen expression and unapproachable posture made most people, at first glance, think she was a man. This was fine by Seven. She did what she could to deter attention, her looks being a major problem when surrounded by hundreds of lonely guys.

"Lance Corporal Michelis." Seven quickly stood and acknowledged her platoon leader, Sergeant Bamforth. "At ease. Where's your other half?"

"In the rain locker, Sergeant," the young woman replied, using naval speak for 'Marcus is in the shower.' "He's meeting me in the gym later."

The beefy sergeant took a seat and motioned for Seven to sit across from him. "They find a space for you okay? I heard there was some confusion, initially."

"Yes, Sergeant. They had to shift a bunch of people around to create more female berthing space, but they got me settled eventually."

"Good. Sorry about that. Even after all these years, seems like we still have to work out the details of having women onboard. Look, do me a favor, will ya? Since your berthing isn't near our platoon, I want you to take extra care and watch your six. This dingy has five thousand horny sailors on it, and the pre-battle adrenaline is running so high the electricity in the air could power the screws. Know what I mean?"

"Will do, Sergeant. Trying to keep a low profile,

but I gotta eat."

"It's not really you I'm worried about." He smiled
at the most surprising talent he'd seen in some time. *"I
know you can protect yourself, I'm just worried that
if some unsuspecting guy gets a little fresh he's gonna
wind up in a body bag. These navy girls know how to
handle the navy guys, but these guys wouldn't know
what they were getting into with you. Try to stay out
of sight, unless you're with us. For my peace of mind.
I can't imagine the amount of paperwork I'd have to
fill out if you beat some poor unsuspecting asshole to
death."* He chuckled a little, so she knew he was only
partially serious. *"You're a killer, Michelis. I can feel
it in you. You're going to go as far as you want in the
Corps. All you have to do is stay out of trouble, if you
can. You're the best I've seen in a long time."* He patted
her on the shoulder, then got up from the table and
walked away.

Seven left the mess deck as the cleaning crew
moved in to do their work. She made her way to the
outdoor gym, looking forward to little sunshine and a
good workout. She pulled a black stretch skullcap over
her head and covered her eyes with a pair of smoke
tinted wrap around shades as she stepped out into the
bright sunlight, thinking how strange it was to have
Sarge get all fatherly on her. What the hell was that all
about?

Seven sat on a weight bench and wondered what
was taking Marcus so long. She was just thinking how
quiet it was in the gym when she felt a feather light
touch on the back of her neck and lifted her head to
see three crewmembers standing uncomfortably close to
her. She could tell by their insignia that they were flight
crew. She sighed internally. Oh great. Pilots. Biggest

egos on the planet.

The leader of the pack sat too close to his prey, uninvited, while his buddies stood closely behind her. "You are, without a doubt, the best lookin' jarhead I have ever seen," he said in her ear, laughing amiably at his own joke. "I always thought it wasn't possible for a woman to look smokin' in BDUs, but damn lady, you look good enough to eat. Mmm mmm."

So how does one tell three guys that outrank me to fuck off? *She asked herself. Deciding on a silent, graceful exit, Seven got up to leave.*

The men tightened up their ranks, making it impossible for her to stand without bumping them. "Come on. Be a little sociable, at least. Just trying to strike up a conversation here. You don't need to be a bitch."

They couldn't see behind Seven's smoked sunglass lenses, but if they could, they would see intolerance for stupidity rapidly rising to the surface. She tried again to stand, her way blocked once more. "Are you Tootsie Roll dicks so pathetic at getting women stateside, you have to harass them onboard where they can't get away?" She glanced around quickly to see if anyone was watching in case she needed her story backed up. There was nobody around.

"Ha! See, I told you Walker. She's a feisty one. I like that. Relax, Jarhead. My buddies and I were just wondering if you'd like to party with us. We know a nice, private place just off the flight deck that would be perfect. Don't we boys?"

"No." Seven pushed to a standing position and faced the leader, who matched her six foot height eye to eye. She felt one of the men behind her brush his knuckles across her ass. The situation appeared to be

rapidly deteriorating.

"Come on, gorgeous. Can you honestly say you can think of a better way to wile away the ocean voyage than to spend it with some great guys who just want to show you a good time?"

"I can think of a million better ways. I said no. Now back away so I can leave."

"My name is Robert. What's your first name... Michelis?" He persisted, looking at the tag sewn over her breast pocket. He touched her nametag with an extended fingertip, then moved it left and fingered a coat button between her breasts. "Come with us, Michelis." He leaned over to whisper in her ear, his finger searching for an open seam between two buttons. "We'll make it worth your while, I promise."

Playtime was over. Sarge said she wasn't allowed to kill anyone, but he didn't mention anything at all about maiming. Seven slowly removed her glasses with her left hand while reaching for his wandering finger with her right. "So you're a pilot, stud? You need two hands to do that job, right?" She whispered back to her pursuer. He gazed into her captivating eyes for the first time and saw something he wasn't expecting. A threat. He saw a feral gleam that told him on an instinctive level he was no longer the hunter, but the hunted.

As her smile widened, so did his eyes. The pressure she applied to his hand was slowly increasing and becoming painful. He stepped back, laughing nervously, and realized too late that he wasn't going anywhere. "Let go of me, bitch," he seethed under his breath so only she could hear a note of panic in his voice. The pilot glanced over her shoulder to his friends for help, but they were unaware of what was playing out in front of them. They noticed for the first time when the pilot *dropped to his knees in pain, the sound of snapping bones and a yell of agony bringing them to attention.*

"Guess you're grounded now, loverboy." Rough hands grabbed Seven by the shoulders and jerked her backward as the two other men moved to protect their friend.

Just as fast, the two men were then jerked backward into a sitting position on the weight bench. "You're gonna thank me for that later, fellas, I promise." Marcus stepped between Seven and the two pilots sitting on the bench. "See, she doesn't know her own strength, and kinda has some anger management issues. Last guy who invaded her space uninvited spent a week in traction, and had his jaw wired shut for a month." He spared a glance for the third guy, who knelt on the deck clutching a broken hand to his chest. "See what she did to your friend? Didn't even break a sweat. She'll do that and ten times worse to you if you don't bug out, and I mean now. You following me?"

The men glared menacingly at the duo. "You fucking whore! You broke my hand!" The pilot on the deck spat out as he ungracefully stood up. The men thought better of further action, now that their bully had been hobbled, and turned to leave. "You're gonna pay for that, cunt." The injured pilot hissed just before he was out of earshot, leaving Seven and Marcus alone in the gym.

Seven slowly put her glasses back on, and turned to her friend nonchalantly. "You enjoy your shower? Took you long enough."

"Yeah. A little bit longer and I would have missed out on your festive little gangbang. Of course, with you, gangbang takes on a completely different meaning. They provide the gang, you provide the bang."

A week after the incident in the gym, Seven was called to a meeting with Sergeant Bamforth. She figured the three jerks would do something in retribution, but had no idea what. Marcus waited outside the door, curiosity getting the better of him.

Getting right to the meat of the matter, the Sergeant said, "Michelis, there have been formal charges filed against you by a Lieutenant Junior Grade Robert DeMarco. He claims to have witnessed you and another female behaving in a sexually inappropriate manner on the Main Hanger Deck, four days ago." *Seven was angry, but she held her tongue, allowing her superior to finish.* "I think you're a top-notch Marine, Michelis, so I'm going to give you the benefit of the doubt and assume these charges are false, but that doesn't change the fact I have to act on them.

"If the accusations are false, then the burden falls on you to prove it so. If you can't, you'll be discharged. You have thirty-six hours to prepare a formal statement, then I will decide on a proper course of action."

"Permission to speak freely, Sergeant?"

"I would expect nothing less."

"This is total bullshit," *she spit viciously.* "Completely unfounded. Last week right after you talked to me about watching my back, that jackass and his buddies came on to me in the gym, and wouldn't let it go. I roughed up that DeMarco guy a little, and this is his way of paying me back. I would never be stupid enough to jeopardize my career so foolishly. I cannot believe my job is on the line because of the lying words of man with a fragile ego. It disgusts me! How can this happen? Does it even say in there who he supposedly saw me with?"

"No. It only names you. He claims not to have

known the other woman."

"Convenient, don't you think?"

"Unfortunately, the way things are in the military, an accusation seems to be enough. You need to come up with something concrete to defend yourself with. Frankly, I don't give a good goddamn who's punchin' your dance card, as long as you're doing your job. And it upsets me to no end that I may lose my best sharpshooter to something so stupid, but it is what it is. This guy has decided to end your career, and he went straight for a head shot. Get me something to work with here, Michelis. It can't end like this."

Seven turned and walked from the compartment without another word. Marcus, who had been eavesdropping, followed her at a run toward her berthing. "Jesus, Marcus. Of all the things that prick could have done, this is worse than anything. Getting booted out after all my hard work is bad enough, but this kind of slander is a curse, and if he wins, I just don't think I can bear it." She slumped against a bulkhead and covered her face with her hands.

"Is there any way he somehow knew you were gay? Or did he take a stab in the dark?"

Seven's body stilled at his words, though she left her head lowered. "How long have you known?" She asked, her voice muffled by the hands over her face.

"Since the day we met, Sev. I have excellent gaydar. Did I ever tell you two of my six sisters are lesbians? And if you add their partners to the mix, that means I actually have eight sisters. Why do you think I'm never lacking in baked goods?"

Seven, never raising her head, did her best to stifle a chuckle, but her bouncing shoulders gave her away. "No. There's no way he could know. I've been discreet my whole life. He just got lucky and hit me where it hurts the most. Marcus, what am I going to do? I can't prove anything one way or the other, but it doesn't matter to them."

"Don't worry my friend, we'll think of something." He knuckled his friend on the shoulder and left to have a private conversion with Sergeant Bamforth.

Seven spent the next couple of days in the shipboard library searching through legal and policy books looking for a loophole or way out. Without eyewitnesses or hard evidence to the contrary, her situation was looking bleak. She went to Sergeant Bamforth to tell him so, and not long after found herself clanking down the metal passageway looking for her partner with a mission in mind. She found Marcus in his bathrobe, just about to enter his berthing, oblivious to her presence due to a towel over his head he was using to vigorously rub water out of his ears. She grabbed him by the shoulder, causing a startled squeak. "Marcus, what did you do?" She demanded, assuming no explanation was necessary.

"Who, me?" He asked innocently. "I have no earthly idea to what you refer. Let a guy put some pants on, why don'tcha."

"Bullshit. Bamforth just told me my case has been dismissed. He didn't give me any details, but implied I should talk to you about it. So what the hell is going on?"

"Please do the decent thing, Lance Corporal, and turn your back whilst I clothe myself," he said cheekily, drawing out the torture before he explained.

"Fine. Go get dressed and hurry. I'll wait for you here."

Marcus returned from his berthing a few minutes later, wearing a freshly pressed uniform and a Cheshire grin. *"Okay. Here's the deal – and if I do say so myself, it was brilliant. I was due for my promotion to Corporal from Lance Corporal, right? So I talked to Bamforth. He pushed through my promotion. Then I signed an affidavit stating there was no way you were where that guy said you were, with some unknown woman, because you were with me. And there was no way you were gay, because we've been having a torrid affair for several months. And...here's the best part...wait for it..."* He paused to draw out the anticipation. *"I told them I broke that asshole's hand while I was kicking his ass arm wrestling, and he was so put out he threatened to get me back somehow. So the Sergeant wrote me up on a fraternization charge, since I confessed to our affair after my promotion, then he demoted me back to Lance Corporal. Punishment for a violation is administered, everybody's happy. Nobody will look too closely at the details. I'm gonna have to wait a little longer for that promotion is all. It's their word against ours. No case. I guess that DeMarco guy has a few hits on his record from before, too, which makes us look even better."*

"So we're sleeping together?" Seven smirked.

"Yeah. Looks good for me, right? You're in the clear, and I'm the new hero of the platoon." He grinned proudly and gave himself a pat on the back. *"I just went from the platoon prankster, to the platoon Ladies Man with one swift blow. I hope you're okay with what I did, but I couldn't let that guy get away with that crap. Of course, now that we've been 'found out' I had to promise the Sarge we'd break it off. For the record. You know."*

"Marcus, you crazy bastard. This could have easily gone bad for you. You did not need to become involved. It could have been the end of your career instead of mine. Plus, to lie like that? On the record?

You're too honorable to lie. You shouldn't have done that for me."

"Hey. Sarge knows what's up. You're his star pupil. He was more than willing to do everything he could to keep you working. And he knew you needed me, so voila. We're back in business. Anyway, DeMarco lied. I just cancelled his bad one out with a good one. I don't regret it."

"I can see why your sisters all love you so much, Marcus." Seven took her friend into a bear hug and kissed him on top of the head. "I never had a brother, but if I did, I'd want him to be just like you. Thank you."

In her unconscious state, Seven's mind journeyed from one memory of her friend to another. She never woke, but if she had, her grief would have manifested itself in the form of wracking sobs. It took unconsciousness to bring down the walls of Seven's psyche as she unwittingly surrendered control to her grief.

❦❦❦❦

The Peace Corps camp volunteers, clinic patients, and locals who were there at the time of Maria's arrival stood silently watching as the two white Land Rovers drove away. There was quiet in the air while everyone digested what had just happened. Then, as if it were choreographed, everyone started talking at once.

People split into small groups, discussing theories and speculating about this mysterious stranger, and about La Loca and her intentions for the camp and its people.

Grace Richards, the camp manager, raised her

voice to get the attention of her co-workers. "All right, folks. Let's get this mess cleaned up, then we'll get together in an hour or so in the dining hall and discuss this latest turn of events." She called JC over and asked him to help Daniel move the patients back into the clinic first thing.

When the area was semi-clear of people, Grace walked over the Jenny and looked very seriously at the young woman. "You shouldn't have done that, Jenny. I fear you have just provoked a very dangerous person. The rumors flying around about that woman are quite terrifying. I don't think this is the kind of person whose attention you would want drawn to yourself."

"Grace, thank you for your concern. I'll be all right. She's crazy though. You're right about that. I took a bunch of undergrad classes in psychology. I'm far from expert, but she definitely struck me as extremely volatile. She was practically vibrating with the need to strike out." Jenny wondered internally if maybe she did make a mistake calling attention to herself. "That woman is not right in the head. It looked like it was causing her extreme effort just to remain in control."

"If what she said about us all being in danger is true, I must seriously consider closing this camp and taking the crew back to La Paz."

Both began to stroll toward Jenny's hut. "To be honest, Grace, I think if there's any danger here, it's from her. If what she says is true, which my gut tells me it isn't, this guy she's looking for would have nothing to gain from harming us. If he's injured, he comes to us, we fix him up, he's on his way. The end. We can't offer him anything of value, except maybe our truck, and if he's on the run from Argulla, he's got a lot bigger things to worry about than us."

They reached the hut and Jenny looked around in disgust. "Well, they sure made a mess of my place. What the hell did they think they were going to find in here? Polaroids of their missing person?" The young woman moved to the center of the hut and began picking up some of her things that had been recklessly strewn across the floor. "Will you contact the local authorities, Grace? Or the area military?"

"No," Grace said, helping Jenny with her things. "From what I understand, everybody in this area is either directly, or indirectly involved with Argulla. It would be pointless to contact any authority, because in a roundabout way they all work for him. That is why I thought we would have no trouble here. Because he is behind us. It never occurred to me he would turn on us like this. It makes our situation here precarious, to say the least."

"Well, in the months we've been here, I have never once felt endangered. Maybe this Velasquez woman is stepping outside her boundaries. Maybe Argulla doesn't know she's harassing us."

"It's hard to say, and I for one don't have the cojones to go knocking on his door to find out. Especially not if that vile woman is there." Grace turned to leave Jenny's hut. "Let's get together in the dining hall in a bit and talk it out with everybody. I'd like to hear what they all have to say."

As Grace opened the door to depart, an anxious looking Juan Carlos was standing on the steps, his hand outstretched for the door handle. "Oh, hi Grace. Are you okay? That was pretty scary. Jenny in there?" He nodded toward the hut he was about to enter.

"Yes, I'm fine. Thank you. I'll meet you all in the

dining tent shortly."

Great. JC. Just the guy I wanted to see. Can't wait to hear what I did wrong this time. Jenny thought sarcastically.

"Hi, Jen. Can I come in?"

"Sure, JC. Grab a chair, though you'll have to pick it up off the floor first."

"I just wanted to see if you were okay. I about had a heart attack when I saw you come flying out of the woods like that." He walked across the room and took Jenny into an awkward hug.

"I'm okay. Are you okay? Did those guys rough you up at all?"

"Not much. What were you thinking, Jenny?" JC couldn't help himself, and finally let loose with his judgment. "You could've been killed. Those guys were armed. And you come out of the woods like the freakin' lone ranger to the rescue. Do you have any idea how everybody would feel if something happened to you? Are you out of your mind?"

Here we go. "How they would feel, or how you would feel?"

"What is that supposed to mean?"

"I don't think 'they' would feel any worse if it were me hurt than if it were Daniel...which by the way, in case you didn't notice, *was* being hurt by that jerk of Argulla's. And what I mean is, you're trying to lay some guilt trip on me, trying to make me feel bad as though I was putting everybody out, when really it's just you who was put out. I wasn't about to stand by and let that guy hurt Dan...and if it's any consolation, I wouldn't have stood by if he was hurting you, either. Or anybody else, for that matter."

"That's ridiculous! I am just worried about you.

Why can't you see that I care about you? I just want you to see that your foolish behavior affects others. It's not just you anymore, Jenny. It's you and me."

"No. JC. I'm sorry. But not anymore." *There, I said it. It's out there now. Can't take it back.*

"What do you mean, not anymore? Look, I know I always seem to stick my foot in my mouth when I'm around you, and you don't seem to be that interested in me anymore, but I can't just turn off my feelings. Are you saying you can just turn me off like some damn nightlight?"

"No, of course not. I care about you, and I always will, but you and I are going back to just being friends because I can't handle you as a lover. I've wanted to tell you this for a while now, but I didn't know how to do it without jeopardizing our friendship and working relationship. Think about it, JC. Once we hooked up, we hardly ever laughed together anymore. If that wasn't a sign we were doomed from the start, I don't know what is."

"Oh, Jenny. Damn it. Don't you even want to try to make this work?"

"No, JC. I don't. I'm sorry if that seems harsh, but the moment we became more than friends, it was as if a door opened that gave you an automatic right to try to run my life. We've only been having a fling for just over a month, and you're acting like we've been married for a decade. We just aren't on the same page. You started suffocating me the instant we got together and I can't take it anymore. Please don't take me the wrong way...what I've said makes it sound like it's all on you, and that just isn't the case. It's me too. Sometimes I think I'm just not cut out to be in a relationship. None I've had have ever lasted very long."

"Well it's no wonder. Who the hell could live up to your expectations?" He said bitterly, regretting the words the moment they left his mouth. "I can try to change if you think you might want to stay together."

"I don't want you to change, certainly not for me. There's nothing wrong with you. A guy like you just needs a different kind of woman, is all. One who wants to be handled. Believe me, they're out there. It's just not me. It's best for both of us that we do this now, before we've invested too much time or emotion. You would have to agree with me, we were much better friends, don't you think?

"JC, don't you think?"

Reluctantly, the young man nodded yes, then looked at his now former girlfriend in the eyes. "I'm not good at this, Jenny. I don't know whether to laugh, cry, or punch a hole in the wall."

"We're friends. And as my friend, you have the right and responsibility to laugh with me, drink with me, let me listen to your complaints, and victories, and you mine. What you no longer have the right to do is pretend like you own me. Can we please stay friends? I don't think I could live with myself if I felt I led you down a path of misery, and we dragged everybody on the team along too."

Jenny took his face in her hands and forced him to look at her. "Please."

She hugged him tightly, and he returned it, lifting her slightly and swingy her gently from side to side. "Yes. Friends. I'd rather have that, than nothing."

Just then, a loud rap sounded on the door at the same time it was being opened. Daniel stuck his head in the room. "Oh goody. WhadImiss? Can I watch?"

Jenny gave Dan the evil eye as JC kissed her

lightly on the forehead and made his exit. "We'll talk more later. I'm glad you're okay."

"Don't cancel the party, just 'cause I showed up," Dan whined to Jenny. "You look too serious to be good, ninja girl. What's goin' down wit'yur bad self?" He plopped himself unceremoniously on the end of her bed and stretched his long frame out.

Jenny sighed heavily. *Shit. Well I guess that could've gone a lot worse.* "You just busted in on me taking the ax to yet another relationship."

"Oooh. Sorry, sis. Bad timing on my part, as usual. You okay? How'd he take it?"

"Surprisingly well. I'm relieved. I don't think we've been together long enough to warrant major fireworks, but I'm glad he didn't blow up. You never know with some people. I know he's got that Latin temper, but he didn't cut it loose, thankfully. Looked like he was thinking about it once or twice, but in the end he took the high road."

"Good. So. Are you gonna tell me how you managed to kick a guy's ass today that was two times your size, and psych out another one who was even bigger?" Dan asked, smirking at his little friend.

"Yeah...how's your arm by the way? Do you need me to check it out? Looked like that guy was about to rip it out of the socket."

"It's okay. A little sore, but fine, nothing's torn. Thanks for the heroic rescue, by the way. Not sure it was worth it for you, though. That bitch with the zebra stripe hair had you on her radar big time. I don't think that's a place I'd want to be. She seemed a little left of center, if you know what I mean."

"I agree. She's the real deal all right. Dangerous."

"I was genuinely frightened for a while there.

When you started goading her, I thought she was going to pop you. She sure looked like she wanted to. You are a crazy woman, you know that? Got some dinosaur-sized huevos on you, that's for sure."

"Just pissed me off, I guess. Seriously. We have only done good here. We are only here to help people. If that psycho wanted to know something, why didn't she just come in and ask? We would have told her the truth. They absolutely did not need to fly in here and start pushing people around like that, trashing our place, and hurting people. It was totally uncalled for, and if I ever see that Argulla guy, I'm going to tell him that to his bullying, drug dealer face." Jenny dropped to her knees and began picking up shards of a broken clay pot she had on the windowsill.

"When you say 'we would have told her the truth,' are you implying that you didn't tell her the truth?"

Jenny was silent for a moment, then looked back over her shoulder at Dan with an evil grin growing slowly on her face. When the smile had reached its full potential, an evil laugh joined it.

"You did not! What do you know, you devious wench?"

"Well, let's just say I didn't share all the information. So technically I didn't lie. Hmm. Okay, maybe I did lie a little."

Dan threw himself back on the bed and kicked his feet joyfully in the air. "Good! Beehotch had it comin'. Tell me everything."

"At first I didn't think anything of it, but this morning when I was in the clinic office I noticed my granola bars and a half bottle of water I left in my desk were gone. I just figured you or one of the other nurses got the munchies, you know? No biggie. Then I found a grubby thumbprint on the doorknob on my way out. That did strike me as unusual, because you know I always keep the clinic spotless. When that woman asked if anything had gone missing, it dawned on me that maybe some other stuff was missing too, I just didn't notice. I haven't had a chance, but I'm going to head over there in a minute and check out my supplies."

"And if you find stuff gone?"

"I'm sure as hell not going to tell La Loca Puta if that's what you're asking."

"Will you tell Grace?"

"No. She's freaked out enough as it is. I'll decide what to do after I know for sure, but here's what I think happened. This guy came in sometime late, picked the lock, took what he needed, and snuck out the way he came in, but instead of heading back down to the river where Maria's goons were looking, I think he headed up path. Also, based on the thumbprint, I think she wasn't lying about him being injured. The smudge had a fair amount of blood in it, by the looks."

"Do you think this guy is a danger to us, that he'll come back?"

"I don't think so. If anyone is a danger, it's this Velasquez character. The fact that she tried so hard to convince us this injured guy is a threat, makes me actually believe the opposite is true. She played her cards all wrong as far as I'm concerned."

"Let's head over to the clinic and check it out. I want to see for myself." Dan popped up and gave Jenny a hand up from where she knelt on the floor.

The sun was beginning to set, and Jenny's stomach growled. A chill breeze blew across her bare midriff and it occurred to her that she was still in her clammy workout clothes. "I have a funny feeling about all of this, Dannyboy. I can't put my finger on it, but something big is going on here."

"You're gonna do something crazy again, aren't you?"

"I don't know. Maybe. You in?"

"I think I feel a fever coming on," he lied, making a joke to get out of whatever Jenny was trying to rope him into.

The young woman laughed engagingly. "You know me too well. No need to commit just yet, chicken-shit. Might as well see what we're up against first." She punched her friend playfully in the arm.

"You never told me about that karate stuff you were doing earlier. I didn't know you could do that."

"Tae-Kwon-Do. Black belt. I've never had to use it in the real world before. Came in kinda handy, don't you think?" Dan nodded to the affirmative. "I couldn't stand the thought of slaving away in a gym when I was in school, so I started doing that instead. It's a good workout and way more fun than treadmills and weight machines. The training helped me work off a lot of stress in med school."

"You impressed the hell out of me. And I thought poor Grace was gonna have a stroke or something. Her eyes were bugging right out of her head."

Jenny kicked a rock along the road as they reached the clinic side door. "Poor Grace is right. I'm not sure with her delicate southern sensibilities if she's cut out to deal with a dirty situation like this. I think she'll recommend pulling the plug here."

"Hey! I have delicate sensibilities, too. But I'm not going anywhere, if you don't. I couldn't live with the constant harassment regarding my lack of manliness. Or as they say in this part of the world...ma-cheese-mo. You're such a manipulative little wench, you know that?" The nurse mocked affectionately, then headed for the office.

Jenny flicked on the light switch as she entered the small room, immediately heading behind her desk. She pulled open all the drawers and took a visual assessment of their contents. Dan moved over to the cabinet and began looking for missing items. "It doesn't look like anything's been messed with. Clean as a whistle," he said, sounding disappointed.

"Oh, there's definitely stuff missing. It's such a challenge getting materials from La Paz, I keep track of every single thing we have. Look here...some bandages gone from this drawer, a roll of tape. Scooch over and let me check the drugs. If he could get in here with no problem, I'm sure the locked fridge was no problem either."

Daniel moved around the front of the desk, clearing space for the determined doctor. After rustling around in the cabinets and fridge for a few minutes, she stood abruptly and moved back to sit behind her desk. "Doesn't make sense, Dan. He took antibiotics, but no painkillers. A whole fridge full of top notch pharmaceuticals and he doesn't lift any of them?"

Jenny threaded her fingers through the cool steel handle, then pulled open the lower right desk drawer and removed her empty box of granola bars. She waved it at Dan as if to make a point. "Guy takes my snacks, but not my drugs. Does that sound like an arch criminal to you?"

"What's that?" Dan pointed to the box.

"Uh...my empty box of Granola Bars. What's it look like?"

"Nooo...on the bottom."

Jenny flipped the box over and stared keenly at a small, yellow post-it note stuck to the bottom of the box. She looked up at Dan unbelievingly, then looked down at the note again. The words on the note were small and neatly written. "It says, Gracías. Lo siento."

"Hmm. How gentlemanly of him."

"Thank you. I'm sorry. Can you believe that? He must have hidden the note there so I wouldn't find it right away. Give him more time to get away undiscovered. Don't you think?"

"I've no idea." Dan looked soberly at his friend. "But I can practically feel the wheels in your head spinning from here. What's going on in that little nugget of yours?"

"Think about it. Velasquez is spewing all kinds of stuff trying to scare us into giving this guy up, but she's nuttier than squirrel shit. She bullies her way in, starts pushing people around, destroys our stuff, etc. This guy on the other hand, comes in, doesn't disturb anyone, takes only what he needs, apologizes, cleans up after himself on the way out, and leaves without a trace. No one the wiser. It may be a bit of a stretch, but...now wait for it...here's the punchline...I'm going after him. I think he's hurt and needs my help, and I can't just let this slide. I've got a very strong feeling that he's a good guy, and if Maria gets her way, he'll be dead in short order."

"You are certifiable," Dan said, exasperated. He knew from the beginning this was where she was headed, but now that the thought was out there, he couldn't believe she would take this kind of unnecessary risk.

"Jenny, I know you would move mountains to help someone in trouble, but please think about this before you react. There's only one reason why you should do this, and at least three reasons I can think of why you shouldn't."

Dan began to tick the reasons off on his fingers. "Number One: You are speculating. You have no idea who this man is. He may be every bit as dangerous as La Loca said. If you find him, and that's not likely in the woods, he could kill you on the spot thinking you're with Argulla's people. Your Spanish sucks. How would you even be able to let him know you're a friend? Number Two: It's a damn jungle out there. It makes me nervous enough that you're running around in the daylight, but there's no telling what kind of night creatures are lurking in those woods. The wild animals in this country can be crazy dangerous. And C: If Grace gets wind of this, or God forbid, La Loca finds out you're out there deliberately disobeying her, I have no doubt she will kill you. It felt like she wanted to kill you earlier just for talking back to her. I can't imagine she wouldn't lose control over something like this."

Strong will and determination failed to adequately describe Jenny when she had her mind set to a particular task. She sat for a moment and pondered her friend's concerns, basically to appease him, though she had already decided on a course of action. "Look, let's head over to the dining hall. I'm starving and it's time to meet with Grace and the others. I'd like to hear what they all have to say, and get a feel for what Grace plans to do. I promise to think about it. After dinner, I'll let you know one way or the other what I'm going to do. Deal?"

"Okay. Please think seriously," he conceded, well aware there was nothing he could do if she had already made up her mind. He looked over his friend's tiny running outfit. "You must be freezing after all this time in those wet clothes. Why don't you grab a shower in here, enjoy the hot water, and I'll run over to your cabin and get you something warm to wear. Then we'll head over to the dining hall."

"See what I mean?" She favored her friend with a broad smile. "Always looking out for me."

♫♫♫♫

Grace called a camp meeting so the volunteers could discuss their options in light of the potential threat of Maria Velasquez. The general consensus amongst the group was to wait and see. Several were of the opinion it was a one-time visit and no real threat. Some were afraid that Argulla's goons would return until they found what they wanted, and were worried the attacks would get worse.

Jenny and Dan were of the wait and see opinion. JC and Grace were of the leaving opinion, but in the end, Grace decided to go with the majority and stick it out for a few more days. She recommended everybody pack up their loose personal items and must-haves, and be ready to go, just in case things escalated.

Jenny and Dan headed back to her hut, talking quietly about her thoughts on what she would now do. She grabbed a backpack from her personal gear and started loading it up with a blanket, towels, food, water, and a few other things she might need if she found the guy. She was planning on heading to the clinic afterward to load up on assorted medical supplies.

"Are you sure you won't change your mind, Jen? I truly believe you are taking an unnecessary risk here."

"Dan, I can't explain it, but I have to do this. It's a very strong feeling I have that it's the right thing to do."

The door to Jenny's hut swung open and JC entered uninvited. He assessed the situation and immediately went on the attack. "I thought I heard you wrong. Surely I must be mistaken, because I thought I heard you say you were going out into the woods to look for this killer Velasquez mentioned. I know I didn't hear you say that, did I? *Did I?*" He demanded.

The guilty parties glanced at each other like kids caught stealing a bike. There was nothing to say, really, now that the cat was out of the bag. "You heard right," Jenny confessed, brushing past him to retrieve a flashlight and some extra batteries.

"Like hell you are!" He yelled, grabbing Jenny by the arm and spinning her to face him. "I will not allow this. You will get yourself killed! Are you totally insane?"

"It's not up to you, JC. I thought we had this conversation already." Jenny looked pointedly at the hand on her arm then back into JC's eyes. "And FYI, if you grab me like that again you're going to be tasting your testicles."

JC quickly removed his hand.

"Look, JC," Dan tried to intercede. "Jenny has reason to believe this guy is a good guy, is injured, and needs help. She thinks if she doesn't help him, he's dead."

"So what? This is not your fight, Jenny. If you become involved in this, you're setting yourself up for major trouble. I sensed, just like everybody else, that the crazy woman has it out for you. Are you trying to give her more reason to kill you? Do you have a death wish?

"You cannot do this alone," JC said, his argument weakening in the face of her stubbornness.

"She's not alone. I'm going with her," Daniel joined in, buoyed up by JC's insulting treatment of his friend.

"I'm not asking you to get involved, JC. Just don't tell Grace, and if Maria comes back, tell her I'm out running or something. You don't have to like it, but I'm doing this. For me, and for him. It's right. I'm going." She smiled at Dan. "We're going, I mean."

"What do you expect me to do when you don't return? Huh? Have you thought of what it will do to us, to the Peace Corps if you go missing?"

"If I go missing I'll have bigger things to worry about than what you guys are doing. Don't get involved. Just don't throw me under the bus, either. Please?"

JC turned and stormed out of the hut.

"Well. That was an unexpected surprise," Dan said sarcastically to his friend.

"Hm. Since you're going with me, super brave machismo man, why don't you grab a backpack and meet me in the clinic. We'll fill it up with everything we can carry and head out to the deep, dark unknown."

"The deep, dark unknown. Yeah. Reminds me of my one and only experience with a woman."

Jenny snorted. "Ow."

Chapter Eight

Raul Argulla sat behind the desk in his study reviewing a spreadsheet of financial information when he heard the front door slam.

"Pinche puta. Yo mataria tu!" Maria screamed, her anger and frustration finally giving way to a full-blown temper tantrum.

He swirled the amber liquid in his glass and rose from the desk, thinking to meet Maria half way across the plushly carpeted room. He was sure she would storm into his den soon, in a full rage, and hoped to calm her temper with a soothing word and a drink before she started breaking things. He could tell by her loud cursing she didn't have any success finding the woman sniper.

The door to the den flew open and Maria entered, sharp eyes scanning the room, searching out her boss in an effort to get the inevitable bad news over with. She met him half way as he handed her a drink. The agitated woman considered slapping the drink from his hand for a moment, before her better judgment took over and she accepted it instead. Calming slightly, she said, "We didn't find her. Wasted an entire day checking the villages when we should have been scouring the riverbanks."

"I don't need to remind you how important this is to me," Raul said seriously, knowing full well Maria would regard this as an insult, but not caring. "I must know what she knows."

At that moment, there was a light tap on the door. A servant entered and began to build a fire in the grate. Maria strode to the window, glancing out, her control slowly returning. After the servant left, Maria continued her story. "None of the villagers had seen or heard anything. The men checked the riverbanks in these areas but found nothing. In the afternoon, we made it over to the Peace Corps camp. Although I couldn't find anything of value, that is where I believe she is. Or, around there, at any rate."

Raul stiffened at the mention of the camp. "What do you mean, you went to the camp? It was not my intention for you to go into that area. What did you do there?"

"I did there what I do everywhere. Intimidation and persuasion. It's what I do."

"And you found nothing, but you think she's there. Why?" He said sternly.

"Because I felt I was being lied to by one of the people there. A woman. Shorter than me. Blonde hair. A doctor. American. She was a cocky little bitch. Made me want to tear her to pieces." She flashed Raul a sneering smile, looking at him under hooded eyes. "I didn't though, *Boss*, because I knew you wouldn't want it." She looked away again, her face now showing nothing but contempt for her current employment situation.

"Good. I want you to leave them alone, and maybe you should consider your motivations. I know how you get about people that pique your interest. Don't think for a minute I've forgotten the fate of my former sous-chef. I let that slide, but I won't tolerate your unprovoked murdering tendencies around here anymore. Especially not any of those volunteers or Americans. If you think I will stand by while your fantasies run wild and bring the U.S. government down on me, you are sorely mistaken. That is the last thing in the world I need now that everything is finally coming together." Raul walked over to Maria and took her chin firmly in his grip, turning her face and forcing eye contact. "Am I making myself perfectly clear, Maria?"

She looked defiantly into his dark, serious gaze. "I am clear on the fact that you are my *temporary* employer, and as such, I will do as you wish. But know this. I will not be controlled. By you, or by anyone," she whispered dangerously, idly fingering the hilt of the knife in her pants pocket.

Raul was not intimidated, though he did understand this woman was a dangerous animal. He chastised himself for getting cocky in regards to her lately, and made a mental note to be more careful in her handling. "So tell me, do you have any real evidence that our sniper is in the vicinity of the camp? Or are you just attributing your feeling to your interest in the young doctor?"

Maria seethed at the implication, but grudgingly admitted he was probably right. "No. We found nothing today at all. It *is* just a feeling, but I truly believe it a valid one. The doctor was holding something back. I would like to pick her up, and persuade her to talk."

"No. Leave her. I told you. We cannot involve those people further. I want you to stay away from the camp."

"And if it turns out I'm right? You said yourself, picking up the sniper could be the most important key in advancing your position. Are you willing to risk her loss by refusing to rough up those Americans?"

Argulla moved to his desk and flipped the top open on his humidor, fingering through several cigars before settling on his choice for the evening. He rolled it lovingly between his thumb and forefinger, testing the freshness before bringing it to his nose for a leisurely sniff. Satisfied with his choice, the man quickly clipped the end and popped the stogie into his mouth, striking a wooden match in one fluid motion. He puffed the cigar while rotating it in his fingers until satisfied with the evenly glowing ember. He used this time to consider Maria's point. *Is it worth it?*

"If we get her, I will get Reyes. She is the key. My ambition in this regard cannot be denied. However, if I stir up a hornet's nest by hurting the American volunteers to get what I want, it is a moot point. In the current U.S. political climate, they will not hesitate to bully and push their way anywhere in the world they wish to go, and squash anyone they deem worthy. I could lose everything. The amount of power and money being tossed around like dice in that country right now is staggering. The U.S. is behaving like a wounded animal backed against a wall. Anyone that makes an enemy of them is a fool."

Maria walked over to where Raul was smoking and removed the cigar from his mouth, placing it sensually in her own. She tried to distract him momentarily, hoping he didn't over think their situation and stall out on her.

"Tell me where the search stands now, and what you plan to do next." He took his cigar back, allowing his eyes to roam at a leisurely pace over her body.

"We were counting on picking up a trail because of her gunshot wound, but that didn't work, at least not that we found. I sent a fresh team out to continue the search through the night. In the morning, I plan to fan the men out on both sides of the river from point of entry, and scour the earth and water until we find some sign, dead or alive, then go from there. If we get nothing from that, we will regroup and come up with a new plan."

"Okay. Then regarding the camp...we compromise. If you have not found the sniper by end of day tomorrow, I give you permission to station a watch in the camp to monitor for suspicious activity. A presence only. No violence at this point. I don't want to draw any unnecessary attention. Do you agree?"

"As you wish, Boss." *I don't care what you want of me, Argulla. My desire for the doctor outweighs the importance of my task for you. I will play along for now, but she will be mine, one way or the other. I will have her. I will crush her. I will hold her anguished green eyes to mine and watch as her life slowly fades away. A shooting star, whose light will quickly burn out. Mine.*

❧❧❦❦

Cold. Wet and cold.
"Hey, lucky number Seven."
"Daddy? Is that you?"
"I'm here, big girl."
"I'm sorry, Dad."
"What are you apologizing to me for, baby? I couldn't be more proud. No father could ever be more proud of his daughter, than I am of you. I love you, Seven. You're brave and strong, everything a parent could ever want in a child."
"I miss you. I wish we'd had more time together.

I wish I knew what you knew, about life, love...living."

"You will, in time."

"Dad, do you remember that time we went camping in the Smokies, and you taught me how to dig in and stay warm?"

"Mmmhmm."

"I tried, but it's just not working. I don't think I'm going to make it this time, Dad. Something happened. Something bad. I made a big mistake and everybody's dead."

"No baby. Not you. You know better. You're gonna make it just fine, you'll see."

"So cold."

"Hang in there, my lucky little number."

"Dad?"

"Mmmhmm?"

"I love you."

"I know, big girl. Hold on just a little while longer. Help is on the way."

☙ ☙ ☙ ☙

Raul stared hypnotically into the blazing fireplace in his library. He was seated comfortably on a luxurious red leather sofa, his hand wrapped around a snifter of fine brandy. Maria entered the room dressed in an elegant low cut black dress, her hair flowing freely down her back, eyes glittering in the firelight.

She almost looks human when she's dressed like that, Raul thought to himself. He rose upon her entrance and handed her an aperitif. "You look absolutely stunning this evening, my dear," he complimented Maria. "Dinner was excellent tonight. Don't you agree?" She nodded her assent as he ran a curious hand down her waist and over a curvaceous hip.

"I have formulated a plan regarding our dear friend Armando Reyes," he sneered. "Would you like to hear it? Or, have you had enough business for one day?" Raul let his eyes wander suggestively to her cleavage. "It involves blood. You should enjoy it."

"By all means. Please continue." She flashed him a suggestive smile, the mention of blood already piquing her interest. There'd been too little of it lately for her taste.

"It's a simple plan, really. I find they're usually best, don't you agree?" His hand moved from her hip to her behind, slowly appreciating the silky feel of the shimmering fabric he gripped. She shifted under his touch.

"The moment that pompous ass walked in my door I have been obsessing over how to turn this situation into an opportunity. My focus was on finding the sniper alive. Getting the real story from her on why she was here, and working from that." He moved a step closer to the young woman, leaning in to smell her hair and positioning himself so she could feel his arousal.

"But I no longer need to speak to our mysterious missing sniper to get information. I thought the information was the key. But now I realize that information doesn't matter. I got all I needed the moment Reyes walked in my door. Tell me, my dear, what was your impression of Señor Reyes?"

"He seemed like a million others I've known. Aristocrats. Superior attitudes. Only...there was one thing different. I sensed a fear in him. Underneath the story he was dishing, he smelled of fear."

"My thoughts exactly." He nodded approvingly. "He signed his own death warrant by confiding in me. It's a beautiful thing."

"So what is your brilliant plan, Raul, or are you"—she rubbed her body against his like a cat on a scratching post—"going to keep me waiting all night?"

"Everybody dies," he said flatly. "Except Manny. All I need from the sniper now is her body...and her weapon, of course."

"I like it already. Go on."

"The Reyes estate is very old. His family going back for generations is wealthy and very well connected. That is why I will never be able to acquire it in its entirety as long as Armando is alive. He would never part with it. He is too proud, and too smart to fall for anything like what I arranged to get my hands on this place." He slid his hand back across her hip and brushed his knuckles over the curve of her breast and up to her throat, appreciating her young skin with his fingertips.

"If I were to acquire his lands, I would become the largest coca grower in Bolivia, with the potential to out-produce some of the more prominent Peruvian and Columbian cartel families. The legitimate sales of the product would provide an excellent cover for the illegitimate production, and the added real estate is ideally positioned to provide a number of promising transfer routes into Columbia, and other more forgiving countries." He dipped a thumb into his snifter and trailed the liquid across her lips, leaning in to taste the brandy in her kiss.

"The sniper is the key to making my plan work. You see, I can't just go in there and kill them all without somebody else to take the blame. Reyes has graciously provided this person for me. Pretty much everybody in Bolivia in a position to ruin me knows how much I have wanted the Reyes lands. So in order for this to work, I absolutely cannot be involved in any way. Reyes must die by the hand of this sniper, or it must at least be made to look so. We only need her body to place at the scene." Maria massaged Raul's thigh through his pant leg, slowly working her way up to a more sensitive body part.

"I'm sure whatever he was wrapped up in will come out eventually, absolving me of any speculation whatsoever. Then, I simply slip in the back door and purchase the estate from young Manny, who is none the wiser. I will be his friend, advisor, confidante. I will take this huge, unwanted burden off his hands for an extremely fair price, freeing him to pursue his life's ambitions." Raul's eyes began to lose focus as Maria increased her ministrations. He moaned softly as her hand made its way to his belt buckle. She placed her drink on the side table so she could focus completely on her task.

"So what is my part in all of this masterful planning, dear Raul?" She said insincerely, but liking the sound of it nonetheless.

"You, lovely Maria, will capture the sniper dead or alive. I don't know whom she is, why she's here, and I don't care. She is the queen in my chess game. Reyes must not be allowed to find her first. You will then use her weapons to kill Reyes and his entire staff, security, cooks, mistresses, everybody. Leave no one alive except Manny. You must incapacitate him first, so he is sure to see nothing that happens. When he comes around, he will raise the alarm and start the ball rolling. You will plant the sniper's body in an obvious place so it looks like she was wounded and died in the attack. The authorities will investigate and will uncover the real reason for her being there and her motive. End of file. Case closed. You get to have your fun...I get to have my land."

Raul removed her hand from his pants and took hold of her waist, turning Maria slowly around and leading her to the high back of the sofa. They both faced the fireplace as he inched the hem of her silky black dress above her hips, and slipped his fingers inside the waistband of her panties, lowering them to her knees as he used his body to bend her over the sofa back. "Raul..." He reached around and placed two fingers in her mouth.

"No more talking."

Chapter Nine

D an zipped his yellow fleece jacket up his neck to ward off the cold, and adjusted the backpack on his shoulders a little higher to redistribute the weight of the load. They didn't even know if they would find the missing man, but Jenny packed supplies for every eventuality, wanting to be prepared for anything.

The friends agreed before leaving camp they would give themselves a cutoff time for the search. If they didn't find the guy before sunrise, they would head back, leaving him to his own luck. As much as Jenny hated the idea, she conceded that it was a mighty big forest, and if the man was moving fast, he could be miles away by now.

They walked slow and deliberately, one on each side of the path, searching the ground and woods for any trace of recent passage. They had been at it now for a couple hours and Jenny could tell her partner was getting bored with it already. They had made no progress yet, not even finding the slightest clue.

"How did you know this trail was back here, D-Mac?" Dan asked, looking to liven up the search with a little conversation.

"I found it about three months ago. It's distinct down by the river. Fades away near the camp, but becomes well-trod again about a hundred yards away from the clinic. I came across it when I was after a photo-op one day. I like it back here. It's very peaceful. Old growth. I've gotten lots of great pictures in this part of the woods. The sunlight barely filters in because the growth is so thick, so when it does the lighting is very dramatic."

Just as Jenny was finishing her sentence, Dan jumped into her at the sound of a loud animal cry in the vicinity. "Shit," he expelled nervously. "That was close. What the hell was that?"

"I don't know." She laughed, partly nervous and partly at her friends jumpy behavior. "But it wasn't that close. Just really loud."

"Too damn close for me. Maybe we should consider heading back before our sunrise deadline. We don't even know if he came this way. It's like finding a needle in a haystack."

"He came this way. I know it. I sure as hell can't explain it, but I feel it. Oh, and in case I forget to mention this later, thanks for coming with me. I really appreciate the company, and you're right. It is a little creepy out here in the dark."

"If we find this guy, do you have any feeling on what we'll find?"

"Not really. But Maria said the guy was injured, and that would have happened a while before he broke into the clinic. Based on the amount of blood in the smudge I saw, I'd say it was a serious enough injury to keep him bleeding for quite some time. A little part of me thinks it's likely the guy has already bled to death if it was a gunshot wound or something equally as serious."

"What's that?" Dan pointed his flashlight just off the trail to a mound partially covered with leaves. It could easily be taken for some kind of large animal droppings.

"It's freshly turned dirt," Jenny said, poking the end of her walking stick into the pile. She rooted around for a second then pulled something to the surface with the tip of her stick. "Yes! Look, Dan. I told you he came this way. These are the empty packages and wrappers from the bandages and pills he took from the clinic. Looks like he covered 'em up so he wouldn't leave a litter trail. Finally. Even I was beginning to doubt my choice of direction."

"Hmph. That'd be a first."

She slapped him playfully, then bent to rebury the trash, careful to cover the dirt with leaves and twigs. "Come on. We're on the right trail. Let's keep moving. Keep your eyeballs peeled for anything out of place. I'm gonna find this guy if it's the last thing I do."

❧❧❧❧

"How come you never told me this stuff before?" Jenny asked, as she looked sideways at her friend, chuckling at his latest story. Another hour of slow progress passed as they continued to examine every inch of the trail and surrounding wood. She stopped for a moment to suck some water from a blue bottle.

"I just didn't think it was appropriate at the time, since you were sleeping with him and all," he snickered, having just relayed an embarrassing JC story to Jenny. "I mean, he is cute 'n everything, D-Mac, but a bunch of us were shocked as shit when we caught you guys coming out of the steamy clinic shower together. I mean, I know the place was supposed to be empty, but that's the best time for the rest of us to use it, you know? You turned so many shades of red, I thought I was going to pee my banana hammock."

Jenny turned red again, just thinking about how mortified she was. "God, that was embarrassing. I didn't really know what I was doing with him either, we just kind of fell into it. He was a good guy though, nice to me."

The big man eyed her mischievously. "How was he?" He asked seductively.

"Dan!" She swatted him in the stomach, laughing. "Let's try to focus on the task at hand, shall we? Look. Man. Dying. Must find. Go!" She pointed up the trail trying to distract him from his latest inquisition.

"Oh come on…can't a guy have a little mantasy?"

"No!" She said, trying not to encourage him further.

"Okaaay. But I'll get it out of you sooner or later. Nala has a huge crush on him. I think she'll be excited to find out he's a free man again. I was just asking so I could give her some pointers on how to handle him," he said and winked conspiratorially.

"Surrrre. Well, if Nala is the kind of woman who likes to be told what to do, then I'm sure they'll be very happy together. But it's not for me."

"Yeah. He was kind a jerk to you earlier."

"Mmm. I'm sure I'm no peach to be around either. I suck at relationships. I'm beginning to believe I don't have what it takes to make one work."

"Sure you do, sis. You just haven't found the spark yet. That's all. You'll get there when your puzzle piece shows up."

"Puzzle piece, huh? Cute. I like that. Is that like a soul mate?"

"Yeah. There's one person out there that is the

yin to your yang. The one piece of the puzzle cut specifically to fit perfectly into you. That's what I believe, anyway."

"I hope I've got one out there somewhere, because if all my future holds is a bunch more relationships like the ones I've had so far, I'd almost rather be single."

"That bad, huh?"

"Yep. The one I was in before JC was a bit longer-lived, and about as much fun as my time with him. Which isn't saying much. The one before that, in college, lasted the longest. I think that was because I was young and thought somewhere inside it would get better. It never did. I broke it off with all three of them. I found out the first time, if you start off a relationship feeling so-so about it, chances are it's not going to get any better with time. It's best to just abandon ship and swim for shore. I think I've become a serial dumper. What do you think? Am I hopeless?"

"Damn. You're asking me? Talk about hopeless. I'm the last person in the world you should be asking relationship advice from. I'm the exact opposite. I fall in love with every guy I'm with, and end up getting dumped."

"You never did get around to telling me what happened with you and your heartbreaker. You promised you would one day when it wasn't so fresh. Now's a good time if you're up for it." They continued to stroll at a leisurely pace, scanning carefully with their flashlights. Dan was internally relieved they hadn't heard any more strange noises in the night since that scare a while back.

"His name was Jerome. Not a ton to tell, really. Your typical heartbreak story, featuring a standard healthy dose of homosexual drama. We lived together for three years. Shortly after we moved in to our apartment, Jerome lost his job. He told me he was really depressed about it. I paid the bills and everything while he got back on his feet enough to start looking for work. He would come home a couple times a week saying he'd had interviews or something. He was a graphic artist. Every now and then, he would get a freelance job or something, but never seemed to find the right job.

"I loved him. I didn't mind that I was supporting him, really, until one day he left me for a better meal ticket. I found out when he left that he'd quit all his jobs, though he told me otherwise. He would just stay in one long enough for me to think he was trying, but really all he wanted was someone to pay his bills. He was sleeping around the entire time. Jerome was a very good little actor. Had me convinced he loved me, but it was all a lie.

"After he left, he came back one day with his new lover and tried to lay claim to all the stuff I'd bought while we were together. And I'm not talking about clothes and stuff. I gave all that to him. I'm talking about tv, stereo, furniture, anything that we bought together, that I paid for, he considered it as much his as mine. I took exception to that. Things got messy.

"I must admit, I would have won the Oscar for drama queen of the year this one day. I was so sick of what was happening, I toted every single thing we had in the apartment out to a dumpster. Couch, chairs, dining table, bed, linens, towels, dishes, tv, stereo, you name it. Everything. I spray painted the side of the dumpster to say 'Here, Jerome! Take everything, you whore, it's all yours now.' Then I video taped myself pouring gasoline over everything, and tossing his engraved Zippo, a gift from me by the way, into the dumpster."

"Wow."

"Mmhmm. That's what the police said. The conflagration was really quite spectacular to behold. I never knew smoke came in so many colors. Took the fire department quite a while to douse the flames. Needless to say, I had to pay a hefty fine, but I didn't get charged with anything because I had a great lawyer. Before they toted all the stuff away, I found the charred and destroyed Zippo in the ash. Lucky find really. I wrapped it up in a box with the videotape and mailed it to Jerome. The rest, as they say, is history. I thought it would be best for my mental health to get a fresh start, get out of town for a while, so I signed up with the Peace Corps. Never regretted a minute of it."

"Jesus, Dannyboy. How are you doing with it all now?"

"Oh, much better, thanks. I'm totally over the whole scene. The lost love hurts. I thought he was it, you know? But what hurts just as bad, but in a different way is being played so badly. It's terribly humiliating to admit blindness and stupidity in yourself. A part of you wants to believe you deserved to be treated that way, simply because you were foolish enough to get hooked into a relationship like that in the first place."

"Oh, Dan. I'm so sorry. That's a truly shitty thing to have happen to anyone. I sure am glad you're here, though. You've made my time in Bolivia an absolute blast. It wouldn't have been nearly as great for me if I hadn't had you to share it with."

They stopped their progress up the trail for a moment and considered each other. Dan wrapped the small woman in a bear hug, before they laughed at their sappy ruminations and moved on.

"Thanks for listening. It actually makes me feel better to talk about it. Makes me see it in a healthier light. I can look back on it a lot more objectively now."

"Your puzzle piece is out there somewhere too, you know. I hope we both find one."

"Well. I hope when I find mine, he looks like Johnny Depp and has a really big di...Ooof!"

"Dan!" She whacked him in the gut again. "How many times am I going to have to beat you up tonight to make you behave?"

"God, I hope I never behave. Where's the fun in that?"

※ ※ ※ ※ ※

"D-Mac, we've been searching for hours, I gotta tell ya, I'm starting to doubt our abilities as trackers," Dan said as he peered of into the deep, dark woods. The temperature was chilly, with a considerable amount of moisture in the air. "Have you thought at all about what you'll do if this guy really does turn out to be dangerous?"

"Kind of. I'm pretty good at defending myself. We are here to help him, so I guess I'm hoping he'll be a decent guy and understand that. And if not, well...I guess we'll cross that bridge if we come to it. Are you concerned?"

"I can tell you what I want to believe. I want to believe your instincts are right, and this is really a good guy. Because I'm gonna be pissed if I find out I gave up a full night's sleep, freezing my nuts off, traipsing around in the woods for some ungrateful criminal."

Jenny stopped to retie her bootlace. She placed

her flashlight on the ground so she could free up both hands for the task. A shadow on the ground created by the close up light drew her attention. "Dan, check this out."

The tall man dropped to his knees beside his friend, and looked at the shadows where she was pointing. "Looks like a hand print. It's hard to say for sure though, with the rain that went through earlier."

"And look here. Two indentions, just below. Like knee prints," she said excitedly, finally having found something tangible. "It looks like he fell here, and landed with one hand."

"This is good. At least we know we haven't overshot anything. We're still on the trail. Maybe we could take a break here for a few minutes before we push on. I could use some snack and drink fortification. How 'bout you?"

"Yeah, let's. I'm gonna go mark my territory behind that bush over there. Be right back."

Dan busied himself pulling out a couple snack bars and his water bottle, after removing his pack to take a break from the weight of it. He wasn't nearly as fit as Jenny, and the long hike was taking its toll. He sighed heavily and leaned back on his pack, taking a well-deserved breather.

Jenny returned a moment later, holding something green under his nose. He flinched at first, sure she was playing some sort of 'smell my finger' prank on him. "Dan, look what I found over there. No way in hell I would have seen this if I hadn't been so close to the ground." She chuckled.

He took the object she held out. It was a small, light green rectangular piece of fabric. "It blended right in, but I noticed it because the shape was too perfect to be natural. It had to come from our guy. I think this means he's hiding out over in that direction somewhere."

"Okay. So we head into the rough next?"

"Definitely. Let's rest for a minute first, though. I could use a few minutes off my feet."

"Jen, what are you planning to do with this guy once we find him?"

"Depends on what we find. If he's dead or alive. How bad is the wound and what kind of wound is it? Will he cooperate with us? There are a lot of potential variables. If he's wounded badly, but okay to travel, I'll take him back to camp and fix him up in a clean environment, then send him on his way. Or maybe we can hide him nearby. If he's not wounded badly, I'll fix him up out here, give him what survival stuff we have, then you and I will go back. If he's dead, I'll search him for some kind of I.D., then bury him as best we can. Or, maybe we'll make a travois and haul him back to camp."

"Just gotta wait and see, I guess," Dan said. He stood and pulled his pack back onto his shoulders.

"Let's separate by about fifteen yards and head into the woods over here." She pointed in the direction where she found the green square of fabric. "We'll go slow, and call out frequently, so he knows were friendly. Look for snapped twigs, broken branches, fresh dirt, anything at all out of the ordinary. Don't get too far away from me...and Dan?"

"Yeah."

"Watch out for snakes." She giggled internally, knowing just how to push his buttons.

"Ohh maaaaan. You sooo did not have to put that image in my head."

అఇఇఇ

Voices. They found me. Dead now for sure. Damn.
Somewhere down deep, there was a vague awareness that she should try to rouse herself, but the task proved impossible. She wanted to survive this trial. She wanted to fight. But no matter how hard she tried, the blackness would not relent.

Voices getting closer.
For the first time in her life, Seven surrendered to defeat.

అఇఇఇ

"Hola! ¿Hay alguien aquí?" Dan hollered from his position to the left of his friend. There was no reply.

"Is anybody here? We're here to help," Jenny tried from her position as they continued to trudge forward. The young doctor startled at something caught at the edge of her vision. "Dan!" She called. "What the heck is that?" Jenny pointed to a large scary shape jutting out of the ground. They walked toward each other to confer.

"I know. Creepy isn't it? Funny we couldn't see that from the trail. Must have been the angle we were at. It's a downed tree, the root structure anyway."

"Scared the crap out of me. In this light it looks like a big monster coming out of the dark." She laughed nervously. "Come on, let's check it out."

"You thinking what I'm thinking?"

"Probably. Make a good hiding place, wouldn't it?"

"Mmhmm."

Flashlights blazing a trail, the duo headed to the fallen tree, both eager to find their prey. Jenny aimed her light along the trunk of the tree while Dan headed for the upended roots. "Jen," he exhaled. "Over here." Now that they were there, he was slightly breathless and afraid. He whispered, "I think I see something down in this hole."

It feels right, Jenny thought to herself. *If I was hiding, this is the kind of place I would choose.* "Hola. Can you hear me?" She called into the hole, hoping for a friendly reply. She aimed her flashlight down and targeted the beam of light on a black, mud-covered boot heel.

"Whew. That's him all right, Dan. Good eyes. He's practically invisible." She slid down the hole and began to gingerly remove the branches and leaves covering the wounded person. "We're here to help you. Can you hear me?"

"Is he dead?" Dan asked, inspecting the curled up figure buried under the tree roots.

"Don't know. Get down here and help me uncover him." The two set to work removing the camouflage until the immoveable figure was totally revealed. Dan stood back to provide better light on the scene before him.

"Oh my," he said, noting the clothing, his mind spinning in multiple directions. "What the heck is he wearing? He looks like a shrub."

"Yeah. This guy looks military. The clothing looks like tactical type gear. He's covered with this camo suit thing, feels like there's a Kevlar vest underneath here, and his face is painted in camouflage, too. He looks like some kind of undercover operator, or guerilla or something. It's amazing we found him at all." She reached over and placed two fingers on his neck, checking for a pulse. "I think we're in bigger trouble than we thought," she said, referring to the possibility of him being military.

"What's the verdict?"

"Still alive, but extremely weak. Heart is racing. Skin is freezing. A quick guess tells me major blood loss by the look of the bandages on the neck, and maybe early hypothermia. He's in bad shape."

"What the hell is that?" Dan asked, pointing to a large shadow just behind the fallen man.

Jenny reached over and grabbed hold of a huge rifle, pulling it free of the branches. "Sweet Jesus," she whispered. "This is a lot worse than I thought, Dan. This guy is serious trouble. This is a sniper rifle. See the size of it, and this huge scope on top? Do you think he was here to kill Argulla, maybe?"

"God, who knows. This is getting worse by the minute. If he's military, we could be getting involved in something really scary here."

"Take it." She handed her friend the large weapon. "And hand me your pen light. I need to get better vitals, then we'll figure out what to do. I'm not sure at this point if he's even going to make it. This changes everything."

Jenny grabbed the sniper by the shoulders and hauled the body around to a more accessible position. "There are bandages taped on the neck, and a tight wrap on the upper left arm that I can see from here." She spoke aloud to Dan as she assessed the body. She quickly felt up the arms and legs checking for broken bones. "Skin is clammy and cold. Heart racing, appears comatose."

Jenny reached over to open the eyelids, shining the small penlight in to check pupil dilation, and froze in place. The young doctor's breathing stopped. Her motion stopped. Suddenly, in her world, the earth ceased to spin. Still holding her breath, she studied the face under the grease paint intently, recognition slamming into her like a runaway train.

She sat back on her heels, rested a hand on the cheek of the unconscious sniper, and bowed her head in a quick prayer to whoever may be listening.

"What is it, Jen? Is he dead?"

Silence.

"Jen!"

"She," Jenny whispered to Dan, barely audible over the sounds of the forest.

"What? Did you say she? How the hell can you tell that by looking at someone's pupils?"

"Because in a million years I could never forget these eyes." She looked at Dan, a tear tracking slowly down her cheek. "I grew up with this woman. She's an American, and a very dear friend. This game just took on a whole new meaning for me, Dan. Thank god I came."

Jenny blinked back tears as she steeled herself for the uphill battle to come. "I will do anything I can to save her. Anything. Do you understand? And she's in really bad shape. Looks like probably a Class IV Hemorrhage, circulatory shock, and comatose. Jump down here again. We need to get her somewhere safe fast, and it can't be camp. I've got to get her on a saline drip immediately, get those wounds closed, get her some blood. We don't have much time. She could go into cardiac arrest at any moment. Now that we know what this is all about, it makes Maria ten times more dangerous in my estimation. I will not allow her to get hold of Seven."

Dan got a good grip underneath the unconscious woman's arms and hauled her ungracefully out of the hole. "Ugh," he grunted. "She's big...and heavy. Damn!"

"Yeah. She was about five-nine at the age of fifteen, so I'm sure she's bigger than that now. Looks like she's about six feet. Come on. Let's get her over your shoulders in a fireman's carry. I'll get the packs and flashlights. Stay right behind me and I'll light your way. We'll make better time that way. I think I know a place where we can go down trail about a kilometer."

"What'd you say her name was?" Dan asked as he bullied her into position over his shoulders and stood to his full height, adjusting her slightly for the walk.

"Seven."

"Weird name."

"Yeah. Suits her though. She's kind of unusual herself."

Jenny pulled her pack back on, swinging Dan's over her front. She grabbed Seven's rifle in one hand, and the brighter of their two flashlights in the other. They shuffled through the brush, heading back toward the path. "Watch your step here, there's a big tree root sticking out. How's it going back there, you okay?"

"Yep," Dan grunted under his burden. "This girl is solid. I am sooo earning a double bacon cheeseburger right now. I've expended a week's worth of calories this one night alone."

They reached the path and began to make good time, heading back in the general direction of camp. "So where are we going, anyway? You said you had someplace in mind."

Jenny checked her watch and picked up her pace. She was going to need to get Seven stabilized, and get Dan back to camp before sunup to avoid arousing suspicion. "Do you remember that spot on the trail where there's a tree growing in the middle and the trail kind of goes around it on both sides?"

"Yep."

"Well, there's a place in the woods near that tree I found by accident a while back. Truth is, the entrance is a hole in the ground, and I almost killed myself falling through it. That's how I found the place. I never told you, because I knew you'd give me one of those 'I told you so' conversions, since you're always trying to get me not to run off in the woods by myself."

"Mmhmm. Told ya so. Could've been bad."

"So I was out running around, taking pictures. I was hot on the trail of a pair of toucans, and all of a sudden I hear wood crack, and down I go. Scared the tar out of me, but I caught myself on the edge before I fell all the way in. I climbed out, couple little scratches, no biggie. I was more worried about damaging my camera. Since I was fine...I, of course, had to investigate." She smiled to herself, knowing without looking at the 'look' her friend was directing toward the back of her head.

"Curiosity killed the cat, you know." Dan shook his head. "Reckless."

"The board I went through was some kind of rotted door in the ground. I used my flash to light the hole and there was a rope ladder that went down about eight feet into a long narrow room. It had been abandoned a long time by the looks of it. I found a small door at the other end I was able to push open from the inside. So it's a little hidey-hole of some kind that was built into the hillside. At first, I thought it was an old hunter's hut or something like that, but based on the debris left behind, I now think it's an abandoned cocaine production lab. There were some plastic tubs and junk left there. Probably been empty since the '80s by the looks."

"How apropos. Hiding from the drug lord in one of his own labs."

"Anyway, it's a train wreck in there, but with a little work we can set up a place to hide her for a few days while she stabilizes. Then we can come up with a better plan. There are some plywood tables, a hodgepodge of wooden stools; we'll bring some lanterns from camp. We're almost there now."

"Jen, do you think she'll make it? She seems pretty bad."

"I'm going to do everything I can to make sure she does. She's an only child. Her father was a Marine killed in action back in 1987. It would be too much to bear thinking of her sweet mother finding out her only child was lost the same way. I won't do that. I'll get her out of this, or so help me, I'll die trying."

Chapter Ten

Jenny and Daniel maneuvered off trail and back into the woods, dodging low hanging branches and underbrush along the way. The tall man's burden had not moved or made a sound since they picked her up from a hole in the ground about a half hour before. "Be really careful here. That's where the rotten wooden door in the ground is. Come around this way and we'll go in the tiny door instead."

Jenny pulled the small side door back, ducking her head so she could see in, and lighting the interior of the long, narrow room. Everything was as she remembered. The bunker was about ten feet wide by twenty long with a packed dirt floor and dirt walls, supported haphazardly by the occasional bowing board. Two support beams in the center of the room held up a planked ceiling, which had long been overgrown with forest floor above. There were a couple overturned, hastily made tables, and some stools lying around on the floor along with assorted debris, dirty plastic tubs of various shapes and sizes. There didn't appear to be any standing water or animal signs, so Jenny felt it would be a safe and acceptable place to hide for a while.

She quickly dropped her load in a corner and walked to the far end of the room, righting one of the wooden tables. "Okay. Drop her here for now and we'll set the other table up for her with the clean linens we brought from the clinic. Move that table over here. There's a couple hooks in the wall we can use to hang the saline and blood from. You work on getting the I.V. ready and I'll prep the table."

They quickly went to work, doing their best to set up the impromptu field hospital. Dan found a small table, covering it with a sterile towel and lining up their supply of medications and equipment. They worked as a team to strip Seven of her ghillie suit and tactical gear, Jenny checking her for further injuries along the way. When Seven was down to nothing but her skivvies and skullcap, they moved her to the clean table and prepped her arms for the I.V., inserting the needles and securely taping them in place.

Jenny removed the bandage on Seven's neck and checked the gunshot wound there, and the one in her arm. "Okay, let's get this neck wound cleaned and stitched. Then we'll get that bullet out of her arm. Looks like this one in the neck just grazed her jugular. Just a fraction more and she would have bled to death, for sure," she said to Dan, who was already pulling together the supplies Jenny would need, drawing a local anesthetic into a syringe from a small clear bottle.

"Dannyboy, let's come up with a plan while we work. You need to get out of here soon and head back to camp. I'm staying for now, but I think we should switch off taking care of her so we can cover for each other at camp. Hopefully she'll be stabilized by the time you return. Go back, grab a couple hours sleep, then act like it's business as usual. If anybody asks after me, 'oh I just saw her in the clinic a few minutes ago, are you sure she's not there?'...'she went running'... that kind of thing. If anybody's really persistent, find out what they want and tell him or her you'll relay the message next time you see me. Okay with you?"

"Yep. What time do you want me back here?" Jenny made quick work of the neck sutures, while Dan tied them off and trimmed the extra thread.

"I'd say early afternoon. Scalpel." Dan handed her the sharp instrument and watched as she went to work on the bullet hole. "That will give me time to get back and be seen for a while. Check in at the clinic, grab a bite to eat, etc. See if you can bring some lanterns and maybe a pair of your sweats or something comfortable for her to wear if she wakes up. More food and water too, might as well stockpile some here. Also, she'll probably need another saline bag by the time you get back."

"What about drugs?"

"We should be able to make do with what we've already brought. Her arm is starting to get infected, but what we've already given her should take care of that. When you get back, we'll chat for a few minutes, catch each other up, then I'll get back there quick. I'll return as soon as it's clear for me to do so, then we'll just keep up a switching routine."

Jenny pulled the bloody instrument from the open wound, a bullet clamped tightly to the end. She dropped the deadly projectile onto the nearby table while her efficient nurse moved to clear the blood from the wound so she could finish her work.

"And Juan Carlos?" Dan asked, dreading the inevitable confrontation.

"What about him?"

"He's in a position to blow this. He saw us leave. Do we tell him what's going on and trust him, or keep him in the dark? You know as well as I do, the minute he sees me he'll make a beeline right to me for information."

"What do you think we should do?"

"Jeez, D-Mac. You're the one who was sleeping with him. Is he trustworthy or not?" Dan could not resist a good tease when the opportunity was so ripe for the picking.

"Yes. I think so. He's a good guy, just a little too cautious for this kind of endeavor. Trust him, but make sure he understands this is now a life and death situation, for me as well as for Seven. Maybe you can suggest he help you in diverting attention away from me. Don't push him, though. He's got to make up his own mind."

"Let's just see if he makes it in the right way. He could easily let Grace know what was happening, thinking he was doing it to protect you. If Grace finds out, she will pull the plug here in a heartbeat."

"Mmm. A wing and a prayer, my friend. We'll see how it all plays out."

"She's pretty big, and strong looking. She could wake disoriented and cause some damage. Do you want to rig a harness for the bed, or maybe some arm restraints, just in case?"

"No. If that happens, I'll probably be able to calm her, or I'll just get out of her way. I gave her some morphine, so that should keep her resting comfortably for a while even if she does come around."

"Watch out for yourself. I know I say that to you all the time...seems to be a habit of everyone at camp, but I mean it. You want me to bring you a snack or something before I head out?"

"I'm okay, thanks. One more thing...when you come and go from here, and when you're hiking through that last bit of rough forest right before the camp, be very careful not to break any branches, and avoid stepping on twigs and stuff. I know it sounds crazy, but we need to try our best not to leave any kind of trail. I don't know how long we'll need to be here for her, but I do know it's just a matter of time before Maria and her gang make it this way. The less sign we leave, the better for us."

"You got it, sweet cheeks."

☙☙☙☙

Daniel was in the corner of the dark dirt room holding a pen light in his mouth as he sorted the contents of their backpacks onto the hard packed floor. He was preparing to leave and wanted to make sure everything Jenny might need was left behind. Clean towels, blanket, cleansers, antibacterial gel, food, water. He laid everything out on the spare wooden table, then turned to his friend who sat next to the unconscious woman, holding her hand.

For the first time since he'd known the young doctor, he saw something in her he had never seen before. Despair. It didn't suit her. "D-Mac, how are you holding up, Sweetie?" No answer.

He walked over to her, seeing she was deep in thought, and placed a hand gently on her shoulder. "Hey."

"Oh. Sorry, Dan. Guess I kinda drifted off there."

"She was pretty important to you, huh?"

"Yes. She was. I was just a kid the last time I saw her. We were close though. It was kind of an unusual friendship. She started out babysitting for me when I was about six. It was fun. We always had a good time together. By the time I was eight and she was fifteen, we were good friends. It was quite a division in age, but she didn't seem to mind. I was mature for my age, and she was a kid at heart, so it was a good match."

"So what happened? You guys have a falling out or something?"

"Nah. Nothing like that. When her father was killed, her mom thought it would be a good idea to move nearer family, since they didn't have any in Virginia where we lived. So they left for South Carolina. We wrote each other for a while, but eventually lost contact.

"You know how you're always teasing me about having a bubbly and ferocious personality?" She asked, smiling thoughtfully at her friend.

He chuckled. "Yeah, it's true."

"Would it surprise you to know that even with my generally good-natured persona, I really haven't had that many friends?"

"Yeah, kind of. But you consider her one of them, I guess?"

"Mm. Not just one of them, but the best one. I was devastated when she left. So sad. I'm sure it seems ridiculous, a kid that young, my whole life ahead of me, but we had a connection that ran deep. We were comfortable with each other, like a twin would be with their sibling, you know?"

"You're scared for her, aren't you?"

"Yes. I'm scared." Jenny paused and looked back at Seven. She reached up and removed the tight elastic skullcap from over her hair. Seven's long black braids spilled out. Jenny smiled and rearranged them next to her head.

"I never really understood the connection I felt for her when I was a kid. It was so strong. But what

I think may be even stranger, is that earlier when we found her, and I realized it was her, that feeling came flooding back like it was yesterday. Like not a single day had separated us.

"It floored me."

Dan put a reassuring hand on her shoulder and gave it a squeeze. "She's gonna be all right, my friend. Don't you worry. After all, she is under the best possible care."

Jenny stood and wrapped her friend in a big hug. "Thank you, Dannyboy. I don't know what I would have done without your help."

Daniel walked to the corner and put his empty backpack on, preparing to leave his friend alone in the deep, dark woods. Fastening it around his waist he turned, "Take care, D-Mac. I'll be back as soon as I can." He waved and headed out the door. Just before shutting it behind him, he glanced back in time to see Jenny place a tender kiss on the forehead of her fallen friend. He overheard her say, "Please come back to me, Seven. I can't lose you again."

⁂

After Dan left, Jenny sat silently for a moment, planning her next move. She decided to clean out one of the plastic tubs that were left behind and see if she could wash Seven up a little bit. Her hands were caked with dirt, much of her body in dried blood and her face was still covered with camo paint and grime from her struggle through the woods. She was a mess. It kind of reminded her a little of that time they got in a mud paddy fight down by the river behind Seven's house. Only minus the blood, of course.

She filled the tub with drinking water and a mild cleanser she carried in a small bottle in her pack. She started with her face, ears, and neck, and worked down from there, removing her blood-crusted bra along the way. She talked in a soothing voice the whole time, retelling stories from their childhood, hoping to help the woman find her way back into consciousness. When she was finished, she tossed the bra into the used water, doing her best to scrub it out. "No way I can lend you one of mine, Sev. We're not even close."

Jenny hung the bra over a stool to dry, and covered her friend with a blanket. She tucked her in around the edges, making sure to keep the catheter hoses for the I.V. clear. She checked the drip again and considered another dose of morphine, but decided to wait until Seven came to before determining if any more was needed.

The young woman made a mental note to search the surrounding area for a stream or water source when it got to be daylight. There was plenty in the area; it was just a matter of finding some. She would spend the time waiting for Dan's return usefully by washing out Seven's clothes so the woman would have something clean to wear when she woke up.

Finally exhausted from trudging around all night, she pulled a stool up to Seven's makeshift bed and rested her head on her arms at the foot of the linen covered surface. *I haven't slept sitting up since college,* she thought then dozed off almost immediately.

༄ ༄ ༄ ༄ ༄

Raul Argulla was sleeping in a brandy-induced haze when there was another obnoxious knock on his bedroom door. He looked over to the naked woman sleeping beside him and noticed she had one, slightly open, but raptor-like eye focused on the door as well.

"*Coño*. What is it?" He yelled at the door, rubbing the sleep from his eyes.

"Sir. Sorry to disturb you, but the forward post has reported one of Señor Reyes' vehicles approaching."

With a long-suffering sigh, Raul swung his legs over the side of the bed and reached for a cigarette. "That son-of-a-bitch. I told him I'd let him know if we found her. Is this going to be a daily occurrence?" He asked no one in particular. He glanced at his gold Rolex. "Six a.m., not even sunrise yet, and that prick is hounding me already. May as well get started early this morning, Maria. I'll see what he wants and meet you downstairs."

Raul donned his silk paisley bathrobe and soft Italian slippers, heading downstairs just as one of his servants opened the door. Raul was pleased to see Manny Reyes at the door and not his asshole of a father. "Manny!" He bellowed over the foyer, as if they were old buddies. "A pleasure to see you. What brings you here? No father hanging over you this time?" He shook the young man's hand and placed a friendly arm around his shoulder, bringing him into the fold.

"Sorry to disturb you so early, Señor Argulla."

"Please. Call me Raul. Come. Let's get some coffee. This is an ungodly hour to be without coffee. You can tell me why you're here, and then...I will show you my new toy while we wait for Maria." He led the young man into the den, where a servant was setting up a gold-plated coffee service on a table by the window.

"Thank you, Señ...Raul. I could use some coffee,"

Manny said warily, as though sleep had not been allowed him recently. "My father sends his apologies that he didn't come in person, but had a pressing matter to attend to. He is most anxious to know if any progress has been made in the hunt for our thief, and if you would possibly reconsider allowing his men to assist your security director."

"We have not found her, but are giving the matter our utmost attention. Since your last visit, our people have scoured every village down the river from your lands. Today, it is our goal to search the river itself and the surrounding wood. I think it would be a good idea for your men to assist, as we will need to start the search on your property at the location she went into the river. We wish to leave no stone unturned, and could use the extra manpower, as we will have people walking both sides of the water."

Manny nodded, happy to have something positive to relay to his father.

"Now, come with me. I have something to show you that a man of your taste will appreciate." He led the younger man through the kitchen and out a back door to a covered walkway, separating his home from a large, matching structure with automatic doors built into twelve arched entryways. They entered through a side door, where Raul flicked on a long row of overhead lights illuminating an impressive collection of beautiful cars. He led Manny to the first one in the row, and was pleased to see the young man's eyes go wide in adoration.

"Bugatti Veyron. Just off the boat from Italy two days ago. Quad-turbo engine. 7-speed sequential. One thousand and one horsepower." There was silence in the room as he glanced at the young man. Raul smiled at the look of vehicular lust in Manny's eyes, certain he could hear a choir of angels singing somewhere in his empty skull.

"Maybe we could go for a spin sometime?"

"I'd love that, Raul. Thank you. It is absolutely beautiful."

"Speaking of beautiful, perhaps we should go check on the lovely Maria. She's been keeping me... company...since my wife has been away." Raul added a personal note to the conversation, trying to make the young man gain trust in him. *Might as well lay the groundwork now.* "I asked my wife to stay in La Paz a couple of days while we sorted this business with the thief out, but she chose to punish me by flying to New York with my credit cards for a little shopping trip instead. God help me. That woman and plastic should never be allowed in the same room together."

They laughed together, like buddies. Manny said, "Maria is beautiful. You're a lucky man. She's not really my type though."

"No?"

"No. I can tell by the way she takes everything in. She's smart. I prefer women a little less sharp and a little more willing, if you know what I mean."

"Oh, she's willing..." They laughed knowingly at their manly joke.

"There's not much action around here. I've wanted to get into the city, but my father won't allow it till this problem is resolved."

"Hm. No problem. What do you like? Maybe I can hook you up here. I have a huge staff, and some of them are very pretty young ladies."

Manny looked over at his host, and smiled. "I like all kinds, as long as they come in quantity." They

laughed together again, their bonding confirmed.
   "Stop by anytime. Mí casa, su casa."

❧❧❧❧❧

   Maria stood on the rock overhang and surveyed
the area where the sniper jumped into the water. No
blood trail was evident, as the previous night's rain
had washed it all away. Reyes' men assured the scary
little woman the sniper had been shot at least twice
that they knew of, having seen her take the hits.

   Maria looked over the high ledge and concluded
that surviving the leap would be possible if you landed
in just the right place. She divided the men into two
groups, assigning each to a side of the river. "You men,
search the far side of the river. Go slowly. It is vital no
detail is missed. Two of you stay down at the water's
edge, and the other two fan out at short distances in the
woods. Look for any trace of disturbance in the moss,
mud, and trees. Look for broken branches, footprints,
skid marks on the rocks, feces, anything you see that is
not a leaf hanging untouched from a tree, call it to my
attention." The men began their short hike upriver,
back to the crossing point. She pointed to the second
group. "You men, same thing, but down this side.
Let's go."

   The terrain was rough in this area and Maria had
to focus on every step over the rocky surface to keep
from falling. She climbed over boulders and fallen
trees, working her way down to the water, her men
and a couple of Reyes' men ahead of her. She agreed to
take them along at Raul's insistence, wanting to keep
from offending anybody's boundary rules.

   The going was tediously slow. Several hours in,

Maria received a call from one of her men on the other side of the river. "Boss, it's probably just animal trail, but there's a spot on the rocks over here that looks scuffed up."

"Did the men find any other sign in the surrounding area?"

"Negative."

"Mark the location on your GPS, and flag a tree in the vicinity. I'll check it out later."

"Will do."

Maria spent the slow passage of time thinking of her new friend, the doctor. A part of her almost hoped they would be unsuccessful today, so she would have an excuse to stop by the camp for another visit tomorrow. Raul did promise, after all. She couldn't get the vision of the prideful woman out of her head. She snapped out of her ruminations at the sound of a gunshot.

Maria heard shouts from her men up ahead. They sounded cheerful, but they were too far away for her to hear exactly what was being said. By the sounds of it, perhaps they'd found the sniper and put her down, cheating Maria of her fun. When she reached the spot on the riverbank where they were milling, her men moved aside to reveal Reyes' guys standing over a dead crocodile. They talked excitedly amongst themselves and gave congratulatory back pats to the victorious reptile killer. Maria was astounded at the idiocy she saw before her. This breach of discipline was unacceptable to the militant woman. Her men would know better. She decided to do Reyes another favor.

Walking casually over to the dead croc, she glanced down at the body, and then up at the proud shooter. She noticed one of her men subtly drop his head, as if he knew what was coming. *Smart man. I should promote him.* She stepped lightly toward Reyes' man, placing him between the water's edge and herself, then smoothly, unseen by those not paying close attention, drew her chrome-plated Nighthawk and shot the man point-blank in the heart.

He stumbled backward toward the riverbank, holding his hand over his chest, a look of utter shock on his face. Maria delivered the final blow, stepping forward and planting a solid kick to the man's middle, launching him backward into the raging water.

"Are we through playing games here?" She asked in an icy tone, looking each man over with her steely eyes, flaring dangerously at them all. No one spoke a word, but as was her intention, the jovial celebration screeched to a halt. "We have a job to do, gentleman. I won't be so kind to the next man who loses focus. Let's go." She nodded to her men, urging them to continue on, and followed a short distance behind.

Chapter Eleven

J enny was pleased to note some color returning to the pale skin of her blood-drained friend. She turned apprehensively toward the little door when she heard a scuffling outside. Dan squeezed through the tiny door with a smile on his cheerful face. "Howdy, pahdnah. How did it go last night? You look like shit."

She couldn't help but laugh. The sound of a friendly voice, even one throwing insults, was welcome after so many hours in isolated silence. "We're good. You're early." She gave him a quick welcome hug. "How'd it go back at camp?"

"Pretty good. Everybody seemed to be totally preoccupied in their own thing. Getting ready to possibly bug out, that is. No one really even seemed to notice you were gone. JC came bustling over the minute he saw me, as predicted. I didn't give him too many details, just told him everything was fine and you'd come talk to him in a little bit. He seemed appeased and took off."

Daniel busied himself finding a couple more hooks on the wall to hang the two lanterns he brought from camp. The good lighting was a welcome addition to the cave-like space. "Any change in our patient? Holy crap, she cleans up nice! You've been a busy little bee, haven't you?" He noticed her long black tresses, which had been unbraided and combed out, were now held together in a single ponytail, the silky hair flowing over her shoulder. "Nice hair."

Jenny rolled her eyes. "No change, though her heart rate is definitely improved and the color seems to be creeping slowly back to her skin. She hasn't stirred at all, though."

"No?" He walked over and picked up the bra, swinging it playfully in circles on his index finger. "Not even for a sponge bath from the lovely Dr. MacKenzie? Pity."

Jenny looked at him as if he'd just grew a pair of purple horns and shook her head. She finally gave in, and started to chuckle. "You're such an ass."

"And you, my sweet, are obviously without your daily dose of a half dozen quarts of coffee. So why don't you vacate, post-haste, and I'll see you back here after dark sometime. Try to grab a couple hours sleep in a real bed before you head back. I'll make sure everything is going smoothly here. Okay?"

"Yep. On my way." She delivered a good-natured hip bump as she passed by, grabbed her pack, and headed toward the small door. "Take good care of her for me, Dan." And with that, she headed out into the afternoon breeze, slightly relieved to be away from the dark bunker, but missing her ill friend already.

The young doctor stepped carefully through the woods until she reached the trail, then set off at an easy jog. She was really looking forward to a shower and a couple hours sack time, but that would have to wait for a little while. She made quick work of the trail, getting back to camp in about thirty minutes, and sneaking into her hut. Jenny threw on a fresh shirt and made her way to the dining tent to put in an appearance. *Must...have...coffee.*

"Hi Grace, haven't seen you around at all today.

How's it going?" She threw out slyly and took a seat next to the older woman, a cup of coffee in each hand.

"Fine, Doctor, and you?" Grace said, looking anything but fine.

"I'm good. I can tell by the look on your face you're questioning your decision to stay, aren't you?"

"Heh. Yes, how could you tell? Fortunately, Ms. Velasquez has not made another appearance today, but I fear she will show her face around here again. If she does, I won't have any choice but to pack us all up and leave."

"I understand. Excuse me, Grace. JC is waving me over. Guess I better go. See you around." Jenny made her way to the other side of the dining tent, stopping to refill her coffee en route.

"Jenny," JC whispered under his breath. "Thank god you're back. I was worried sick last night. Are you okay? Did you find him? Dan didn't really tell me much."

"Everything's fine. Let me grab a sandwich and we'll go over to my hut so we can talk in private. The situation is a lot more complicated than we originally thought."

JC squeezed his eyes shut as if attempting to will away any further problems. "Let's go." He stood and escorted Jenny over to pick up some food. "I'm glad you're okay," he said, as Jenny snarfed her sandwich. They reached the hut and Jenny immediately began to peel off her dirty clothes, turning the lukewarm shower on full blast. She couldn't wait one more minute for a shower, and was not bashful about being naked in front of JC. She could tell by his slight blush, however, that he now felt awkward about it. She thought for a minute that perhaps she was sending mixed signals, then blew the thought off.

As she stepped into the shower, JC averted his eyes. Jenny filled him in on her most recent activities, not leaving out a single detail. She wanted to be sure he felt connected to what she was doing somehow. If he did, maybe he would come to feel a level of responsibility for what she was trying to accomplish. When she got to the part about conveying her deep feelings toward the injured woman, she made sure to emphasize just how much she meant to her. More than anything, Jenny wanted him to understand this wasn't some bullheaded lark.

JC listened silently until Jenny had finished her story. "Sounds like a dangerous game you're playing, Jen. Maybe we should just toss her in the car and drive her to La Paz, so she can get away from here."

"She's not in any condition to travel at the moment. Right now, the best thing we can do is just keep her hidden. With any luck she'll be up and around in a few days. Then we can come up with a plan to get her out. I'm sure Argulla is not going to let this drop, so we need to fly under the radar as much as humanly possible."

"And if that psycho shows up here again looking for you? The longer they go without finding her, the worse things will get around here. If Velasquez truly is desperate to grab this woman, she'll probably start escalating the pressure, which means Grace might pull us out then. Have you thought about what you'll do if that happens?"

"Honestly? No. But I can tell you this. Everything in my life, including this Peace Corp assignment, takes a back seat to me getting her through this safely. I will risk everything. I'm all in. I know you think I'm nuts, but I have no doubt you'd do the same if it was your brother, or somebody you felt this strongly about."

"Well, you're right about one thing. I do think you're nuts. But it's obvious this is very important to you. I'm not happy about it, Jenny. Those drug people could easily wipe us off the face of the earth and no one would be the wiser. They run the show in this area and it scares me. I'm scared for you. I'm scared for all of us, actually."

"I know, JC. I'm scared too, but I'm doing it, regardless of the outcome."

"I knew you were going to say that." He watched her dress, looking on with a touch of pity, thinking she couldn't help being this way. "Okay. What can I do to help?"

"Nothing, really. But thanks for asking. The fewer people involved, the better. Dan and I are going to switch off taking care of her, so there might be windows when he or I are missed. We're planning to run a little subterfuge on that score. If you'd like to help, it'd be good, especially if Maria shows up. She might not notice Dan missing, but I'm sure she'd be looking for me based on yesterday's little show. So if anybody asks, you saw me head out with my camera or something."

"Coño," JC whispered, dropping his head into his hands.

"Hey. Don't look so glum, chum. It's all going to work out, you'll see. And on a happier note,"— she nudged him knowingly—"a little bird told me somebody cute in camp has a big crush on you."

"With my luck, it's probably Dan."

Jenny chuckled, glad for the lighter shift in mood. "No. It's Nala, but you didn't hear it from me."

JC looked up with interest, a slow smile spreading across his face.

❧ ❧ ❧ ❧

It was late evening by the time Maria returned to the Argulla Hacienda. She was exhausted from a fruitless day of trudging through muck and forest with nothing to show for it except a little sport with one of Reyes' morons.

Normally she cared about nothing, but found herself dreading the lecture that would come when Raul found out she was unsuccessful once again. She was rapidly becoming frustrated with her failure in this search. She did not like to lose, and could not understand how this adversary had managed to escape detection so thoroughly. Her position with Argulla was wearing thin on her nerves as well. She thought perhaps it was time to quit his employ and head to more fertile ground. *Mexico, maybe. Things are heating up there.*

She removed her muddy boots in the foyer, leaving them for someone to take and clean, and headed straight upstairs for a much-needed shower. Her efforts to delay the inevitable confrontation with Raul were stymied when he stepped out of the den, catching her half way up the stairs.

"Common courtesy dictates you at least tell me if you've found her or not. I can assume since you're slinking up the stairs unannounced you failed?"

"I need a shower, and a change of clothes, Raul," she replied, fingering the knife in her pants pocket, willing her temper to stay where it belonged. "I will be down shortly to fill you in."

⚘⚘⚘⚘

Raul walked into his study and was followed soon after by Marcelo. "Car coming, sir. Looks like Reyes again."

"Terrific. What have I done to deserve such attention?" He said sarcastically to no one in particular. "Marcelo, is his son in the car?"

"Yes, sir."

"Tell the housekeeper to have her two young helpers...the twins...what are their names?"

"The Garza twins, sir."

"Yes, the Garzas. Have her dress them and place them in the den to serve cocktails to our guests when they arrive. Quickly now, they're almost here."

Maria arrived downstairs a short while later to find her amused looking lover and a beet faced Armando Reyes facing off with each other. There were two attractive and busty young women at the sidebar serving a drink to the very attentive Manny Reyes. "Ah. Maria. Please join us. We'd like you to fill us in on the events of the day."

"You!" Armando hollered, pointing an accusing finger at the deceptively placid looking woman. "What is the meaning of your behavior today? You had no right to kill one of my men, on my property, no less!"

Raul leaned back on his desk casually, crossing his arms over his chest, perfectly happy to let Maria defend herself. He was enjoying being witness to his pathetic rival's breakdown. It was the most fun he'd had in ages, and couldn't wait to see what Maria had to say for herself.

"You asked for my assistance, Señor Reyes, and

I've given it to you. I rid you of a fool. You should be thanking me," Maria replied. Raul turned his face to hide his silent laughter.

"What do you mean by that? He was a good and loyal servant."

"He was an idiot who jeopardized our mission by not paying attention to his task, and announcing our presence with an unnecessary gunshot. Is my action toward your man more important to you than the success of our quest?"

Reyes chose to say nothing in response. It was obvious Maria's point had been made.

Raul elected that moment to intercede. "Maria, perhaps you can fill us in on any new information you have found about the woman. If anything."

"We have three potential leads off the river. One indicates she may have got out while still on your property, Señor, I will give the GPS coordinates to your man before you leave, so your people can search that area tomorrow. The second is about a kilometer further down river. I checked that one out myself earlier, and found nothing. The third is a little further down, yet, near an outpost of volunteers we will head into tomorrow."

She made a point to look directly at Raul in understanding. This was Maria's version of an 'I-told-you-so' and it irked him that she was probably right.

Raul strolled over to stand by his new buddy, Manny, giving the young man a knowing look and nodding toward the twins. Manny's smile widened in understanding.

He suspected Maria lied about finding a trail on Reyes' property. She would want him out of the way, and did not intend to allow his people anywhere near the sniper when they captured or killed her. If they had found her today, she would have just killed all of Reyes' men on the spot, and told him some story about an epic gunfight.

"I cannot have any more delays. I must find her!" Armando dispensed with the respectful titles, his distaste for the younger man finally leaking out. "Argulla, are you sure you're doing everything you can? I will have two dozen men searching the wood tomorrow. I can have two dozen more here for you in the morning if you'll just say the word."

Raul turned from the side bar, staring dangerously at his condescending neighbor. "Try not to forget your manners, Señor. I am doing you a favor, after all. I will put every available man into the forest tomorrow, and we will flush this woman out."

Armando turned and stormed from the room, "Manny! Leaving! Now!"

❧❧❧❧

Doctor MacKenzie reached up to work a kink out of her neck, a product of sleeping upright on a splintery wooden stool for the second night in a row. It'd been about twenty-four hours since she first put her friend on an IV, and her color, blood pressure, and heart rate were showing measured signs of improvement.

Jenny re-adjusted her position and put her head down on her arms once again, moments away from drifting back to sleep, when all hell broke loose.

Seven awoke and was completely delirious. She sat bolt upright and began to rip the I.V. tubes out of her arms before Jenny had time to react. The big woman swung her legs to the floor, kicking Jenny in the head on the way by.

Seven looked around in a panic, eyes darting every which way, but completely unfocused. It looked as if she was about to make a run for it.

"No no nonono. Seven!" Jenny yelled. "Calm down. It's okay. Everything's okay." Jenny frantically tried to calm the panicked, incoherent woman. She grabbed Seven by the shoulders, attempting to pressure her back onto the table, but the strong woman overpowered her with no trouble. Seven forced herself to a standing position while trying to untangle from the blanket and make her escape.

Delirious, Seven took an uncoordinated swing at the enemy between her and the door. The fist barely missed Jenny's head as she ducked out of the way just at the right moment. The sniper forced two steps toward the door, while the doctor tried her best to restrain her movement, failing miserably at getting through to her senses. "Hold on, Sev...it's okay. Calm down. You're safe, Sev, it's okay. Noooo."

Seven looked down at the short blonde, unrecognizing. "Marcus!" She blurted out, then collapsed, unconscious once more into the arms of the doctor.

The impact of Seven's dead weight in her arms practically brought Jenny to her knees, but she struggled successfully to return her to the table. "Welcome back, friend." She leaned over and kissed the unconscious woman on the forehead, before covering her up with the discarded blanket, and setting to work reinserting the I.V. hoses. "Hope you come around soon. I can't wait to say hi."

Chapter Twelve

A deal was a deal. Raul specifically said if they didn't find the sniper the day before, she could go back to the Peace Corps camp and station personnel there to watch. He said no violence. *Fine. I'll just look around.*

Yesterday when they searched the riverbank for clues, the best set of tracks they found were scuffs and scrapes in the muck just a little upstream from where the camp's small dock was located. Maria knew the moment she saw the marks this was the place. She sensed all along her prey was in this area, and now she would have her. *And the blonde, too, for that matter.*

She arrived at the outskirts of the camp before sunup, wanting to see the place again before it was swarming with busy bees. She left her men, over a dozen now, just down the road in a couple of Argulla's Land Rovers.

It always seemed to Maria that the time of day just before sunrise was the darkest. She liked that. She liked to hunt in these hours. It was quiet. People were sleeping, or relaxed, their guards down. She crept into the camp at the edge of the tree line, careful not to make any noise grinding her boots on the dirt road. One by one, she entered the small buildings and crept along in the shadows, taking in the scents and sounds, sometimes stopping to watch someone sleep.

She tested a door here...picked a lock there...

whatever instinct told her to do, she did. In the clinic, she spent an extra few minutes looking around the doctor's small office, familiarizing herself with the scent and space of the room. Next, she headed to what she knew to be the doctor's hut.

She pressed her nose to the seam of the door, drawing a deep, slow breath through her nostrils, trying to catch the scent of the woman inside. The door was locked. She considered picking it briefly, but decided against it, afraid she would not be able to restrain herself from taking the woman's life if she was alone with her. Instead, she settled for walking around back and peeking in the window of the small space.

She wasn't there.

Hmm. Very, very interesting. Where are you, doctor? Don't bother playing cat and mouse with me, my arrogant little blonde. I never lose.

She continued her scouting trip, slithering to the perimeter of the camp and looking around the edges for anything of interest.

Maria did not see that just a stone's throw away from her position stood a man in the night shadow of a tall tree. He watched silently as she moved with stealth around camp, eventually heading down the road, before he came out of the woods and darted for the clinic's side door. Once inside, Dan took a moment to collect himself, silently thanking the powers that be he saw the woman, before she saw him.

❧❧❧❧❧

An hour after sunrise, Maria returned, only this time accompanied by two truckloads of men. The residents of the peaceful camp watched with trepidation as she lined her men up in the middle of the road and began ordering them around with different instructions.

Grace Richards was relieved to see the groups of men leaving the camp in various directions, but incredibly disturbed to see the Velasquez woman back. She had made a deal with herself and the other volunteers, that if the woman returned they would pull out. This saddened the camp leader a great deal. Their work here had been very successful. The people were friendly, and the location excellent. She was sorry to see it go, but it was obviously no longer safe.

Maria chose that moment to approach Grace. She nodded a greeting then began her explanation of the unfolding events. "Good morning, Ms. Richards. We have physical evidence our criminal is in the area, so we will be searching more thoroughly in this vicinity, and leaving a presence here in camp for your protection."

Grace said nothing, but stared at the woman, the sadness evident in her eyes. She would tell the gang after this vile woman left to get their things ready. They would be leaving as soon as possible. She could not tolerate even the remotest possibility they might be in danger.

"I have sent men down the road in both directions to fan out and search all the way to the nearest towns. I will also have a team searching from the river to here, and in the surrounding forest. I will be placing two men in this camp to guard 'round the clock. They have been instructed not to interact with any of your people. They are merely here to watch for the criminal. You have nothing to fear from them."

Yeah, right.

A soft wheezing noise to her left woke the slumbering woman, who struggled internally to shake off a deep, groggy sleep. She kept her eyes closed, attempting to assess what she could of her situation before alerting anybody in the room to her wakefulness. From what she could tell, it was extremely quiet here, except for the light snores of one other person nearby. She could hear the rustle of leaves in a breeze outside. The room felt close and had an earthy, somewhat musty smell to it. The surface she lay upon was hard and uncomfortable, but at least she was warm.

Seven slowly and deliberately flexed each muscle in her body, starting from her feet and working her way up, trying to determine if she was restrained, or in good enough shape to fight if need be. When she got to her forearms, she felt something foreign there, and a little painful. She flexed her upper arms next, and barely stifled a gasp as a bolt of pain shot through her body. It quickly came back to her that she was shot in the left arm. She was happy about the pain. That she could feel it meant she wasn't too drugged up to be alert. Everything else from there seemed to be in good working order.

She tried to recall what she could of recent events. Her memory was foggy, but she remembered being captured and feeling as though she'd lost the fight. People had found her. *So,* she thought, *I must be a prisoner here. But why would they bother to keep me alive?* She pondered a vague recollection of somebody talking to her. Telling her stories, or something like that. It didn't have a negative feel, but a positive one. *Strange.*

She thought back to the horrific events that got her here. Her grief for Marcus washed over her like a tidal wave of sorrow. She thought of Ty, and how he tried to save her, throwing himself between her and one of the gunmen coming out of the woods. She knew Ty had never liked her, and was somewhat surprised at his heroic actions. Unlike Marcus, she realized she never actually saw Ty die. Shot yes, but dead? With Marcus, there was no question. He was definitely killed.

Seven slowly inhaled a calming breath and replayed the event over and over again in her mind, looking for any flaw in their plan or execution. She could think of nothing. The only possible explanation was that someone from Black Flag Company had sold them out to Armando Reyes. Obviously, the price for such information would be high, and money was an excellent motivator.

Seven decided it was time to open her eyes and get a visual on the room and occupant. Somewhere in the back of her mind, she had a vague recollection of hearing her name called. *That's impossible. Nobody here knows who I am or why I'm here.* She had no form of identification on her whatsoever. Maybe she dreamt it. Or, maybe whoever sold them out gave her name along with all the other information. That thought reinforced Seven's belief that she was being held captive.

She slowly opened her eyes, peeking surreptitiously around the room. *Low ceiling. Dirt walls and floor, like a hole in the ground, maybe. Low light.* Down at the foot of the table she was lying on, was the blonde head of a person that appeared to be sleeping. *Small, muscular body, probably a woman. I should be able to take her if it comes to that. Funny. She doesn't look like a threat. Not exactly thick and Latin like the rest of Reyes' men. And blonde? What's with that? This is Bolivia...blonde is not what I would call a prominent hair color here.*

She glanced at the hoses of the I.V., wondering what on earth they were pumping into her, and took a moment to reevaluate how she felt. She didn't feel sedated or lethargic in any way, so it was probably not drugs of any kind. *Hmm. Leave 'em or pull 'em?* Seven debated with herself for a moment, trying to decide if she should just knock the woman's block off and make a run for it.

Or, what if the blonde was a prisoner too? It's possible. She looks like a foreigner. She recollected two voices talking, and hearing the name DeMack. *That definitely doesn't sound like a Latin name. But that doesn't mean anything. She could be Irish and still working for Reyes. He is a wealthy man and probably employs people all over the world. Or maybe I'm not a prisoner. Maybe I somehow won the 'shot in the jungle lotto,' and got rescued by good and innocent people, just in the nick of time. Yeah, right. Definitely a prisoner.*

Her mind swirled with new images of Marcus' death, and she wondered about the fate of Ty Cooper. She blinked back a few tears, and focused on what her next move should be. *What are my options? One: knock her out and run for it. Two: wake her up and see what happens. Three: I can't think of a three.*

Okay, let's think about this. Pros and cons for acting on number one: I can catch her unawares and make a quick getaway, assuming I can get out of here somehow. But I don't know what kind of shape I'm in or if I'll be able to run, if there's security around, etc. Pros and cons for acting on number two: If I wake her up, I'm probably not in any immediate danger. They wouldn't have kept me alive if they didn't want something from me, or to use me for something. Why the heck did they keep me alive anyway? They sure didn't seem to mind me dead a little while ago. If she's not an enemy, she could help me. If she is the enemy, I would only be expediting whatever they have planned for me. Crap. Okay. Number two it is. Too many things don't add up. I have to take this chance.

꙲꙲꙲꙲

The man they called the Chairman stood solemnly staring out the plate glass window in his office, contemplating events that led to the decision he was about to make. He was a man who showed many hard lines on his face, making him appear much older than his forty-nine years. Bushy graying eyebrows covered a wrinkled brow set in a seemingly permanent frown.

Black Flag Company was specifically set up so he would no longer have to make these kinds of life or death decisions. That was one of the reasons he agreed to take on this job in the first place. He had killed enough to last a lifetime. *Hell will probably spit me back out,* he thought as he watched a cardinal chase another bird from its perch in the tree outside his window.

In his mind, each team of the BFC went by a Greek letter. It was a way for him to compartmentalize in his thoughts the different teams of four and their specialties. The department was new, and experimental, and already his plans were unraveling. *How did this happen?*

Team Epsilon was a sniper hit squad made up of Team Leader Michelis, S., Johnson, M., Cooper, T., and Takashi, T. The squad was a well-mixed group of talent assigned to address a Bolivian businessman. A person of interest allocated to the team several weeks ago.

If everything had gone according to his plan, Delegate Takashi should have filed the paperwork on the details of this mission yesterday. He did not. The Chairman picked up the phone and dialed the extension for Team Alpha.

"Smith," a man answered.

"Team Leader Smith. This is the Chairman. I need to clear your schedule. I have a situation in Bolivia that needs to be addressed."

❧❧❧❧

Seven steeled herself for potential disaster but decided it was time to bite the bullet. She elected to start with the most basic question…where am I? The sniper reached down and brushed her fingers lightly across the blonde's arm. "Hola. ¿Me puede decir dónde estoy, por favor?"

Startled by a voice suddenly coming out of the quite room, Jenny leapt from her stool, prepared to ward off another attempt at her patient's escape. She stumbled clumsily backwards, flailing her arms for balance, and caught herself just before going down. Blushing furiously at her ungraceful entrance into wakefulness, she blurted, "Ohmygosh… you're awake! I'm…um…I'm awake too…now…sort of…um." She blushed again and looked at her feet, shaking her head to ward off the fog of sleep.

Seven could not help but smile at the Keystone Cop routine. *Oh yeah. She's a tough guy all right.*

"S...Sorry. What did you ask? My Spanish is pathetic."

Hmm. American. Or Canadian, maybe. Things are looking up. "I asked if you could please tell me where I am?" Seven noticed she was looking into the most intense and lovely green eyes she had ever seen. Even in the dim light, they appeared to sparkle.

"Yeah. Um. Bolivia, still, unfortunately for you. We're hiding you in an abandoned coca lab." She glanced around at their shabby surroundings. "Which explains the fancy digs."

A smile crept slowly over Jenny's face, reaching her eyes, which spoke of an unsaid surprise she couldn't wait to share. Her friend was every bit as hypnotic as she remembered. She had a deep, melodic voice with a very slight southern accent in the timbre she must have picked up in South Carolina. Her eyes were intelligent, and shone like glacial ice even in the mellow lantern light.

Seven nodded that she heard the reply, but it didn't seem to answer the question of whether this chipper young woman was a friend or foe. *She's got to be a friendly, or she's one twisted individual, smiling at me like that.*

"Unfortunately, why?" The injured woman asked, determined to get the truth one way or the other.

"Because there's some really nasty people out looking for you, but fortunately, we found you first."

Realization dawned on Seven. *Ah. Friend.*

"You're from that little medical clinic I broke into, aren't you?"

"Indeed I am. Let me help you sit up. Easy now. Don't want you to pass out again." Jenny retrieved a bottle of water and handed it to her patient. "Here. Drink up. You lost a lot of blood and need to hydrate as much as possible. Do you think you could eat something?" The patient nodded, yes. "This is probably going to sound stupid, considering the trauma you've been through...but you're very lucky. You lost enough blood to kill most people. I think your excellent physical condition probably saved your life."

Seven tucked into a peanut butter and jelly sandwich the young woman handed her. "From where I'm sitting, it looks like you saved it." She took hold of an apple with her free hand, wincing at the shooting pain in her arm.

"I haven't given you anything for the pain in quite a while. Would you like something now? I can give you some morphine intravenously, if the pain is bad, or if you'd rather, I have Percocet."

"No. Nothing thanks. It hurts, but I need to stay alert. I'm usually a pretty fast healer." Seven realized she wasn't wearing anything and pulled the blanket tighter around her body. "Where are my clothes?"

"Over there," Jenny pointed to the other corner, where several articles lay over the table and stools. "I scrubbed them, but they may still be a little damp. I emptied out all the pockets. Your stuff, including the gun, is in that white bucket on the floor over there. Your really big, scary-lookin' gun is over there in the corner." She nodded toward the door. "I have a sweatshirt and pants you can put on while you're here. You were covered with blood so I took everything off to clean you up."

"And you undid my hair, and by the looks of it, gave me a manicure." She raised an eyebrow and smiled inquisitively at the younger woman.

Sheepishly, Jenny admitted, "Yeah. Sorry. I got bored."

"That's okay. At least you didn't paint them." She looked down at her clean and filed nails. "I would've had to kill you if you'd painted them," Seven said to Jenny in a deadpan tone, looking up from under her eyebrows to see if she got the joke.

"Ha! You'd have to catch me, first." Both women chuckled, as Jenny walked over to the table and grabbed the sweats Dan brought from camp.

Seven looked more closely around the dark space. Sure enough, her rifle sat in the corner. She couldn't believe this woman would just give her weapons back like that. *How can she assume she is in no danger from me? Maybe this is some sort of game and I'm being played. She's trying to gain my trust. She doesn't seem the type though. Don't trust her. Give her small bits of unimportant info only, just enough to draw her out into giving up info of her own.*

"What's in this drip, anyway?" Seven indicated the I.V. still attached to her arm. "Can I get rid of it now?"

"Sure. That bag is just about empty anyway. Give me a second and I'll take it off." She removed the tape holding the needle in place, and carefully extracted the sharp object, placing a bandage over the hole. "It's a saline drip. I gave you a pint of blood yesterday, plus you've been getting the saline since we got you here. I've also given you a couple doses of morphine, yesterday, after I took out the bullet, and some antibiotic for your arm, which I checked not too long ago and it's looking good.

"You've been in a coma since we found you. I was pretty scared for you," Jenny relayed, wanting Seven to understand the seriousness of her situation. She helped the taller woman wriggle her injured arm into the sweatshirt.

Seven looked down at her hands, which were resting on her knees. The words hit home. She'd been in dangerous situations since she was nineteen, but this is the closest she'd ever come to buying the farm. Her body betrayed her stoic behavior and silent tears streamed down her face. She relived the disaster of her recent trauma all over again in her mind. *Oh, Marcus. It's not fair that I'm here and you're not.*

Jenny didn't push her friend. She figured Sev would tell her what was going on when she was ready. She handed her a towel to wipe her eyes. Seven looked down at the sweatshirt she now wore and shook her head. "Great. West Point. You couldn't find me a Citadel shirt, or just a plain one to wear?" She joked feebly.

"Is that where you went? The Citadel?"

"Go Bulldogs," she said dryly.

Seven hesitated to say too much, still not a hundred percent sure about this woman. "How long was I out anyway?"

"Well, you broke into the clinic three nights ago. We found you two nights ago, but don't know how long you were out when we found you. So at least a day, plus some."

"Damn, damn, damn. I was afraid of that." She sighed, the weight of her troubles rested heavily on her broad shoulders.

"What is it? Something I can do?"

"No. Thanks. I had a small window of opportunity to catch a ride out of here yesterday morning. I've missed it. It's just as well, I guess. There's something I have to do here now." Seven thought again of Ty, and how she didn't actually see him die. "Maybe you could fill me in on what's happening out there. You mentioned before some people were after me. How much do you know?"

"I know what you are, if that's what you're asking." There was a moment of silence in the room as Seven wondered why the young woman was being so casual about this knowledge.

"But what I don't know," she continued, "is who you're after or why. I'm not sure I want to know, frankly. The person looking for you is named Maria Velasquez. She is a seriously bad apple, and works for the local coca king. His name is Raul Argulla. Our Peace Corps camp sits in the middle of his vast land holdings. It's generally a peaceful area, and he even helps us out from time to time, but now everything has changed. His attack dog, Maria, is on the hunt looking for you. I guess I kind of assumed it was Argulla you were after."

"No. This isn't about drugs. I have no interest in Argulla. I have no idea why he would be after me." Seven's mind was spinning with a million questions. *Maybe we didn't get sold out. Maybe I screwed up and landed us in the middle of some drug king's operation. No. Not possible. We were on target to reach the Reyes Hacienda as planned. Is there a chance we got caught in the middle of something else? No. The attack was too precise. Too premeditated.*

"Do you want to try standing? It's soon, but it

might make you feel better to stretch out those muscles a little. You may be a little unbalanced at first, so you should lean on me." She moved over to stand beside Seven, placing her arm around her waist for support. Seven stood slowly on shaky legs, then took a couple deep breaths and stepped forward.

"We're about a thirty minute jog from the camp here, so if you can think of anything you need I can try to get it for you. You're doing well, by the way, but even if you are a fast healer, I still have to recommend you stay here under our care for a couple of days. At that time, if you want, we can discuss your options. I'm happy to help in any way I can."

"I don't know if I can wait a couple of days," Seven said, lying exhausted back onto her makeshift bed. The woman forced another bottle of water on her to drink. Melancholy washed over the injured Marine as she drifted back to sleep.

※.※!※.※

Everywhere outside her field of vision was swirling darkness, undulating shades of gray and black with no horizon or point of reference. She was running. Hard. She looked to her left. Nothing. She looked to her right. A figure running next to her was there as though he'd been there all along. It was Marcus. He ran full out, just like her, but didn't appear to be expending any effort whatsoever. He laughed, but his voice sounded strange. Marcus said, "Why are you running?" At that moment, a bullet smashed into his head from behind, leaving a gaping exit wound in his forehead. He smiled at her before falling face down and sliding several feet to a stop.

Grief.

Unbelievable grief.

Her hand reached out to touch the shoulder of her fallen friend. She rolled him over. It wasn't Marcus at all, but her father. "Noooo!"

"Hey! Wake up. Wake up. It's okay. You're just having a bad dream." Jenny grabbed the woman before her, shaking her gently into wakefulness.

Seven sat bolt upright, gasping for air, sweating, and confused as to her whereabouts. She looked into the gentle eyes of the woman standing concerned next to her bed. Everything came back to her in a flash.

"Are you okay? That seemed like a pretty intense dream. I had a hard time waking you."

"Yeah," Seven said, sheepishly. "Sorry. It was really vivid. I don't usually have nightmares."

"Here...drink some more water. Might help to wake you up a little."

"Thanks." She took a long, refreshing swig. Looking around the room she asked, "Um...I'm kind of in need of a bedpan. Got one of those around here anywhere?"

"Yeah." Jenny smiled. "It's called the bush of your choice, just outside. Come on. I'll walk you out till you get your sea legs, then leave you to it."

Outside the bunker, Seven got her first look around at their location in the daylight. Looked pretty much the same here as it did in the area they were originally dropped. Same basic foliage, terrain, temperature. It suddenly occurred to her how incredibly lucky she was to fall into the hands of someone who cared and knew enough to save her. A guardian angel was definitely sitting on her shoulder when he sent a doctor into the woods to find her.

Seven realized she didn't know for sure if the woman even was a doctor. In fact, she hadn't even thanked her, or introduced herself yet. *Ungrateful wench. Bad Marine. Where are your manners?*

Seven wondered if she could trust this woman. She knew nothing about her, really. She seemed very trusting of Seven, though she had no reason to be. The woman's instinct told her the girl was okay, but the skeptic in her said be careful. She walked back into the bunker, standing still for a moment while her vision adjusted to the dim light. The young woman came near and squirted some sanitizer gel into her hands on the way by. "Thanks." She chuckled. "You think of everything."

She touched the young woman on the shoulder. "Hey. It just occurred to me I never properly thanked you for the heroic rescue. I really appreciate it. I'm Seven, by the way." She held out a freshly sanitized hand. "Michelis. That's my last name."

The doctor took the proffered hand. "You're welcome, Seven. It was my pleasure." Her eyes twinkled with mischief.

"Are you a doctor at that little clinic I broke into?"

"Yes. I'm a Peace Corps volunteer. I've been stationed at that camp for about six months. Before that, I was in La Paz. Ninety percent of what we do there is education and immunization. Not much excitement till you showed up, but it's feel good work, you know?"

"So should I call you Dr. DeMack? I think I remember hearing that name while I was out. Is that you?"

Jenny rewarded her patient with a hearty laugh. "D-Mac. No. That's just a nickname my friend Dan

calls me. Dan is the nurse who's been helping me here."
She chuckled again. "You don't have to call me that...
in fact, please...don't call me that." She smiled and
turned her back to the woman, greatly anticipating the
next question.

"Well, what should I call you? You have a name?"

Jenny turned back toward her friend, holding
her eye contact as she did her best to suppress the
smile growing across her face.

"You can call me Pumpkin Head."

Jenny watched intently as her unsuspecting
friend rapidly processed this new information. She
swore she could see the neurons flying around behind
those intelligent eyes. In order to drive the point home,
she added, "D-Mac is short for Dr. MacKenzie."

The long silence was deafening. Jenny's smile
grew wider in tandem with Seven's eyes, Seven's
mouth hanging slack jawed in disbelief.

"Bu...you...wh...Je."   Seven   pointed   a
finger numbly at the girl, and shook her head as
if to relieve herself of the cobwebs in her skull.
"Holymarymotherofgod." She expelled a huge lungful
of air. "You have got to be freakin' kidding me!" She
grabbed the girl by the shoulders and pulled her close,
gazing intently at her laughing captive.

A massive smile grew onto her face as she pulled
the girl to her in a crushing hug, overdue by fifteen
years. Some minutes later, she leaned back and took
the uncontrollably chuckling Jenny's cheeks in both
hands, looking over every detail of her lovely face.
"Didn't anybody ever tell you Pumpkin Heads have
red hair?"

The two women held each other at arm's length
for some time, reacquainting themselves with the

adults that had replaced the children they once knew. The long lost friends hugged each other again. Neither wanted to be the first to let go. Seven lifted her friend from the ground, twirling her in a slow circle. "Only you could do this to me, Jenny MacKenzie. Only you could make the worst thing that's ever happened to me into a cheerful occasion. How the hell do you do that?"

For a brief moment, both women forgot the danger they were in, and were content to just be happy in each other's company.

Chapter Thirteen

I just can't believe it, Jenny. God, you grew up nice, too. Look at you. You're beautiful. And a doctor at twenty-four. I always knew you were brilliant. I used to tell mom you were going to be something special when you grew up." She beamed with pride at her friend, unable to take her eyes from the younger woman. "What are the odds? It must be some kind of divine intervention that brought us back together after all these years." She looked around at their not-so-luxurious surroundings. "Especially in place like this."

"It's crazy, isn't it? Come over here and sit. You need to eat and drink some more water." She led Seven back to her table and sat her down. "I had no idea what I was getting myself into when I dragged Dan in the woods to look for you. I only knew it was something I had to do, and I wasn't taking no for an answer. The moment I realized it was you, well...I...um...gosh, I can't even explain the emotion that washed over me. I was so happy, and so sad all at once."

"It's so good to see you. It makes me regret even more losing contact all those years ago."

"No worries, my friend. We won't let that happen again. Now. Why don't you tell me what the heck you're doing down here. Are you with the military?"

"Department of Homeland Security. Though I was with the Marines for twelve years."

"Wow. Like father, like daughter, huh?"

"Something like that, yeah. I found out my dad was a scout sniper with the Corps when I was about sixteen. It shocked me at first. I didn't really understand it. But my Uncle Nick explained it to me. After a while, I couldn't stop thinking about it. Then I decided I had what it took and wanted to do what he did. I enlisted right out of high school, served for few years, then got accepted into a program that allowed me to go to college and become an officer."

"So you're telling me the guy who used to give me chocolate chip cookies and swing me around in your front yard was a sniper?" Seven shrugged her shoulders and smiled. "So how'd you end up with the DHS?"

"Got recruited in 2002. It's a new agency, so they were filling it with people from all branches of the military, law enforcement, and government agencies. They were pushing hard, and I was ready to move on. They needed my talents. I saw it as an opportunity to settle down. I was thirty when I got my first apartment. How strange is that?"

"So you grew up and became a...what's the proper terminology? A hit man...er woman, I mean?" Jenny laughed at her own ignorance.

"It sounds kind of ridiculous when you say it like that...but basically, yeah. I kill people for a living. On behalf of the good 'ol U.S. of A., that is. We're in a different kind of war now. A lot has changed. I know what you're thinking. I can see it in your eyes. That's exactly how I felt when I first found out about my dad. Do you still believe in your childhood fantasy that the world's problems could be solved in a winner-take-all boxing match?"

Jenny laughed at her youthful innocence. "Of course!" She chuckled indignantly. "I mean, I'd much rather see a bloody nose than someone's head blown off. Wouldn't you?"

"Depends on the head," Seven said, wryly.

"I have to admit, I'm a little traumatized by your choice of careers. I'm trying to remain objective, but it's hard. I've dedicated myself to saving lives, and you've spent yours taking them. How can you do that?"

"I know it can be hard to swallow, but try to think of it as harm reduction. The world will never be at peace, Jen. It's not possible. All we can do is try to make it better than it could be by eliminating people in a position to make it worse. Yes, I kill people. But if I can stop one guy who is in a position to hurt hundreds, or even thousands, isn't that worth it? In my own way, I'm actually saving lives too. It's an extreme case, but think of Hitler. If you could go back and kill him, before he did what he did, wouldn't you?"

They sat in silence for a moment, while Jenny digested this information about her friend. She figured something like this already, the first time she saw the rifle, but it was something else entirely to hear the facts.

"I guess I understand. Though you know my opinion on war hasn't really changed much since I was a kid. I think our views on the best way to accomplish furthering the greater good have gone in drastically different directions. Though I guess it's comforting to know that even if I don't understand your tactics, I certainly appreciate that you're trying to help people. So for now, if it's okay with you I think we'll just agree to disagree."

Seven smiled in understanding. She knew it was

a lot to digest.

"So what is the DHS's interest in Bolivia?" Jenny asked.

"Can I trust you, Jenny?" Seven asked seriously. "I'm sorry to ask. I don't mean to be mistrustful, but it's the nature of my job. If I'm going to trust you with classified information, I need to know you're not going to say anything to anyone. Not even Dan."

Jenny nodded. "You can trust me with your life, Seven. I would never do anything to put you in danger or undermine you in any way. I feel as connected to you now as I ever did, and I value your life and friendship much more than any politics."

Seven gave her friend a brief hug. "Thanks. I was after a man named Armando Reyes, but the op went bad. I won't go into much detail, but suffice to say, he was deemed a threat to our national security. Do you know of him?"

"I've heard the name. I think he is in the same league as Raul Argulla. The guy I told you about whose people are looking for you. Tell me what happened."

"My team of two and I were moving toward the Reyes Hacienda, still about three miles away when we were ambushed. They killed my friend and partner, Marcus, and shot my other guy, Ty, as well. I was shot and had to run. I saw Ty go down, but I can't be sure he's dead. That's why I have to leave here as soon as I can. I have to be sure about Ty one way or the other before I can get out of here."

"They were trying pretty hard to kill you. What makes you think this guy could possibly still be alive? It doesn't sound to me like they were interested in prisoners, only bodies."

"I don't think he's alive, but I can't leave until

I'm sure. He was under my charge. The guy threw himself in front of a bullet for me. Even if he didn't, I cannot leave this way…with everything hanging. I owe it to Ty and Marcus to see this through to the end. No matter what."

"Do you have any idea what happened? How it could have gone like that?"

"Believe me, I've been thinking of little else since I started running. My theory is that somebody at home sold us out to Reyes. Not many knew of our mission, only one for sure. Our organization is set up so only the team directly involved knows the details. That way, if something goes wrong, it's a limited liability, controlled damage kind of thing. But there's one other guy who could know. The problem is, I can't call home for help because I don't know which one to trust. Whoever did sell us out took a huge risk none of us would survive to tell the tale. If I don't make it out of here, this whole thing gets swept under the carpet, and no one pays the price."

"Maybe you should just think about leaving. Live to fight another day. You had a very close call here, Seven. You almost didn't survive it yourself, and with that crazy woman hunting you, you're not out of the woods yet. No pun intended." She smiled again, despite the seriousness of the conversation. "I'm sorry about your friends." She put a reassuring hand on Seven's arm.

"This was my team, Jen. My operation. Mine to direct. Mine to control. Mine to lead to success or failure. I've been lucky my whole life in that I've never failed at any mission I've undertaken. With this one failure, I've made up for a lifetime of successes. It's a bitter pill to swallow." Seven stared at the empty water bottle she twisted idly in her hands. Another tear found its way down a high cheekbone. "Marcus was my best friend."

Jenny could feel the grief radiating from her companion. She found she was on the verge of tears herself, in sympathy for this woman heaping the burden of loss solely on her own shoulders. She reached over to wipe the tear away, her hand coming to rest on a broad shoulder. "Well, since the position is available, I'd like to apply for the job."

This forced a reluctant chuckle from Seven, as she dried her cheeks with the back of her hand. Jenny always had a way of snapping her out of self pity. "You're hired. But I warn you, the hours are long and sometimes dangerous, and you may be required, on occasion, to answer punk rock trivia."

"Hmm. Hard core punk, or new wave?"

"Both. All new hires must undergo an entry exam. You ready?"

"Hit me...wait...considering your profession, let me rephrase that," she smiled, slyly. "Go."

Seven laughed and shook her head. "Name the bass player for the Sex Pistols."

"Ha. Easy. Sid Vicious."

"Girlfriend?"

"Nancy...something that starts with an S."

"Close enough. Lead singer?"

"Johnny Rotten."

"Okay, you're in. You can start immediately."

The women smiled at each other in comfortable silence, enjoying familiar company. Jenny crossed the room and tested Seven's washed clothes for dryness. "Almost there. Not exactly Downey fresh, but at least they won't stand up on their own anymore."

Seven stood and walked carefully over to the bucket containing her loose items. She dumped the contents out on the nearby table, reviewing the inventory. Jenny watched, fascinated at the expert movement of Seven's hands as she removed the clip in her handgun and popped a round out of the chamber, inspecting the weapon top to bottom for damage. She picked up her belt, grabbing it by a holster and removed a vicious looking stainless steel knife. She wiped the blade clean with a nearby towel, flipping it around in her hand like a circus performer.

"Why do you need a knife if you're loaded to the teeth with guns?" Jenny asked, curiously.

Seven paused in her equipment check. She casually flipped the weapon over in her hand so she held it by the blade, and whipped her arm out with lightning speed, not bothering to look at her target. The deadly projectile flew across the small room, implanting itself with a thud and a small poof of dirt into the far wall, spearing an empty saline bag along the way. "A gun runs out of bullets," she glanced over her shoulder at Jenny, a wicked glint in her eye, "but a knife is always sharp."

"Jesus." She expelled a lungful of air. "I'm glad you're on my side." Jenny laughed nervously, having just seen a side of her friend she'd never seen before. *She's a professional killer. You've chosen a seriously intimidating friend for yourself, doctor. Not exactly the kid you knew when you were eight, is she? Can you handle that?*

Seven noticed her friends wide eyed stare as she walked over to retrieve her knife from the wall, wiping the blade again before sheathing it. *Showing off, Seven? Yep. Bad Marine.* She grabbed up her rifle and began to inspect it for damage.

"I noticed you didn't have a passport or anything in there." Jenny motioned her head toward the now empty bucket.

"No. I have no money or identification on me at all. So if we're caught or killed on a mission we can't be identified. It's a risk we all take. That will present me with a bit of a problem now, though, since I've missed my ride out."

"That's gonna be a challenge. Can we contact the U.S. embassy or something?"

"Can't. If I contact the embassy, word will get back to my department immediately that I'm alive. I can't have that. I'm going to have to find another way out after I've visited Reyes."

"We."

Seven squinted suspiciously at Jenny, sure she heard wrong. "We, what?"

"After *we've* visited Reyes. You're going to need help getting out of the country, and I'm it. *Stop!*" She held up a hand to halt Seven, mid-protest. "Don't even bother. I'm going. Feel free to ask Dan when you meet him what happens when somebody tells me I can't do something. I won't get in the way when you go find out about Ty, but after that, I'll be helpful, and you know it. I can hold my own. I have money. I'm fit. I can travel fast and I have a black belt in Tae-Kwon-Do. If you don't believe me, take a swing at me right now and see how fast it lands you on your ass. Don't think for one minute after all we've been through that I'm going to walk happily away, and leave you swinging in the wind."

Jenny's heartfelt tirade took Seven aback. She decided then and there it was better to diffuse than to argue. "Got any more peanut butter and jelly sandwiches over there? I'd like a snack before you land me on my ass."

Jenny laughed. "Sorry, but it's not up for discussion."

"Stubborn. You didn't even give me a chance to protest. How'd you even know that's what I was going to say?"

"Please. It's the story of my life. Now...why don't you tell me how you're feeling? Sit down and let me check your heart rate and blood pressure."

"I feel pretty good, considering. A little woozy when I first stand up."

"You're doing great, but you still need to rest and rebuild. I think if we can get away with hanging out here for a couple more days, you'll be cleared for takeoff. Oh, come on. Don't play those baby blues on me. You've already missed your ride, so what's two days going to matter?"

"Ty. I admit I'm in no condition to go barreling into this kind of mission right now, but if I'm feeling better tomorrow, you may have a more difficult time keeping me here. If there is any chance at all Ty is alive, the longer he is in captivity, the worse chance of survival he has. Not to mention that, if he is alive, he's probably being tortured for information. The sooner I can get there, the better chance I have of saving him, if I can."

Jenny was just about to comment further when Seven raised her finger to her lips in a shushing motion. "Something moving outside," she whispered, and sprang into action. She grabbed Jenny by the shoulders and positioned her down behind the table. Grabbing her gun, she popped a clip into the 9mm and moved to the corner shadow by the door in one fluid motion, positioning herself to strike.

The rustling noise outside increased in volume enough to where Jenny could hear it too.

The small door was pulled slowly open as the tension built within the dirt room.

Dan ducked in and looked around curiously, not spotting Jenny or her unconscious friend. The doctor popped up from her hiding place and threw her hands out to signal Seven it was okay.

The man startled at the sudden appearance of his friend. Following her gaze, he turned to look over his shoulder and wound up eye to eye with a terrifying menace he never heard step up behind him. "Eeek!" He squeaked out and stumbled backward, flailing his arms before he could control his reaction.

He backed quickly away, eyeing the tall woman holding a gun. "Holy crap!" He breathed heavily. "You scared me half to death."

Jenny started to giggle as Seven approached Dan, gracing him with a brilliant smile. "I'm sorry, you must be Dan. I didn't mean to scare you."

He looked over to his friend for reassurance then back to the imposing woman wearing his sweat suit. "Damn." He looked her up and down as she tucked the weapon in a pocket. "Gorgeous *and* deadly. I soooo want to be you for Halloween next year." He smiled back and shook her hand.

Seven chuckled. "Thank you so much for everything you did for me. Jenny told me all about it."

"Oh yeah? Did she tell you I bitched and moaned the whole time, and she had to drag me out there by my nostrils?" He grinned, looking affectionately toward his friend.

"She may have left that part out."

"Well, listen kids...I hate to break up your reunion, but things are heating up back at camp. I think you need to get back there and be seen, D-Mac. I would've come back an hour ago, but I had to sneak away with the utmost stealth." Dan looked very serious as he made eye contact with his friend.

"I think it's over for us here, Jenny. Grace is pulling us out. Maria came back to camp today and brought a dozen or so guys with her, then sent them off in all directions to search for Seven." He glanced back at his new acquaintance. "Grace is freaking. She told everyone to pack up. I think she plans to pull out as soon as tomorrow. She feels the risk of danger is too great with Maria, and I think she's right. This morning, when I was heading back, it was still dark in the camp and I spotted her sneaking around before I came out of the woods. She was actually peeking through the window of your hut, Jen. There's something seriously wrong with that woman, and she sure as hell knows you weren't there."

"I guess I better get back and make an appearance. I should probably talk to Grace, too. Tell her I won't be coming."

"Oh God, Jen. Please tell me you didn't just say that."

"Don't bother," Seven piped in. "We've already been through it."

Dan sighed in total exasperation. "Be careful in the woods. Her men are everywhere."

"Will do. Seven, get some rest. Drink. The more the better for you, understand?"

"Yes, doctor." She saluted as Jenny made her way out the door, leaving two sets of admiring eyes in her wake.

≈≈≈≈≈

Jenny was able to make pretty good time through the woods and was fortunate not to see any of Maria's men along the way. She slipped into her hut unseen, and quickly changed into her running gear, jogging in place long enough to break into a healthy sweat, then strutted through the middle of camp looking like she'd just returned from a long workout. She made sure everybody got a good look at her, especially Maria, who was watching from a distance.

Jenny headed to the dining tent, looking for Grace. She did not intend to tell Grace what she'd been up to, but wanted to find out first-hand what her plans were regarding departure. She saw Maria striding toward her from one side, and JC coming at her from the other. *Oh, this'll be entertaining.*

JC got there first. "Jen. Good to see you. Is everything okay?" He gave her a brief hug.

Jenny sent him a subtle signal to keep quiet. "Great! Just got back from a nice, long run. How are you this morning?" She asked a little too cheerfully, designed for the oncoming woman to hear.

Before JC could answer, Maria interrupted. "Good morning, Doctor. Can you tell me where you were this morning, please?"

Jenny dismissed her as if she were being interrupted in the middle of an important conversation. She didn't know what it was about this woman, but she felt compelled to annoy her. It was akin to poking a snake with a stick, but for some reason she couldn't help herself. "No," she said, flatly. She turned back to

JC and asked if he wanted to grab something to eat.

Maria's eyes flashed at the curt reply. She was not accustomed to being handled in such a way, and it only served to increase her interest in this reckless woman. Most people feared her too much to look her in the eyes, let alone speak to her in such a manner. "Please," she ground out once more, through gritted teeth.

Jenny turned back around and looked herself up and down, raising an eyebrow in question as if it were perfectly obvious where she'd been. "I was running, of course. Your presence here is unwanted, Ms. Velasquez. You're making these good people nervous. Why don't you take your party elsewhere?" She knew the attempt to get her out was in vain, but she tried it anyway.

Maria was visibly agitated. Jenny noticed the knuckles on her hands going white. With lightning speed, she moved so close to Jenny, she could smell the woman's hair products. Maria whispered for the doctor's ears only, "You're involved in this. I know it. I'll have you, and my prize as well." Before pulling back, Maria tilted her head slightly, breathing in the young woman's scent with some strange pleasure. It gave Jenny the heebie jeebies, but she held her ground.

"Don't blame your failure to locate your lost stranger on me, Ms. Velasquez." Jenny nearly flinched at what she saw cooking in this psycho's eyes. For the first time, she thought perhaps she'd made a big mistake provoking her so much. For the first time, she considered the real possibility that she truly was in personal danger from Maria. *All the more reason for me to get the hell out of here.*

It was late afternoon before Jenny could slip

away again. She grabbed as much extra food as she could without raising suspicion, before triple checking her surroundings and sneaking back into the woods.

Jenny never did find Grace. JC told her she was out in the field and was planning to wrap things up and take the troupe back to La Paz sometime tomorrow. She would deal with that when the time came. But now, Jenny couldn't help but smile at the prospect of seeing Seven again. Even though it had only been six or seven hours, she couldn't control the unexplainably giddy feeling she had just thinking about being in the captivating woman's presence. She tried to dissect that feeling a little as she walked through the woods, keeping a look out for Maria's men. She thought her feelings bordered slightly on obsession, but in the end, wrote it off to just being happily reunited with her long lost buddy.

She quietly announced herself outside the door, so as not to scare anyone, and entered, making immediate eye contact with Seven. A brilliant smile greeted her, and she thought for the briefest moment that she saw the same thing in that look that she herself was feeling. Joy and obsession. Dan noticed the exchange, but said nothing. She greeted him, gave them both a brief update, and sent him on his way with a kiss on the cheek.

"Welcome back." Seven smiled again. "I like Dan. He seems like a good man. Didn't get to talk to him much because I slept most of the time you were gone, but we got along well."

"He is. He's been a good friend to me. It looks like Grace will be pulling the team out tomorrow. I'll be sad to see him go. No telling when I'll see him again. He'll probably be re-assigned to another country."

"I'm sorry, Jenny. If I weren't here, none of this would have happened. The failure of my op is having a far-reaching effect on you. I feel really bad about it."

"Don't take the blame for this on yourself, Seven. Whatever Argulla is up to probably has very little to do with you. Why would it? From what I've heard, he's a business competitor of Reyes', not a friend, so his reasons are probably self-serving."

"What kind of fallout will there be from you leaving the Peace Corps like this?"

"I have no idea, but once I tell Grace what's going on, I'm sure she'll cover for me as best she can. She really cares about people, more than just about anyone I've ever met." Jenny moved to Seven's side and began testing her heart rate and blood pressure. She removed the bandage from Seven's neck and arm to check and re-bandage the healing wounds. Satisfied with the progress, she handed her patient another bottle of water. "Drink. How are you feeling? Still woozy? Winded?"

"Not as much. I feel a little clearer in the head after that last bit of sleep."

"How's the mobility in your arm?"

Seven gave her injured wing a test drive, wincing a little, but trying to hide it as she moved it around in a circle.

"Good. I brought you a jumbo turkey sandwich with all the fixins', so eat up. Regain your strength. I'm pretty sure you're going to need it." A strange look crossed the younger woman's face, not unnoticed.

"What is it, Jen?"

The doctor took a moment to look around the dingy little cave they were in, thinking it somewhat appropriate to their dire situation. "This woman that's looking for you, Sev. She's not right in the head. I've been pushing her buttons a little, and maybe I shouldn't have. She's a few clowns short of a circus, ya know? She said she was going to get you, and me too. She doesn't have any real knowledge I'm helping you. She just wants me. For whatever reason, God only knows, but I've got to admit I'm a little freaked out. She's got a Hannibal Lecter quality about her."

"I'm not going to let anything happen to you, Jenny. If she gets anywhere near us, I'll take care of it. Okay?"

Jenny nodded in solemn understanding.

"Now," Seven stated, after swallowing a gargantuan bite of her turkey sandwich, "Let's get off the subject of my health and our dicey situation for a little while. Frankly, it's depressing. Why don't you fill me in on what you've been doing since Virginia."

"You want to hear about me?" The tall woman nodded affirmatively. "Well that should take about two minutes." Jenny laughed in a self-depreciating way. "I've pretty much spent my life till I joined the Peace Corps with my nose stuck in a textbook. My parents retired and moved to Jacksonville, Florida when I was twelve. I accelerated through high school and finished with honors at sixteen. Got a full scholarship to University of Miami, pre-med, and finished in three years. Got a full ride through UM med school too. That was a bit of a surprise, because they don't give out many of those, but I was thrilled. After I graduated, I wanted to do something with it, before I settled down to a life of office visits and trips to the E.R., so I volunteered to come to South America."

Seven smiled affectionately at her friend. "This must be a veritable vacation for you after all that studying."

"Mm. Yeah. I've enjoyed it. It's been an eye-opening experience. The people here are very nice, simple people. It's quite a difference from Miami, that's for sure."

"Is that where you'll practice when you get home? Miami?"

"I don't think so. I don't really have anything there, and truthfully, it's kind of a crazy city. Fascinating...but kind of nuts. I'm not sure where I'll settle. How about you? I guess you're in DC, somewhere?"

"I rent a brownstone in Old Town Alexandria, kind of near where we used to live. I can walk down to the Potomac from my place. It's a pretty cool little area. How's your family?"

"Okay, I guess. My dad is in his seventies now, conservative as ever. Maybe even more so. You know how they say whatever your personality traits are when you're younger only magnify in old age? He was fifty something when I was born, so he never seemed too involved with me when I was growing up. Unless I messed up, that is. Then he always came down hard. My little brother, Philip, kept him busy in that department most of the time."

Seven raised an eyebrow at the mention of Philip, Jenny's hyperactive little brother who she also babysat from time to time. He was an obnoxious little shit if she remembered correctly. "How is Philip? Did he ever grow out of that 'Tasmanian Devil' stage? I'll never forget the time he launched himself off the couch as if it was a trampoline, and shot straight into the plate glass window. You have no idea how relieved I was when he bounced back and hit the ground instead of going through it."

"I remember that. He was wearing a red cape. That was in his superhero stage. Just be lucky you weren't there for his 'I'm going back to juvenile prison for the third time,' stage."

"Oh nooo." Seven chuckled. "He was always wild."

"It was his way of getting Dad's attention, I guess. It worked. He got plenty, just not the kind most kids dream of, probably."

"What's he doing now?"

"Never the same thing for long. He didn't turn out to be a criminal or anything, fortunately, but he has trouble doing any one thing for too long. Gets bored easily. Or so he says. He's a good kid, just searching for something. I guess we all are, really," Jenny said rather wistfully.

"What are you searching for, Jenny?" Seven reached out to lift her friend's chin, so she could see into her expressive eyes.

The young woman looked up, getting lost for a long moment in the caring face staring back at her. She felt something unexplainable. Somewhere inside, a small voice said, *This.* She shook off the thought and replied with a sad shake of her head. "I find myself wondering that quite frequently of late."

"Whatever it is, you'll find it," Seven said as she released her chin. "So compared to Philip, your parents must be incredibly proud of you."

"I guess. They don't seem that interested, really. Whenever I tell them what I'm doing, they give me the 'That's nice, dear' line. As long as it's not embarrassing to them in some way, they're happy to live in their own little world. That's okay, though. Everything I've done,

I've done for me. I don't need a cheering section."

"Well, if it means anything this late in the game...I am incredibly proud of you. I can hardly wait to get back and tell Mom all about how remarkable you turned out. I will be sure to gloat about my keen powers of observation."

Jenny laughed lightly and took her friend by the hands. "Thanks. Actually, coming from you, it means a lot."

Jenny released her friend and reached over to grab her backpack, unzipping a side pocket and spilling forth a small mountain of pre-packaged brownies. "Dessert?" She smiled, remembering Seven's fondness for sweets.

"Oh my lord! Why didn't you tell me you had these sooner? I wouldn't have wasted my appetite on a turkey sandwich." She snatched up two to start, ripping at the plastic with her teeth. "Wh ab u ofer buvr?" She asked through a mouthful of gooey brownie.

"Was there a question in there somewhere?" The doctor laughed. "You could at least swallow what you're chewing before you take another bite."

Seven's shoulders shook in silent laugher as she washed her brownie down with a big swig of water. "Sorry. Old habits. Marines generally frown upon good table manners. We tend to squash and swallow. Gotta get down as much as possible, as fast as possible, because you never know when you're going to get another chance to eat."

"I hope the first thing they taught you in boot camp was the Heimlich Maneuver."

"I said, what about your other brother?"

"Neil. He's a good guy. Got a nice job with some big corporation. One of those high-paying positions that nobody actually knows what he does. I fall asleep every time he tries to explain it to me. We were never close when I was growing up, since he was sixteen when I was born. But I got to know him a little better when I was in school. I visited him in Texas for spring break a few times. Got to know his wife and kids. She's nice, daughter of some big wig Houston oil guy. They've got a nice house in Dallas."

Four brownies later, Seven was contemplating just one more when Jenny reached across the space between them and wiped a crumb from her cheek with a fresh towel. "Some things never change." She smirked. To herself, she thought, *except that I can't seem to stop finding excuses to touch you.*

❧❧❧❧

"Miguel, how much longer must we walk around out here in these damn woods?" Another of Argulla's men asked his compadre, as he wiped the palm sweat from the handle of his gun with the tail of his shirt. "Ten hours looking for this puta in one day is enough. I've got a blister on my foot and it's getting dark now. Maybe somebody else has already found her. How would we know? I say we head back to that camp and see if the boss wants us to continue on through the night. At least we can get something to eat."

"Shut up, Nino. You've done nothing but whine all day long. You bitch like a little girl. I have blisters on my ear drums from all your pathetic complaining."

"We don't have flashlights. How are we supposed to search in the dark without flashlights? If we don't head back soon, we won't be able to find our way back in the dark."

Miguel conceded this point. They would have to head back. He tucked his gun into the waistband of his pants and removed a small electronic device from his shirt pocket, along with a pencil and a piece of paper. He took a reading from the GPS and made a note on the paper. "Okay. You are right about the flashlights. We can't do anything without them. We'll head back and see what the boss wants us to do. We'll start right back here, later, where we left off. I think she'll at least be happy we found this trail, even if we didn't find the missing woman."

From a dangerously close distance, Seven watched the two men fade away down the trail before retreating back into her hole in the ground. She quietly manipulated the slide of her pistol, removing the chambered round from its dangerous position. Seven looked over to her friend who was crouching wide-eyed in the corner behind a table, waiting for all hell to break loose. "It's okay," she whispered. "They left. I overheard one of them say they'll be coming back this way, though, so we may want to think about getting out of here soon. I'm not sure how much longer it will be safe to stay in one place."

"Hell of a way to wake up from a nap," Jenny said, her voice shaking slightly.

"Yeah. Nothing like a little adrenaline to get the heart rate going. Zero to sixty in three seconds, flat. Are you okay?" Seven asked, seeing Jenny stand numbly in the corner with a glassy look in her eyes. She walked over and took the woman into a reassuring hug.

"I'm okay. Thanks. Freaked me out a little is all. I guess they caught me off guard."

"Jenny?"

"Yeah?"

"Those people are here to kill us, and now that you're with me, I definitely mean *us*. I know you're aware, but this isn't a game. If we're going to run together, neither one of us can afford to let our guard down, ever. Understand? You have to be prepared to do and to see anything, or we'll never make it. If I have to kill people to save us, I won't hesitate to do it. If you're not up for that, it's not too late to reconsider coming with me."

Jenny took the words seriously and nodded that she understood. "I don't think I can kill anybody, Seven. I want to save lives, not take them."

"That's absolutely fine. I don't expect you to. I just want to make sure you don't shut down on me if I have to do some damage. It could be dangerous to both of us if you do."

"I won't. I'm going. No matter what," she said, and took a deep breath to steel herself for future trials. "I'll just consider this little freak-out a learning experience. It won't happen again."

"I know you're fearless, Jen. I remember." She smiled fondly, holding the young woman at arm's length and giving her an encouraging squeeze on the shoulders.

༄༅༅

In the quiet of the night, Jenny and Seven lay silently, attempting to rest. Engulfed in the darkness of their dank space and dour moods, each woman's varying thoughts won out over the struggle for sleep. Jenny was nervous and excited about entering an unknown world of danger for the first time in her young life. Seven puzzled over her team's betrayal, and the oddity of Jenny's appearance, standing by her side, ready to risk her life.

Seven heard a soft sigh in the gloom. "Jen, are you awake?" She whispered, just in case she wasn't.

"Yeah. Are you?" They both chuckled at the inane question.

"I need you to do something for me tomorrow. It might be kind of risky with that Maria woman hanging around your camp."

"No problem. I live for danger." Seven grinned at the sarcasm.

"I need you to get to a phone. I've been thinking about this for days, and the only thing making sense is that one of my own guys sold us out. It's the simplest explanation, which usually tends to be the right one. I'll tell you where to call, what to say, what to listen for. I think the result will tell me for sure what I need to know."

"I should go back early, before sunrise, hopefully before Maria shows back up. I can grab one of Grace's vans and drive over to a little town about thirty miles south of here. I'll call from there."

Jenny made a mental list of the bare minimum of her things she'd need to bring. She and Dan had managed to stockpile some food and water over the last couple of days, so they had a decent supply for the journey to Reyes' Hacienda. She felt keyed up and in need of something to calm her racing thoughts. "Seven?"

"Hm?"

"Will you tell me something?" She asked to the darkness.

"Sure. What would you like to know?"

"Anything. How's your mom? What've you been doing the last fifteen years? A story, whatever."

"I'm not much for storytelling, Jen. I thought that was your department."

"How's your mother doing?"

"She's doing great, actually. She finally broke down and remarried about three years ago. A nice guy she met through my Uncle Nick. Not a military guy, which I think she was pleased about. She was kind of funny about it. Mom thought I would be upset, but I think she was just using that as an excuse to stay single all those years. She told me Dad was it for her, the love of her life. She never wanted to be with anybody again. I told her I didn't think that was any reason to go through life alone. She may never find what she had with him again, but that doesn't mean she can't have happiness and companionship with someone else. Then she met this guy, and they hit it off."

"That's great. I'm happy for her."

"They moved to Charleston a couple years ago. Mom opened up a little gourmet café and cheese shop there. It's a small place, only about eight tables. She serves wine and cheese plates, cold sandwiches, but the place is packed all day. Loving every minute of it. I'm really proud of her for stepping forward like that. She deserves to be happy."

"I always liked your mom, Sev. She was very kind to me, even though I know I was an obnoxious pest, hanging around all the time."

"Nah. She didn't mind."

"How'd she feel about it when you joined the Marines?"

"In a word...resigned. When I was little, she called me 'Daddy's little clone.' I don't think she was happy about it, but I don't think she was surprised, either."

"She was probably worried about you. I'm sure she knew you wouldn't be happy with some pencil pusher type of job."

"I didn't tell her what I was doing for a long time. I knew if she found out I really had followed in Dad's footsteps she would have gone ballistic. It all came out in the wash when the President awarded me the MOH in '99. She found out everything then. I didn't want her to read about it in the papers, so I gave her the Cliff notes version of what I did to earn it, and took her with me to the White House."

"What's a moe?"

Seven chuckled in the dark. "M-O-H. Medal of Honor. In the military, it's a big deal. They rarely ever award it to a living person. My commander put me up for it."

"And what, pray tell, did you hurl yourself into to get that?"

"Uhh." She groaned, not able to bring herself into rehashing that tale yet again. "Some other time, Jen, over a few beers. Okay?" That was Marcus' favorite story.

"It's something that's going to make me hyperventilate when I think about it, isn't it?"

"Probably. Anyway, we were at the after party. The officer I served under was there, and he was bragging to a couple other people about what I'd done. My mom overheard. I saw her across the room and she was white as a ghost, staring at me with this strange look on her face, as if she didn't even know me. I saw whom she was standing next to, and that's when I knew she'd heard the gory details. I remember thinking if she was going to lose it, now would be the time."

"Did she?"

"Yes and no. She didn't freak out or anything, which is good, since she just found out her only daughter was some Rambo-like killing machine. That's what my C.O. used to call me, anyway. She came over and whispered in my ear, 'I'm proud you're my daughter. Your father would be very proud of you too,' and then she left me there. She couldn't deal with what I'd become. We're okay now. It was just a lot for her take at the time."

"Do you think your father would be proud you followed in his footsteps?"

"I don't know. I wonder from time to time. I think he would understand me. He definitely understood how powerful the call to serve your country could be. I hope he would be proud, and not think me foolish for spending so many years there."

"He would be proud. I have no doubt. I remember how much he used to dote on you. You could do absolutely no wrong in his eyes." Jenny smiled at the memory. "I was always jealous of you for that. Our Dads were total opposites. Yours was barely ever home, but when he was, he paid attention to every little detail of your life. Mine was always home, and never spent any time with me at all."

"Turn that lantern on, would ya? I might as well see you since we're talking."

In the dark, Seven heard Jenny rustling around for a minute before the lantern illuminated the room. "So when you moved to South Carolina, did you like your school? Meet any interesting people? Cute boyfriends? Did you ever get married?"

"No. School was the same there as everywhere. I went out for sports and stuff, but never was very sociable. I would hang out on the base with Uncle Nick sometimes. I joined up at eighteen. With the exception of Marcus, I always kept to myself. Relationships in the military are not usually a good idea." *Especially for me.*

"So you and Marcus were never an item?"

Seven smiled, fondly remembering the antics of her longtime partner. "No. He loved for people to think we were, though. Said it was good for his reputation as a ladies man. He was almost a full head shorter than me, so we made quite the odd couple." A wave of sadness washed over her. "He was in love with a fantastic girl from Charleston. They were living together in a little apartment in Georgetown. She saw him for what he was. Heart of a lion. Heart of gold. He was going to ask her to marry him when we got back from this op.

"How 'bout you? Married...divorced...single?" Seven asked.

"Chronically single, I think. I seem to be connectionally challenged. I've been in a few short relationships, but I just can't seem to find a guy I can stand to be around for more than a few months."

"That's a few months longer than I could stand it." They laughed. Man bashing seemed to be a favorite pastime of women all over the world.

"This coming from the woman who spent over a decade with thousands of men? It's no wonder you feel that way."

That's not the only reason I feel that way. "That's one of the reasons I left the Corps. I was ready to feel what it's like to live a normal life. Get my own place?

Check. Find someone to share it with? Still working on that part." *That position is available as well, if you're interested. Stop that. Bad Marine.*

"Did leaving the Corps have anything to do with what you do, exactly? Being a sniper, I mean. That's got to be a hard thing to take sometimes, psychologically speaking."

"It can be, but that's not why I left. It's easy for a civilian to separate what I do from what a regular soldier does, because what I do is so much more calculated. Engaging in a battle as a group seems less personal, and therefore, acceptable. But what scout snipers do is really not much different. It's just an alternative form of warfare, and there are many forms. The U.S. knows 'em all, and we put them to good use. Even terrorism is a form of warfare. We don't use it, we don't condone it, but for some countries, it's the only way they know. They don't give a shit about what we consider fair or not. They could never compete with us on a level playing field. Not many countries could. So they do what they can."

"Does the violence of it ever get to you?"

There was a long silence as Seven gave serious thought to the question. "Sometimes." She sighed at the confession. "More so recently. I've seen a lot of death. Lately I haven't been able to shake it off like I used to. Sometimes you have to stake out a target for days. You watch him eat, sleep, laugh with his people. You get to know him, in a way. If your walls aren't up, you can get so you're relating to him on a personal level. Then when the order comes down to shoot, you're in trouble. You have to stay removed, or you can't survive. For most, it's harder to do that when they're new, and easier as they get older. For me, it was the other way around."

"But you're still doing it?"

"I still believe in the basic principle. Some people out there live to cause pain, be it for power, money, religion, or any number of objectives. They will steamroll over innocent people for no other reason than their own selfish goals. Before, these guys were in other countries, doing bad to other people. But now, I'm after the ones who have a hand in hurting the U.S. directly. It's a different ballgame, but important to us. We're attempting to be more proactive in stopping the threats against us before there's a body count. 9/11 changed everything."

"Seven, is the real reason we're going to the Reyes Hacienda so you can kill Reyes?" Jenny asked, afraid she already knew the answer.

Seven stalled momentarily. She knew her friend wasn't going to want any part of what she may do. "No, Jen. But I won't lie to you. If I get the opportunity to finish the job, I'll take it."

"Why? You said yourself the mission was a wash. Why not let another team finish it? Maybe you should examine your motives, Sev. Is it revenge for Marcus? Pride? You can't stand that you actually lost this time? Duty? Why? Please make sure you know before you act on it."

God she's cute when she gets fired up. "What is it about you, Jenny? You've somehow gotten me to talk more in one night than I've talked in a year." Seven changed the subject, not prepared to argue over her intentions. *I love that crooked little smile. Stop that.*

Jenny chuckled, recognizing the change of subject for what it was. *Okay, but you'll have to answer me sooner or later...can't get rid of me now.* "Come on.

Let's try to get some sleep. I've got to get up in about three hours, and something tells me I'm going to need all the energy I can muster tomorrow." She reached over and dimmed the lantern. "Sleep tight, Sev."

"Same to you, Pumpkin Head."

Chapter Fourteen

Jenny MacKenzie stood in the predawn blackness cast by an ancient mahogany tree, trying to convince herself that her mind was playing tricks on her. She needed to sneak from her hiding place in the woods to the next dark shadow, graciously provided by her own hut just thirty yards away. She didn't see any mysterious men lurking around, or Maria for that matter, but she was very nervous about getting caught this close to her escape.

The time had come to put up or shut up. She gathered her backpack close to her chest and ran for it, breathing a sigh of relief when she reached the shadow of her hut unnoticed. Jenny paused to catch her breath and listened for any activity that might be going on around her at this ungodly hour. She heard nothing but the sound of crickets and a monkey howling from the treetops somewhere far away.

Quickly entering her hut, Jenny deposited her pack and snuck back out, walking quietly in the direction of the volunteer's dorm. She leaned over her friend's sleeping form and whispered for him to meet in her hut, then crept out the same way she'd entered. A short while later, Dan came in, still rubbing the sleep from his eyes.

"Well, aren't we up bright and early this morning?"

"Good morning to you too. Thanks for coming."

"How many hundreds of miles did you say it was to the nearest Starbucks?"

Jenny chuckled and smiled fondly at her good friend. She was going to miss him terribly. He had the gift of always being able to turn her mood around to a good one. "Two hundred and thirteen miles...in other words, too many. It would definitely be cold by the time you got back."

"So you left our charge alone in the woods? You're not afraid she'll take off on you?"

"Actually, yes. I wouldn't put that past her for one minute. She would think she's protecting me by leaving, but I don't think she fully understands the danger I'm in from Maria. I get the feeling I am, anyway. She's not very good at covering up the crazy. I think Seven will wait, though. I've either managed to convince her she needs me to get through this, or she just wants my company. Not sure which."

"Or maybe you want hers," Dan said slyly, watching his friend for reaction. She didn't deny it.

"I need to take the van and run a little errand. I should be back in a couple of hours max. I've got to tell Grace what's going on and grab a few things, but then I'm out of here for good. Will you take the stuff I leave behind when you go?"

"Of course," Dan said sadly, the reality of their separation just now hitting him. "How are you going to manage all that with Maria lurking around?"

"Just gonna wing it, I guess. Thanks for sacrificing your pack. Here's a list of stuff to carry back to the bunker that we'll probably need. I'll see you there once more before we take off. Do me one more favor? Give Seven a thorough check up when you see her. I need an unbiased opinion on how she's really doing."

"Jenny, are you sure about this? You could just come with us back to La Paz. I don't think Maria would try anything with you if you're with us the whole time. She'd have to kill us all. Do you think she'd really do that?"

"Maybe, and that's too big a risk to take. Besides, I can't leave Seven. She's not a hundred percent and she needs me. Even if she didn't, I wouldn't leave her."

Dan resigned himself to Jenny's departure. "She's lucky to have a friend like you, you know?"

Jenny hugged her friend quickly and headed for the door. "And I'm lucky to have a friend like you. See you in a bit." Jenny closed the door softly behind her, leaving Dan to ponder his surroundings.

He glanced around, his gaze coming to rest on the pack Jenny left behind with her essentials packed haphazardly in the main compartment. Walking over to the dresser, he picked up her once beloved and now forgotten camera and tucked it carefully in her pack under a fleece jacket. Dan went through the drawers, tossing the rest of Jenny's things onto her bed, preparing to pack. He intended to have a serious word with this Seven person when he saw her. She was taking Jenny away, and needed to understand just how precious her cargo was. If Seven let anything happen to his beloved D-Mac, it didn't matter how scary she was, he would kill her himself.

⁂

Jenny shifted the van into drive and pulled slowly away from the camp, trying hard to make as little noise as possible. Once she was well away, she hit the gas and headed to the nearest town, the cool wind blowing in the open window shaking the last remnants of early morning haze from her brain. Her focus was now off Seven and Maria, and on to her upcoming phone call. A task Seven considered of the utmost importance to determining their future course of action.

She had to know if her suspicions were well founded, and together, they determined a way to test her theory. She would be calling the offices of Black Flag Company in Washington, and asking for the fourth member of Seven's team, Takeo Takashi. Seven's suspicions led her to believe this man was the most likely to have betrayed them. He was the only person she knew of with exact details of their operation, and would have been the only survivor of their team, had Reyes' men succeeded in their ambush. Seven was assuming at this point that Ty was dead. If it turned out he wasn't, then he could be suspect as well.

There was an old and often used technique in psychology that involved leading a person into a truthful confession by convincing them you already knew the answer to the question. You wouldn't give them the chance to deny their wrongdoing, but accept it and approach the person from a position of non-judgmental knowledge. It was really just a simple trick, but worked more often than not.

Jenny would not ask Tak directly if he did this thing, but would ask *why* he did this thing, then sit back and listen. It wasn't so much what he said, but how he said it that counted. His reaction would either clear him, or condemn him. Seven's take on the man was that of a skilled computer technician, but not a smooth operator or experienced in the art of deceit. If it were indeed Tak, he had gambled everything that Reyes would be successful. They were hopeful his reaction to her direct attack would tell them if he was responsible for the betrayal or not.

Jenny arrived in the small town as the sun was just beginning to arch over the treetops. The streets were coming awake as sleepy looking people opened curtains and doors to the morning light. She parked the van on a dusty street and entered the front door of a cantina the volunteers frequented, walking directly back where she knew the owners' office to be. She offered the man twenty dollars for the use his phone. He happily complied and vacated his space, this not being the first time the doctor had come to call.

Jenny sat at his desk and took a deep breath to collect herself. She placed a piece of paper in front of her, and grabbed a pen to take notes with, scratching a few marks in the margin to get the ballpoint rolling. She intended to jot down her immediate impressions and Tak's responses for later review, as it might be some time before she'd be able to discuss it with Seven. Next to the paper, she placed her watch, with the time set to zero. She would hang up the call before it could be traced to her exact location, though she was sure they'd get the country and vicinity pretty quickly. Three minutes was her limit.

Jenny dialed the number in D.C., followed by another on a pre-paid calling card. She punched in the extension and waited nervously, her stomach fluttering, a slightly nauseous feeling lurked somewhere in her esophagus. After the third ring, a deep and confident voice answered abruptly. "BFC, Takashi."

"Good morning, Mr. Takashi. I'm calling on behalf of Seven Michelis."

There was a long silence on the end of the phone. Jenny made a note of it on her paper. *Seemed genuinely shocked you were alive.* Finally the deep voice choked out, "Who is this? Where are you calling from? Where is she? Is she alive?"

"She was unable to make it to a phone, so asked that I call you instead."

"Unable? Is she wounded?"

"She is seriously injured, Mr. Takashi."

"Tell me where she is," he demanded. "I can help. Tell me exactly where she is, right now. I'm not kidding. It's for your own protection." *Demanded your exact location over an unsecured phone line.*

Was that relief she detected? A trace of panic? She made a note of her impressions. *He never asked about the other team members. Why? Because he already knew their fate?* She and Seven had decided a little extra subterfuge couldn't hurt their cause, so meant to leave the impression that Seven was injured so badly she was in a stationary location.

"Mr. Takashi, I have a very important question to ask you. She needs to know before it's too late. Why did you do this?" Jenny left the question to hang heavily in the air.

A burst of statements from the other end of the phone ended a long silence. "Listen, lady. I don't know who you are, but you better give me her location right now or you're in some serious trouble. You are interfering with an investigation of the Department of Homeland Security and if anything happens to our operator you will be held personally responsible and dealt with accordingly."

Voice is elevated an octave. Pressured, rapid speech.

"What are you playing at? Don't you realize the kind of danger she is in? I've got to get her out of there, now before it's too late. Help us to save her and no criminal charges will be filed against you. Don't think for a minute I won't find out exactly who you are."

Voice not excited you survived, but agitated, threatening.

"Why did you do this, Mr. Takashi?"

"What the hell are you talking about? Do what? Who do you think you are? I didn't do anything. What are you accusing me of, exactly?"

Exhibiting defensive posture.

"Mr. Taka…"

"You are seriously undermining the security of this operation."

"Mr. Taka…"

"I'm sending another team down there right now to arrest you. And make no mistake, I will…"

Click. *Time's up.* Jenny hung up the phone and continued to write her impressions. She wrote everything he said she could remember, and reviewed her previous notes, making additional notations in the margins. *He's the guy, all right.*

࿇࿇࿇࿇

"You have absolutely no right to speak to me that way, Mr. Takashi. We had a business arrangement, and I believe you have been paid accordingly. The rest of the team will be eliminated shortly. We are on the trail now." Armando Reyes' voice was calm, and he struggled to keep it that way as this ass on the phone was attempting to shatter his last remaining nerve.

"Do you have any idea what I have risked? I saved your pathetic life and you're lying to me?" Tak screamed into the phone.

"Let's not twist the facts, Mr. Takashi. You sold me information. I paid. You're not exactly in the business of saving lives, are you? Now, as I said before, we will have her shortly. She will be dead. You have your money, and my name will be cleared from your records. End of story."

"I cannot believe you can be so glib! You are not hearing me, Reyes. My freedom, my life is riding on you being able to take out all three of the team. The entire team! Our plan only works that way. Period! I demand to know what is being done to capture her. Damn it! Fool! I told you she was dangerous, but you didn't take it seriously enough, did you?" He yelled every other word as if that would somehow make his complaint better understood.

"Calm down, Mr. Takashi. I assure you, everything that can be done is being done. We will have her. She will not get out of Bolivia alive. I have much more to lose than you. Please try to remember that."

"You have no idea what you're dealing with, do you Mr. Reyes? She's probably out of Bolivia already. In fact, I wouldn't be one bit surprised if she had her rifle sighted between my eyes right now. If the conversation stops and you hear my phone hit the ground, you'll know why," Tak said, still not believing Reyes could screw up such a simple task. It was an easy gamble. Easy money. "All you had to do was take out three people. You said you had an army to do it. This thing would be done and over, everybody's happy. But no! And why the hell didn't you contact me? I had to find out she was alive via a phone call from some stranger?"

"The situation is under control. It is too risky

for us to be speaking, Mr. Takashi. I will contact you again in forty-eight hours if we have not yet captured her, so you can plan accordingly."

"Let me make something perfectly clear to you, Mr. Reyes. You have an extremely limited amount of time to hold up your end of the deal. If you don't, everything we discussed is off."

"Our 'deal' is not off, Mr. Takashi, until I say it is."

"Oh, it's off all right. You see, if Michelis lives, you will more than likely be dead, and shortly thereafter, so will I. Therefore, it's pointless to even be discussing our 'deal.' Who is this woman that called me, by the way? She led me to believe Michelis was gravely injured. If that's true, she shouldn't be hard to find."

There was an uncomfortable pause on the line. Reyes knew the truth would result in another screaming tantrum. "We believe she is being helped by an American doctor who is here as a Peace Corps volunteer. We didn't have anything concrete to go on before, but now that you have informed me of this phone call, we will pick her up for interrogation. I feel confident with the right persuasion she will lead us to the sniper."

"Has it occurred to you that if she's being helped by a doctor, she's probably anything but gravely injured?"

"Every scenario has occurred to us, Mr. Takashi. As we speak, this Michelis woman is the most hunted person in all of Bolivia. Trust me. We will get her."

"I wouldn't be so sure of yourself, Reyes." Tak said sadly, already feeling his tentative grasp on success fleeting. Unlike Armando Reyes, Takeo Takashi was well aware of his boss's capability and determination.

"What else would you have me do?" Reyes asked, wanting nothing more at the moment but to end this call.

"I would have had you succeed in your initial assault, then this conversation would not have been necessary."

"What's done is done. Now we can only fix it, or pay the price for underestimating her."

"I fear we both may be paying that price, Mr. Reyes. And sooner than we think."

❧❧❧❧

Dan was finding it increasingly difficult to laugh as hard as he was laughing, and remain quiet at the same time. Seven had been thoroughly entertaining him with childhood stories of his friend Jenny, and he loved every minute of it. "I can't wait to use this material on her next time we're out drinking. If I play my cards right, I can probably get her to buy every round of drinks just to keep me quiet. This is some terrific blackmail material. Thanks."

Seven chuckled. "Don't mention it. It's the least I could do. Consider the lifelong supply of free drinks a token of my everlasting appreciation for saving my life."

"I can't get the visual out of my head of her running down the road stark naked in nothing but her mother's rubber rain boots. What I wouldn't give for a picture to back up that story." He laughed some more.

"Okay, now it's your turn. Tell me everything you know about Dr. Jenny MacKenzie. Don't leave out any of the gory details. I want it all." Seven smiled charmingly at her new buddy, Dan. She tried to act casual, but was dying of curiosity about the fair young doctor. She wanted to squeeze every detail from Dan before they were parted.

Dan began to weave the tale of how they'd met in La Paz, threading his way steadily through their building friendship and working relationship. Dan watched closely as Seven devoured every tidbit of information, stopping him frequently to elaborate on a particular detail. He sensed almost immediately the woman behind that stunning smile was interested in more than just a casual way.

He continued to talk, as he tried to determine in the background of his mind how he felt about this new development. *Jenny could certainly do worse.* This woman was graceful and gracious, witty and seemed very intelligent. What was initially a very intimidating appearance gave way totally when she relaxed and smiled, leaving the opposite impression of a kind and incredibly lovely woman. Her laugh was deep and infectious, and her eyes glimmered with mischief. She had a charming way of expressing her thoughts not with words or smiles, but by arching her eyebrows one way or another, together or separately. She had very talented eyebrows.

Dan smiled. He had suspected for some time what Jenny was longing for, what she was struggling with, was really the first stepping-stone to finding out whom she really was as a person. He suspected it hadn't occurred to Jenny she might be gay because of her conservative upbringing and general lack of having gotten around much. That, and she hadn't met anyone until now who brought those thoughts to the surface.

He didn't know Seven very well, but she was definitely lustful material. She was the kind of woman who could bring Jenny out of her closet for sure, if Jen opened her mind to it. She might not realize it yet, but Dan was sure she'd get there soon. Ever since they'd found Seven in the woods, Jenny had acted slightly manic and obsessed with the woman. When the three of them were together, he had seen looks pass between them that were charged with more than friendship.

"...so, the moral of the story, Seven, is don't bother arguing. Just save yourself the heartache and agree to whatever she wants, because she's going to get it with or without you."

Seven's lips curled into an indulgent smile as she thought of her friend's stubborn streak. Dan was right. She'd seen it for herself already. "She's always been that way. No hesitation. She makes up her mind, and that's the way it is." She laughed at the thought. "One time when she was sixish, I was babysitting Jen. Her parents left supper, and made me promise to see she ate everything on her plate. I told her she couldn't leave the table 'till everything was gone. Four hours later, she was still sitting there. Livid. The next time I went back to check on her, she was gone and the plate was empty. I found her asleep in her bed with her clothes still on. When I went back down to clear the table, I noticed her napkin was missing. After a little searching, I found it tucked behind where she was sitting in the drawer of a sidebar, all the food she didn't want scraped into the napkin." Seven smiled at the memory. "That little monster. I told her to empty her plate, and she did."

Dan snickered at the story, having seen similar streaks of stubbornness in his friend many times.

Suddenly, his expression turned serious as he looked pointedly at the woman sitting across from him. "Seven, what are your intentions toward Jenny?"

The directness of the inquiry took Seven aback. Her first instinct told her it was an innocent question regarding their upcoming journey. But when she looked at Dan, she knew that's not what he meant. She hadn't realized her thoughts were so transparent, and felt uncomfortable for a moment, that this stranger would presume to ask her about something so personal. After a moment, she gave way, realizing his prying was only because he cared deeply for his friend.

It's obvious Dan's gaydar is fully functional. She sighed and attempted to form a reasonable and comforting answer.

"Sorry if that seemed a little forward, but I care about her. I don't want to see her get hurt, and I'm not just talking about the impending danger of being hunted through the countryside. I can tell you've been around a bit...and...well...she hasn't. I just want you to understand that she's precious cargo. A lot of people, including me, will be really upset if you don't handle her with the utmost care."

She hesitated. Talking like this was breaking new ground for Seven. She never even spoke to Marcus of her personal feelings before, let alone a veritable stranger. "Dan, Jenny and I have shared something powerful since we were kids." She took a deep breath and looked up at the ceiling, trying to collect her thoughts. "I can't really explain it. Neither can she. We've tried to talk about it a couple times, but it just sounds strange. There is something there, though. A connection that runs deep. We understand each other on a level neither one has ever experienced with anybody else. It's always been that way, almost as if we're a part of each other, somehow."

Seven paused to take a long swig from her water bottle. "Dan, I can't believe I'm going to say this...my friend Marcus would razz me for months if he heard me, but here it is. I'm damn good at what I do. One on one, I like my chances against almost anybody... even one on ten for that matter. But if it makes you feel better, I want you to know this. I would willingly bring considerable force to bear on anyone that tried to harm her. I would give my life for her, and I won't surrender my life easily."

"Seven, I don't doubt..."

The woman smiled and held up her hand to stop him in mid-sentence. "Please. Let me finish," she said. "As to your other concern, I care about her a great deal. I think she feels the same, but more than likely, that's where it stops. Why would someone as special as her ever be interested in someone like me? I'm just another jarhead. If she should ever decide she wants more from me, I'd happily give it, but that's her decision to make, with no outside influences. She would have to come to terms with that on her own. I would never risk our friendship by making those kinds of assumptions about her feelings toward me."

"She believes in you, Seven. And if she does, I do too. She hasn't said anything to me about it, but I think her feelings run deeper than friendship." He smiled warmly at the pleased look in Seven's eyes. "Forgive my protective streak, but I just wanted to be sure you weren't the type of woman to push her into anything she might not be ready for. It's hard on people coming to terms with certain realities, when they're pushed into them. I know firsthand. There's an innocence about Jenny. It would break my heart if anybody ever did anything to take that from her."

"So you think she's…"

"Yeesss. I certainly do. But like you said, she's got to get there on her own."

Seven casually stood and strolled over to her gear, her mind whirring with the possibility that Jenny might actually like her as more than just a friend. It seemed impossible to believe, but the more she thought about it, the more appealing it sounded. *Don't go there, Sev. Don't get your hopes up. There's way too much going on here for you to be thinking about romance. Keep your eye on the ball, get out of this alive, and then if she's still around you can think about it.*

In a soft, barely audible voice, she told Dan, "I will never be the one to cause Jenny pain."

Dan walked to where Seven stood by the table. He placed a hand on her shoulder and turned her slowly toward him so they were eye-to-eye. "Take good care of her, Seven. I couldn't stand it if anything bad happened to her."

She reassured him. "I won't. I promise. Now why don't you tell me what's going on at your camp, and what this Maria character is up to. Do you think Jen's fears are justified?"

"I think so. This woman claims to be looking for you, but her behavior seems more like she's stalking Jenny. She sends her men out in all directions to look for you, but she stays behind in camp and lurks around her. She's a freak. It's a good thing you guys are getting out of here, because I think she's getting more and more bold about her obsession."

"How are they handling her at camp?"

"Grace, our camp director, is freaking. She's convinced this woman poses a threat to us, and is planning to pull us all back to La Paz today. Jen is going to tell her she's not coming, and is hoping Grace will cover for her. I have no idea how Maria will react to that. We want to make her believe Jen is leaving with us."

"I cannot figure out why this woman is involved at all. From what Jen told me, she has nothing to do with Reyes. Do you have any ideas about that?"

"Not really. But if I had to make a wild guess, I'd say it's probably a territorial thing. Rumor has it Argulla and Reyes hate each other's guts, and we're sitting in the middle of Argulla's land holdings."

"Whatever the reason, I am anxious to get moving. It's not safe to stay in one place too long, and from the sounds of it, Maria is ratcheting her search up a notch. I don't think we're safe here any longer. In fact, I think we should have left this morning."

"I probably won't see you again anytime soon. Please take these contact numbers and let me know when you're back home safe and sound." He gave a small slip of paper to Seven and hugged her quickly.

Together they began stuffing the backpacks with supplies for Seven's escape.

≈≋≋≋

Jenny slammed the van into park and hopped out at a run, heading straight for Grace's hut. Now that the phone call had been placed, she was fairly certain the proverbial shit was about to hit the fan. Her immediate mission was to explain the situation to Grace as quickly as possible, say her goodbyes, and get the hell out of Dodge.

She spied Grace walking out of the dining tent, a steaming cup of coffee in hand, and headed for her at a run. "Grace."

"Oh, good morning, doctor. You're up bright and early as usual. Are you all packed up and ready to head out?"

"That's what I came to talk to you about. Can we go to your hut?"

Both women turned and headed in that direction. "Of course. Is there a problem? Something I can help you with?"

"Grace, I'm not sure where to begin. I guess I'll just spit it out, and you can make of it what you will. I'm not coming with you when you leave today."

"Wha..." Grace stopped dead in her tracks.

"The person Maria is looking for? I found her. Yes, her. It turns out, not only is she a she, but she is an old friend of mine, here doing something for the U.S. government. I can't say what exactly, but it's top secret."

"You've been helping her, like Ms. Velasquez thought? All this time?"

"Yes. I'm sorry I didn't tell you sooner, Grace, but I honestly believed the fewer people that knew, the better. This is extremely important. She is in mortal danger, and I am going to help her get out of the country. We're leaving this area as soon as I can grab my things and go."

"Now listen here, Jenny. I have a serious problem with this," Grace said angrily. Jenny was thrown off her rapid-fire explanation, never having heard the good-natured Texan lose her temper before. "Your safety is my responsibility. I must insist you come with us.

That woman will have your head when she finds out you've been deliberately thwarting her. I fear she will kill you."

"She might, Grace." A mischievous grin was on her face. "But she's going to have to catch me first."

"This is no laughing matter, doctor. I am very seriously concerned about the stability of your judgment at the moment."

"Don't be. I've never been more sure of anything. The woman I'm helping is a very skilled operator, Grace. I'll be fine. If anybody can keep me safe, she can. We'll help each other through this. She is a very dear friend, and I won't abandon her, so don't bother arguing the point. My mind is made up."

Grace grunted her disapproval, as well aware of Jenny's stubborn streak as the rest of the team. From across the camp, JC spotted Jenny and Grace, and made a beeline in their direction. He tapped Jenny on the shoulder then accepted a hug and a sad smile from her. "JC, I'm glad to see you."

"Hi, Jen. How are you? How is everything going?"

"Don't tell me you knew about this, too?" Grace asked disgusted, but resigned.

"Only because I forced it out of her." The two shrugged in exasperation at their stubborn friend. Jenny wondered briefly if she was being laughed at, then pushed on.

"I'm leaving, JC. I've got to go now, because the next time Maria comes back, I think she'll be coming for me. My friend and I are taking off. Don't bother asking, the less you know the better."

"You really are nuts, Jen, you know that? I can't believe after all the good we've done in this area it's come to this."

"That psychotic *bitch* is to blame!" Grace blurted out. Jenny and JC laughed at the absurdity of profanity coming from the mouth of the angelic Texan.

"You know I'm going to be worried sick about you. Please find a way to contact us as soon as you're safe, okay?" JC asked, sincerely distressed.

Grace straightened her shoulders in defiance of their world unraveling. "What can we do to help you, Jenny?"

"Please make sure the Peace Corps people understand I entered into this situation completely aware and of my own volition, and partly because I think I'll be safer from Maria if I disappear. Also, when Maria gets here this time, she's probably going to be pissed. Don't provoke her. If there's any way you could load up a van and send some of the guys away now, you may be able to convince her I left already. Try not to lie directly to her in case she finds out, but maybe just insinuate I'm not here and that a van's already left for the city. I don't want to give her any reason to strike out at you guys, or hinder your departure. And for God's sake, be careful. I'm really going to miss you guys."

She hugged Grace. "I promise to contact you as soon as I'm safe. I'll leave a message with the home office, hopefully within a few days. Please. Please be careful."

She hugged JC goodbye and planted a tender kiss on his cheek. "Thanks for everything, my friend. I'll miss you. Please say goodbye to the rest of the gang for me after you're well away." One last hug, and she turned to jog across the small compound toward her hut, wiping a few errant tears from her cheeks.

❧❧❧❧❧

Having to endure another evening of humiliating conversation regarding her apparent failure was the final blow to Maria's formerly collected wits. Tires spun on the gravel road, kicking pebbles into the nearby trees as she punched the gas for more speed. She didn't bother waiting for her men, assuming they would collect vehicles and follow her.

The gloves were coming off. She was taking this fight to those American bastards at the camp, now convinced beyond a doubt they were hiding the sniper. Reyes had called to tell them a woman had placed a call to Washington on behalf of the missing person, and Maria knew without asking it was the doctor.

Raul had finally relented and given his permission to grab the American doctor and extract the information by whatever means necessary. He would find some way to cover it up so as not to incur the wrath of the U.S. government, but he was very clear the others were to be left unharmed. *We'll see.*

Maria skidded the Land Rover to a halt in the middle of the camp and jumped out of the truck, fuming. She looked around under a hooded glower for the object of her desire, but was disappointed as usual. Walking briskly toward what she knew to be the doctor's hut, she took two quick steps up the stairs and violently kicked the door open.

The sound of nails being wrenched from dry wood was enough to make a person's skin crawl. She stomped into the small hut and yelled, "She's not here! What a surprise!" The psychotic woman tore at the dresser drawers and hurled the small piece of furniture to the floor, finding the room empty of not only the doctor, but her belongings as well.

She stopped her frantic actions abruptly and took two steps toward the bed, lifting the small pillow to her face and breathing deeply. With one hand, she reached down to her leg holster and removed her skinning knife, bringing it slowly up to the pillow and forcing the blade tip deep into the fabric. Two quick thrusts sent feathers flying all over the small room as the woman released a gut wrenching howl that could be heard throughout the entire camp. Birds left the trees for safer perches, recognizing the screech of a dangerous animal when they heard one.

Maria released the snap on the holster of her Nighthawk and removed the 9mm, caressing the slide as she righted her shoulders and marched with a determined step to the center of camp. She flipped the safety off and fired three rounds rapidly into the dirt. The noise had the desired effect. Everybody in the camp came running to see if someone was in trouble. Maria leveled the gun at the remaining volunteers and several locals who were in the area, capturing each of them in turn with her blazing eyes. "Where are the rest of you?" She asked, her voice somehow more frightening when calm than it was in its regular state of agitation.

Silence was their response. Every man and woman in the group understood that speaking up could equal a death sentence. Maria finally singled out JC, recognizing him as a friend of the doctor's. She snaked a finger between the buttons of his shirt and tugged at the fabric, pulling him forward to stand in full view of the small crowd. She stood dangerously close and spoke lightly. "Where is the doctor?"

The man kept silent. He probably thought he was being heroic. She turned her back to him and spoke loud enough for everybody to hear. "Where is the doctor?"

When nobody answered, she spun quickly and hammered the butt of her 9mm into the side of JC's head, dropping him to the ground clutching a gash over his ear. She grabbed the lapel of his shirt and dragged him back up to his feet. "Want more? Where is the doctor?" She reached her arm back to strike again, when JC decided to answer.

"Gone. She's gone. For good."

Maria felt it to be true. Her rage at the loss was like a white-hot flame burning behind her eyes. She drove her fist into the stomach of the bleeding man and met his nose with her knee as he doubled over. She kicked him again in the stomach for good measure before grabbing his lapel and hauling him back up to his feet. "Where are the others?"

"Gone," JC choked out, defiantly. He nodded toward their white van, indicating she should notice one of them was missing. "We're leaving here. Leaving this place where people needed us, because of you." This earned him a backhanded slap across the cheek, the action causing a spray of crimson from his profusely bleeding nose.

"You see, I have this theory," Maria stated matter-of-factly, now pacing in front of the others like a prowling cat. "If I find the doctor, I find my missing person. If I find my missing person, I find my doctor. I would like to have the set, you see?" She glanced up at the cloudless sky and took a refreshing, calming breath, looking over her shoulder at the approach of two truckloads of her men coming to aid in the search.

The bleeding man in front of her was now sporting several impressive looking cuts and bruises, along with a broken nose, yet he stood defiantly before her. The only thing giving away his pain was a trail of tears running down his blood-spattered cheeks. Her expression was flat as she withdrew the sharp blade from its holster and pressed the cold steel tip under JC's ear.

"Enough!" Grace shoved herself in between Maria and JC. The tension was so thick it felt like air was electrically charged. "If you think I'm going to stand by and watch you abuse my people for one more minute, you are sorely mistaken, you vile excuse for a human being." She practically spit the last words into Maria's face.

It hurt to smile, but JC couldn't help himself. Grace was something else when she was fired up.

"These are good people here, doing good work. It's because of you the people of this region will suffer. It won't affect you! Why should you care? Oh that's right, you don't! Well perhaps you'll care about this. I placed a call to our home office a short while ago and named you and Mr. Argulla, personally. If anything happens to us, the full force of the U.S. government will be knocking on your door. There's nothing the American people tolerate less than the abuse of good Samaritans. I would think somebody in Mr. Argulla's position would frown upon that kind of recognition, don't you?"

If Maria had a sense of humor, she would have laughed at the balls on this suddenly ferocious woman. She raised her weapon and aimed the barrel right between Grace's eyes. "I'll tell you what, Miss Richards. Answer three questions honestly for me, and if I'm satisfied you're telling the truth, I will leave you alone. If I'm not satisfied, I will start with you, and work my way through your precious volunteers until not one is left standing."

"And who is to judge if I'm lying or not? *You*?" Grace snorted with disgust.

"I will know if you're lying, Miss Richards. I always know."

Grace willed herself to play this smart, trying her best to ignore the gun barrel pointing at her head. It wasn't easy. "Ask."

"Is the doctor truly gone from this camp for good?"

"Yes."

"Was the stranger I am looking for ever here, under your care?"

"No." *Technically true.*

"Did the doctor and my quarry leave this camp together?"

"No." *Also technically true, since Jenny was alone when she left.*

"Did…"

"Three questions, Ms. Velasquez. I answered them truthfully, as promised. Now please leave us to the business of closing up this camp."

Maria stared at Grace for a long, silent moment. The evil woman quivered like an alarm clock strapped to a ticking time bomb, her body wound so tight she could barely control its need to explode. Argulla would be very upset if she killed them. Then she would probably have to kill him, too. That might hinder her ability to get another job if word got around. *Coño.* "Ernesto!" She yelled over her shoulder, never taking her eyes off the feisty Texan.

The man ran quickly from where he stood next to his vehicle waiting. "Yes, boss?"

"Take a truck and four men down the road to La Paz. Go fast. When you come to a van matching that one,"—she indicated the large white vehicle with a nod—"run it off the road." Grace gasped.

"Yes, boss."

"Bring Dr. MacKenzie to me. Alive. Understand?"

"And the others?"

"Let them go. If she gives you any trouble, bind her. Tight." She added with a smile, the thought of the arrogant woman being in pain was very appealing.

"On my way."

Grace turned her back on Maria and took JC by the arm, leading him toward the clinic. She nodded for Nala to follow. To the rest she said, "Grab the rest of your stuff, everybody. Pack up the van. We're leaving shortly."

Under her breath, the young nurse Nala whispered, "Daniel is not back yet, Grace."

"He'll get here, Nala. I have faith."

Maria called her remaining men together. "The person we are searching for is in this area. So far, our search has been too broad. We will start here, and work our way out in tight groups. The first man to pick up a trail will be rewarded with 25,000 Bolivianos." A cheer rang out amongst the men at the prospect of such a generous reward. Maria hoped this would be enough to motivate them into fierce action.

"You two,"—she pointed at two men whose names she didn't know— "take this camp apart. If you find any trace or trail here, let me know. Miguel, take your man and head to the trailhead you found northeast of here yesterday. If you find anything of interest, report back to me immediately and we will shift the group in that direction."

"You." She pointed to a large group of men. "Head back down to the river. Pick up the trail from the water's edge and work your way out from there. The rest of you, begin walking the edge of the camp and work your way out. Let's move it people. I want this finished today."

Maria wanted nothing more than to find this woman and end this charade. If her men were unsuccessful in picking up the trail, she would take MacKenzie apart, piece by piece, until she got the information she needed. Either way, this circus would end soon. Then, she would leave Argulla's employ and get the hell out of this damn country. *But not before I've had my fun.* She smiled for the first time that day.

꙰ ꙰ ꙰ ꙰

"Fathe..."

"Silence." Takashi senior commanded his son.

Takeo Takashi held his tongue. He hesitated at the entrance to the dining room of his father's home. Removing his house slippers, he proceeded onto the tatami floor of the traditional Japanese dining room in his socked feet. Tak bowed respectfully to the old man and seated himself on a red cushion on the floor.

Against his nature, he waited patiently while his old man poured tea at the low, cherry wood dining table where they sat. Takeo was a magna cum laude graduate of UC Berkeley computer science, and considered himself a genius in the art of hacking and programming. At twenty-one, he graduated and took a position with the State of California, which eventually led to his discovery by Mitchell Lebo, the same nightcrawler who recruited Seven into the DHS.

Now twenty-six years old, Takeo's bad habits of sugar and cream-laden coffee, Red Bulls, imported beer, and pizza at all hours of the day and night were catching up with him. His hair was still jet-black, but the paunch of his gut and his bottle thick glasses made for a much older looking man.

After the tea had been served and his father raised his own cup, Tak reached for his and took a sip of the mellow brew. He waited for his father to speak first. This was the custom in his family, regardless of what needed to be said.

"I have dedicated my life to respecting the ways of our ancestors. Of making sure my family did not forget where we came from in this new land, which plays by these new rules. And still, my son, you ignore my teaching and barge in unannounced demanding an audience with me."

"Father. You asked to see me. I did not barge in unannounced."

The old man sighed. "This is not open for debate, my son. If I should call you, you come when I say, not whenever you feel like it. You must learn respect. You must behave in a manner befitting your Samurai heritage. You are a direct descendent of a proud Samurai warrior. You need to start acting like it."

"Yes, father." Try as he might, Tak always felt like a little boy whenever he was in the older man's presence. Nothing he ever did was good enough. He realized a long time ago nothing he did would make the man proud, so the best he could do was try not to embarrass him.

The old man stood and walked to the wall where

his Samurai ancestor's katana and wakizashi hung proudly displayed. He looked lovingly on the weapons, their intricately carved sheaths pulled back slightly to reveal the gleaming, razor sharp steel underneath. "This daisho is a symbol of everything we are, my son. Of who we are. It is what you have above all others. It is what you were born with and what you will die with. Everything else in your life can and will shift and change, but not this."

"What did you want to see me about, father?"

"Your mother and I have decided it's time for you to marry. She has compiled a list of suitable young women in our community for you to pursue. Also, you need to do something about your weight. You're starting to become an embarrassment to us."

Tak closed his eyes, willing himself not to scream. Usually when his father called him over, it was so he could lecture him about what he should be doing with his life, but this? Damn. How the hell was he going to get out of this one? His parents were so incredibly traditional. He wouldn't be surprised if the girls his mother found came with dowries.

"It's not a good time for me to consider this kind of thing right now, fath..."

"Your mother and I will handle the wedding arrangements. You merely have to choose a bride, and of course, produce a grandson to carry on our family line."

Tak stood and bowed respectfully to his father. "May I be excused, father?"

The old man nodded his assent as the younger retreated to the doorway, donned his house slippers and left. Once free of his father's stare, Tak's face fell into a brooding scowl as his thoughts turned again to his real problems. His parents and their issues could wait. *What I really need to address, right here and now, is Seven fuckin' Michelis and how to get that bitch dead.*

Earlier that morning, Takeo filed the mission paperwork to the Chairman. He was two days late in the filing. Tak wanted to wait to be sure Michelis was dead before he sent in the mission failure report, but realized that holding off any longer would only generate suspicion in his direction. If Reyes hadn't screwed everything up by missing Michelis, everything would have gone off without a hitch. He decided a change in tactic was necessary, and felt if handled properly, it could be done to suit his purpose.

Before Reyes blew it, he planned to state that Michelis made a gross error in judgment, the mission failed, their cover was blown, and she and her team were killed. He had manufactured the necessary documentation to prove it true. Now, with some clever hacking, his paperwork would prove Michelis sold the team out and then Reyes double-crossed them. He would tell the Chairman that Michelis was either alive and on the run in Bolivia, or dead. He thought the odds were good the Chairman would send a team after Michelis. She would be made a kill-worthy target for her betrayal. With any luck, the Chairman would be the one to clean up the mess Reyes left behind.

Reyes had assured him last time they spoke that Michelis would be dead within the day. He couldn't afford to wait for a confirmed kill. He knew his report to the Chairman would result in prompt action in Bolivia, but Tak felt precautionary measures must be taken at home as well, in case she escaped Reyes' nets and found a way out. His life and future were riding on his deal with Reyes.

Tak had made arrangements to meet a professional 'fixer' in the park by his apartment. He intended to make sure if Michelis made it back, she wouldn't live long enough to kill him first. If Reyes fucked up, which he already had in Tak's opinion, he would clean up the mess and bill the bastard. *Never send amateurs in where a professional is obviously needed.*

Tak arrived at the park early since he had allowed more time to visit with his father. With any luck, the guy he was meeting would show up early also, then maybe he'd have time for a little Texas Hold 'em and to place a couple bets with his bookie Sal before he went home for the night. He was ten grand up last time he played with Sal's boys, so things were looking good.

He looked around the green expanse under overcast skies and settled his focus on a distant vehicle with two men behind the wheel. He was being watched. He made an immediate assumption the men in the car belonged to the man he was due to meet at any moment. Tak wouldn't know if they weren't. He wasn't experienced in these covert types of maneuvers. He was just a computer whiz with a gambling problem. It didn't really surprise him he was being watched. If he did what the man he was meeting did for a living, he would take out insurance as well.

No sooner had the thought left his mind then he heard a voice behind the bench where he was seated. "Mr. Takashi?"

"Yes. That's me." Tak looked up into the lifeless black eyes of the killer with no name. He was a smallish, mousy looking man with slicked back dark hair and a tightly trimmed goatee.

"Make it quick, Mr. Takashi. I don't ordinarily

like to meet in open places."

Tak handed the man two envelopes. One was large and had all of Seven's personal information including her home address, her mother and uncle's addresses, favorite hangouts, etc. Several photographs and her service record were also included along with her current suspected location. The other envelope contained a down payment of $50,000 in cash. How the man with no name spent the funds was up to him as long as his mission was accomplished. Tak would double the money upon completion, and throw in a bonus if the kill was made to his specifications.

Michelis must be wiped from the face of the earth with no trace. He didn't care when, where or how, as long as it was done before she had a chance to do it to him. Takeo had no doubt whatsoever Seven would set her rifle sight between his eyes at her first given opportunity.

"She may already be dead. If she doesn't show back up in the United States, the 50k is yours. If she does show up, do what you have to do and the rest will be paid along with a bonus." Without further comment, the man with the goatee took the envelopes and walked away.

Across the park, two men in a black truck watched, taking an occasional picture of Takeo Takashi and his associate. The man in the driver's seat flipped open a cell phone and spoke a few words. A few minutes later, another vehicle pulled alongside. The man with the camera hopped out of the truck and ran around to the passenger side of the second vehicle. They drove away, soon out of sight around a copse of trees to the other side of the park.

Chapter Fifteen

Jenny was slightly winded, but excited to be on her way as she bounded into the bunker with a flush in her cheeks and wearing a bright smile. "Whew! I made it!" She beamed at the two amused stares drawn from the other side of the dank room. Her boundless energy never ceased to amaze Daniel. "What?" She asked, suddenly self-conscious due to the mischievous grin Dan was sporting.

"All right. What's up? Spill it!"

"Oh nothing." Dan smirked. "I'm just picturing you in an overlarge pair of rubber boots running willy-nilly through the streets, all naked and free and such." The two conspirators chuckled in sync.

"Sev! You didn't! How could you? I'll never hear the end of this, now." Jenny's already rosy cheeks flushed pink with embarrassment. "Oh well. At least you didn't have the picture."

"There's a picture?" Dan jumped up excitedly. "You are sooo going to show me that picture someday, my little D-Mac. I will not take no for an answer." The trio laughed together, Jenny shaking her head in denial.

She dropped her backpack unceremoniously on the ground and headed over to take a seat next to Seven on her bed/table. "Well, what's the verdict, Nurse Daniel? Is our patient ready to fly?"

"She's flyin' whether she's ready or not," came

the low mumble from near her right shoulder. "How'd it go out there today? Did you run into your stalker?"

"No. Thank God. I was out of the camp almost as soon as I got back, and she hadn't shown up yet. I spoke to Grace briefly, said goodbye to JC then took off. They said they would attempt a little subterfuge on my behalf, which was nice. Grace didn't like it, but she came around in the end."

Dan watched the two women interact and thought they made a nice looking couple. *Jen and Seven. Heh. Sounds like a cocktail.* He directed his question to Seven. "So where do you go from here?"

"I have something I need to do before we can leave, then Jenny is going to help me sneak out of the country. Don't know how yet, but we'll work it out. I don't have any money or I.D., and I can't go to an embassy without alerting people back home. I'm not sure who I can trust back there yet."

Dan looked at her quizzically.

"Don't ask, Dan. The less you know, the better. Maybe someday we can get together over a margarita or two and I'll tell you the whole sordid affair."

"Good. I like sordid affairs." Sarcastically, he added, "Whatever you do, don't tell me anything now. I absolutely *hate* knowing juicy information. I really *love* being the only one in a room that doesn't know what's going on. Makes me feel special, you know?" The friends laughed at his overly dramatic act.

Seven popped up from her seated position and adjusted the hang of the camouflage pants she wore. She squatted down and tightened the lace on her black combat boot. "I'll let you two say your goodbyes. I'm going to scout the area a little before we take off, and try to get a feel for the terrain we'll be heading into.

Jen, I'll be back in about a half hour. If it's okay with you, we'll pack up then, go over a quick plan, and head out." She stood and stuck her hand out toward her new acquaintance. "Dan, it's been a pleasure. Take care of yourself on the way back, and thanks again for everything."

He said goodbye, smiling affectionately and took her strong hand into his own. "I'll take you up on those 'ritas anytime, beautiful." He gazed meaningfully at his new friend. "Take care of our girl." The sadness and worry was evident in his expression.

"I will, I promise. I'll make sure she calls you when we find our way home." She gave him a reassuring pat on the shoulder, then turned to leave.

Silence followed in her wake, as the two remaining friends watched the gracefully departing gait of the tall warrior as she ducked out the small door.

Dan sighed heavily at the sight. "Well, I have to hand it to you, D-Mac. You know how to pick 'em. She is something else. What I wouldn't give to see her in a little black dress, stilettos, and that big, honkin' rifle slung over her shoulder."

Jenny laughed at the visual, thinking to herself that *would* be kinda hot. "She is something else, you're right about that."

"She cares for you a lot. She told me you had a connection. Something deep."

A slow smile crept all the way across the young woman's face. She couldn't stop its progress until the muscles in her cheeks were maxed out. Dan laughed aloud at the sight. *You're a goner,* he thought, knowing for certain now that she sensed it too. He figured, *what the hell, I'll help it along.* "She couldn't stop drilling me about you while you were gone. Wanted to know everything about the fascinating and beautiful Dr. Jenny MacKenzie."

"Get out." Jenny laughed, dismissing his silly comment.

"Nope. Not going anywhere. I'm serious. You better be careful there, I think she's interested in you. Wink wink, nudge nudge." Dan laughed and poked his friend in the shoulder.

"Oh please. As if. Why would somebody as great as her be interested in somebody like me? Anyway, I'm sure she's straight. She's probably got half the men in D.C. drooling over her every day of the week."

"Funny, that's what she said about you."

"She did not!" Jenny was incredulous, a blush creeping up her neck. "What are you up to anyway? You are up to something, aren't you?"

He skillfully changed the subject. "Since when does having 'half the men in D.C. drooling' mean a person is straight, anyway? Do you know for sure? Have you asked her? I mean, look at me. I'm a gorgeous hunk of man-meat, and have half the women in L.A. drooling over me, but *I'm* not straight." Dan teased, having fun pushing every button he could reach.

"Well I am!" *At least I think I am.* "Do you really think she's interested?" Jenny dropped her head into her hands. "Oh God, what am I saying? Damn it Dan, you are totally messing with me, aren't you?"

"Look. You said you were unhappy. Searching for something. I'm just trying to encourage you to keep an open mind. You said you never enjoyed any of the relationships you were in before, and now all of a sudden, here is this gorgeous creature in your midst who you can't keep your eyes off of."

"Oh god," Jenny whined. *So busted.*

Dan grinned knowingly at his embarrassed friend.

Finally, Jenny looked up from her hands, smiling sheepishly. "She is kinda nice to look at, isn't she?"

Dan quickly covered his mouth to stifle the sound of him busting out with laughter. He doubled over, clutching his stomach as his shoulders shook with mirth. "I knew I wasn't imagining it. You've thought about it, haven't you?"

Jenny didn't reply, but merely made eye contact with him, and grinned conspiratorially.

Shoulders still shaking, he asked, "What are you going to do about it?"

"Nothing!" She began to chuckle as well. "Anyway, she's straight. I'm straight. Everybody's straight, remember?"

"No. She's not. She likes the girls."

Whoosh...and just like that, the conversation was no longer funny. "Are you just saying that to tease me, or do you know for sure?"

"We've been to some of the same clubs in L.A. I'm not teasing."

Jenny's suddenly serious expression concerned Dan. She dropped her elbows to her knees and stared at the laces on her hiking boots. A harmless fantasy was one thing, but to know for sure it had the real possibility to be more was something else entirely. It elevated her thoughts to a new level. Jenny was feeling slightly stunned at the notion.

"Jenny. What's wrong?"

Here, right in front of her, was something that could be real if she wanted it to be. She knew somewhere in the back of her brain she was making an assumption that Seven would be interested, but instinct told her she was. All she had to do was be brave enough to take that step. Could she? The thought was terrifying and fascinating all at once.

"You never had a problem with me being gay; I guess I just assumed you wouldn't have one with her, either. I'm sorry. I guess I shouldn't have stuck my nose in where..."

"No no no. Sorry, Dan. I don't have a problem with it. Of course I don't." She placed a reassuring hand on Dan's forearm. "It's not that. I think that information just made this little game I've been playing with myself a bit more real is all. Brought it home, so to speak."

"What do you mean?" Dan was relieved beyond measure he wouldn't have to reevaluate his feelings for his friend.

Jenny took a moment to collect her thoughts. To voice them to Dan would make her feelings more tangible. There'd be no backing out of this once she told him. If she stopped now, she could deny everything. Blow it off as a lark. No biggie. But if she said the words? She'd have to face the words.

"You were right...before...when you were teasing me. I've come to terms with the fact that I do have a thing for her. Kind of an obsession, really. I can't stop thinking about her. When I'm not with her, all I can think about is getting back. When I am with her, all I can think about is how to make her smile, so I can see her face light up again. It's confusing to me. But before now, it was just a game. To find out it may actually be for real, means I'm not going to be able to push this under the carpet. I'm going to have to face it. Face myself. I'm not sure I'm going to like what I see."

"Wow. You're deeper in than I thought," Dan

said, somewhat surprised at her heartfelt confession.

Jenny took a swipe at her eyes, the motion alerting Dan to just how seriously she seemed to be taking this new revelation. "Hey now. Why so glum, chum?" He scooched over to her side and wrapped a beefy arm around her slumped shoulders. "This is a good thing. Why are you upset? The D-Mac I know grabs the bull by the horns and gives it what for." He paused, revamping his previous statement. A wicked smile crept up his face. "Or in this case, grabs the bull-dyk...oof!" Jenny backhanded him in the stomach.

"Dan!"

"Ow!" He laughed. "You didn't have to hit me so hard." They grinned at each other, the maudlin mood departing. "Why wouldn't you like what you see? You are one of the most fantastic people I've ever met. What's not to like?"

Jenny dried her cheeks with the backs of her hands. "My family means a lot to me, Dan. I think if I did this, if I became this, I would lose them."

"If it's who you are, it's what you are, Jenny. It's not about becoming anything. If you choose not to follow your heart, to pretend to be something you're not, that's the choice. Not this, if this is who you were born to be. But ultimately, it is up to you to know what is real and what's pretend. You've got to choose which path you take."

"When I was growing up, there was this guy in my dad's office. A permanent bachelor with a 'roommate.' He wasn't out, so to speak, but everyone in the office knew, or at least speculated that he was gay. My parents were very conservative as you know, but the anti-gay garbage they would spew always made me feel bad. They used this man as the fall guy, or the butt of every joke. He was an ever-ready punch line. All anyone ever had to do was say his name, and they'd all crack up laughing. It makes me sick to think about it now. But that's the kind of bigotry I was raised with."

"That's not you, Jen."

"No, but it is them, and they are mine. Lumps and all. When my dad is ranting about something, it's not unusual for him to throw dykes and communists in the sentence together, as if they're one and the same, and the cause of all the world's troubles. How do you think it would go over if I brought a girlfriend home?"

"I don't know what to say about that, Jen. Fortunately for me, it's not an issue I ever had to deal with. My mother told me she and my father suspected I was gay from the time I was four years old. My mom said I was standing in the driveway watching all the kids play, but wouldn't join in. When she asked me why, I told her it was because I didn't want to get my hands dirty."

Jenny cracked up at the previously unheard story, Dan chuckling along with her.

"Do you think I am, Dan?"

"Only you can say for sure, sweetie. Just promise me you'll keep an open mind and follow your heart, regardless of the outcome. It's a huge heart. Plenty of love to go around. If you do that, I have no doubt you'll find what you're looking for. Which in my opinion is happiness with a sprinkle of contentment thrown in for good measure. What does your heart tell you?"

"I never really considered it before. I'm just not sure. But I can't deny how I feel about Seven. I've always felt strongly about her. Even as kids, I never understood why I wanted to be around her all the time. As an adult...it's so much stronger. I've never felt this way about anyone before, not even close. Those so-called relationships I had can't touch what I'm feeling now. It's almost laughable by comparison."

"But…?"

"But I'm *terrified!*"

Dan smiled at her exaggerated response, watching as she threw her hands in the air like an exasperated child. "So you're scared. Of being gay? Getting seriously involved? Getting hurt? Hurting her? Being disowned? Who isn't? That's not a very good reason to sit still. You gotta see where the world takes you, or the world will spin right by. I know you well enough to know you don't want that."

"It feels so strange, Dan. What if I encourage this, and it turns out to be wrong for me? How would that affect her? Us? What if this is nothing more than my childhood infatuation rearing its ugly head? What should I do?"

"Well, you know if you ask me that question, what I'm going to say. You should go for it, of course! You're putting so much weight on your shoulders over this. Give it a shot. Try it on for size. If it doesn't work out, chalk it up as a life experience and move on. That's what I'd do."

"I can't do that. I could never lead her on in that way. I think it would break her heart, and I could never be responsible for doing that. She's searching too, Dan. If I lead her to believe what she's searching for is me…she's going to take the bait. I feel it. Our friendship is too deep to be marred so casually."

"Come on. Are you telling me it's all or nothing?" Incredulous.

"If I encourage this, I think it could be, yes. If I open myself up to her, I have to be prepared to commit for life, if she'll have me. Otherwise, I won't do it. That's the decision I need to make. I couldn't live with myself if I hurt her. I'm scared of repercussions with my family. I'm scared this is all in my head, and maybe it's not right for me. How would I know? On the other hand, this could very well be my one shot at true happiness, Dan. I don't want to blow it. God, I'm so confused."

"It seems you're damned if you do, and damned if you don't. So you may as well just stop thinking about it so much and act. See what happens. Let the chips fall where they may, as they say." Dan smirked at his mildly clever rhyme. "Jen, this issue isn't going anywhere. Why don't you let it germinate for a while, and see how it sits with you? If she's all-that-and-a-bag-of-chips like you think she is, she'll be there when you're ready. Or not. My guess is she's struggling too. The only thing I know for sure is that you both care very much for each other. Don't over think it, sweetie. Just let it happen. If it's right, your heart will tell you. If it's not...well...you can cross that bridge when you get there."

Jenny took a long, quiet moment to look deeply into Daniel's eyes. *My God, I will miss you,* she thought. *I don't know what I would do without a shining star like you to lean on, my friend.* She didn't say these words aloud, because she was certain they were too sappy, even for him.

"Well Dannyboy, looks like it's going to be a WWF match from hell." Jenny held an imaginary microphone up to her mouth, doing her level best to imitate an obnoxious emcee. "Ladies and gentlemen... in this corner...battling preconceived notions about herself...I give you the *amazing* Jenny MacKenzie...

Versus...tonight, for one show only...attempting to come to terms with what she really wants...the *Deee-Lightful D-Mac*! Yaaa. WooHoooo. The crowd goes *wild*!"

"Stop. You're hurting me." Dan grinned, smacking Jenny playfully on the arm.

They shared a moment of companionable silence. "Thank you, Dan, for everything. It always makes me feel so much better when I talk to you. You've been a true friend."

Jenny hopped up from her perch and grabbed Dan in a heartfelt hug. "I'm really going to miss you, ya big lug. I guess you should probably get going now, huh?"

"Yeah. No telling what's waiting for me in psycho-ville. I'm gonna miss you too, D-Mac. Thanks for always taking my bitching with a smile. I wish it wasn't coming to such an abrupt end." He took her by the shoulders and looked at her seriously. "I'm incredibly worried about you, crazy girl, so please promise me you'll be careful. No unnecessary heroics, okay? Leave that to Rambette out there. Promise?"

"Promise." She laughed. "You know me too well."

"Mmhmm. That I do. About the other stuff... don't feel bad if you're freaking out a little. That's some pretty emotional territory you're treading on. Just trust your instincts and follow your heart. Whatever comes will be good if you stay true to yourself, because *you* are good. God, I sound like a cheesy greeting card." They walked hand in hand toward the door, as Dan said one last goodbye and ducked out.

"Be careful, Dan. Take care of Grace, okay?"

"You got it, Sweet Cheeks. See ya around."

Dan stepped over a fallen branch and ducked under another as he picked his footing carefully, making slow progress back up to the trail. He got his bearings, then headed back toward camp at a quick pace, hoping to grab a bite to eat before Grace packed up the entire camp.

His thoughts drifted to Jenny and Seven, and he said a little prayer for their safe delivery back to the States. He didn't consider himself a religious man, but a little prayer, just in case, could never hurt. Dan was just wondering if the Peace Corps would transfer him out of Bolivia when a motion at the edge of his vision snapped him back into the present.

His heart jumped into his throat as he bolted off the trail and hid behind a large tree. *Holy shit, here they come. Breathe. Easy. Stay quite. Don't move. Oh, thank God. I don't think they saw me.* Dan opened his mouth slightly and took slow, even breaths, trying to remain as quite as he possibly could. The two men walked slowly along the trail, chatting quietly. Dan noticed one of the guys was big and held a gun firmly in one hand. The other was smallish, seeming to talk and move his hands around incessantly, constantly inserting and removing his gun from a pants pocket.

They were right on top of him now, less than ten yards from his hiding place. He could smell stale tobacco and unwashed clothes from his position in the rough. As they strolled by, searching the shadows, his thoughts turned once more to Jenny and her friend. *Oh my god, no. They're heading right for them. Shit, what should I do? I need to warn them somehow. Take it easy, Daniel, if you do anything rash you'll blow this whole thing. Just stay where you are. Trust Seven to take care of her. You need to get out of here, and have faith they'll be doing the same.*

He waited for the men to pass from view, crossing his fingers and slinking back onto the trail. He estimated he was still another ten minutes or so from the camp if he really hoofed it. His concern now lay with Grace and the others. The presence of the two goons meant La Loca was undoubtedly back in town, and probably really tweaked by now. It was definitely time to vacate. Dan picked up his pace, making a beeline for home, hopefully followed soon after by the safety of La Paz.

⚜⚜⚜⚜⚜

Miguel and Nino couldn't believe their luck. They got back to the trail where they'd left off yesterday and immediately found a clue just off the path. Nino lamented momentarily that if only they'd seen it yesterday, they could be back at the Hacienda right now watching the Bolivia vs. Uruguay football match.

What Miguel noticed was half a boot print coming onto the path from the eastern side of a tree dividing the trail. This was good. If they were the ones to find the sniper, maybe Maria would give his old job back, and let him be the one to fire that son-of-a-monkey, Ernesto. He motioned for quiet, and indicated to Nino they should enter the brush at this point and walk east, down the slope.

He knew he was on the right track two minutes later when he heard a faint voice coming from somewhere up ahead. He motioned for Nino to stop and listen. He would be the one to take the boss's prize back to her. He would get the money. He would get the praise.

"Do you want me to help you?" Jenny asked, as Seven sat on a stool and braided her long black hair into tight ropes.

"Nah. Thanks. I've had years of practice. How's the food and water supply looking?"

"Good. We've got enough food to be relatively comfortable for about three days. I've also got a small bottle of purification drops for when our water runs low, a couple blankets, sheet of plastic, rope, a decent amount of medical supplies, and assorted other goodies. I've separated the weight out between the two packs. Hope that's okay with you. I was going to put all the heavy stuff in mine, since you've got all that other stuff, but thought you would probably appreciate me being faster as opposed to carrying more."

"Good thinking." Seven twisted her braids onto her head and pulled her tight black skullcap over the crown of hair, securing everything neatly in place. "Got any of those brownies left?" She asked with a touch a mischief in her melodic voice.

"Oh sure, now you ask me. After I've already packed all the food!" Jenny laughed at Seven, who sported a perfectly innocent, angelic look on her face.

"Just kidding. Come over to the table here... let's look over the map so you'll know where we're headed. Just in case we get separated somehow. We're here now." She pointed, indicating the approximate location of the Peace Corps camp. "We're going to head down hill, due east until we reach this plateau." She traced her index finger along the laminated sheet, as Jenny focused not so much on the map, but on tan, elegant hands. "Then we'll change course slightly and head southeast across this river here, and on toward the Reyes Hacienda. It should take us 'till about this time tomorrow to get there. We won't stop for the night, but take periodic short breaks instead."

"What happens when we get there?"

"I'll scout the area and determine the level of security. I'm hoping it will be light, since his guys are probably all out looking for me. Then I'll sneak in and look for signs of Cooper."

"And Reyes?" Jenny had a hint of disapproval in her voice. "Will you kill him?"

"If the opportunity presents itself, yes."

"Even if it means alerting them to our presence?"

"I'm sorry, Jenny, but this is not open for discussion. I said if the opportunity presents itself, not that I was going to specifically hunt him down. The man is a pig. The U.S. targeted him for good reason. He was heavily involved in the funding of the 9/11 terrorist attacks. He killed my crew and is hunting me through the woods like an animal. The question is not will I kill him…but why shouldn't I?"

A battle of wills ensued before Jenny gave way and lowered her eyes to the ground. "I just think it's risky, and you're too close to it. That's all. It just seems at this point, it's not duty, because your mission is a wash, so it must be either pride or revenge, and both of those are hollow reasons to kill. I'd rather see you live to fight the good fight another day, than charge in there and get hurt. I didn't…I didn't mean to sound so judgmental. I'm sorry."

"This is a lot to take, Jen. I know it is. You've been thrown into the middle of a violent situation, and it sucks. Please, just trust me, okay? I promise not to kill anybody unless I have to. My primary mission at this point is to confirm Cooper's death and get us out of here safely. That's it. If Reyes happens to step in front of my rifle sight, then goodie for me. He's probably not even there anymore. Knowing what he undoubtedly knows about me, he'd be crazy to stick around."

Seven buttoned her camo jacket and tucked the map into a breast pocket, reaching next for her hip holster. She thought about Jenny. She was so used to being a loner, being with people like herself, having to think about things from a civilian's perspective seemed so foreign. *Try to be a little more understanding of how she may be feeling, you big dumb ox. She's probably scared out of her wits.*

She turned to her friend. "I don't know why you're with me, Jenny, but I'm glad you're here. Please forgive me if I seem a little abrupt. It's not intentional, and it's not directed toward you. How 'bout we get our stuff and get the heck out of here. The sooner we move, the sooner we'll be sitting in a pub somewhere chowin' on a couple of juicy cheeseburgers. You can tell me about your phone call to Takashi while we walk."

"Oh yeah, I think that went..."

"Shh." Seven, who was facing the side of the bunker with the rope ladder, suddenly went wide-eyed, as a sprinkling of dry leaves drifted lazily through the opening. She grabbed Jenny by the shoulders and reversed their position, placing herself between the ladder and her friend. She pressed a fingertip over her lips, indicating silence, and whispered urgently, "There's someone out there, Jen. Go to the door and get ready to run. Head up trail away from camp as fast and hard as you can. Hide where you found me, and I'll meet you there."

Jenny knew no-nonsense when she heard it, and was suddenly very frightened. The thought of protest never crossed her mind. She was way out of her league here, and she knew it. Grabbing her pack, she walked quickly and silently toward the small door, preparing to push it open at Seven's signal.

She never got the chance.

She glanced back at her friend just as a big man in black dropped unceremoniously down the hole. In a flash, Seven was on him, knocking the weapon from his hand. He was much bigger than her, but her strength in this hand-to-hand battle was undeniable. She was fierce, and her fighting skill commanding. Strangely, it even looked like she was enjoying herself. The man was incredibly outmatched. Jenny couldn't tear her eyes away from the fight. She was witnessing something raw and powerful in Seven she had never seen. Scary, yet exciting. It was thrilling to see.

"Go!" Seven yelled, snapping Jenny out of her trance. She turned toward the door, just as it was pulled open, and another smaller man charged in, pointing a gun directly at her. Before she could react, the man grabbed her by the shoulder harness of her backpack and spun her around. She struggled, but he held fast around her throat, pointing the gun over her shoulder toward the fighting pair.

Miguel sensed he was losing the upper hand and doubled his efforts in the battle for his prize. The banshee he was fighting had managed to get around to his back and was forcing his arm into a painful position. But more disturbingly, she had managed to wrap his neck in a hold that was cutting off his oxygen.

He slammed backward into a wall hoping to dislodge her. It didn't work. She wrapped her vise-like legs around his waist and squeezed. He wanted to tell Nino to shoot the bitch, but no words would leave his mouth.

Seven released his arm and used her other hand to assist in the crushing of his windpipe. An instant before she broke his neck, it occurred to Miguel that he wasn't going to win this fight. The notion seemed preposterous, then his world went black.

Seven kept her assailant's body between the little man's gun and herself. She was okay with the idiot's position as long as he didn't point the gun at Jenny. He seemed frightened and focused solely on her, which was just what she wanted. With a couple of powerful steps, she heaved the dead man across the remaining space and into the pair as a deafening shot rang out in the small space. She could tell by the jerk of the dead man's body the bullet had struck him, but did not impede his motion as he fell into them, knocking Jenny and her captor to the ground.

The move accomplished the desired effect. Jenny was pinned, but the small man was separated from her, leaving him clear to take out. He attempted to right himself, drawing his weapon around for another shot. With one swift motion, Seven slid her knife from its holster and launched it, imbedding the blade deep into the man's chest. He fell to his knees with a shocked expression on his face, before slumping lifeless in the dirt.

Only the adrenaline induced panting of the one fighter left standing broke the eerie silence in the room. She rushed to Jenny's side, freeing her from the heavy body sprawled over her. The woman seemed slightly dazed, but incredibly relieved as they hugged each other in silence. She pulled Jenny to her feet. "Are you all right, Pumpkin Head?"

"Sev." She panted, trying to catch the breath that was knocked from her. "Oh my god."

"I know. I know. It's okay, now. Everything's okay. I've got you."

"It happened so fast. I just froze."

"No no no. You did fine. Sorry I had to force you to duck." She smiled at the incredulous snort that came out of Jenny.

"Is that what you call having a body thrown on you?" She laughed nervously.

"Did I hurt you?" Seven checked her over for injuries.

"No. I think I landed on my pack. Your brownies are probably squashed to oblivion, though. How are you? Did you get hurt?" She looked Seven up and down, noticing a couple raw looking marks that would soon be bruises.

"No. I'm fine. All in a day's work. We better grab our stuff and get out of here though. These guys will be missed, and there'll be more to follow. We need to put as much distance as possible between them and us. Are you okay to go?"

"Yeah." Jenny brushed herself off and readjusted her pack as Seven removed her knife from the dead man and wiped the blade on his shirttail. Jenny pretended not to notice, but the simple, nonchalant maneuver turned her stomach slightly. Seven re-sheathed the blade and grabbed her rifle and pack from the floor. She attached the rifle to the pack and slung both over her shoulders, taking one last look around before nudging Jenny toward the door.

"I'm sure it's futile to ask, but any chance you'd consider taking one of these guys' guns with you for protection?"

"You're right. It's futile to ask. Anyway, why would I need a gun with you around?"

۞ ۞ ۞ ۞ ۞

Maria had watched from a distance as the man they called Daniel helped the Richards woman pack the last of their things into the van and leave. Now that the camp was deserted, she was free to roam from building to building at her leisure, touching things, destroying things, whatever was her pleasure. Technically, she could have done so before, but one must maintain appearances.

She was sure Raul would be upset with the departure of the do-gooders, but at the moment, that was not her primary concern. All would be forgiven once Reyes was dead and Raul had acquired his precious estate. Allowing the volunteers to place their camp on his land gave him an opportunity to present in a good light to the powers that be. Not that he needed it. Money usually did his talking for him, but it never hurt to have positive deeds to fall back on.

It was getting late in the afternoon. The men were still searching; a couple small new clues had been found outside the camp, but Maria remained frustrated. She knew the sniper was here. Tiny clues didn't mean anything to her anymore. She thought for sure she would have heard back from Miguel and his partner by now, but they must have hit a dead end with their trail.

What she was anticipating more than anything

was the forced return of the doctor. The departed volunteers couldn't have had more than a two-hour head start, so her men should be back any minute. She needed results. *Damn it.* She thought she had trained her staff better, but was beginning to wonder if perhaps she had overlooked some critical detail in their education.

No. They were just inept, like everybody else.

She would need to develop a new plan that played to their strengths, eliminating their obviously poor tracking ability. The sound of gravel crunching under truck tires reached her ears and her foul attitude dissipated immediately. *Finally, the doctor is mine.* She smiled and reached for the door handle of what was once Grace Richards' hut.

Maria walked briskly toward the truck, reveling in the fear she would soon see in those defiant eyes. Her man Ernesto jumped out of the driver's seat. She noticed immediately that instead of looking triumphant, he was the one who looked afraid. She planted her feet and waited for him to approach her, preferring to receive bad news on her own ground.

"We found the van, boss. She wasn't there."

Ernesto waited for his boss to blow her lid, but his statement was met with silence. He eventually worked up the nerve to raise his eyes from the ground to meet hers. Amber eyes flashed and bore into his, but still she said nothing. He shifted nervously from foot to foot, unsure of what to do next. Perhaps she was waiting for more information.

"We overcame the vehicle about two hours from La Paz. We ripped it up, forced them to talk, but we believe they were telling the truth. They said she had never been with them. They said the Richards woman asked them to pack up and leave early this morning, but didn't say why, just that they would meet them in the city."

One of the other men from the vehicle slowly approached Ernesto from behind carrying a small duffle bag. He nodded at his boss as he came within sight of her. "We found this amongst their things, miss." He opened the bag to reveal some running clothes, and other assorted items most probably belonging to the doctor.

Without so much as glancing at the duffle, Maria looked at the second man. "Your name?"

"Rene, miss."

"Rene, take the other men in the truck and torch this camp. I want nothing left standing."

"Yes, miss."

Ernesto thought she was handling the news surprisingly well. He turned, intent on lending his assistance to the others, hoping beyond hope he'd gotten a pass on this one.

"And Ernesto…" *Coño*. Ernesto turned back to face his boss.

Maria smoothly pulled her 9mm from its holster and shot him in the head. "…feed the worms."

The shocked stares of the other men followed her as she turned and made her way to the truck. "Rene." She called her new man over, now visibly shaking in fear of her. "Make a note and pass it to the other men. If I ask you do something, make sure it gets done, or don't bother coming back."

"Yes, miss."

≈≈≈≈

Seven had to admit, even under these dire circumstances, she couldn't recall ever feeling quite so at ease. Something about being around Jenny calmed her nerves. Her focus didn't seem to suffer for it either, which made it even stranger. The young woman chatted amiably as they trekked through the woods, about anything and everything. It was like a balm to her soul. Marcus used to drive her crazy when he chatted like this, but for some reason, with Jenny she enjoyed it.

She had always preferred solitude to active company, finding it easier to withdraw into her thoughts than force a conversation about something she wasn't necessarily interested in. Her mother once called her introverted, but in Seven's opinion, that was okay. She needed to be a loner to survive in the Marines anyway. Unreachable. So no harm done. With the re-introduction of Jenny in her life, she found a desire to come out of her shell. She wanted to talk, to hear the young woman's opinions about her theories and experiences. She was interested and wanted to hear all about who Jenny had become as well.

"Hey! Did you hear a word I said?" Jenny laughed and punched her friend playfully in the arm.

"Oh, sorry. Guess I drifted off there. Nice walking stick. Where'd you find that?"

"'Bout a half mile back. Just my size, don't you think? Nothing like having a solid walking stick when you're in the woods. Saved my ass from wiping out more than once, not to mention essential in the spider web-clearing department. You want me to find one for you?"

"Nah. I've got enough to carry. How you holdin' up, by the way? We've been making pretty good time."

"Good. I'm used to running a lot, and I haven't much lately. It feels good to be moving. How are you feeling? Any residual nausea or dizziness?"

"I'm all right. How'd it go with Takashi? We never got a chance to talk about it earlier."

"Exactly as planned. I think your instincts were dead-on. He fell right into everything we discussed as if it were scripted." Jenny relayed the entire conversation to Seven as they walked, reading the slip of paper she'd stashed in her pocket so as not to forget any details. The more she talked, the more her companion fumed.

"He's a dead man," Seven finally announced, looking off into the distance under angry, hooded eyes.

Jenny ignored the comment. "Does this mean we can contact them for a way out, since you know to avoid him?" The surprisingly innocent question brought a smile to Seven's face.

"Not yet. There's one other guy I need to be sure of before I can make my presence known. My boss, actually. He felt like a good guy to me, but you never know. He won't be as easy to figure out as Takashi was. Probably have to do a little recon and surveillance on him when we get home to see if he's dirty. Plenty of time to work that out later." Seven suddenly stopped in her tracks, her senses prickling, a taste of danger in the air. She held an arm out to stop Jenny's progress and squatted in her tracks, urging her companion to do the same.

Seven reached slowly back and removed her pack, quietly setting it on the ground in front of her. She noticed Jenny was wide-eyed and hardly breathing. She smiled to herself. She didn't mean to scare her, but silence was critical if they were going to enjoy this rare sight. With a quick precise motion borne of years practiced, she removed the scope from her rifle and flipped the protective cover open, bringing the attachment to her eye.

Smiling, Seven handed the scope to her friend and moved behind her. She nodded for her to hold the scope to her eye and positioned herself behind so she could see down the length of the device. Placing a supportive hand over Jenny's, she directed her line of sight to a low hanging tree branch some forty yards away.

After a moment of adjusting their position, Jenny gasped and jerked her head around to meet Seven's eyes, wide in wonderment, a massive smile gracing her lovely face. Seven couldn't help but feel a grin growing herself at the sheer joy and zest for life evident in Jenny's body language. Just ahead of them, on a low-slung branch, rested a majestic spotted jaguar with two adorable fuzzy cubs. They were snoozing in the late afternoon sun, the mother's massive legs hanging limply off a thick branch.

"Oh...my...God," Jenny whispered, quivering with excitement. Seven chuckled under her breath, happy to provide a pleasant distraction for a change, instead of blood and violence. "Can we stop for a minute so I can take a picture?" She pleaded quietly.

"If she cooperates." Seven released her hold on Jenny, instantly missing the contact, and backed quietly away so she could retrieve her camera from the backpack. She watched silently, admiring her effervescent demeanor as she set to work capturing the powerful animal in a still shot. *Focus. Click.* Jenny's innate cheerfulness couldn't help but seep to the surface, even under the most serious conditions. It made Seven admire her even more. For a brief moment, she forgot where she was and just felt happy.

Jenny tucked her camera back in her pack and hefted the bag in place, securing the plastic clasp at her waist before turning to face Seven. She threw a hug around her neck and planted a light kiss on her cheek, which earned her a brilliant smile. "Thank you. I have been hoping to see one of those since I got here and she totally exceeded my expectations. She is absolutely fantastic. I'm so glad you spotted her."

Seven was overjoyed at the gratitude, so pleased to have been the one to cause such happiness in her charming friend. "You're welcome. Now we better get going before she decides it's time to feed those cubs."

"You can say that again. Let's boogie." The pair headed away, trying their best not to disturb the furry family. Their silence eventually evolved to whispered talk, which in turn shifted to regular speech. "Seven, do you mind if I ask you a personal question?"

Uh oh. Step out of character and be nice, Sev. "Um. Sure? You saved my life, seen me naked, and given me a manicure. How bad could a question be?"

"I guess that would depend on how you feel about this particular question."

"Oh boy. Now you're scaring me."

Jenny grinned. "I was just wondering how you knew. Um, about you...I mean...I...um...what I mean is...god I sound like an idiot," she blurted, exasperated. "What I meant to ask was, how did you know you were gay? How old were you? Did something happen, or did you just wake up one morning and know?"

Ah, so Dan told her. She's still with me, so that's a good thing, I guess. "Well, let me see. I was sixteen when I figured it out. Every guy on the basketball team in my small town, South Carolina high school was trying to get me to go with them. I think they had some kind of bet or something going to see which one could get me first. I thought it was kind of funny initially. I figured with an entire team to choose from, eventually I'd meet someone I would be interested in."

She took a swig from her water bottle and continued. "It never happened. Then I joined the volleyball team and realized I had developed a crush of sorts on our young coach. She was married, unusual for a gym teacher, I know." Seven snickered at her joke. "She was about twenty-two or so. Nothing ever happened, but the attraction was enough to deliver the wake-up call. I found I was completely disinterested in the jocks hunting me down in school. It was a pretty easy realization."

"Dan told me his parents suspected when he was four. He didn't want to play with the other kids, because he didn't want to get his hands dirty."

Seven laughed. "Sometimes it's easier for guys. They seem to be much more aware of themselves that way."

"So how did you handle it? Seems like at the age you joined the military you would have been one big raging hormone. They don't exactly look kindly on that kind of behavior."

"No. They don't. I told my uncle of my intention to join and explained about me. It came down to choose either a personal life, or a career in the Corps. We both agreed it would be impossible for me to have both. I chose the Corps. He was the one who suggested I try to keep my head down overall. Not get involved too closely with men, either. There was a lot of bullshit that went on. I knew of this one girl in another platoon. I'm pretty sure she wasn't even gay. Some guy came on to her and she brushed him off. Next thing she knows, she's being drummed out for being a dyke. The guy lied as some kind of adolescent payback and just like that, her career was over before it even began."

"I can't believe that."

"Believe it. It's a government-sanctioned witch-hunt. They didn't even require proof. Just an accusation was enough. It woke me up to just how careful I needed to be, though. I lived with that hypocrisy for a long time, and ultimately it was the main reason I left. I was sick of living under a rock like some second-class citizen. I put my life on the line, just like everyone else. You get enough hateful thinking dumped on you, eventually you start to believe it. I don't believe it, and I never will. When I grew up, I realized I was looking for something more."

"Did anything like that ever happen to you?"

"Yeah. Actually it did. When I was young, nineteen or so. I got out of it though. I wouldn't have if it hadn't been for Marcus going to bat for me. I was lucky I had a friend willing to stand up."

"I find it hard to believe you went all that time without getting involved with anyone. You've never been in a relationship?"

This was getting uncomfortably personal for Seven. She never spoke of herself in this way to anyone, not Marcus, not her mom, nobody. She thought for a moment before answering, finally deciding that Jenny was probably the one person she actually was willing to talk to about it. "How about you? Tell me about this JC guy you were with. Dan mentioned him."

"Ha. That was a very not-so-clever attempt to change the subject. We're talking about you. But if you must, I will happily tell you all the sordid details of my failed relationships after my curiosity about you is fully satisfied."

"Jeez, Jenny. At the rate you're going that could take all month."

Jenny whacked her playfully. "Come on. Spill it."

"I've never been in a long-term relationship, no. You were definitely right about raging hormones, but I found a way to deal with it that wouldn't compromise my career. Every two-week leave period, I would go visit mom for a few days or a week, then travel somewhere far away from home for the rest of the following week. Toronto, Denver, Dallas, L.A., Vancouver, you get the picture. Didn't matter where really, as long as the city was big enough to have a club scene to get lost in. I'd check myself into a decent hotel, then go find someone to spend the week with."

The women came to the edge of a rock outcropping, standing on the ledge of a ten-foot drop. Seven tied their packs off and lowered them down, then climbed down herself and helped Jenny do the same. "The first time it was a little scary, but I knew what I wanted. Someone older, to show me how to be. It took me a few days to find a woman I was comfortable with, but eventually I did. I was in Montreal. She was in her late thirties. I was just nineteen. She understood I was young and just passing through. It was kind of great, actually, once I got over my initial awkwardness."

She helped Jenny reseat her pack. "After that I went to a new city every time. I never led anyone to believe I was going to be around for a relationship. In fact, I made sure they knew I wouldn't be. Some were fine with it, some weren't and left. Some would stick around for a night, some would stay with me all week. It was a shallow existence, but fun when I was younger. I could be whomever I wanted. Say whatever I wanted. Everything was a game to me."

"So what changed?"

"I did. I grew up, I guess. It stopped being enough. When I realized what I wanted was something solid, something to call home, I started looking for a way out." *What I wanted was someone like you.*

"Have you found it?"

"No. With all the training for this new job and everything going on, I haven't had time. Got my place in Alexandria I told you about, but that's as far as I've gotten to anchoring myself."

"Will you go back there, to that job, after everything that happened here?"

"I don't know. I have to wait and see how things play out. I must admit I'm a little disenchanted with everything right now. I may want to get out of government work all together. Do something different. I have no idea what, though. Sneaking around in the woods is pretty much all I'm qualified for."

"Oh, I don't know." Jenny smirked. "You may consider a career as a professional wrestler. I saw how you threw that big guy around."

Seven laughed and took a turn at whacking Jenny playfully in the ribs. "Okay, your turn. Tell me about JC."

"Urg. Must I?" Jenny made a face that got them both chuckling again. "Well, there's not much to tell, but know this...a drunken party does not the foundation for a successful relationship make," she said. "In other words, valuable lesson learned...never get bombed with co-workers, because what seems like a great idea when drunk rarely turns out to be one when sober."

"Wise words, to be sure."

"Other than being a little on the controlling side, he was a decent guy though. It seems like I'm always telling them the problems are with me when I drop them." Jenny was suddenly serious. "Every relationship I've been in, it's like I get bored so easily. They start off mediocre and rapidly descend to bad. Why is that, do you think?" *Please make it easy on me and tell me what I want to hear.*

Seven smiled down at Jenny and dangled a comforting arm around her shoulder. *Is she trying to tell me something?* "You just haven't found the right person, yet, Jen. Don't worry so much about it. You're young. You've got so much going for you. The right one is out there. I promise."

"This girl I knew in college said I have to pretend to be what they want, to make it work. But I don't buy that. If I can't be myself, I'd rather be alone."

"Just be yourself, Jenny. If that's not good enough, then they don't deserve you." *I think you're absolutely perfect just the way you are.*

"Come on. We should probably pick up the pace a little. When we get a bit farther along, we're going to make you a ghillie suit so you can be invisible when I go check out the Reyes place. Or maybe I'll leave you with mine, and I'll just go in au naturale."

"Hey, Sev?"

"Yeah?"

"Sorry if I stuck my nose in where it doesn't belong. I appreciate you answering my questions. Helps me to think things through."

"Anytime." *Do I mean that? I actually do. Heh. Go figure.*

Chapter Sixteen

The atmosphere in Raul Argulla's study was cold despite the crackling fire in the hearth. The lights were dimmed as the man sat staring into the fireplace with a drink in one hand and a cigar in the other, the long ash threatening a drop to the plush carpet at any moment. Under normal circumstances, the low light and warm fire might be construed as romantic, but one look into the brooding eyes of the room's occupant would quickly dispel such notion.

Seething, he awaited the arrival of his employee and soon to be ex-lover. If she didn't pull a rabbit out of her hat, she may very well be his formerly alive employee and ex-lover. One day, maybe two he could understand. However, failure after failure and a mounting body count was unacceptable. He didn't care who she was…it was embarrassing. He wouldn't tolerate being embarrassed.

Even though he had his own agenda regarding Reyes, he resented being made to look inept in front of the man. He had insisted Maria take responsibility for the search, and her failure meant his failure in the eyes of his nemesis. It didn't matter that Reyes would soon be dead, and he would own his property. All that mattered right now was that Reyes was alive and blaming him for the botched search.

The soft click of the door latch followed by light footsteps over carpeting alerted him to her presence.

He silently watched the dancing flames, not standing to offer a drink as was his custom. The first words out of her mouth had better be good, he thought, or she wouldn't make it out of this room alive.

Maria didn't like to lose, but what she despised most was admitting it to the likes of Raul Argulla... or to anyone, for that matter. Groveling was not her strong suit. Raul was normally an easy man. She could read his mood shifts, and adjust her foreplay to turn him to her will. She could tell by his posture that tonight she would need to bring her "A" game. He was livid, and she was to blame.

She stood silently behind him for a moment, choosing her words carefully. Maria knew she couldn't do what she really wanted, which was stab him in the heart and leave. She decided on a tactic that would play to his ego. Something all men were susceptible to, no matter if they were street sweepers or presidents.

"Perhaps you should be your own Chief of Security, Raul. You would undoubtedly do a better job of it than I have done these last few days. I should have listened to you. My deepest apologies. If you can forgive my recent rash of ineptitude, I'd like for you to hear my new plan that guarantees our success within the next twenty-four to thirty-six hours."

Well, that's a new tactic, Raul thought. *Instead of having a tantrum, she's kissing my ass. That might have just saved your life, you murdering cunt.* "You should have figured out I was right two days ago, but you were blinded by your lust for the doctor. I'm considering having your things moved to the barn so you can sleep with the rest of the animals." Raul looked relaxed, but his senses were on high alert. Not many people could get away with insulting Maria

Velasquez in such a way and live to tell the tale. He was prepared to deal with her if she decided to strike.

"Come now, Raul. You hired me to do a job, and I intend to do it. What will any of this matter once Reyes is dead and you have what you're after? Then, if you are no longer happy with my services, you are, of course, free to release me."

Maria walked slowly around the sofa toward the mantel, making sure to brush his arm with her hip on the way by. She took her time getting there, knowing he would have difficulty resisting the urge to stare. She missed their usual dinner together, but took the time to dress anyway, slipping into a tight, shimmering golden gown that hugged every curve and detail of her curvaceous body. It matched her eyes perfectly, and together they practically sparkled with feline intensity. This was her sexiest dress. She knew he wouldn't be able to resist her in it.

She pretended to look at something on the mantle, giving him ample time to appreciate her bare back, stretched calves, and total lack of undergarments. She was willing to take his insults and his sex if it meant she would get what she wanted. It may be in her best interest to feign disinterest with the doctor now, as it was undoubtedly a sore spot with her employer.

She turned to face Raul, pretending an adjustment with her hem so she could bend and give him a good long look at her cleavage. She noticed with some satisfaction, even though he was still scowling, his other parts were beginning to betray his true feelings. She moved to his side, close enough for him to smell her subtle perfume, the shimmering fabric of her dress whispering ever so lightly against his pant leg. "May I?" She reached down and removed the drink from his hand, bringing it to her own lips.

"Why the hell should I trust you to finish this job?" He barked, angry at his body's betrayal. The sight of this dangerous and beautiful woman never failed to stand his manhood at attention. "How do I know you're not just using this situation to hunt for your little blonde? I think you couldn't care less about the sniper or what I want. Need I remind you, again, who you're working for?"

Maria leaned seductively over Raul to place his glass on the table. He used her weaker position to grab her roughly around the wrist and squeezed painfully, dragging her eyes down to meet his. His arousal may have betrayed his true emotion, but the intensity in Maria's eyes betrayed hers. She wanted him dead. He could feel it. She struggled half-heartedly for release, knowing for sure she had him now.

Her teasing didn't fool Raul, but that didn't mean he wasn't going to take advantage of it. The manic gleam in her fiery eyes aroused him even more. A slight smile at the corner of her mouth betrayed how much she was enjoying this little struggle of wills. They never broke eye contact as he stuffed his now unlit cigar in his mouth and used his free hand to undo his belt and ready himself. He released Maria's wrist, grabbing her around the throat with his free hand, and forced her slowly to her knees.

Maria pretended to struggle. Argulla growled deep in his throat, a warning that she had better comply, or else. She fought him a moment longer, not wanting to appear to give in too easily, before lowering her eyes and her head to his lap. She had won. Later, when he'd had enough, he would listen to her plan and allow her free reign to hunt the doctor.

❧❧❧❧

Seven shuffled around a large tree trunk, careful to avoid its bark, which was covered in massive two-inch thick thorns. The forest was so dense in some areas, it was like an imaginary world on another planet. Jenny had stopped a couple minutes before to snap pictures of an adorable squirrel monkey chattering at her as if they were old friends.

At that moment, their movement was slow and treacherous. It was dark and the forest thick, but they pushed through, wanting to make the most of their time when others probably wouldn't be following.

The moon was bright tonight, which was a big help when they hit a clearing. Seven could tell her companion was finally wearing out. For the first time that day, Jenny wasn't chatting. It was time for a rest, but that wasn't going to happen until they got out of this mess.

"Do you hear that?" Jenny asked, nodding in the direction they were heading.

"Mmhmm. Sounds like water. Must be a small river. I'm pretty sure we won't reach the big one I came down until tomorrow sometime. Maybe we can find a place to crash around there for a few hours. I don't know about you, but I'm ready for a break." She really didn't need one, but could tell Jenny did.

They trudged along, finally breaking through the thick patch and ending up in a small, moonlit glade. Even with just moonlight and shadows, Jenny could tell it was beautiful. A shallow stream ran through the middle of the glade, a small pool forming at one end before spilling back into the forest. There were some substantial looking rock formations on the other side, but it looked as though they could easily go around. It was a surprisingly lovely oasis in the middle of the woods.

"Rest here for a minute, Jen. I'm going to cruise the perimeter, and make sure there's nobody else lurking around out here but us monkeys. Be right back."

Jenny sat down and watched the moon light Seven's way as she ran across the open space, hopped a couple of boulders over the stream and disappeared into the forest.

Jenny was wiped out. People always accused her of boundless energy, but Seven looked like she just woke up. She didn't want to admit it to her friend, since she'd made such a big deal about tagging along, but they'd been going about twelve hours straight and she needed a break. She rolled her head around in circles, attempting to loosen muscles made sore from long hours carrying a pack.

A short while later she spied her friend walking back into the glade. Seven removed her pack and dropped it where she stood, crouching down and scanning the water's edge, surface, and surrounding area with her flashlight. Satisfied, she put the flashlight with the rest of her things and began removing her clothes. She waved Jenny over to join her.

Jenny picked up her things and headed to the other side, wincing as she stood at the stiffness in her back. It was quiet, so she knew her voice would carry. As she was heading for the boulders, she asked, "Seven, what on earth are you doing?"

"You mean before with the light? Or right now?" Off came the jacket and shirt.

"Both."

"I was looking to see if there were any crocs or gators in the water. They're easy to spot at night with a flashlight because the light makes their eyes glow red like little neon signs. They usually hang out on the bank, but sometimes they'll float with just their nostrils and eyeballs sticking out. Looks clear. I didn't see anything." She hopped on one foot and pulled a boot and sock off the other.

"And now, I'm taking off my clothes, because it so much better to swim without them on." The other boot and sock landed near the first set.

"Are you kidding me? It's damn cold out here, and I'm guessing that water is freezing too. You're actually planning to get in that?" She neared her friend, looking into the water apprehensively.

"Come on, chicken. Last one in 'sa rotten egg." Her pants joined her boots and socks.

"Oh no, no, no. I don't think so. There could be piranha or snakes or something in there."

Seven laughed like a kid skipping school. "Piranha are overrated in the scary department. It's gonna be great. Besides, don't you want to be clean? Get the grime off? You've put in a lot of miles since your last shower."

Jenny turned away as her friend peeled off her bra and underwear. Seven laughed again. "Nothin' you haven't seen before, Doctor MacKenzie. Anyway, I'm not bashful. Come on. I bet you anything the water is warmer than the air."

Jenny turned back to face her friend as she headed for the water's edge. *My god, she's a goddess.* Jenny looked bashfully at the ground, a blush creeping up her neck. She was sure Seven could sense the butterflies swarming her abdomen at the sight of her nude form bathed in moonlight.

Seven took the plunge, silently screaming at the freezing assault on her bare skin. "It's not bad... really," she lied. "Look at it this way. We're going to be sleeping close tonight 'cause it's cold, so do me a favor and bathe, would ya?"

She had a point. Jenny did want to avoid being smelly if she could. "You're just saying that to get me in that freezing water so you don't have to suffer alone."

She always was a smart kid. "You'll get used to it after a minute or two."

Jenny relented and started to pull off her boots as Seven chuckled in victory. Jenny paused just before removing her shirt, suddenly feeling exposed. "Turn around!" She commanded, blushing.

"Are you bashful?" Seven teased, laughing as she turned away.

"Hell yes. Are you kidding me? My face is hot pink right now. You just can't see 'cause it's dark."

"Didn't you ever have to take a shower in gym class with all the other girls?" She couldn't resist the opportunity to bait her young friend.

"No. I dressed in a bathroom stall." Both women giggled like schoolgirls at the thought.

"Okay. I promise I won't look." She crossed her fingers under the surface and snuck a glance over her shoulder as she heard her enter the water. She turned quickly back around so Jenny wouldn't see her mouth hanging open. *Holy freakin' abs, what a body! Jesus.* She had to close her eyes and shake the vision from her mind before Jenny spoke to her. She was afraid she might stutter if she didn't collect herself. *You are the complete package, my little friend. Everything a girl could ask for and so much more.*

"You are a shameless liar, Sev," Jenny complained, voice shaking from the chill.

Uh oh. Busted me lookin'. "I have no idea what you are talking about." She mustered her best innocent angel look.

"This water is freezing is what I'm talking about. Warmer than the air, my ass!" She floated over next to Seven and treaded water, teeth chattering. "And how the hell can you just float there like it's bathwater? You don't even look cold."

"I am a human furnace. Self-warming. If I stay in here long enough, the water will probably heat up."

She's right about that. She's definitely hot. Oh dear lord...where do these thoughts keep coming from? "You were right about getting the grime off, though. I'm sh..sh..sure I'll thank you for that later, w...when I get warm. Can we get out now?" Even in the cold water, Jenny could feel her face heat up as it suddenly occurred to her she was naked, floating mere inches from Seven...and finding it...thrilling.

"Sure. I'll stay in a little while longer so you can have some privacy." Seven turned around, thinking that technically Jenny didn't ask her not to look this time. *Stop that. Be good.*

An evil grin spread over Seven's face as she lowered herself into the water so only her eyes were above the surface. She turned silently to watch Jenny leave. *It's a good thing I'm already in cold water,* she thought, and smiled at her inner voyeur. She got a sense that Jenny had no idea how stunning she was. She seemed shy and embarrassed about herself, but in reality, she was an absolute knockout. Watching beads of water on Jenny's skin sparkle in the moonlight was enough to take her breath away. Seven committed the vision to her all-time memory bank before turning away. She called out, "So if you're Bashful, which one of the Seven Dwarfs does that make me?"

"Um...Dopey?"

"Don't do drugs."

"Was Lurch a Dwarf?" Jenny giggled at her own insulting 'tall' joke.

"Ha freakin' ha."

"Well, I'm pretty sure none of the Dwarves were six feet tall."

"Guess you'd fit right in then."

Jenny laughed at the banter. "Okay, you can come out now." She looked up, startled to see Seven already heading her way, dripping wet with an impish smile planted firmly on her face. Just like that, the blush was back. *Thank goodness for darkness.* She was caught staring for a long moment before she collected herself and looked away.

Seven's smile grew wider. *Guess I'm not the only one looking.* She dried her face and neck with a small hand towel before beginning the arduous process of pulling dry clothes over a wet body. "I found us a safe place to crash for a few hours over behind that outcropping if you're interested. Or we could push on."

Jenny zipped her jacket and pulled the collar up high for added warmth, still shivering visibly. "Sleep sounds good, actually. I think I could use a little recharging if that's okay with you."

"Absolutely. Gotta grab it while we can. No telling what tomorrow will bring." She tightened the laces on her boot, slung her pack over her shoulder, and headed in the direction of the forest. Along the way, she removed her knife from its sheath and cut a handful of low-slung branches from the trees as she walked. Jenny was curious about why, but assumed she'd find out eventually.

They arrived at the spot Seven had chosen and squatted as she aimed her light under a small rock outcrop about three feet off the ground and going back about double that distance. "It's a tight squeeze, but we'll both fit and I can cover the opening with branches for camouflage. Put on anything else warm you have, stuff your pack back there for a headrest, and crawl on back. I'll come in behind and arrange the branches for cover."

Jenny worked herself as far back into the tiny cave as she could, curling up into a fetal position trying to get warm. It was far from comfortable, but she was too exhausted to care. Seven rustled about for a few minutes, trying to arrange herself into a sleeping position before finally settling down with a deep sigh.

"Jenny, I can hear your teeth chattering from here. Roll over."

"S...sorry. Can't seem to warm up." She rolled over obediently, assuming Seven meant to dampen the noise by requesting she face the wall. Without warning, a strong arm curled around her waist and pulled her back into the curve of a warm body, covering them both with a blanket commandeered from the clinic. One arm slid under her head in a makeshift pillow, the other was around her waist, and knees were tucked behind her legs, instantly nestling her from head to toe in a full-length body heater.

Initially shocked at the abrupt turn of events, Jenny was at a temporary loss for words. A moment of awkward shyness passed. The constant chattering of her teeth slowly subsided as she relaxed into the physical warmth of Seven's embrace. It was more than just warm here, she thought, it felt like a good fit. Comfortable. "Thank you. You were right, you are a furnace. I feel much warmer already."

Seven was thinking their bodies fit together like two pieces of the same puzzle. "Jenny, can I ask you a question?" Her eyes started to drift closed.

"Mmhm."

"Do you ever write stories anymore? I always liked your stories."

Warm breath caressed the back of Jenny's neck, sending a shiver up her spine that had nothing to do with being cold. "I don't really write them down much anymore. Mostly I just think them up in my head when my mind is drifting." She yawned.

"I never told you this, but that story you wrote for me about my dad...I still have it. I never told you how much I appreciated it and what it did for me. I had all this sadness pent up inside, but your story did something. Helped me to let it out. I'm not sure how or why, but in a way I think you saved me back then, too."

Jenny didn't respond, but instead took hold of the hand wrapped around her waist, giving it an affectionate squeeze.

"Maybe you could write some of your new ones down for me sometime."

A sleepy grin went unseen in the darkness. "Sure."

❧ ❧ ❧ ❧

Maria handed Raul an icy drink to cool his forehead as he lay panting and spent on the plush carpet of his den. The fire had burned down to nothing but glowing embers, much like his temper. He was thinking that this woman was surely gifted in the art of fucking. Every time he thought he'd done it all, and seen it all, she would find a way to push him to new levels of ecstasy.

She stretched, self-satisfied, back into her golden dress and walked to the bar, retrieving a moist towel. Returning to the side of her employer, she placed the towel on a slightly bleeding wound in his leg, ruptured by the heel of the gold stiletto shoes she bought especially to go with the dress. She glanced over to see a matching wound on the other side as well. Some men liked it when she used her heels like spurs when she rode them. Raul didn't seem to notice the wounds at all. She lit a cigarette and stuck it between his lips before taking a seat on the couch.

"Would you like to hear my revised plan regarding our slippery friends?" Maria interpreted his lack of response to mean she should continue.

"We have determined the doctor and the sniper are traveling together, heading for Reyes' estate. This plays right into our hands. I have no idea why the doctor is with her, but it is of no concern. It will be to our advantage in the end. If we fail to find and kill them before they reach the estate, then the doctor will be the key to capturing and/or killing the sniper once they are in the vicinity, thereby succeeding in our set up of the Reyes massacre." She paused to take a sip of her drink. Raul remained silent, still lying completely naked and limp on the floor.

"Tonight I will go to Reyes, enlisting the use of

his force along with ours, and suggest the use of his helicopter as well. I will make sure he understands the sniper is heading back in his direction to motivate him properly. All the men, about fifty total, will be dropped at the crossing that intersects his estate with the direction the sniper is coming from, and fan them out to specific areas. We will swarm the forest with bodies. I will have detailed records of which pairs go to which coordinates. They will report back to me every two hours. I will be able to track the sniper's location and movement by which pairs of men do not report back. I have no doubt her superior skill will best them, though it's possible one of the teams will get lucky. Either way, we get what we want."

"And what if Reyes' men get to them first?" Raul flicked his cigarette butt toward the fireplace without looking.

"I will be waiting at the rendezvous point to pick them up, at which point I will kill the men and take the sniper's body for our plan. This is the primary objective. I believe we have the greatest chance of success capturing her in the forest with this many men. But I have a backup plan in case we don't."

"Reyes is no fool. What makes you think he's going to roll over and let you take charge? You failed in your attempt so far. Why would he trust you to succeed now, when it's even more important?"

"In his mind it wasn't me who failed. It was you. I will ingratiate myself to him. Play to his ego. Explain that I am not happy in my employ with you, and my hands were tied. He will buy into anything bad I have to say about you because he wants to believe it. He doesn't need to trust me. He just needs to accept that I'm the best person to organize the final hunt."

Maria rose from her position on the couch and strolled to the bar, refilling her drink. She brought a fresh one for Raul, before reseating herself. Raul finally stood, lit another cigarette, and pulled on his pants, squinting his eyes to the smoke curling off the freshly lit tobacco held between his lips. "I will convince Reyes the sniper is returning to kill him, though I don't believe that is her true intention. He will probably want to run, but I will make him understand he is better off hiding deep within his hacienda, well protected by all of us. Then when it is time, I will kill him myself."

"Why do you think she's not going back to kill Reyes? If she is, we should just let her and be done with it. Then we really wouldn't be involved but our goal is still accomplished."

"I believe she will assume Reyes has fled after the attempt on his life. And frankly, if there wasn't something else going on, he should have. But he is afraid of something else. Something more than whomever this woman represents. He is trying to squash this attempt personally and quietly for a reason. In my opinion, she is returning to make sure her teammates do not require rescue. She either wants to save them, or erase them. I will give her what she wants by instructing Reyes' men to recover and burn the bodies somewhere she is sure to find them, thereby lulling her into a false sense of security. If she even gets that far."

"What makes you think she won't slip in and back out undetected? She has managed quite nicely to elude everyone so far."

"That's where my back up plan comes into play. If the men don't get them in the forest, we will pick up the doctor when the sniper leaves her to search for her people." Maria secretly hoped this was how it went. She longed to possess the tenacious do-gooder. "With the doctor in our possession, the sniper will come to us. With Reyes' men all out searching, the hacienda will be emptied of most of his security, making it much easier for us to kill him and the remaining staff, and set up the scene to suit our purpose."

"What makes you think the sniper will part from the doctor?"

"She is a hunter. She will need to hunt alone, without the burden of watching out for another person. She will leave her. I am certain of it."

"And what is my role in all of this?"

"Oh, your role is critical, my dear Raul. Our original plan called for Manny Reyes to be attacked but left alive at the scene. I believe now, that with all the action and manipulations required at the hacienda, Manny should not be there at all. You will entice him to come here, where you will ply him to his heart's content with women, drugs, whatever you deem necessary to make sure that when he wakes in the morning, he will think he had the time of his life. Of course, everything will change when he returns home, but by then our men will be long gone, the sniper's body will be planted, and you will be beyond suspicion."

"The success of this entire scenario depends on your ability to convince Armando that you are the only one who can deliver the woman. If you fail, everything fails." Raul made eye contact with Maria and held her gaze. He wanted to make sure she understood failure was no longer an option. Her life now rode on her ability to succeed. Maria stared back, unintimidated by the non-verbal threat. "Fine. Go ahead with it. Do not fail me again, Maria. The time for games is over."

"I never play games."

֍֎֍֎

"You snore."

"I most certainly do *not* snore," Seven said. Both women laughed, their shoulders shaking with mirth.

"Mmhmm. Little tiny snorts. Such a cute tiny little sound coming from such a big, bad soldier. Sooo intimidating." Jenny laughed.

"Oh yeah, well, you fart in your sleep."

"I do not! That is just rude!" Jenny looked thunderstruck, her face immediately pinking up. Seven couldn't help but burst out laughing.

"Just kidding...just kidding...don't panic." Seven quickly ducked out of the way as Jenny took a playful swat at her. They continued to walk, the taller woman still chuckling as she went.

The friends woke several hours earlier, wanting to put some miles underfoot before daybreak. A slight blush crept up Seven's neck, as she thought back to how they woke. What started out as a completely plutonic spoon for the sake of warmth, at some point while she slept, turned into a tangle of arms and legs, her lying practically on top of the younger woman with her face buried deeply in Jenny's warm, sweet smelling neck. She was thankful Jenny was still sleeping, as she extracted herself from a potentially embarrassing position.

What she didn't know, was that Jenny was awake a half hour before, and went back to sleep with a smile on her face.

"Don't be surprised if we run into trouble today," Seven reminded Jenny. "I'm sure they realize where we're headed by now and are probably concentrating their efforts."

"Ya think? Seems like they'd be looking for a needle in a haystack to me. This forest is massive and dense. How could they possibly find us in here?" Jenny's naiveté made Seven smile.

Adorable. Look how she squints on one side when she smiles. That's so cute. "Trust me, it's possible. Just keep your eyes open and be ready to run, duck, whatever. Do we have any of those granola bars left?"

"Oh yeah. If there's one thing we have plenty of, it's granola bars. Sev, do you think there's any chance at all Ty is alive?"

"Realistically...no. But I have to know for sure. Those guys tried their hardest to kill us all that day. If they wanted us all dead, they would have no reason to keep him alive."

Seven ripped the wrapper off a chocolate chip granola bar and bit it in half, sighing in appreciation of the chocolate chips. The forest was lush and green in this particular spot. Seven pointed as she walked toward a pair of colorful parrots standing side-by-side on a distant branch. They had a close encounter with a snake about an hour before, which kept Jenny jumpy, sure now there would be one around every corner. Seven was thinking if they weren't in so much trouble, it would have made an excellent prank opportunity. She decided no snake jokes would be forthcoming, seeing as how a blood-curdling scream could possibly give away their position.

She tucked 'fear of snakes' away in her memory bank for future use and smiled wickedly to herself.

The sound of a bullet thunking into a nearby tree trunk reached their ears a split second before the crack of the gunpowder exploding. Seven spun around, taking Jenny to the ground and tucking her behind a cluster of undergrowth. "Jenny," Seven breathed heavily, collecting herself before the fight. She pointed in the opposite direction of the shooter. "I want you to run that way as fast as you can. Don't slow down, but try to be aware of your surroundings. Try to keep a big tree between where you are and me. Don't stop. I'll catch up with you. Keep low. Go!"

Like a rabbit avoiding a hunter, the young woman darted out from the greenery and bolted as fast as her muscular legs could carry her. Seven ditched her pack and ran in the opposite direction, closing the gap between herself and the shooter as quickly as she could. The gunman saw her coming, and for a moment looked like a deer caught in the headlights. He didn't seem to know whether to run, stand, or move toward the oncoming train. He decided too late. A fact he realized as two bullets smacked hard into his chest, dropping him to the ground.

Seven skidded to a stop and reversed her direction, running full speed after Jenny. It would be unwise for Reyes' men to travel in the forest alone, so she strongly suspected there was another man in the vicinity.

Jenny had only run about seventy-five yards when a mostly toothless and particularly rank smelling goon jumped out from behind a tree and grabbed her. Her momentum caused her to slam into a nearby tree before she fell. Dazed by the blow, she became alert just as the man removed a gun from the back of his pants and swung his arm around toward her. From her position on the ground, she kicked out and nailed him in the forearm, sending his weapon to the dirt.

With a growl and a toothless grimace, he leapt on her, pinning her to the ground and reaching to wrap his hands around her throat. Jenny bucked and struggled with all her might to throw him before she willed herself to calm down and think. Her Tae-Kwon-Do classes kicked in and with a couple decisive moves, she found herself on top and pushing herself up and off the disgusting man. He jumped to his feet and charged her once more. His crotch met her foot and as he doubled over, his nose met her knee, the final blow knocking him bleeding and unconscious to the ground.

Seven ran up to the scene in a crouched, combat position, aiming her 9mm at the unconscious man's chest. She placed herself between him and Jenny before kicking his weapon far out of reach. Her fierce expression left no doubt that she was prepared to kill. Jenny could see in an instant how others could be intimidated. She was like a whole other person when her fighting gene kicked in.

Seven shoved the man with her boot to see if he'd come to. When he didn't, she backed herself and Jenny to a safe distance and asked her friend if she was okay, her gun sight never leaving his body. Jenny placed a comforting hand on her shoulder and assured her friend she was fine. "Good job, by the way. You kicked that guy's ass." Though still serious, she flashed a brief smile at Jenny. "You're one tough little cookie, Doc. I am impressed. Sorry I didn't get here sooner."

"What are we going to do with him, Sev?" Now that the guy was down, it didn't seem right to hurt him further.

"Jen, I know what you're going to say. I don't want to kill him either, but if I don't, he'll give our position away as soon as he comes to. It's too dangerous. We're miles away from any kind of civilization and have nowhere to hide."

"Can't we just tie him up or something? Leave him out here?"

"Do you think he'd be better off bound to a tree and helpless against the big cats and other meat hunters in these woods? This place is crawling with dangerous animals, insects, snakes, you name it. Seems to me that kind of suffering would be worse."

"Maybe we could take him and drop him near a road or something, if we come across one."

"No way, Jenny. I understand you're compassio..." Seven stopped mid-sentence as their captive came to. He looked around dazed, and wiped blood from his nose with the back of his hand and looked at it. The goon glanced up at the pair and slowly rose to his feet, mumbling curses under his breath. The blood ran into his mouth, covering his few teeth with red, making for a gruesome site as he growled menacingly at them and began shuffling backward toward his gun.

Seven growled back. "Don't even think about moving, asshole. Stop. Alto."

The man continued to slowly inch backward and shouted at them. "*Pinche puta. Ojala qu mueral. Vete a la chingada. ¡Puta!*" He dove for the ground and rolled, attempting to retrieve the weapon and come around for a shot.

Seven's sight never left the man as she squeezed the trigger and stopped him in his tracks. She moved to his side, picking up his gun and flinging it deep into the woods. Jenny came over and check for a pulse. "Fool. What did he think he was doing, anyway? You had your gun pointed right at him and he acted like you weren't even there."

Seven holstered her weapon and turned to Jenny, about to suggest they move on. She indicated the direction they should go with a nod. "Sev, what was that guy saying to me, anyway?"

"You really want to know?"

"Yes. Seemed like he really meant it whatever it was. I mean...if he knew they were his last words, I would hope they would be worth knowing."

Seven buried a chuckle under her hand. "Okay, I'll tell you. He said something along the lines of 'you like to have sex and take money for it...he hopes you meet an untimely end...and he suggested you should consider having intercourse with yourself."

There was a long silence while Seven tried her hardest not to laugh.

"Verrry funny. Something tells me he didn't say it quite like that."

"Nope."

"Jeez. I hate to speak ill of the dead, but what a moron."

"Yep. Just the way I like 'em...ruthless and toothless."

⚜ ⚜ ⚜ ⚜

The pair reached the white water river around noon, taking a small break on the bank while they decided the best way to cross. Seven thought she should go first, taking the rope, then Jenny should follow after she got across and secured the line. Jenny thought they should secure the line first, then go over together so they could help each other through the rough parts.

Each had valid points, but in the end, Seven won out. Her logic that they wouldn't be able to take the rope with them otherwise was the deciding factor. After one end of the line was secure, the older woman tied the other end around her waist and prepared to find a safe path across. The near side would be the easiest to negotiate, large boulders scattered generously, making the traverse more about hopping than wading or swimming.

Seven had just started her journey, hopping as gracefully as possible from one rock to the next when a sound on the wind caught her ear. The raging water was very loud. She thought for a moment it was a figment of her imagination when she saw what caused the sound off in the distance, and heading their way: Reyes' big blue Sikorsky executive helicopter.

"Shit!" She waved frantically at Jenny to head into the cover of the woods as she hopped back the way she'd come as quickly as her feet would move. The chopper was crisscrossing back and forth over the river. Seven just managed to dive headfirst behind some tall brush when the powerful rotors blasted the treetops overhead into a sea of dancing greenery. She was close enough to see the pilot and the passenger as they searched the surrounding open space for their prey. She motioned for Jenny to remain very still; any movement at this close range would surely draw their focus.

Once the chopper had traveled a little further upstream, the pair relaxed and nodded in silent understanding, acknowledging their successful brush with another close call. Seven whipped the pack off her back and began to unfasten her rifle. Her hands flew over the weapon with a confidence gained from years of practice. She attached the scope, adjusted the bi-pod, and slammed the magazine holding the long distance .300 Winchester magnum cartridges home.

Seven's professional, no-nonsense actions fascinated Jenny. Watching this was like watching her fight. Something about seeing her shift seamlessly into this other persona was electrifying. "Sev...um...hate to bother you, but what are you doing exactly?"

"Just a little target practice," she said, nonchalantly. She lifted the heavy rifle and placed the bi-pod on a nearby boulder, kneeling behind the scope and flipping the protective cap up. The chopper was getting further and further away, but the slow, steady pace and occasional hovering suited her needs just fine.

"Are you going to shoot those men?"

"Nope."

"Then what are you going to shoot?"

"I'm going to shoot down Reyes' multi-million dollar toy, is what." Seven took aim, making adjustments for wind speed and distance, taking into account the target was moving.

"But won't you kill those guys?"

"Depends."

Jenny was getting frustrated. "On what?"

"On how good a pilot he's got."

"So, you're saying..."

"Jenny! This isn't the best time to be having a conversation. I need to take this shot before he's out of range."

"Why?"

"Because having eyes in the sky will be a very real and very serious hindrance to us, and because it'll really piss that pig Reyes off. Now, if you don't mind...shhh."

"So if I tickle you behind the ear right now, that wouldn't be good, right?"

With that, Seven completely lost her focus and turned to Jenny, sighing heavily in frustration. She couldn't help but smile at the stubborn look staring back at her. "Jenny, I wouldn't tell you how to remove a spleen, or that you shouldn't. This is a covert op, and for some strange reason that eludes me, you're here by choice. I'm something of an expert in these matters, so if I say the chopper's gotta go, can you please trust my judgment?"

"You get a cute a little crinkle right between your eyes when you're frustrated." Jenny chuckled to herself at Seven's astounded expression. "You're right, I'm being an ass. I was just hoping you wouldn't shoot them if you didn't have to. Please...by all means... carry on."

"If I didn't have to, I wouldn't. It's too big of a threat to have in the sky." She figured Jenny was trying to stall her, thinking the bird would be out of range soon.

Seven went back to lining up the shot, re-adjusting the dials to accommodate the new distance. She breathed slowly to calm her heart and pressed her eye a little tighter to the scope. She held her breath, depressing her index finger slightly on the trigger waiting for just the right line up. *Three...two...*

"So if you're not going to shoot the pilot, what are you going to shoot?"

Seven let out her held breath. "One good shot

to the rotor system will drop it like a moth in a bug zapper. And don't bother trying to distract me. It's not going to work. I know what you're up to, trickster, but I could pick you up, toss you in the river, and still have time to come back and make the shot. So don't waste your breath."

"Won't other people in the area hear your rifle?" One last-ditch effort.

"Built in sound suppressor. Something I wish I had for you at the moment."

"Very funny." Jenny smirked, thinking the chopper was way too far away to hit now.

Seven made a couple new adjustments and lined up the shot again. Taking a deep breath, she held and waited for the perfect moment. She was determined not to let Jenny distract her again. *Three...two...one... fire.* The rifle kicked slightly and was followed almost immediately by a loud *ping* off in the distance. Seven stood and began to disassemble her rifle before the helicopter showed any signs of fading from its position in the sky.

Jenny stood silent for the first time in hours, her mouth hanging open in amazement as she watched the bird's rotor seize, and the craft arch toward the canopy of trees in what seemed like slow motion. A crash of breaking branches and a tremendous thud could easily be heard over the volume of the nearby rapids.

Seven didn't bother to watch, but packed up her things, knowing the feel of a successful shot when she took one. She saw Jenny in her peripheral vision alternating between staring at her, and staring at the hole in the sky where a helicopter used to be. "What?" She asked without turning around, feeling Jenny's eyes on her back.

"I…I…can't believe…you…how did…that thing must have been a mile away! And moving! How the hell did you do that?"

"Not quite a mile. You thought you stalled me long enough for them to get away, dincha?" She chuckled. There weren't very many civilians that ever got to see a scout sniper in action. If Seven hadn't been doing it herself for such a long time, she might be impressed too. "Come on, Jen. Click your jaw shut and let's move out. We still have about ten more rough miles to cover and there's no telling what's between them and us. The sooner we get out of this area, the better. Place'll probably be swarming with Reyes' people soon."

"But…but…"

Seven grabbed Jenny's pack and helped her into it. After securing her own pack, Seven headed back toward the river's edge, hopping up and over the big boulders with the energy of a billy goat. After a bit of tricky maneuvering and a good soaking up to the hips, she made it to the other side. Jenny undid the secured line and tied it around her waist, shimmying up the rocks and beginning her arduous journey across the treacherous rapids.

Jenny attempted to keep her mind off how scary this was as she scooched, hopped, waded, slipped, and prayed her way across the rough water. Her mind drifted to Seven, where she found a safe haven of thoughts that calmed and helped her to forget her fear for a little while. Her friend was on the opposite shore holding tightly to the rope, looking apprehensive, watching her almost fall a couple times. Seeing the caring and concern in Seven's expression, Jenny couldn't help but wonder if a life with Seven was what she'd been waiting for all along. *Maybe it was always meant to be.*

The emptiness she felt just a week ago was no longer there.

Jenny found as she became closer to Seven, the trepidation and reservations she expressed to Daniel seemed less and less serious, and the feelings she had about Seven and her own happiness became more important. She weighed the pros and cons of becoming involved with Seven, then chastised herself for always finding a way to slant almost every issue into the pros column. *Hell, Jenny. If that doesn't tell you what you really want, what will?* Her mind drifted to earlier that day when she woke up with Seven wrapped around her like a lover. At first, she felt disoriented and a little embarrassed, but that quickly turned to feelings of happiness, warmth, and security with a healthy dose of butterflies mixed in for good measure.

She reached the trickiest part of the traverse. She would have to slide slowly off the rocks into the rapids, try to find a secure foothold and get her balance before leaving the security of her dry perch. Seven moved as far out into the water as she dare go, wanting to be as close to Jenny as possible in case she fell.

Inch by inch Jenny worked her way toward the waiting arms of her patient companion.

Chapter Seventeen

I haven't really been around much. I mean… this job in Bolivia was my first chance to get away and see the world a little, ya know? For obvious reasons, it didn't really turn out like I thought it would." Jenny smiled in Seven's direction.

"Guess I kinda threw a wrench in the works, huh?"

"Don't you mean a wench?" Jenny laughed as Seven took a turn swatting her. "Hey, is it just me, or is this last leg taking longer than we planned?"

"It is taking longer. I changed our course a little. We turned south a ways back. I want to come toward Reyes from a different direction. I think by now they know where we're headed, so I don't want them to know from which direction we're coming."

"Okay, so back to your earlier question. My favorites are alternative, new wave, punk, but not so much the hard core stuff, classic rock, and last but not least '70s R&B. I know you like punk and new wave, because you used to make me listen the Clash and the Smiths all the time."

"And the Sex Pistols."

Jenny laughed. "And the Sex Pistols. Are you still into that kind of music?"

"Yep. Punk rock girl. Okay, here's another trivia question for ya. I'll recite a verse, and you tell me the singer and song title. Ready?"

"Go."

The pair played this new game back and forth for some time, wiling away the hours trudging through the forest. Seven was obviously the expert, but Jenny held her own.

Running out of easily accessible trivia, Seven jumped back to their previous discussion. "I'm not sure I understand the R&B thing. I never really listened to it. What is it you like about it?"

"Hmm. Well, it's passionate. And sexy. Mood altering, really. New wave is boppy and fun, but if you ever want to escape into another world, try a little Marvin Gaye, Ashford & Simpson, Luther Vandross. It's got a motion all its own." Jenny closed her eyes for a moment, remembering the music in her head and promptly tripped over a root, sending her flying into the woman in front. Seven caught and helped to right her.

"A motion all its own, huh? Does that motion include flying headfirst through the air?"

Jenny looked sheepish and chuckled. "Only if you're jumping onto a waterbed. Sorry. I'll play some for you when we get home. I think you'll like it."

"I'd like that."

"Did you keep playing guitar?"

"Yeah. When I can. I still have that old 6-string my dad gave me. I like to play. It relaxes me." Seven checked her GPS and made another adjustment to their direction.

"What do you do for fun when you're not on duty? Or working? Or whatever you call what you do now. Besides being an international bar-hopping chick magnet, that is."

"Um...well when I was still with the Corps, I

used to take a lot of advanced tactical courses. Special operations certifications and the like. I always enjoy doing that kind of stuff. The HALO course was a thrill and a half. That stands for High Altitude-Low Opening parachuting. You jump from so high, you need to breathe from oxygen bottles. It's a trip. That's how my team and I got into Bolivia. It's a great way for covert entry because radar can't pick up a flying body. You're practically invisible if you come in at night."

"That's insane. I suspected all along, but now I know for sure. You *are* crazy."

"Maybe you'll let me teach you how to parachute when we get home. I think you'd like it." Seven stepped to the side and paused for a second so Jenny could walk next to her. "You can't fool me. I know you're fearless. That kid that used to hurl herself bodily out of the swing is still in there."

The corners of Jenny's mouth twitched up into a grin. "Okay. What the heck. If you're with me, I'm sure it'll be safe. I guess it does kinda sound like fun."

"It is. I also like to cook, but since I've never really had a kitchen until recently, I've just started to learn. Do you like to cook?"

"I like to eat. Never had much time for cooking. I do appreciate a creative chef, though."

"Marcus used to always tease me. We were quite the pair. We'd be tucked in a hide in some backwoods country somewhere, stuck in the dirt for three days. To pass the time, I'd be flipping through a dog-eared copy of *Bon Appetit* and he'd be doing the same with his copy of *Better Homes and Gardens*. The other teams used to give us a never-ending amount of shit about it."

"You like to cook. I like to eat. A match made in

Heaven." Jenny laughed it off, but Seven caught her blushing a little at the unexpected innuendo.

"How 'bout you? What do you do for fun?"

"I liked to go running on the beach when I lived in Miami. It's really wide and the area farthest from the water is packed hard like a road. The water is beautiful, and great people watching too. You wouldn't believe how entertaining people can be just being themselves in a place like South Beach. It really brings out the crazy."

"So you like Miami? I got the impression the other day you didn't care about going back."

"I do like it. I love it, actually, but it's a hard place to live. There are a lot of contradictions there. The ocean is beautiful, the culture is fascinating, but the crime is unnaturally violent, the politicians are more corrupt than the criminals, the hurricanes need no explanation. It's like a little piece of Heaven *and* Hell on earth."

"So you're not going back?"

"I'm not sure what I'm going to do, Sev. I'm open to suggestion."

"That makes two of us."

Jenny halted her forward motion and turned to face her friend. "What does that mean? Have you decided not to go back to the DHS?"

"I don't know. I guess I'll wait and see how everything unfolds. I just know that what I want out of life now doesn't revolve around how I make a paycheck."

"What do you want out of life, Sev?"

Seven took a moment to contemplate her answer, not sure how personal she wanted to get. "I guess I want what my parents had before my Dad died. They loved each other, were bonded to each other. It's like they were two halves of a whole. I'm tired of separating myself from the world. It takes a lot of effort to be an island. I want to share myself with someone who wants what I have to give, and wants to give it back."

Seven had to stop for a moment and think about what she just said. She didn't think she'd ever thought about it, or verbalized it quite that way, but it seemed to come together for her now more than ever. That was what she wanted. "I guess it sounds simple, but when it comes right down to it, I want what everybody wants. To find someone that I'm excited to spend the rest of my life with." She blushed slightly at the admission.

They walked on in silence, each lost in thought. Jenny spoke first. "Guess you're not so tough after all, huh?" She smiled and poked her friend in the arm. Every single step seemed to bring her closer to Seven.

"Nah. It's all an act." They looked at each other and grinned in mutual understanding.

"Sev, you've done some amazing things in your life, but you're human. We all are. You saw something special in what your parents had and want the same. You'd be crazy not to. What you've done with your life so far is work, but now it's time for you to live. Don't be ashamed to admit it. I think you've separated yourself from the human race for so long in order to survive, you don't know how else to be. But you shouldn't worry. Who you really are will come back and eventually it will get easier for you to open up. To be you. To feel free."

"You see me, Jenny." Seven was somewhat amazed her young acquaintance could understand her so well, and wasn't afraid of what she saw. "Even when we were kids, you were the only person that ever seemed to really get me."

"I always felt the same way about you too, Sev. Maybe it has something to do with our 'psychic hotline.'" Jenny used air quotes to emphasize her joke about their connection with each other.

"Maybe." Seven slowed her pace as she checked their position on her GPS.

"Hold up here for a minute, Jen, it's time to get down to business." Seven squatted and pulled the ghillie suit from her pack. "We should be able to see the Hacienda just over that ridge up there." She handed Jenny the suit, and dropped her pack on the ground. "Put this on and make like a bush. I'm going to scout that ridge. Be right back."

Jenny squirmed into the suit, suddenly nervous, and squatted down to wait for Seven's return. She was pleased and a little surprised her friend opened up to her, confirming what she already believed. Seven was searching for something, just like she was.

"I think I was right about them all out looking for me." Jenny jumped, startled by the voice near her ear she never heard coming. "Sorry, didn't mean to sneak up on you," Seven said, sheepishly. "Grab your stuff, we're moving. I spotted a good place about another quarter mile around to the south where we can hide. There's good cover and I can get inside from there also."

Jenny hopped up and donned her pack once more. Seven had to do a double take at how outlandish Jenny looked in her way-too-big camouflage suit. *Cute.* "We're really close here, Jen, so from here on out you've got to be extremely careful, and very quiet. Don't speak unless necessary. Stay very close to me, move slowly, and keep low. We'll find a place to settle in and watch for a few hours before I make my move."

⁂

Raul listened in from the next room as Maria addressed a select few of her best men. So far, her plan had played out almost exactly as she had predicted. Two men went missing, and shortly after, along the same direct line, Reyes' helicopter was grounded. He smirked at the thought, imagining how bad it would sting to have lost something so valuable. Maria held up a map of the Reyes Hacienda.

"They are coming from this direction. I don't expect them to stay on this course, however, because they know we will be looking for them there." She pointed to ten different locations around the perimeter of the property. "I want one of you in each of these locations. Go slowly and be extremely careful. Make no mistake. This woman is a professional and if you are careless, she will have you before you even see it coming. Sweep the area. They will probably be dug in anywhere from twenty to one-hundred and fifty meters from the perimeter, but wherever they are will undoubtedly have a clear line of sight to the hacienda."

Maria stopped for a moment, taking a sip from a clear water bottle on a table nearby. "The first one to spot them, do not...I repeat...*do not* approach or attempt any heroics on your own. You are to retreat to a safe distance and contact me immediately. Do you understand?"

Several heads nodded in agreement. "I will come to you. I will deal with it myself. From your drop points, move in a counter-clockwise direction, sweeping as you go. When you reach the next drop point on the map, turn around and work your way back, altering your search pattern in case you missed something. You will all be contacted to meet back at the rally point after they're found. If you don't hear from us, keep searching. Don't stop until we have them."

Raul had heard enough. He turned away and walked to his desk, taking a seat in his comfortable leather chair and reaching for his humidor. He was expecting Manny to arrive sometime in the next couple of hours. The groundwork had been laid. A limo full of beautiful women was on its way in from La Paz, a couple of his favorite cars had been prepped for a little racing, and an excellent meal would be laid out for the young man. All this in addition to enough high-grade cocaine to keep a hundred people dancing and fucking twenty-four hours a day for a month, and Manny was guaranteed to have a night he'd never forget.

≈≈≈≈

The man she saw walking the hacienda perimeter looked like a basic security patrol, so Seven made a note of his position and shifted her scope to a new target. She reached up and snapped an irritating twig that was poking her in the left temple, then resumed her position behind the eyepiece.

She and Jenny were buried in a natural ditch, covered by branches and chunks of shrub, making them virtually invisible to the casual observer. She had been spying on the compound for some time now, noting the activity and movements of the occupants, trying to get a feel for the comings and goings of the staff and residents. About thirty minutes earlier, she watched as Armando Reyes himself escorted his son to a black Mercedes Benz that was parked near the front of the Hacienda. They were in the midst of a heated discussion when Armando turned and stormed back into his house. Seven couldn't believe the guy was still here after everything that had happened.

Jenny had been dutifully silent for hours and Seven could tell the restriction was driving her crazy. She noted on more than one occasion the young woman open her mouth to speak, then snap her jaws shut in frustration, mouthing a silent opinion to herself instead. Jenny didn't know it, but Seven was enjoying her own private joke. In reality, it was probably okay if they spoke in whispers, but Seven had a bet with herself on how long Jenny could hold out before she couldn't tolerate the silence anymore.

She glanced behind her and smirked, her shoulders shaking in silent laughter. That was the straw that broke the camel's back.

"What?" Jenny whispered, no longer able to contain herself. "What's so funny?"

This only increased her mirth as her shoulders now shook uncontrollably, a light wheezing joining the fray.

"You sound like Dick Dasterdly...or was it Mutley? What the hell is so funny?" She demanded as strongly as she could, while still maintaining her whisper.

"Sorry. Nothing. How you holdin' up? Need anything?" Seven did her best to get her grin under control. She was growing dangerously fond of this young woman. More and more she seemed to be fighting the urge to wrap her up in a big hug and hold her until she begged for mercy.

"So it's okay if I talk now?"

"Yeah." She snickered again. "Just keep it to a whisper like you're doing."

"Ya know...I get the distinct impression you're laughing at me, and not with me. Go ahead and tell me it's true so I can pay you back in kind when the opportunity presents itself." Jenny squinted her eyes in distrust, certain she was the butt of some unknown joke.

"Do you want to see what's going on? Scooch over here and take a look through my scope. Tell me what you can see."

Happy for something to do after hours of sitting still, Jenny willingly complied. "Hmm. Nice place. What am I looking for exactly?"

"Nothing in particular. Just tell me what you see."

"Classic Spanish architecture. Arches, red barrel tile roof, huge circular driveway, audacious water fountain, tiled balconies, multiple chimneys, stables, no longer needed landing pad for a helicopter..." This elicited a chuckle from Seven. "I can barely see the front doors. I see several smaller side doors; the one toward the back painted a rust color is probably the kitchen."

"What makes you say that?"

"The door itself and area around it looks more worn than the others, like a delivery receiving area. Plus there appear to be extra exhaust pipes near it."

"Good observation."

"There's a smaller cellar door near there too, a wine cellar maybe? I see a gardener working on flowers near the water fountain, the very edge of some other kind of building on the other side, and I count four other visible people outside and have seen a couple more pass by windows on the inside. You'd think if they knew we were coming they would have beefed up security or something. It looks a lot lighter than I would have expected it to be."

"I think so too. I'm sure they're all out looking for me, but if they are, why aren't more of them close to here? I can't help but wonder if something fishy is going on."

"I also see the corner of a swimming pool over in back there…looks like there's a very well-endowed and very attractive naked woman just climbing out."

Seven snorted a sip of water down the wrong pipe and coughed. She flipped over so she was facing the direction Jenny was looking. "Where? I didn't see any pool." Seven was focusing intently on the back of the house when she realized Jenny's shoulders were shaking silently, her face turning red with the effort to contain laughter.

A blush crept up Seven's face. "You are so gonna pay for that," she threatened, her eyes squinting with evil intent. "Sometime, somewhere, when you least expect it…look out."

"What? You can dish it out, but you can't take it?"

"Oh, I can dish it out all right. You'll find out soon enough just how big a plate you'll need."

"Ohh. I can hardly wait." Jenny clamped a hand over her own mouth. "I never realized how difficult it was to laugh without making noise," she whispered between gasps for air. Seven finally relented her evil glare and joined in.

"So what's the plan?" Jenny finally asked, having

exhausted her teasing.

"Wait till after dark and sneak in. You'll stay here like we talked about before. I'm going to start with those outbuildings on the other side of the property. Looks like a stable, garage, according to my earlier research the security dorm is over there too. It's a likely place for them to keep a live prisoner. If I don't have any luck there, I'll scout the perimeter and grounds for a burial site or something suspicious. If I still don't find anything, I'll head down into that cellar and check the house. If he's there, they're probably keeping him underground."

"What if they didn't bring the bodies back here?"

"They wouldn't have left them out there. This guy is going to want to cover his tracks. Make like we were never here. He would need to make sure the bodies were buried in a secure way or disposed of so there was no trace or sign for another team to find. Like on his property, for example. Out in the woods where we were attacked is just too risky."

"Sev, I want to apologize to you for before."

"What for?"

"For giving you a hard time about killing Reyes, the helicopter, everything. I want you to know I do understand it's what you do, your job. At first, I had a hard time coming to terms with it, but I don't think I fully understood the seriousness of the kind of life you live. This is some scary shit and you deal with people who want to kill you every day. I had no right to say the things I said."

"It's all right, Jenny. Not many civilians understand what any soldier's life is like on a daily basis. Most people can't imagine this existence. Like it or not, it's a necessary evil."

"In any case, I want you to know I think I understand better now. Do what you have to do, whatever it is. For our safety, the country's, I'm sure it's for the best."

Seven smiled. "I would have anyway, but thanks."

"What should I do while you're gone?"

"I'll leave you the scope and rifle so you can watch. I won't need them for what I'll be doing. I just want you to hang out here until I get back. I wouldn't worry, unless the sun comes up and I'm still not here."

"Oh, Jesus." A sudden wave of fear washed over Jenny as the thought of potential disaster gripped her gut. "Please, please be careful, Sev. I don't know what I'd do if anything happened to you. How would I even know?" A slight accent of panic was creeping into her voice.

Seven took her hands into her own and pulled the woman around to face her. "Don't be scared, Jen. And whatever you do, don't panic. No matter what. If you hear a gunfight, or I don't come back by sun up, you'll know something went wrong. Then you're going to need to get the hell out of here, and I mean fast. No. Don't say it. Listen..." Seven placed a finger over Jenny's lips to silence her protest. Looking deeply into concerned eyes, she couldn't resist taking the sad face into her hands, gently caressing Jenny's cheek with her thumb.

Jenny's determination crumbled and she slumped forward, her forehead a hair's distance from Seven's lips. Seven tilted her head slightly and placed a gentle and comforting kiss on her forehead, wrapping her arms around Jenny and pulling her into a reassuring hug. She wondered for the umpteenth time how incredible it would feel to kiss those soft, full lips.

"I'll be careful, Jenny. I promise. But if something happens, you've got to get yourself out. Stay off the roads. Work your way to the nearest village, which is about fifteen miles west of here, and take a bus or whatever kind of transportation you can find to either La Paz or south to Sucre. Fly out of Bolivia on the first available plane."

Jenny wrapped her arms around Seven's waist, taking immeasurable comfort from the temporary closeness. She sniffled and wiped away a tear, embarrassed by her show of weakness.

"Please promise me you will get out. I can't go in there and do what I have to do if I don't think you'll do what *you* have to do."

For the longest time Jenny said nothing. Seven held fast and did not intend to give up her position. Finally, Jenny nodded her agreement. "I promise." She wiped another tear from her cheek. Seven caught the one coming down the other side.

"Good. Now why don't you curl up with me for a little bit and we'll try to get some rest before it gets dark." Seven hunkered down into the ditch and put an arm around Jenny's shoulder, pulling her close. Neither slept as one thought chased another around the synapse racetrack of their minds.

For the first time in her life, Seven wished she had made a different choice at the age of eighteen and done something else with her future. Something that wouldn't have led her to a life that included dead friends and endangered loved ones. It took her fifteen years to learn enough about herself to figure out what she wanted out of life, and now that she knew, she ran the greatest risk of losing it all.

It was coming on strong. She recognized her

feelings for Jenny were growing fast and hard, unbelieving that something like this could happen under these extreme circumstances. She tried to focus on her upcoming task, but her mind continued to drift back to the woman, barely more than a girl, snuggled safely in her arms. She decided right then she would not allow herself to think of Jenny in a romantic way. It was too risky to give her heart to someone that hadn't yet figured out what they wanted from life. It was hard enough to be alone, but brokenhearted and alone was unbearable.

༄༅༄༅

Jenny hunkered down, enjoying the warmth and security of Seven's embrace. She refused to dwell on the possibility that this situation might go bad. The implications of what that would mean were too much for her to bear. Instead, she turned her thoughts toward defining the feeling she got whenever Seven smiled and laughed. She'd had a lot of friends, and done a lot of laughing, but this feeling was something entirely new. Many friends had touched her many times, but when Seven touched her, rational thought flew right out the window. Her cheeks turned pink, her brain scrambled, and the most inane and completely unexplainable things seemed to exit her mouth without permission. Jenny blushed just thinking about all the stupid things she'd said since they'd been together. Seven seemed to understand her every mood, her opinions, she 'got' her in a way no one else ever had.

God help me, I'm falling in love with her.

Separately but together, both women shared the same thought.

≈≈≈≈

A cloud bank slowly inched across the sky, blocking out the last of the setting sun. It was just before dark when Maria Velasquez took up position behind a large Jacaranda tree and leveled her binoculars in the direction indicated by her man, Rene.

"Okay, talk," she whispered.

"You see the cluster of rocks on top of that small ridge, there." He pointed in a northeasterly direction.

"Yes."

"Count three palm trees to the left of the rocks and about ten meters toward the Hacienda from there."

"Okay. Not seeing anything."

"Sweep the area. Look for a cluster of shrubs and branches that look unnaturally tight together."

"Ahhhh. Yessss. I see it." Upon closer inspection, Maria could just make out the barest hint of flesh tone under the canopy of branches. It appeared they were sleeping. Closely. *Hmm. Well that explains why the doctor left with her,* she thought, snickering silently to herself. If there was something between them, it only further ensured her plan would succeed. With that, the sniper would truly be invested in sacrificing herself to save her little whore.

She watched for several minutes as the couple slumbered in perceived peace, having no idea how close they were to danger. *I could kill them both so easily right now. But alas, I cannot!* Maria chuckled silently to herself, reveling in her imminent victory. *I would not want to rob myself of the memorable experience I will have with the young doctor.* She gloated to herself as she imagined the terror that would invade those arrogant eyes when the young American realized her fate at the end of a very sharp knife.

"Boss," Rene whispered, trying to draw her from her prolonged musing.

"Mm?"

"Should I collect the others so we can move in on them?"

Silence was his answer. Just as Rene was beginning to think she was deliberately ignoring him, he opened his mouth to ask again. She stopped him with a wave of her hand.

"No. I've got something else planned for them, Rene." Maria gave only a moment's thought to killing them both now. If she did, it would all be over. She immediately dismissed the notion, not having come all this way to complete her agenda without getting what she wanted out of the deal.

"Okay, boss."

"I will stay here and watch them. I want you to back away to a safe distance and contact the others. Have them meet you where you are, but don't come back up here. When I have what I need, I'll meet you."

Rene hesitated for a moment, not wanting to leave her alone with these obviously dangerous people who already killed Miguel, the strongest among them. He debated with himself, then decided to leave, fearing her wrath more than her death.

❧❧❧❧

"Sir, we're definitely on the right track. I don't think just anybody could have made a shot like this."

The Chairman sat in the comfortable leather

office chair at his home in the Maryland countryside. The weather outside had turned foul, the Chairman's only light coming from the green glow of his computer screen. He complained silently to himself about the gravely noise coming from his phone. Unfortunately, satellite technology just wasn't there yet, and he was lucky to understand every other word coming from his man in Bolivia. He decided to just listen and do his best filling in the blanks later. "Tell me what you've found so far."

"We traced the phone call made to the BFC to a cantina in a small town about one-hundred and eighty miles from La Paz. The owner there said an American doctor from a nearby Peace Corps camp would sometimes pay him to use his phone. We went to the camp, but it had been recently evacuated due to threats of violence from a local drug lord. My partner contacted the Peace Corps people in La Paz. One of them said the doctor, a woman by the name of Jenny MacKenzie, didn't come with them, but left another way. They speculated she was involved somehow with attempting to rescue someone this guy Raul Argulla was hunting. They also said she was being personally threatened by a woman named Maria Velasquez."

The Chairman didn't think the combination of a drug lord and a doctor sounded like it had anything at all to do with Team Epsilon, but he couldn't deny the possibility that it was the doctor who called the BFC. There was no such thing as coincidence. It seemed as if the two were unrelated, but the evidence couldn't be denied. Somehow, this group was tied to Reyes. "It sounds coincidental to me that our team would be operating in the same area as this drug lord and the missing doctor. Why do you think Michelis is involved?"

"We triangulated the location of the Camp with the sniper team's drop site and the Reyes Hacienda."

"And?"

"We began our search by cruising all the back roads we could find within that triangle. A short while ago we spotted smoke coming up through the forest canopy. It took us a while, but we hiked in from the road and found a helicopter, recently shot down. Pilot and passenger dead in the crash. Looks like a single shot to the rotor took the bird down. I don't imagine there are many out there capable of a shot like that, so it's got to be Michelis. I can't tell about the rest of her team, but that shot had to be hers. She's alive, sir. We think she is the person the doctor may have left with."

"Any idea on how or why Michelis could become involved with this drug lord? Or why this doctor would become involved with Michelis?"

"No sir, but right now our focus is on finding her and working out the details later."

"Keep tracking. Call me when you have more." The Chairman hung up his phone and reached over to the keyboard on his desk. He pulled up his priority clearance search engine encompassing all U.S. government, Interpol, and available international databases and keyed in the doctor's name. After a short while, he did the same for Raul Argulla and Maria Velasquez.

Chapter Eighteen

Seven spent a peaceful moment before the storm staring down at the sleeping face of her young friend. She thought briefly of Jenny's fate should something bad happen, and was flooded with an emotional need to protect her like a bear protecting a cub. She leaned over and pressed a tender kiss to her head, drawing in the scent of her hair, her skin, closing her eyes and letting her mind wander to what could be.

How could someone like this ever be interested in me? I'm such a lug. A social idiot. I wouldn't say two words a year if I weren't asked a direct question. I'm damaged goods, and she's so...so...opposite of me. I'm darkness and she's light. Don't even go there, Seven. She's too good for you.

It had been dark for some time now, and activity around the hacienda had slowed to a trickle. She thought if she was stealthy and fast, barring any run-ins, she should be able to search the outbuildings and grounds, and if necessary the hacienda in about three to four hours. If she found Ty alive, she would eliminate whoever held him and get him out of there on the spot. If she found a fresh grave, she'd dig it up. Finding no trace at all would be the worst scenario, because all this would be for nothing. If she found no trace, she would collect Jenny and get out of there. If it were just her, Seven would probably stick around for a few days, hide out, and raid at night until she found what evidence she needed. It was one thing to risk her own life, but to risk Jenny's unnecessarily was not an option.

She squeezed the young woman lightly on the shoulder. "Jen, wake up. Time for me to go."

Sleepy grumbling and a brief smile greeted her. "Oh. Gosh. I didn't realize I'd fallen asleep. What time is it?"

"Midnight."

Jenny was suddenly wide-awake as the words 'time for me to go' sank in, and she remembered where she was. She took a deep breath to calm herself. "Sev, I'm scared. Please be careful. I don't know what I'd do if something happened to you."

They held on to each other for several minutes, neither wanting to be the first to let go. "Just get away from here like we talked about, like you promised. Remember?" Jenny nodded her assent.

Seven rose to her knees and began arranging what she would take, keeping the weight and items to a bare minimum in favor of stealth and speed. "If you have to run, just grab your pack and go. Leave the rifle and my stuff here. You won't need any of it, anyway."

She moved the branches and shrubs away from overhead and popped effortlessly out of their ditch hideaway. Glancing back, she saw Jenny open her mouth to say something, then close it quickly, changing her mind. Jenny reached for her hand instead, and wordlessly placed a light kiss on her knuckles, giving her hand a final squeeze before settling back down into the ditch to wait.

"Be right back," Seven said, then turned and moved like a shadow through the night, disappearing from view in a matter of seconds.

Jenny shifted over to where Seven had left the rifle with the scope still open and facing the hacienda. She peeked through the lens, wondering if she would be able to see her friend in the distance as she moved from place to place. She didn't hold out much hope, knowing as she did it was Seven's job to be invisible. Just as the thought passed through her mind, she caught a flash of movement. A small smile crept onto her face as she witnessed Seven make a low dash from the cover of one copse of trees to the shadows of another, working her way stealthily around the forest's edge.

Seven controlled her breathing, getting her heart rate under control as she stood ghostly-still, allowing the air to settle around her. Only her eyes moved as she took in the immediate area. She held her position for several minutes to be sure no action was taken to defend against her intrusion. Once satisfied, she planned her route and headed in the direction of the stable, making quick work of the latch and slipping silently inside.

Like a deadly apparition, she glided down the long corridor using all of her considerable senses to direct her motion. She wedged into a shadow and breathed, listened, felt the space around her. Satisfied there were no guards, she checked each stall and room for any sign of human life or foul play. She discovered nothing, and snuck back into the night, moving from shadow to shadow toward the next building.

Jenny, having lost sight of Seven quite some time ago, settled down to wait. She was too nervous to sleep, so instead pondered the different scenarios that could happen and their outcome.

One scenario never crossed her mind.

A twig snapped mere inches from her head. She whipped around to the source of the sound and found herself staring into the barrel of a shining silver gun, held casually by a woman with a Cheshire grin.

⁂

Jenny woke up an undetermined amount of time later with the coppery taste of blood in her mouth. Her head, still hanging loosely, felt as though it had been bashed with a cinder block. Her brain throbbed as she let her eyes flutter open. She didn't raise her head, wanting to assess the situation before giving away her consciousness. The slightest movement forced an uncontrollable gasp from her mouth as pain shot through her shoulders and wrists as though they were being wrenched from her body.

Realizing the gasp would have given her away if there were anybody around, she lifted her head and gazed for the first time at her dire situation. She was in what looked like a large, underground cellar of some sort. The floor was dirt. There were large support pillars spaced evenly down the length of the room, and a few low watt light bulbs swinging unadorned from large wooden crossbeams overhead. There were some plastic wrapped bales of something stored off to one side stamped with the Reyes Estate logo, but for the most part the room appeared empty.

I must be under Reyes' house. Why would Maria have brought me here? I guess she was closer, or Argulla was closer to Reyes than we thought.

She was alone. She looked up, and down, getting a sense for the source of her extreme pain. Her wrists were handcuffed and hanging over a thick chain secured over a ceiling crossbeam. Her feet barely reached the ground, which put almost all of her body's weight on her shoulders. It was excruciating.

Her thoughts drifted to the woman who had captured her, and she was afraid. Try as she might, she could think of no way out of this situation. There wasn't even anyone around she could talk to, or try to convince to release her. What would happen when Seven found her missing? Would she assume Jenny had left, not able to handle the pressure of waiting?

She heard a small noise in the distance and strained her ears, trying to pick up the sound. That's when she heard a faint noise coming from behind her for the first time. Breathing. The dank and musky smell of the underground room slowly shifted, the scent of something feral and dangerous creeping into the mix.

Jenny tried hard to clamp down on a surge of fear as the something behind her stepped closer and sniffed her, breathing in deeply. It was Maria. She knew for sure now, sensing the same quivering, barely controlled energy flowing off the woman.

Maria glided silently around, looking her over from head to toe as she smiled to herself. Jenny knew she was crazy, but now saw something in her eyes so dark and unfeeling it took her breath away.

"I'm sure I'm going to regret asking this question...but what the fuck do you want from me?"

Maria's smile broadened. "Ahhh. Doctor. Defiant to the end, eh? Good. I would be disappointed otherwise."

"So this is the end, huh?"

"Mmm. Not quite. But you'll get there soon

enough. No need to rush things." Maria walked around behind her once more and leaned in to smell her hair. She ran a lazy hand down Jenny's back, sliding it over her behind, down her thigh and around to the front. The hand slid slowly up her abdomen, over a breast, her neck, and came to rest under her chin, lifting so their eyes met. "I think I may just enjoy you more than any of the others. So much life. Such a bright future for me to steal."

Maria reached down to her leg holster and removed her favorite skinning knife. She slid it slowly into Jenny's shirt between two buttons, letting the doctor feel the cold steel on her bare skin, never taking her eyes off her victim's face. The fear from earlier had unfortunately been replaced by a mask of calm. But no matter, it would return soon enough. She flicked the blade, sending a button flying, then another.

Soon her shirt lay open, hanging loosely from her raised arms. Jenny had never felt so exposed. Maria slid the flat of her blade up between her breasts and with a flick of her wrist, sliced through her sport bra, leaving it hanging open as well. The feel of Maria's touch as she ran her knuckles over her bare midriff sent shivers up her spine. It was, without a doubt, the creepiest, sickest thing she had ever felt in her life. No matter what, she would not give Maria the satisfaction of knowing the effect she was having on her.

"I'll have you, my dear doctor. But first, I will use you to get the sniper. Once she comes to me and is taken care of, you and I will leave this place and have our fun. You will be my reward for a job well done."

"You're way out of your league, Maria. You only think you'll win that fight."

Maria ignored the remark, but her nostrils

flared. "You are the key," Maria said. She lowered her head and took a long, slow sniff up Jenny's bare torso. "With you in my possession, she will come crawling. I have but to wait a little while, and she will be dead. My mission accomplished. I will finally be free to spend a leisurely amount of time on my personal hobby. Which, at the moment, is you."

"You haven't answered my question yet about why you are doing this. You don't even work for Reyes."

"No. I don't work for Señor Reyes. He does have something I intend to deliver to Señor Argulla, however. And that, my dear doctor, is his blood on my skillful hands. I am here for the simple purpose of killing him and placing the blame firmly on the shoulders of your sniper friend. Or is it lover?" Maria snickered into Jenny face as she roughly tweaked one of the doctor's breasts.

Jenny turned her head as far from the repulsive woman as she could, a look of disgust on her face. The motion caused her shoulders to scream in agony. She barely managed to stifle a cry, not wanting to give Maria the satisfaction.

Maria rested the tip of her knife just below Jenny's sternum. "He wants this land, and Reyes won't part with it. So Argulla found a way to get it, which absolves him of any foul play. They hate each other, you know. Reyes is such a fool, he enlisted our help to find the sniper, but thought us ignorant enough to buy his pathetic story of who she was. Of course, that just inflamed Raul's interest, and led him to pursue this action instead of just giving the man what he wanted. Perhaps if he had trusted us enough from the beginning, this would all be over now. I guess he'll never know."

Her eyes drifted to the ceiling as though she was looking through to a room upstairs, a wistful expression on her face. She was looking forward to the bloodbath she would soon perpetrate. "Which reminds me...not that it matters, really, but why is your lover trying to kill Señor Reyes? Raul and I have been unable to find out. What is her name? Whom does she work for?"

Jenny said nothing, but continued to stare off into the distance, praying silently for a miracle.

"No matter. My own personal motivation is different, however. What I get out of this little adventure is you. Raul will leave me alone while I take my time with you doing what I do best. Which, in case you haven't figured it out, involves me draining the life slowly from your arrogant green eyes. It's the closest thing I get to pleasure, and I love to be pleasured." Maria chuckled at her own comment. "You're going to give that to me. It is something I have desired since the moment you stuck your nose in my face. I knew then you would be mine, and now you are. Things tend to work in my favor."

Maria pressed the tip of the knife in slightly, drawing a tiny drop of blood. She watched the deep red fluid trickle out, her eyes glowing with anticipation.

Jenny closed her eyes at the sting of the blade and willed herself not to hyperventilate. The thought of being a victim of this butcher, of hanging helplessly while this woman cut her to pieces was, to say the least, unappealing. She found her mind wandering in crazy, fear induced directions. Hearing her mother's voice saying, 'I told you not to go to South America. Why can't you just take a train trip across Europe like everybody else?' Wondering what would happen with her student loans. Thinking how upset Dan would be. She didn't know what this woman had planned for her, but she hoped it didn't happen until after Seven entered the fray. At least then, she may have a chance.

Unexpectedly, Maria retracted the knife. She pinched the blade between her thumb and forefinger, sliding her fingers slowly to the tip, capturing the single drop of blood that stained the point. She massaged the blood between her fingers as though testing the viscosity, then brought it to her nose, inhaling deeply.

Jenny watched the sick ritual with trepidation. She knew this woman was nuts the first time she spoke to her, but she now feared even 'psycho' was not strong enough a word to describe the vibes Maria was giving off.

Maria wiped the blood and the blade on Jenny's shirt before placing the knife back into its holster. "Unfortunately for me, my fun will have to wait just a little bit longer. Anticipation makes everything so much sweeter, don't you think? Now, if you'll excuse me, doctor, I have some business to attend to upstairs."

☙☙☙☙

The group of six men stood unspeaking in an alcove, towering over the small woman who was testing the weight and balance of a very long and well-made sniper rifle. Maria removed the clips and held the scope to her eye, pulling the trigger to test the action on an empty chamber.

She smiled, liking the power and balance of the finely crafted German-made DSR-1, having a new respect for its owner. The scope was state-of-the-art and allowed her to see clearly far into the distance. It was unfortunate she wouldn't have time to try the rifle outside in the daylight. Built-in sound suppression would certainly come in handy. The power of it excited her, and she couldn't wait to feel this beast buck in her arms.

She wished she could test her might one on one against the sniper, but it wasn't meant to be.

Maria popped the clip back into place and slid the bolt back, chambering a round. Her nostrils flared at the sound of the bolt locking down, the thrilling anticipation of the coming attack was almost too much for her to bear.

She gathered the men closer, and dropped to a knee like a coach about to give one last pep talk. She reached into a pack near her feet and pulled out a handful of identically matching, six-inch bladed military knives. She handed them around to the men, taking the last for herself and sliding it into a leg pocket, next to her favorite blade.

"No guns unless absolutely necessary. If you find you must shoot someone to survive, go for one bullet in the head. Gunshots will alert the staff and cause trouble, so avoid them. I want you to cut their throats. Right handed, from left to right. It is important everyone appears to have been killed in the same way, by the same person. Also, don't strangle anybody. Do your best to sneak up from behind, a clean cut, and move onto the next. Is anybody here carrying anything other than a 9mm?" The men shook their heads. "Put on your gloves, and make damn sure every one of these knives gets brought back to me when we're done. You will all accompany me to where I have Reyes tucked away. Once I have killed him, you will spread out to your pre-assigned areas and search the entire place. Kill everybody you find. Not one single person must survive. Do you all understand?"

The men nodded, a couple of them shifting nervously from foot to foot. Rene was thinking it was one thing to defend Señor Argulla's property, or hunt this assassin, but unprovoked murder was something else entirely. It made him a little sick, but he wanted to prove himself worthy to the boss.

Maria checked her weapons once more, then signaled for the men to follow her. With stealth, they crept down a side corridor toward the center of the house where Señor Reyes kept a small, windowless office belonging to his head house servant.

≈\≈\≈\≈\

Armando Reyes was not a patient man. The previous evening when he'd met with Maria, she convinced him to wait in this small room while she made good on her promise. He was content to do so at the moment, because everything the woman predicted so far had happened exactly as she said. Reyes got over his initial distrust and dislike of Maria when she explained the reason they had been unsuccessful in capturing the sniper so far was that they thought her a simple thief, and greatly underestimated her abilities. She explained how upon discovering the woman's real purpose, her search plan had been adjusted accordingly, leading them back here.

It was all a lie, of course, but Reyes bought into it completely, fearing for his life once more. It was obvious Maria's skill and experience far outweighed that of his security force, so he decided to accept her.

She assured Armando the sniper was heading back for him, and he should remain safely out of sight while she led his men in her capture or death.

It was the middle of the night and he was tired and sick to death of being in this little room, but soon it would be over. He had no doubt. Argulla and his clever little killer seemed to have come in handy after all. The phone rang, startling him slightly in the quiet of the night. He snatched it angrily from its cradle.

"Yes?"

"Ah. Good evening, Señor Reyes. Sorry to call at such an ungodly hour. This is Raul Argulla speaking. I was calling to inquire as to the progression of our little venture?"

"You tell me. I would have thought your pit viper would have kept you better informed. She is here, somewhere, but I have not seen or heard from her in hours. She promised the matter would be ended before morning, so I can only assume something is being done."

"Yes, she assured me as well. She will deliver, you have my word." Argulla waited silently for a moment, wondering if this prig would thank him for the time and effort he dedicated to helping him, even though he lied. He smiled to himself, knowing full well the man wouldn't have the stones to suck it up and say it.

"Ah, here she is now," Reyes said into the phone. He stood as Maria entered the room holding the sniper rifle. "It's about time, Ms. Velasquez. I was beginning to wonder if you were going to make me wait here all night. Can I assume by the looks of that rifle that you've captured the sniper?"

"Yes, Señor Reyes." Her eyes were cold, but crinkled flesh around the edges hinted she was smiling at him somehow, even though her mouth didn't look it. "This is her weapon." She spoke clearly, so Raul could hear the conversation over the phone.

"Good. Good. So she is dead, then? Or did you capture her alive?" Reyes still held the phone, the call now forgotten as he waited for the good news.

Maria slowly raised the muzzle of the rifle until it was apparent to Reyes she was pointing it toward him on purpose. He was stunned, but realization dawned on him immediately why her expression was as cold as ice.

"Wha..."

The impact from the large caliber bullet at close range slammed into his chest, sending him forcefully backward over the office chair and into the cabinets behind. Maria thought the look on his face was priceless as she pumped the spent cartridge from the rifle and slammed another one into position. She looked dispassionately at the rifle's sound suppressor, thinking she missed the chaotic noise the shot would have made, but glad that a loud gunshot would not interfere with her future plans.

She walked to the desk and picked up the phone. Raul had wanted to hear the event as it unfolded. "Did you enjoy the show?"

"Describe it to me."

"He was...surprised, I think. The look on his face even now attests to that."

"Ha! Good. I enjoyed that. Thank you for my evening's entertainment, Maria. Now. Tell me what is happening over there."

With a signal, Maria waved her men off to carry out their duties. She returned to the phone. "We have the doctor; it's just a matter of time before the sniper comes for her. The men are moving through the house and outbuildings now, taking care of the rest of the staff. When she comes, they'll be waiting for her. Everything is going as scripted. How is young Manny faring?"

"Eh. As expected. Last time I looked in on him, he was being blown by one woman, snorting coke off the ass of another and had two more behind him waiting their turn. He'll be here all night."

"Good. To the hunt, then. See you in the morning." Maria dropped the phone and walked silently from the little office, looking for more fun to have.

⚜ ⚜ ⚜ ⚜

Several rooms away, the man known as Armando Reyes' head house servant tightened the string on his pajama bottoms and slung a cotton robe over his shoulders. He was a light sleeper, and was used to prowling the large hacienda's many halls in the wee hours of the morning. He sometimes would use the quiet of the night to make lists in his head of household chores needing to be addressed, or supplies he needed to stock up on. This night, an unusual noise woke him from his light slumber. The sound had filtered away by the time he was fully awake, but he could swear something crashed in the vicinity of his office.

He opened his bedroom door and stepped quietly into the hallway. As he turned down the hall, a motion flicked into his peripheral vision in tandem with a quick, cold, jerking feeling at his neck. It all happened so quickly. Startled, he opened his mouth to squawk, but no sound was forthcoming. Something warm and wet flowed freely down his chest. He reached for his neck as the first tinges of pain began to make themselves known. He looked over his shoulder to see a man he didn't recognize standing over him with a very large knife. Fear gripped him. The servant wavered for just an instant, staring intently into dark, brooding eyes, before he dropped to his knees and gasped desperately for air. Darkness came quickly as he continued his short journey to the floor, face first in a pool of his own blood.

Chapter Nineteen

Seven crouched in the cool, dark shadow of a low hung tree, unscrewing the lid of her water bottle and taking a well-deserved swig. She had scouted all the outbuildings, and was making good headway in her search of the grounds when she decided a short break was in order.

The night was cool and the sky, overcast. The conditions were perfect for what she was up to, Seven thought as she scanned left to right across the estate. Bright moonlight could put a real damper on stealthy outdoor activities.

She had easily skirted all contact with humans so far. Her closest run-in had been with a guard watching TV in a small six-bed dormitory by the garages. She had snuck in through a back door and checked the building thoroughly, right under the man's nose. As she was creeping out the same way she came in, he seemed to look into the darkness right at her. She stood breathless, sliding her knife from its sheath, preparing to kill him if he tried to sound an alarm.

It occurred to Seven the man couldn't see her standing there because his eyes were blinded to the darkness by the bright TV screen. She released her breath and smiled to herself before sneaking out the door, a mere instant before the guard reached over and flipped on the light switch. She scooted into the shadows and watched as he shrugged and went back to his game.

As she squatted under the tree reviewing her course and planning her next move, a light breeze kicked up and shifted directions a couple times, settling on a southeasterly course. She caught a whiff of something in the air that sent a chill to her very soul. The scent was faint and it had only been there for an instant, but it was a smell that once experienced was never forgotten.

It was the smell of battlefield death.

She caught the scent again. There was no mistaking the charred, almost sickly sweet smell of scorched corpses. A brief feeling of nausea swept through the woman as she considered the implications. Seven flashed back to the first time she had encountered this unpleasant aroma. She could've lived without that experience.

Her platoon was on patrol in northwestern Kuwait when she was just twenty years old. The Gulf War had been somewhat anti-climactic for the ground troops, most of the war being waged from the air. They were walking through the hot, empty desert toward a cluster of black specs they could see in the distance. When they reached the specs, it turned out they were Iraqi tanks destroyed by a bomb blast. The ground and equipment were burnt black, as were all the soldiers unfortunate enough to be in the vicinity. There was one soldier who was literally hanging out of a tank hatch, burned alive while trying to escape the inferno inside. The smell was atrocious.

The scent was gone now, but she was sure it wasn't her imagination. She screwed the cap back on her water bottle. Warily, she changed her search grid, now heading into the direction of the breeze. A half hour passed before she detected the smell again. Seven felt for sure she was getting closer to the source, as the stench was getting stronger by the minute. The closer she crept, the more dread she felt crawling through her belly at the prospect of what she might find.

She came upon the source a short while later. A large pit in the ground just behind the tree line had been dug on the northwestern edge of property. It appeared to contain the remains of at least one scorched body. The swirling ash, dark colored dirt, and low light made it impossible to tell.

There was no heat coming from the pit. Seven deduced this had been done sometime within the last week, making the timeframe right for the victims to be either Marcus or both of her men. She had to be certain. With swift, sure movements, the woman snatched a bandana from her coat pocket and wrapped it around her face to keep from breathing in the ashes. She grabbed a sturdy stick from the forest floor in one hand, a flashlight in the other, and dropped herself into the grave.

She planted the stick firmly in the pile and began to drag it through, turning up pieces of bone and the occasional chunk of fabric too black to be identifiable. She bit down on the small flashlight so she could dig with two hands, and as she turned her head to the side, a glint of something shiny caught her eye. After a couple minutes of searching, she found the object that had captured her attention.

Kneeling heavily in the bottom of the pit, Seven lifted Marcus' engagement ring into the beam of her light. She rubbed the grime off with her thumb as tears began to flow freely, soaking the bandana under her eyes. She knew he was dead. She had seen it happen.

But kneeling here, so close to his remains, holding what was to be his future in her hands brought her to grief like she had not known since the death of her father. This man was the brother she never had.

Seven wasn't sure how much time had passed when she finally ran out of tears. She zipped the ring into a secure pocket and continued to search through the fresh grave. Eventually she uncovered enough evidence to confirm that indeed, both of her teammates were dead. The proof in the form of partially burned boots gave it away. When she found the third boot, there was no longer any doubt.

Dejected, Seven climbed from the pit and sat heavily a few yards away. She needed to clear her head, and get herself back under control. She never really got to know Ty very well, but he was a brave soldier, just like Marcus. He took a bullet aimed for her. She grieved his loss and vowed their friends and families would know what heroes they both were.

A fury was simmering under her skin that wanted release. As she sat thinking, an obvious target came to mind. She told Jenny she would return as soon as she found the evidence so they could make their escape. Jenny didn't want her to go after Reyes, but on the other hand, she also understood Seven would do what she had to. She now felt, without a doubt, finishing Reyes was what she had to do.

A niggling thought in the recesses of her mind told her this was no longer about duty but revenge, just as Jenny had suspected. Seven didn't care. Her temper and grief was roiling and needed to be satisfied. She could not just walk away. *I'm sorry, Jenny. I'll be back soon.*

With that, the warrior resigned herself to a

healthy dose of future regret about this kill, but shrugged it off, prepared to deal with it later. She did not intend to look Marcus' fiancé in the eye and tell her she let the man who killed him go. This was justice that required no court of law.

Her decision made, she darted from shadow to shadow, creeping steadily toward the hacienda. She would kill Armando Reyes after all.

⚜⚜⚜⚜

Jenny said the maroon colored door was the kitchen door. That seemed like as good a place to start as any. She made quick work of the lock and crept silently through a large walk-through pantry and into a spacious kitchen. The woman hovered silently, listening in all directions for any hint of movement. The house was quiet.

It seemed strange actually, as though something was off kilter. She had the feeling several times already this night was playing out in a way that just didn't fit. If Reyes knew his life was in extreme danger, which it was, where was his security? Why wasn't this place crawling with guards? For that matter, why was Reyes even here? Seven thought if she had the U.S. Government after her, she sure as hell wouldn't be sticking around in one place.

Her research of Reyes and his home told her he kept a minimum of six to ten security guards working around the clock, as well as cooks, maids, gardeners, stable hands, mechanics, every type of personnel required to efficiently run an estate of this size. Even more if he was in residence. So, where the hell was everybody?

She crept the length of the kitchen, listening to the silence all the while. She knew from her research Reyes' bedroom was on the second floor. According the architectural plans, there was a servant's staircase on this side of the house she could use to get there.

She cautiously stepped out of the kitchen into a hallway with several doors when her right heel slipped out from under her. Nimble reflexes kept her from crashing to the ground as she planted her hand and left foot to stabilize herself. Looking down at the offending obstacle, Seven saw her boot heel had slid through a pool of something black. Peeking around the corner, she saw the source. A man lay face down on the floor with his throat cut.

Seven held her breath, shocked and not understanding what this was all about. She continued down the hall, a faint beeping noise attracting her attention. The noise was coming from a small room with the door hanging slightly ajar. She poked her head into the room long enough to determine the sound was that of a phone off the hook. Gun drawn, she stepped more fully into the room, eased the door shut, and flicked on the light switch.

From where she stood, she could see a man's leg flung over a fallen chair, and a considerable amount of blood spatter on the cabinets behind a small desk. She eased forward.

It was Armando Reyes.

By the looks of it, he had been shot by a very large caliber bullet at very close range.

A large calib...oh god. Oh my god. My rifle. Jenny!

Seven felt as though lightning had struck her as she bolted from the room, the worst possible scenarios flashing through her mind like a film reel in slow motion. All pretense at stealth was gone as she ran through the house, out the kitchen door, and flat out toward the forest where Jenny was hiding.

Oh god, no. Nononononooooo. Please, Jenny, please be okay.

Gasping air into her lungs to fuel her exertion, Seven plowed into the woods, leaping logs and barreling though the underbrush as fast as her legs would be pushed. She reached the small ditch they were using as a hideout and ripped the cover branches aside, praying beyond hope Jenny would be sleeping comfortably inside.

The ditch was empty. All her things were gone.

The only thing left was a small, white square of what looked like paper. She crawled down into the ditch, picked it up, and turned it over. It was a Polaroid instant photo. She didn't think they even made these anymore.

Seven plunked heavily to the ground as she stared dumbly at the image. She didn't think she had any more tears to give, but the sight of Jenny in this condition made them flow freely once more. She couldn't tell from the photo if Jenny was dead or alive. *And this is all my fault. It's all my god damned fault!*

Seven abruptly rolled to the side and vomited.

I'm such a fool! All this time I thought this was about Reyes and me. Now Jenny is paying the price for my ego and ignorance. This isn't about me. Jenny warned me. She told me that Maria woman was after her, but it seemed like a small consideration at the time. Insignificant. This was about her...and I left her alone like bait. Even Dan warned me to take the woman seriously. How could I have underestimated her like that?

Seven studied the picture again. Jenny's body was hanging by the wrists, beaten, bloody, and unconscious or dead.

Oh God, what have I done? I'm so sorry, Jenny. I promised I would protect you and I failed. You're a fucking idiot, Seven. Why did you let her come with you in the first place? How could I have discounted this Velasquez woman so thoroughly?

I cannot live with this. I cannot accept this. You're so innocent, so good. To have someone like you in my life, only to lose you, and it be my fault, my carelessness, my ego. This is not acceptable.

Seven's mind swirled with emotions, self-loathing being chief among them. She must save Jenny. Her own existence depended on it. Without any doubt, Seven knew she couldn't live with herself if she failed. Not that she would have to. She would give her life to save Jenny's, so either she would die trying or she would succeed. There was no middle ground.

Seven crawled from the ditch and settled against the trunk of a nearby palm tree. Anguish drained her of collected thought. She removed a water bottle from her coat and rinsed the taste of vomit from her mouth. A handful of water refreshed her face as she tried to collect herself into clear thinking.

Seven looked more closely at the Polaroid, this time to decipher a location. Glancing toward the hacienda, and back to the picture, it became apparent Jenny was being held somewhere underground, inside that house. She was certain she recognized the space from the blueprints she had studied for her mission. Seven thought for a moment about trying to come up with a plan of action, but determined no plan was necessary.

Anybody that stood between her and Jenny would die. That was the only plan she needed.

⚜⚜⚜⚜

Maria slapped her hard across the cheek.

Jenny jerked awake, the sting of the slap still fresh on her skin. Her shoulders screamed as she lifted her head and stared into the face of evil. "A simple 'wake up' would suffice," she said through clenched teeth.

Maria laughed at this woman's unerring audacity. She loved it.

Jenny looked around her earthy prison and noticed blood-covered men now populated the room. The shock of this sight sent her mind reeling, fearing desperately for Seven and the innocent people in this home.

There must be no God, because He would surely never let loose a woman like this on the world.

"What have you done?" Jenny whispered, so only Maria could hear.

"Gentleman," Maria addressed her men. "This is the young doctor who so kindly volunteered to act as our bait this morning. Please be so kind as to make sure her sacrifice is not in vain."

Maria paced down the length of the sub-basement and back, looking at the state of her men. Some appeared to have struggled in their task, some not so much. "I take it you all were successful in eliminating the staff?"

"Yes, boss," Rene spoke up for the group.

"How many did you find, Rene?"

"I found two, boss. The others found a total of

ten including a couple of guards in the outbuildings."

"Every door was opened? No room left unsearched?"

"Yes, boss."

Maria was satisfied her orders had been carried out in full. She turned to address the men as a group. "The sniper we have been searching for will be here shortly. Do not underestimate her, gentleman. She is a skilled operator. You know me and have worked with me long enough to fear my gift for killing. Treat her as if it were me you were hunting. We are the same."

"Ha! What a load of shit!" Jenny barked from behind her. "There's a difference between a professional and a psychotic murdering bitch, you know?"

Her opinion earned Jenny another hard slap across the face. "Shut up!" Maria's veneer of calm slipped off. For a moment, Jenny saw into the blankness that was her soul.

Jenny considered the possibility that if she could taunt her, insult, threaten, cajole, perhaps she could pull the woman off her game enough to lose focus with regards to Seven. *What the hell. I can't get out of this. She's made it abundantly clear she plans to kill me. What does it matter if it happens now or later? In fact, might as well get them all doubting.*

"Not one of you will leave this room alive. You know that, don't you? This psychotic bitch is comparing herself to someone she has never seen and never met. None of you have any idea what you're up against. She is the best of the best the U.S. has ever trained, and you think you have a chance? A pathetic bunch of security guards? Ha! Half of you will be dead before you even know she's in the room, and the other half will wish you were by the time she's finished!"

Jenny could see her words were having the desired effect. She could tell from watching the men that the one Maria addressed as Rene was translating for them. Their eyes grew larger with every passing sentence.

"Shut up!" Maria spun and slapped Rene on the face, then marched to stand in front of Jenny, jamming the barrel of her gun in the woman's mouth.

Jenny looked pleased with her small triumph. Maria repaid by punching her in the stomach.

Maria turned back to continue her address. "You must not shoot her. I want you all to stay hidden until she is in the middle of the room then overwhelm her all at once. Knock her out. I would like to position her in a certain place upstairs and kill her a certain way to pull off our deception."

Jenny added, "You might as well say goodbye to each other now. You won't have a chance once she gets here. There's still time to write a little farewell note to the wife and kids."

Slap! "You are trying my patience, doctor." Maria snatched her knife from its sheath and grabbed the tail of Jenny's shirt. She pulled the tail down and sliced a large piece of the fabric off, wadding it up and stuffing it in her captive's mouth.

"This is it, men. Pass or fail. There will be a very substantial reward in it for you when we have completed this task. Señor Argulla will recognize you all for a great service rendered in his name. Now... each of you take up position behind a pillar, and make no noise. There is only one entrance to this basement, the same way we got in. She will come down those stairs, and will either walk down the middle straight toward her friend, or move to the side and sneak around. Either way, her goal will be to free her friend. Pay attention to her movement. If she shifts to the side of the room, those nearest must slowly move around your pillar as she comes near. I don't want anyone to jump her until she is centered between us. Then, you should all jump at once. One on one she will be too much to handle. Questions?"

"Yes, boss," Rene spoke up. "What if she starts shooting when we jump her? Can we shoot her then?"

"If you do this right...according to plan...you should be able to take her down before she can get off a shot." Maria was prepared to sacrifice a couple guys. She figured the sniper would get at least two before they would subdue her. "It is important she not be shot. Our goal is to put the blame for the Reyes household massacre onto her. If she is riddled with bullets, our plan will fail. This we cannot have. It must appear as though a guard got off one lucky shot and killed her as he was dying."

Maria stepped closer into the circle of men. "Trust me, gentlemen. Señor Argulla will make you all wealthy men if you pull this off. Your master is putting his faith in you to succeed. Don't let him down."

☙ ☙ ☜ ☜

Seven stretched out on her stomach, weapon in hand, and pressed her ear as close to the sub-basement hatch as she could get it. The door was open and the voices, though muffled, could be heard clearly.

When the woman known as Maria Velasquez told her men the sniper would be there shortly, Seven hooded her eyes, flexed her grip on the gun handle, and whispered, "I'm already here, Maria, and you're about to meet me up close and personal." Seven was wound tighter than an anchor chain on an aircraft carrier.

When Seven heard Jenny start talking smack, she almost laughed aloud. She was beyond relieved to hear that Jenny was not only alive, but still in good enough shape to dish out some attitude. It brought a tear of extreme relief down her cheek, her fierce eyes closing briefly in a silent prayer of thanks.

She listened as Jenny told the men half of them would be dead before they even knew she was there. *Good idea, Jen, although I think I'd rather it be all of them.*

When Jenny started talking the second time, Seven used the opportunity of their drawn attention to poke her head down the hatch. Jenny was at the far end of the room, chained overhead as she was in the photograph. There were a half dozen men of various shapes and sizes; none appeared to be seasoned commandos. They looked like typical security thugs.

She got her first look at the Velasquez woman just as she was slapping Jenny hard across the face. She looked young, somewhere between Jenny and herself in age, late twenties maybe. She wore knee high boots, pocket pants, and a khaki shirt with the sleeves rolled over the elbows. Her long curly black hair was streaked with highlights. She was well built, but didn't look particularly muscular, and Seven had at least a head in height on her. She looked scrappy, though. If it came to hand-to-hand, she had no doubt the woman would put up a good fight.

Maria had made a critical error, and Seven smiled, a plan of attack now taking hold in her mind. The woman told her men there was only one entrance into the sub-basement. She was wrong. There were two. In her research of the Reyes Hacienda, the architectural plans were studied thoroughly in case it became necessary to enter the home.

She visualized her position in the hacienda and made a mental calculation as to the location of the other hatch. It obviously didn't have a set of stairs like this one did, or Maria would have spotted it when she was familiarizing herself with the room. Seven crept away, and ran silently down a long hallway toward the other end of the house.

Seven reached the area she suspected held the hatch and began searching the floor for any signs of it, trying to calculate its whereabouts based on her new position. There was a large Persian carpet on the floor, and several pieces of antique furniture. She unplugged a lamp, and moved a couple Victorian chairs and an oval marble-topped table to the side. She rolled back the carpet and was pleased to discover, well-disguised in the floor, the other door.

She turned off and pocketed her flashlight, secured her weapon, checked that her knife was in place and firmly positioned, then grabbed the hatch handle and moved it as slowly and quietly as she possibly could. Silence was imperative. If she gave away her position, she would be dead before she ever hit the ground.

Once the hatch was open, Seven could hear Maria offering last words of instruction to her men. She went head first through the hole, gripping the edge with her hands and swinging her torso and legs through after, dropping silently to the ground. Maria's voice covered the muffled landing as she encouraged her men to take their positions.

The stealthy fighter crouched unmoving in the darkness as she gained her bearing. The shadows and pillars in this poorly lit room would serve her purpose well. Quickly, she darted behind the closest one, now positioned behind and to the left of her bound friend.

She drew deeply through flared nostrils, preparing mentally and physically for the battle to come. She would work her way down one side of the room, come back to the dark area behind Jenny, move across and work her way down the other side. With any luck, Maria would find herself completely alone before she even knew Seven was there.

The unknown factor was Maria herself. If she stayed stationary and on the other side of the room, this plan would probably work...but if she moved? She would probably come across a body, and then a full-frontal battle would ensue. *Oh well.* Seven felt perfectly capable of playing either game. The key was not to get Jenny hurt in the process.

She was behind the first man and into position before she had any time to second-guess her battle strategy. The man was mere inches away, focused intently in the opposite direction as Seven covered his mouth and slit his throat in one smooth motion. She gripped the man tightly to keep his struggling to a minimum. When he stopped, she lowered him to the ground and tucked his body unseen against the pillar.

She inched slowly around the large round concrete support until she was at the very edge of Jenny's line of sight. Only a moment passed before the young woman's gaze drifted in her direction, then shot wide open as Seven raised a finger to her lips and gave a reassuring wink to her friend.

As Seven snuck back into the shadows, Jenny

closed her eyes and dropped her head dejectedly to the ground so as not to give away her extreme relief and joy at seeing Seven coming to the rescue. Jenny prayed for Seven's success, her hopefulness of surviving this situation now ten times what it had been just moments before. Somehow, her clever friend had found a way into the room that Maria didn't know about. Jenny wanted to scream with glee right through her gag, but kept it all inside.

She tipped her head forward, watching surreptitiously under her brows for any activity she might catch in the shadows of the room. She wondered how long Seven would get away with her activities before something occurred to blow her cover. She hoped a long time, because she had no desire to be a victim of Maria's twisted fantasies.

As if the thought brought the devil forward, Maria chose that moment to leave her hiding place and walk boldly through the center of the room toward her. She hadn't seen it happen, but somehow Seven had gotten herself on the right side of the room. Jenny caught a glimpse of her friend closing in on the man nearest to her at the same time Maria was closing in on Jenny.

The captive tried not to betray anything with her eyes, but couldn't help watching glimpses of the quiet struggle taking place behind the nearby pillar. Maria reached her and snatched the gag from her mouth. "Well doctor, perhaps your friend isn't so interested in saving your life after all. She certainly is taking her sweet time getting here."

Jenny's mouth was so dry her tongue felt like a paper towel. She didn't know whether to tell Maria to fuck off, or try to distract her in some way. The sound of Maria speaking to Jenny brought Rene's attention around for a moment, to see what was happening behind him. A furtive motion two pillars away caught his notice and he jumped from his position, yelling a warning for the other men to attack.

In an instant, the room was in chaos. Rene and the man next to him ran toward where he'd seen the sniper moving among them. Maria ran to the center of the room commanding the others join the attack. She herself moved in the direction of the fray attempting to help also, until she realized no one else was coming. She moved cautiously around one of the large pillars to see only two men attempting to subdue the sniper.

She could tell with a glance that the American's superior fighting skill would end in defeat for her remaining men. She watched as the tall woman forcefully kicked the head of one man back as she stabbed the other man in the gut. Seeing as how silence was no longer an issue, the sniper removed her sidearm and shot the first man in the head.

Maria ran quickly behind Jenny for protection, leveling her gun at the doctor's temple. As they watched, the man named Rene stumbled to the center of the room clutching his gut and whimpering in agony. He pleaded with this tall demon to go away and for Jesus to end his suffering. As he lay on his back clutching his gun in a shaking hand, he attempted to kill her one last time. He should have listened to the blonde. Shakily he raised the weapon to the unseen ghost that had bested them all.

Seven walked from the shadows for the first time, a blood-covered specter, eyes charged with murderous intent. She stood to her full height, moving slowly and deliberately toward the man lying in agony on the ground.

Maria found she was holding her breath. She had to admit, this creature was impressive. Graceful. Deadly.

Seven didn't look at the man at her feet. She was zeroed in with laser-like intensity on the maniacal woman holding a gun to Jenny's head.

Without ever looking down, she crushed Rene's gun and the hand holding it into the earthen floor with her boot, the sound of breaking bones adding to his continued whimpers.

As Seven lowered her weapon toward the injured man, she and Maria looked into each other's dark eyes. Coldly, and without so much as a twitch of emotion on her face, Seven shot the man twice in the chest, his moaning coming to an abrupt halt.

The deafening volume of the gunshots reverberated around the enclosed space. Jenny had never considered it possible, but she found her feelings numb to the violence she was witnessing. It was hard to have compassionate feelings toward people who treated others with so little consideration. It was easy to judge violence as not being the answer when you weren't a victim of it.

Maria was captured in a grim stare so filled with purpose and intent, for the first time she felt something she had never known in her adult life. Fear. Given a choice, it was not the emotion she would have chosen to feel after all this time, but to feel anything at all was like a breath of fresh air. She smiled, gleeful at finally having met another who could inspire her so.

"That was quite entertaining. I thank you for a most enjoyable show," Maria said, the smile on her face mirroring the amused tone of her voice.

Seven walked slowly toward them, her gun held loosely at her side.

A brief image of an old west gunslinger flashed through Jenny's mind.

"Allow me to state the obvious!" Maria barked, not wanting the threat to move any closer. "You will do what I say now, or I will put lead through this pretty head." Maria held the gun fast to Jenny's temple and snaked her other hand around to her abdomen. She slid the flat of her palm sensuously upward until her fingertips were making slow circles over the small knife wound she had left near her heart. "I wanted to spend a little time alone with her in the future, but I will not hesitate to make the sacrifice. You do understand my position, of course."

"Of course," Seven said calmly, standing her ground.

The depth and timbre of the sniper's voice captivated Maria. *Oh how I would love to have you too, my dangerous beauty.* "Drop your weapons." She yelled at Seven. "Get on your knees and put your hands behind your head. Comply with me. No struggle, and I will let her go."

Seven didn't believe Maria for an instant. She could tell by the look on Jenny's face that she didn't believe it either.

Seven hesitated for just an instant before tossing her gun to the ground. She made eye contact with Jenny, apologizing with a look. Even if she didn't believe Maria, she couldn't take that chance. She had no doubt Maria wouldn't hesitate to shoot Jenny if she put up a fight.

"And the knife..."

Seven's blade joined her 9mm on the dirt floor.

She dropped to her knees and placed her hands behind her head.

"Good. Now we can get down to business." To Jenny she whispered, "I guess you and I will have our time together after all."

Maria leveled the gun at Seven as she walked slowly around Jenny's body. She stood with her back to the girl as she reached around and removed another set of handcuffs from her back pocket. Throwing them toward the kneeling woman, she indicated with a nod to put them on.

Jenny was petrified their chance for survival was waning. If Seven allowed herself to be bound, there was no telling how Maria would capitalize on her concession. She had to do something. She had to take the upper hand back before this bitch could kill them both.

Jenny moved her head slightly to the side, a motion intended to quietly draw Seven's attention to her. Seven met her stare as she slowly reached for the handcuffs with one hand.

Maria was panting with excitement, her adrenaline pumping at the prospect of being the one to finally cage this wild animal. Her eyes were razor sharp as she zeroed in on the sniper's every minute movement.

Jenny motioned toward Maria's gun with a slight tilt of her head, hoping Seven got the hint. This would be the shortest ruse in history if she didn't. Her hands were numb from being overhead for so long without blood to circulate feeling into them. Her shoulders were searing in pain with the weight they carried. She just barely reached the ground with the balls of her feet, so it was with tremendous effort that Jenny was able to stifle a cry at her own painful actions. She grasped the chain above her handcuffs with all the strength she could muster and swung forward, kicking viciously upward toward Maria's gun hand.

An instant before she made contact, Seven launched herself to the side, in case the shock of impact caused Maria to fire her weapon. The gun didn't fire, but flew several feet into the air, followed by the unbelieving eyes of its former holder.

In a flash, Maria's mirth turned to wrath as she spun around to face the woman whose life she so desperately desired to take. She screamed a blood-curdling curse and stepped toward the young doctor, drawing her skinning knife as she went. All thought of Seven and her mission for Argulla seemed to have left her, so intent she was on impaling the woman in her sights. Too long had she gone without sating her desire. Too long had this arrogant woman taunted her. She would have the doctor. *Now!*

Jenny watched wide-eyed and helpless as Maria turned toward her with a maniacal look on her face. Something blank and inhuman had replaced the mask she usually wore. The knife came up, and just as Maria's arm swung down to plunge the blade into Jenny, an unbelievable force slammed her body sideways.

Seven flew from the shadows like a demon possessed. If she could have hit this woman hard enough to turn her to dust, she would have. Instead, she took her out like a linebacker pile-driving a quarterback into the ground.

Maria screamed again as her body impacted the dirt floor. Her knife hand slashed wildly and without reason, attempting contact with anything in its path. She felt it strike flesh just before her wrist was grabbed and something slammed hard into her face.

Both women were frenzied in their attack of each other as Jenny watched helplessly from her hanging prison. Seven rolled to her feet as Maria slid from her grasp and lunged once more toward the doctor, her deadly intent made clear in her lifeless eyes. Mere inches away from reaching her target, Maria was jerked backward as her opponent dug a powerful fist into her long hair and pulled her off her feet. Seven wrapped her arms around the manic woman's neck and waist, twisting her body and flinging Maria several feet through the air, far away from Jenny, to tumble in a heap on the ground.

Maria was wild-eyed and snarling like a rabid animal when she faced off against her tall opponent once more. She seemed to look right through Seven and focus on her ultimate goal, the sniper being nothing more than an obstacle for her to overcome. An inhuman mewling sound was building in volume as it morphed into a scream that shook the rafters. Maria launched her body toward the sniper, slashing her knife blade toward the woman's face.

Seven dropped to one knee, and with all her might slammed her fist firmly into the oncoming woman's solar plexus. Maria's momentum hurled her forward as she crumpled to the ground and Seven leapt on her, wrestling the knife from her hand.

Maria fought with inhuman energy, striking, kicking, biting, anything she could call on as the weight, size, and ability of her opponent slowly, but steadily overwhelmed her.

Tiring and desperate for her kill, she suddenly found herself locked in the position of being planted face down in the dirt, the flow of oxygen to her lungs being firmly terminated. Her glower never left the doctor's as her world faded to black. Maria's last thought was to wonder what it would've been like to watch the light leave her own eyes.

Chapter Twenty

Fear and adrenaline made for a powerful combination. Seven's fear slowly subsided as the woman beneath her finally stilled. It had been an incredible battle. The ex-Marine had fought many men and women in her days with the service, but had never experienced anything quite as unhinged as her struggle with Maria.

She lay across the motionless body, attempting to catch her breath, still winded from the fight, her body quivering with an excess of adrenaline. A quick physical assessment told her she was bleeding from a knife wound on her arm, but it didn't feel that bad. Relief flooded her emotions. She rose up to her knees, quickly removing an unseen tear from her own cheek before turning to her friend.

Jenny watched in horror and fascination as they struggled. It seemed like a lifetime since she'd found Seven unconscious in the forest, and it all came down to this. Either Maria would win and they would both die, or Seven would win and they would make their escape, together.

Tears of relief ran freely down Jenny's cheeks as Seven finally looked her way and stated with a slightly shaking voice that she was okay. She felt her tears turn into wracking sobs as the pain, relief, fear, and trauma of the last day washed over her in an uncontrollable wave.

Seven frisked Maria's shirt and pants pockets, looking for the key to Jenny's handcuffs, finally finding it tucked tightly in a coin pocket. She snatched it up and turned to release Jenny from her painful bonds.

Seven stepped in front of Jenny and wrapped a supportive arm firmly around her waist. She pulled the small woman tightly to her with one arm, testing that she held her full weight before reaching up with the other to release the cuffs. She knew the pain as the blood flowed back into her arms and hands would be incredible, and didn't want her to collapse into a heap on the ground.

Jenny cried out through her sobs as she collapsed into Seven's body.

"Shhhh, Jen. It's okay...it's okay. I've got you. Everything is going to be okay now. Shh shh shhhh." Seven sat cross-legged on the ground and cradled Jenny in her arms, rocking her gently in an attempt to calm her. She cried a little herself as she whispered soothing encouragement to the young woman.

Jenny seemed so small and fragile. "I'm so glad I found you. I was so scared, Jenny. I'm so...so sorry. I never should have left you. I'm so sorry." Seven kissed the top of her head and pressed her cheek into blonde hair, adjusting slightly to hold her tighter still. Jenny wrapped her arms around Seven's waist and sighed deeply as her sobbing slowly subsided.

"I knew you'd come," she sniffed, wiping the tears away with the back of her hand.

"I thought you were dead. I thought she'd killed you. I was so scared." The women held each other tightly, finding comfort and relief in each other's warm embrace.

"Thank you for saving me," Jenny said in a small

voice.

"Oh, Jenny." Seven kissed her forehead lightly and brushed the hair back from her face.

"I thought I was a goner there for a little while. Sorry I'm falling apart on you like this."

"Are you kidding me? You rocked! I heard you talking shit to her. It sounded to me like you weren't fazed at all. She was so tweaked you weren't afraid of her, I think that really threw her off. It was great. You were great."

Jenny giggled a little through another teary sniff. "You think she was tweaked?"

"Definitely. She wanted to see your fear, and you didn't show it to her. You withheld what she wanted most. You're very brave and fearless, as I've always suspected."

Jenny leaned back and looked at her friend, smiling for the first time in quite a while. Even with red, puffy eyes, Seven thought she was beautiful. Jenny hugged her tightly around the neck, then leaned back once more and placed a tender kiss on Seven's lips. "Thanks." Her kiss was meant to be chaste, but she wondered immediately upon leaning back if perhaps it wasn't her subconscious at work.

Seven's eyes seemed to change color. For a brief moment, she forgot all her promises to leave Jenny to her own path. With warm fingers, she caressed Jenny's cheek, then leaned in to continue the kiss. It lasted for just a moment, barely long enough to be past chaste. Jenny's eyes closed, then grew wide in realization at the same moment Seven became aware of her actions.

"Ohmygod." Seven jerked backward and quickly lifted Jenny and herself into a standing position. She flushed in embarrassment. "Ohmygod. Jenny, I'm so sorry. I just...I just...I didn't mean...oh god," she whined pathetically.

Jenny chuckled at how flustered her perpetually cool friend suddenly became.

"I...I..." Seven tried to scrub the blush away with her hands.

"It's okay, Seven." Jenny chuckled again. "Really. It's all right. Just caught me a little off guard, that's all. I should be apologizing to you. I started it."

"I'm so sorry, Jenny, really. It's just...sometimes I get so keyed up when I fight. The adrenaline gets me going, it's like I lose my mind a little. I didn't mean to press you like that."

"Sev, I'm serious. It's all right. Now maybe we should be thinking about getting out of here, yeah?" Jenny seemed to be enjoying how uncomfortable Seven was.

Relieved to have something else to focus on, Seven nodded her agreement. "Yeah. We definitely need to get out of here before somebody shows up and starts finding bodies all over the place. The police won't stop to ask questions, especially from me. We need to get as far away from here as possible."

Jenny retrieved her backpack from the corner of the room where it had been unceremoniously tossed and put it on. Seven's was there as well, right next to where her rifle had been placed up against the wall. She removed Dan's sweatshirt from her pack and wiped down the weapon, placing it back up against the wall.

"You're going to leave it?"

"Yeah. I hate to, but if we're picked up, it won't look good for me to have Reyes' murder weapon on me. Both our prints and Maria's are on it. At least this way it leaves a question hanging. The weapon is untraceable. Still, it would be better all around if we just got the hell out of Bolivia before any questions are asked. I'm not supposed to be here. If I get caught, there won't be any trial."

"Where are we going to head now? La Paz? Maybe Dan and those guys could help us somehow. Do you think Argulla will keep coming after us?"

"First things first. Let's get out of here." Seven urged Jenny toward the stairs and they climbed into a pantry that opened to the cellar hallway. Once outside, Seven directed Jenny to one of the far outbuildings. "There's a large garage, storage area in this building. When I was checking it out earlier, I saw a dust covered dirt bike tucked back in one corner. Probably belonged to Reyes' son once upon a time. More than likely, they won't even know it's missing for a while. We need to get five or ten miles from here, then if you're up to it, I'd like for you to stitch my arm. We'll talk then about what's next, okay?"

"Do you think you can get that bike to start?"

"Hope so. That's the beauty of a bike like this. Even if it's old and unused, just get it rolling and pop the clutch...you're good to go."

☙ ☙ ☙ ☙

Jenny held tight to Seven's waist as she maneuvered the bike up a bumpy gravel road. She was feeling a little sick by the time her friend slowed and pulled the vehicle into the forest, turning it off and pushing a good way back into the woods.

During the ride, Jenny couldn't help but let her mind drift back to their brief kiss. Seven seemed angry with herself about it. It was entirely possible that Jenny had completely misread her. She chastised herself for being egotistical enough to believe this amazing woman would just be waiting for her to give the go ahead.

She's angry because you drew her in and then acted shocked. No. It's because she's not interested in you and is pissed she made a move when she was vulnerable. Jenny, you're such a fool. Why did you do it? You've probably blown it now. Everything was going along just fine, and now, because of you, there's this big elephant flying around us with little pink angel wings.

She spent a few bumpy minutes thinking about the kiss itself. That had been the first time Jenny had ever kissed a woman. She smiled to herself. Almost as soon as it started, it was over. But that was enough. It was nothing at all like kissing a man. With any guy she'd ever been with, the kiss seemed rough. Rushed, as though it was just something for him to get past so he could get what he really wanted. Seven's kiss...was about the kiss. Nothing more. Nothing hidden. It was honest and peaceful like a cool breeze in the heat of a summer's day.

It was somewhat amazing, really, that in the midst of all the chaos, pain, and violence, something as simple as a small kiss could dominate her thoughts so thoroughly. It was scary, but felt very right at the same time. *Well, Jenny, if that doesn't tell you what you need to know about yourself, what will?*

She watched Seven as she tucked the bike behind some underbrush and sat up against a tree trunk, rifling through her pack for the medical supplies. She took out a bottle of water and a small kit before unbuttoning her coat and gingerly removing it from her injured arm. She removed her shirt and pants, also, tossing them into the bushes nearby. She was being very quiet, Jenny thought, too quiet, even for her.

God, I really did blow it. She won't even look at me. Relationship Kryptonite, Jen, that's you. I don't know why I'm surprised. I'm such a big mouth dork. Short, high-strung, opinionated, needy, of course she's going to run for the hills. What was I thinking? I wish I could've tried that kiss out one more time before she wised up. Seven's friendship is the most important thing, Jen, don't lose sight of that.

Seven glanced up to see Jenny staring at her with a blank look on her face. She appeared deep in thought, because the young doctor had made no move to tend her injured arm.

Seven's mind was racing with thoughts of her own. *I don't blame her for not wanting to touch me. She probably thinks I'm some kind of sexual predator now or something. God, Seven, you really freakin' stepped in it this time. How could I have done that? Poor girl is having a hard time as it is, let alone being hung from a ceiling by a lunatic poking her with a knife, and what do you do? Rescue her so she can then turn around and deal with a lesbian come-on? Idiot. What was I thinking? That's just it. You weren't thinking. You blew it. You'll be lucky if she doesn't dump you like a hot potato the second we get out of this country. You'd deserve it too.*

"Jen."

Snapping out of her trance, Jenny jumped into action at registering that her friend was sitting partially naked on the ground, her arm still bleeding. "Sorry. Zoned out there for a minute." She cleaned the wound and pressed some clean gauze to it, stemming the flow of blood. "Hold this why I get the needle ready. It's not so bad, probably only needs five or six sutures. What is it about being around you that makes me feel like I'm working in a MASH unit?" She tried to lighten the mood a little.

Seven smiled at her attempted humor. "Just lucky, I guess."

Jenny stitched the wound, noting Seven didn't make a peep, even though she was working with no anesthetic. "You're pretty tough yourself," she said with a smile.

Seven grunted an acknowledgement, still not looking Jenny in the eye.

She's so stubborn. Jenny placed two fingers under Seven's chin and raised her head until their eyes met. "Doctor to patient. Tell me how you're feeling. You lost a decent amount of blood. Not a dangerous amount, but enough to make you lightheaded. Like, maybe you shouldn't be driving a bike, lightheaded."

"I'm fine, Jen. Thanks for patching me up, yet again."

"You're welcome, of course. It's the least I could do for my hero." She grinned rakishly. Seven rolled her eyes and looked wryly at Jenny. Refocusing on her medical duties, Jenny ripped open a package containing a wet towel and began cleaning the blood off Seven's arm. "Let's get you cleaned up and dressed. You must be getting a chill by now." They made eye contact again, and both started laughing. "Oh, that's right. Human furnace. I forgot."

Grow up, Seven. Stop acting like a humiliated child.

"So what's our plan, oh tall, brooding one?"

With that, Seven relaxed and chuckled. "Cochabamba."

"Gesundheit." They both laughed for real at that one.

Seven reached over and tugged the sweat suit Dan gave her out of the pack and put it on. "You told me before Argulla's only interest in this was killing his rival and gaining his property, right?"

"That's what Maria said."

"Then I have to assume he won't continue his chase. There's no reason, unless the authorities try to pin the deaths on him. By the time they get around to that, we'll be long gone. If he were to chase, however, or if he sends the cops or military after us, he would probably assume we were headed to either La Paz or Sucre. So we'll head to Cochabamba. It's not too far, and I want us to get lost in a city that's big enough to disappear in until I can come up with a plan to get out."

Seven reached over to where she'd tossed her camo jacket and unfastened a pocket. "Jen, will you hold something for me? It's important and I don't have a secure place for it." She removed Marcus' engagement ring and handed it to her friend.

"For me? Really? Gosh, Sev, we haven't even been on our first date yet. Aren't you jumpin' the gun a little?"

Seven chuckled, but it was with a sad smile. "Are you implying we will be going on a first date?"

Jenny smiled innocently and batted her eyelashes doing her best to look angelic.

"This belonged to Marcus. He was going to propose to his girlfriend Alicia when we got home."

"Oh. Um. Sheesh, I'm sorry, Sev. I didn't mean

to make light of it."

"S'okay. Funny though. That's almost the same thing I said to Marcus when he showed it to me. Something about an engagement ring really brings out the smartass in people, huh?"

"So you found him then?"

"Yes."

"And Ty?"

"Also dead. They dumped and burned the bodies in the woods outside the northwestern part of the groomed property."

"Oh God, Seven, I'm so sorry. I'm glad for one thing, though. At least now you know. When we get home we can work on getting this trauma put behind you."

The 'we' in Jenny's last remark didn't slip by the listener.

≈≈≈≈

"Look, it says here we shouldn't leave Cochabamba without visiting the Cristo de la Concordia." Jenny sipped her Coke, looking incredibly disheveled after the long ride, but happy nonetheless.

After Jenny patched up Seven's new wounds, they drove the bike a couple hours before stopping, deciding to ditch the stolen vehicle about five miles outside the city. They hiked along the road for about a half hour before hitching a ride in the back of a flatbed the rest of the way into town. The truck driver would accept no payment, and insisted on dropping them off in a plaza near a beautiful Roman Catholic Cathedral.

Seven laughed at her friend's undying enthusiasm. "Spoken like a true tourist. I personally, could stand to skip the Big Jesus. I'm more interested in talking to Nick and finding a shower and a pillow."

"Killjoy." Jenny rustled around in a sack containing their first hot food in several days.

Seven was eyeing the sack suspiciously, but she was starving, and therefore eager. "I hope that's pizza in there. I don't think I'm in the mood for barbequed Llama."

"Just be thankful I didn't get you the Changa de Cobayo." The blonde pulled out several pocket-shaped pastries and a handful of napkins.

"Are you serious? Guinea pig soup? That is nasty. Might as well make it with kittens." The scruffy looking woman in the dirty West Point sweatshirt snatched up a pastry and helped herself to an ungraceful bite. "Mm. Ith goo. Wa ith thith?"

"Was there a question in there somewhere?"

Grinning around a large mouthful of food, Seven swallowed and repeated herself. "I said it's good and was asking what it was."

"I'm gonna have to talk with your mother about your bad manners. Talking with your mouth full is very unladylike."

"Like hell you will. And last time I checked, being ladylike wasn't exactly high on my priority list." Seven made a pretense of looking suspiciously over her shoulders. "Anyway, I don't think the cotillion police are watching."

A grin curled the corner of Jenny's mouth. "This is Latin America, honey. They're always watching. It's called a Salteña, by the way. It's kind of like a Bolivian version of the chicken pot pie meets the Cornish pasty, chicken, potato, corn, peas, good stuff wrapped in a crust."

"I lie ie. Ga aiey ngoe?"

"You like it and want to know if I have any more?"

"Mmhm."

"You are merely pretending to be an adult, aren't you Seven?"

"Mmhm. Gimme."

Jenny watched amused as Seven snarfed two Salteña and polished off the second half of one of hers. She looked around at the lovely Plaza 14 de Septiembre where they were sitting and took a moment to admire the stately cathedral across the street. The sky was beautifully blue with little puffy clouds, and with the tiniest bit of imagination, she could almost pretend to be on vacation.

"Sev, do you mind if I ask you a personal question?"

"Does it have to do with me eating like a pig?"

"No."

"Okay. Then go ahead."

"When you figured out you were gay, did you tell your mom? How did she react? Did she totally freak?"

Oh boy. I feel a sensitive chat coming on. "Yes, I told her. My family knew about me almost as soon as I figured it out myself. Maybe even sooner. My mom was okay about it. Great, actually. My uncle dropped a couple of hints to me early on that he was accepting of it, so he must have sensed it in me. Based on that, I would have to assume he and my mom discussed it. When I finally told her, she said she was worried. Not because I was gay, but because of the trials I would undoubtedly have to face because of it. Bigotry, discrimination, etc. I was young, though, and therefore bulletproof. I thought I could deal with it. I did, but after a while it got old."

"I was just wondering…well…do you remember my parents at all?"

"Your mom, but not so much your dad. I never really interacted with him much. When I was babysitting, she always called me and paid me. Why?"

"I was just curious about how you think they would take that kind of information?"

"Probably not well, but you never know about people. They can surprise you. Your mom always struck me as the uptight sort. A 'too concerned' about what the neighbors might think kind of woman. Conservative, you know? Am I wrong?"

"No. Unfortunately. And compared to my father, she's down-right liberal."

"Just 'cause she's like that Jen, doesn't mean you have to be, even if she may have raised you that way. You're your own person. Be who you want to be. Speaking for myself, I didn't want to look back on my life when I'm old and gray, and regret not doing or being something because I was worried about what people thought. Anybody. Even the people that mean the most to me."

"Maybe you were able to have those strong, to-hell-with-the-world feelings because of the kind of house you were raised in. Maybe if your parents had been like mine, you wouldn't have been so sure of yourself."

"Maybe."

Silence reigned for a few moments as Seven drained half her Coke in one swallow and her friend sat struggling with her own demons. Jenny hadn't actually come out and expressed her fears about possibly being gay, but Seven knew that's what she was thinking. Dan had said as much. Until Jenny brought it up with her personally, she would remain impersonal. She didn't want her feelings for Jenny to interfere with the young woman's decision about her own self and future.

"Sev, you told me before you weren't seeing anyone back home. Why is that, do you think? I mean, now that you're free to do what you want, I would think you'd be beating 'em off with a stick."

"It's easy to find someone to sleep with, Jen, if that's all you're interested in. Finding someone who excites you so much on every level you want to spend the rest of your life with them, is not so easy."

"What kind of person would that be for you?"

Jenny had unwittingly backed Seven into a corner. *Someone just like you. Should I tell the truth, or lie?* Neither was an acceptable option. *I guess that leaves Plan C: subterfuge followed by running for the hills.*

"Jen, I think it's time we split up."

"You're breaking up with me already? We were just getting to the good part," Jenny said with a sly smile, fully aware how uncomfortable she had made her friend. She was graceful enough to admit poking her nose where it didn't belong. This time anyway, she would retreat to Seven's timely and convenient change of subject. Jenny knew what she wanted Seven's response to be when she asked who would be right for her. She wanted her to say 'someone like you.'

"Okay, so what's next for us, Sev? Got any plans on how we're going to get out of here?"

"You got that Cochabamba guidebook we picked up handy?" Seven scooched around so they were sitting side-by-side, and looked at the booklet Jenny produced from her bag. They flipped through the pages, looking for a viable option. "Here's one. The Gran Hotel Cochabamba. It's not too far from here."

Jenny looked on and nodded her approval.

"Grab a cab and head over to this open air marketplace, La Cancha. It says you can get everything there. Buy us some clothes."

"What kind of clothes?"

"Just jeans, or something nondescript. I can't wear this sweat suit around. It's filthy and it's all I've got. Maybe some fresh socks, underwear, a couple t-shirts. Definitely a toothbrush. I don't have anything but this, so I can only go up from here."

"Shoes?"

"Nah. I'm okay with my boots."

Jenny made a mental shopping list then figured out how much money she would need, and how much to give to Seven. She dug into her backpack and pulled out a wad of cash, giving Seven enough to get her through the day.

"When you're done, head over to Gran Hotel and get us a room. See in this picture here?" Seven pointed to the guidebook photograph of the hotel. "This gazebo thing on the lawn, that's where we'll meet. I'd like to not go through the lobby, so while you wait for me, see if you can find another way to the room. I'll meet you at that gazebo in five hours. That's 5:30ish. If I don't show up, come back to the gazebo and look for me at midnight. If I'm not there at midnight, something's happened, and you need to get gone. Before you even say it, don't argue. If we're going to be separated, we need a contingency plan. This is it. If I don't show, you leave the country. Grab the first flight out of here."

"What are you going to do?"

"I'm going to the opposite side of town from where you are to call my Uncle Nick. I want to be far away from where we're staying in case Takashi has his line tapped. He and my mother are my only family, so it's possible. I'm not sure if he thinks I'm dead or alive at this point. I'll have Nick get to a secure line then call me back in a hotel lobby or something. I'm going to tell him what's going on and see if he can get us back somehow. It's going to be tricky as hell getting into the states undercover and without I.D., especially since 9/11."

"I hope he can help us."

"He will, Jen. Don't worry. He's very well connected. Even though he's retired, he has a lot of friends in high places. If anyone can help us, he can."

⚞⚞⚞⚞

Armando Reyes, Jr., Manny to his friends, stood open mouthed and staring at the blank eyes and macabre blood splatter in the small office down the hall from the kitchen. His heart was pounding furiously. He seemed frozen in time, unable to take action of any kind; even a simple step forward toward his father, or backward to run from the room seemed impossible.

Some minutes passed in the unearthly silence of the Reyes Hacienda. That was the first thing he noticed upon his return from partying at Raul's last night. The quiet was unnatural. He had never been close with his father, but noted his emotions, or lack thereof, seemed to be having trouble settling on anything in particular. Was he sad? Angry? Scared? Free? In shock? He was at a total loss, and strangely felt nothing but blankness and confusion.

He had never really been on his own before and found it to be a little unnerving. Alone. He didn't know what to do. He would call his new friend, Raul, and have him come over. Raul would know what to do. He was a wise and successful businessman, a friend, experienced with this kind of thing.

Manny moved closer to his father and replaced the beeping receiver of the telephone back in its cradle. He picked it back up, listened briefly for a dial tone, and then called Raul Argulla.

⁂

The beat-up silver minivan careened around the roundabout, honking obnoxiously as it went. Seven glanced up at the driver to see what had so upset him, and he looked perfectly calm. *Don't need any real reason to lay on the horn here, I guess.* She had the cabbie drop her at a non-descript looking building on the far side of town. She looked up at the hotel sign, satisfied this was the place she was headed and walked into the lobby.

This was Seven's third stop. She had collected hotel lobby phone numbers from two previous hotels so she would have a place for Nick to contact her once he got secure.

Seven approached the lone hotel employee behind the counter and slid a hundred and fifty Boliviano across the counter. That was somewhere between twenty and twenty-five bucks, U.S., but here, a small fortune. In Spanish, she said, "I need to make a long distance call. It will be brief. Would it be all right if I used your lobby phone?"

"Sí," the man nodded, eyeing the cash.

Seven took a seat facing the door and picked up the phone, dialing Nick's home number.

"Michelis residence," a deep military voice boomed over the line.

Thank god he's home. "St. Nicholas, this is Deanee speaking." When Seven was a child, her uncle often teased her with a nickname. He said she was so much like her father, he was going to call her Teeney Deanee. The nickname never really stuck past her twelfth birthday, when she was no longer teeny, but Seven knew her uncle would remember. She also knew if she used this old name, he would be smart enough to know there was a damn good reason behind it.

There was a long silence on the line, and for a moment, Seven feared they'd lost the connection. "Well, Deanee! What a pleasant surprise. It's been years. How's the flower shop business?"

They didn't have any code they spoke to each other, but she knew this was Nick's way of saying he understood not to call her by name. "Excellent, Nicholas. As a matter of fact, a customer just walked in and is vying for my attention. Bad timing, huh? Do you think you could call me back?"

"Absolutely." Nick understood she meant from a secure line or different location.

"Great. How long?"

"About fifteen minutes. You got a number where I can reach you?"

Seven read off the number to one of the other hotel lobby phones she had visited. "I'll look forward to doing a little catching up." She hung up the phone and headed out the door, flagging the first taxi she saw.

Several minutes later, Seven parked herself in front of her chosen lobby phone and waited for Nick's call. She picked it up on the first ring. "Seven, you old warhorse, you have no idea how glad I am to hear from you. I should have known you'd be a hard kill," Nick said. "Your mother got a call just this morning from somebody in your department who called himself the Chairman. He told her you were missing and presumed dead. I can't wait to let her know you're okay."

A wave of guilt washed over her for the sorrow her mother was undoubtedly feeling. "Well, it wasn't pretty, Uncle Nicky. I lost my whole team, but I'm still here. For now, anyway. It looks like someone from BFC back home sold us out, so at this point I'm not sure whom I can trust at Black Flag. I'm stuck in Bolivia with no identification, and can't call for professional assistance. In other words, I'm screwed."

"Are you hurt? Are you safe right this moment?"

"I'm okay right now. I was shot twice when my team was ambushed, but got patched up all right. Back to fightin' form now. I have a friend here who's helping me at great personal risk. A civ doctor. The two of us are in Cochabamba, Bolivia and need to get out and back home somehow. Do you think you can help?"

"I'll figure something out, Seven. I'll get you home."

"My friend has cash and credit cards, but we can't use any public transportation of any kind. I think it's possible I may still be hunted. The sooner we're out of here the better. There could be some major fallout in my direction when what happened this morning hits the media."

"Describe your friend in case I need the info."

"Her name is Jenny MacKenzie. She's five foot, four inches, blonde, green eyes, twenty-four years old. American, born in Virginia."

"Sounds cute, you old dog. Just like your father."

Seven sighed and rolled her eyes, unseen by her Uncle several thousand miles away. "How long before we should talk again?"

"Give me a couple hours to come up with a plan."

Seven read out the phone number to the next hotel with a promise to be waiting for his call in two hours' time. "Thanks, Nicky. Tell mom I love her, okay?"

"Will do, shorty. Talk to you in a couple."

Seven dropped the receiver in its cradle and headed out the door to occupy herself for a little while. She decided that instead of taking a cab to the next hotel, she would walk and check out what she could of the city while she was killing time. As she walked, something in a shop window caught her eye and she immediately turned into the store, smiling wickedly. After all, no trip would be complete without a souvenir to remind you of the time you had.

Across town, Jenny was being escorted to her room at the Gran Hotel after several pleasurable hours spent bartering for goods at the market. The bellhop carried two backpacks stuffed with new clothes and sundries, enough to give them both fresh duds for at least a couple more days. She tipped the boy and he left, as she checked her watch. One hour until she met Seven at the gazebo. That was time enough to have a nice, long, well-deserved shower. She could hardly wait to feel the hot water on her aching shoulders.

An hour later, freshly scrubbed and feeling better than she had in days, Jenny waited patiently for her friend to show up. It was only five minutes after the time she had agreed to meet, but her anxious nature let her imagination get the better of her. Doomsday scenarios were building in her head as she felt a light tap on her shoulder.

🙖🙖🙖🙖🙖

"Smith here, Chairman."

"Talk."

"There was a massacre at the Reyes Hacienda, sir, somewhere between fifteen and twenty dead. The place was a ghost town."

"Did Michelis do it?"

"I don't think so, sir, but it's possible. Based on her file, I don't see her as the type to kill innocents, but if it was a revenge thing, maybe. Most of the vics had their throats cut."

"Go on."

"Reyes was killed by a large caliber rifle, which we found later in a sub-basement along with seven other corpses. The rifle was the same make and model Michelis used. We believe it to be hers. Of the descriptions you sent us, only the Velasquez woman's body was among the dead. There was a struggle."

This news did anything but absolve Michelis of treachery. Something about Takashi's report mixed with what he knew of Michelis, and the addition of Dr. MacKenzie into the mix just didn't add up. Something stunk, and he intended to find out what.

"And what of Michelis?"

"We have her, sir. We followed the freshest tracks on the dirt road as far as we could. They led in the direction of Cochabamba. A credit card check revealed the missing Dr. MacKenzie registered alone into a hotel here. We've had a tail on her and she just met up with Michelis on the hotel grounds. They are in my sights. Do you want me to proceed with eliminating them, sir?"

Silence.

"Chairman. I repeat. Do you want me to eliminate Michelis and MacKenzie, sir? I have them in my sights, and am ready to take the shot."

It would be so easy to clean this mess up and sweep the whole incident under the carpet. Make Team Epsilon go away, problem solved. Eliminate Michelis and Takashi and it wouldn't matter who was lying and who was telling the truth. *It would matter to me.*

"No." The Chairman decided to let the drama play out.

"They're moving, sir. I'll lose my line of sight in ten seconds."

"I said no. Keep following and keep me posted on their activity." The man in Washington hung up the phone.

Smith turned to his second. "Stand down, Vargas."

The sharpshooter lowered his rifle. "Thank god."

❧ ❧ ❧ ❧

"You're clean and you actually smell good. I hardly recognized you," Seven said, a devilish grin on her face.

Jenny swatted her in the stomach, relief evident in her smiling eyes. "Come on. Your turn. A shower feels incredible." She led the way to their room, checking out the bag in Seven's hand as they walked. "What's in the bag?"

"A surprise."

"A surprise? For me?"

"Not tellin'."

"Well, what kind of surprise is that?"

"A surprise surprise."

"Fine. Be that way. Here's our room. They didn't have a double. Only this king suite was available. Hope that's okay. We'll have to share."

"The last time we slept it was under a rock. I think I'll survive. Thanks."

The door closed behind them and Jenny threw her arms around Seven's neck and hugged her fiercely. Seven hugged back and lifted her briefly from the ground. Jenny pulled back and said, "I'm so glad you made it. I have to admit I was a little worried something would happen while you were gone. I'm really happy to see you're okay. Were you able to get in touch with your Uncle?"

"Yep. We now have an official plan. By tomorrow night, we'll be in Peru. I'll fill you in over dinner. Do they have room service here?"

"Yes, Ma'am."

"Great. Let me get cleaned up and then we'll order. Okay with you? I can't wait to wash my hair." Seven, not one for modesty, dropped her bag on the couch and started peeling off her clothes and boots. Jenny plopped on the bed and pretended not to watch as Seven headed for the bathroom in her underwear.

Once in the bathroom, Seven checked her watch and made a bet with herself how long Jenny would hold out before looking in the surprise bag. She was rewarded almost immediately with a startled scream, followed by laughter. "You rat!" She yelled from the other room. A hand-carved and realistically painted snake curled lazily inside the small plastic bag, waiting forever patient to scare the living daylights out of its next victim. The laughter in the other room continued as the black haired woman shook out her braid and stepped grinning into the steaming shower.

Several minutes later, freshly clean and pink from the hot water, Seven stood wrapped in a towel brushing out her hair as Jenny berated her for the evil prank. "Well, I had to get some kind of souvenir of our trip to Bolivia." She snickered. "There's something else in there too. Did you look under the snake?"

"Hell no. What is it? A tarantula?"

Seven reached into the bag and took out a small package wrapped in plain brown paper. She sat on the edge of the bed and handed it to Jenny. Still suspicious, the young woman took the package and opened it to reveal an exquisitely carved and hand-painted leopard with two cubs lying peacefully in tall grass.

Jenny was speechless.

"I wanted you to remember that your time here wasn't all bad."

"It's beautiful, Seven. Thank you."

"You gotta take the snake too though, it's a package deal," she said, laughing once more as a pillow flew across the bed and whapped her in the head.

"Now. Where are the clothes you got me? There's no way I can put that sweat suit back on. That thing could stand up on its own by now."

"Those two bags there." Jenny pointed to the end of the bed, now attempting to keep a straight face. She turned on the television and pretended to watch, waiting with great anticipation to reap the reward of a little fun of her own.

Seven dumped one bag unceremoniously onto the

bed. She opened a package of underwear and socks, pulling both on in short order before dropping her towel and pulling a fresh sport bra over her head. There were a pair of black jeans in the bag and a pair of black cotton work pants. She pulled the cotton pants on, happy with the fit, and searched the bag for a shirt. Not finding one, she dumped the other bag onto the bed and stood wide-eyed and staring at something completely improbable.

"You got me a sky blue polyester blouse covered in red and yellow hibiscus, with ruffled cuffs? Are you out of your mind? What, about me exactly, says 'floral patterns' to you?"

Jenny looked over to her friend, her eyes fairly sparkling with glee. It was all she could do to contain herself. The expression on Seven's face was absolutely priceless. She didn't have the heart to push the joke so far as to actually make her put it on, though. After a minute of painful silence, she broke out laughing so hard tears streamed down her cheeks.

A polyester projectile hitting her squarely in the face was Jenny's reward. Still wheezing, she said, "I don't know what's funnier. My fear of snakes or your fear of flowers." Seven joined in and they laughed at themselves and each other. It went a long way to alleviate the strain they had been under for so long.

Jenny got up and handed her friend another bag. "Here. I got you some plain white t-shirts, a plain blue oxford, and a loose black leather jacket. I thought you might like to have a coat in case you wanted to carry your gun on you. I think there's a belt in there somewhere too."

"You really had me going there for a minute. These are great, thanks. The jacket is perfect. I was thinking you'd get us something to get by, you know? But this is above and beyond." Seven ran her fingers over the cool, smooth leather. She always had a thing for black leather. Did she mention that to Jen, or did the girl just know?

"What's that?" She pointed to a bottle sitting on the side table.

"Ah, yes. It's a bottle of Chicha, the local beverage of choice. It's made from fermented corn, or so the vendor said. I thought we might try it. I know it's not wise to get hammered, considering we're still in enemy territory, but after everything we've been through I could really use a drink. You game?"

"I'll get the glasses."

Jenny sat comfortably cross-legged at the head of the bed, while Seven lounged with her head at the foot, facing her. They sipped their drinks and waited for their room service order to arrive. Seven could tell by the look on Jenny's face she was struggling with herself again. Finally unable to take it anymore, she decided to push the issue a little bit.

"Jenny, whatever it is, spit it out. If you've got something to say, say it. If you want to talk through something, I'll do my best to be a good and impartial sounding board."

That was all the encouragement she needed to open the floodgate. *Okay. It's now or never.* "Be careful what you ask for, Sev. You may not want to know this."

"Try me."

"The shower felt good, didn't it?"

"Mmhm."

"Do you like the drink?"

"It's okay."

"I ordered us steak for dinner."

"Sounds good."

"The thing is, Sev…" Jenny's heart hammered in her chest. She could feel the heat climbing up her neck and into her cheeks. She took a deep breath and nervously jumped in with both feet. "I…I seem to have developed a very serious crush…on you."

Silence. Seven processed this new information, overjoyed she hadn't scared the girl off after all.

"So I wanted to apologize for my erratic behavior. I shouldn't have kissed you earlier. I mean, that was probably inappropriate and I…well…I don't want you to think I was just playing you or anything. I mean, well, I hope my behavior didn't make you hate me, or not want to be around me. This feeling is new to me, and kind of scary. I mean, I don't know how you feel. I'm kind of an idiot, I know, but I'm so conflicted. I've never felt so comfortable and happy around anybody before."

She buried her face in her hands, now completely embarrassed at her own behavior, and kept going. "Dan says I should just follow my heart no matter the outcome, and so I am and it keeps leading to you, and…oh crap. Maybe I should just shut up. I'm rambling now. I guess I'm scared. I don't want you to feel because I'm saying all this you have to say anything back…but…well…the thing is, I really liked that kiss. I didn't know this about myself before you. It never even occurred to me that I might like girls. And really, I'm not even sure if I do, maybe it's just that I like you. I'm absolutely certain my family will disown me. So I was wondering…like…what you thought. I'm mortified that I'm throwing myself at you, and you might just think I'm a tourist, or just a foolish kid or something. Oh, god. Why can't I just shut up?"

Seven sat up and silenced Jenny's rambling by lifting her chin and placing a thumb over her lips. She looked deeply into distressed eyes and smiled. She let her true feelings show on her face for the first time, her previous reservations out the window.

As they gazed at each other, Jenny's worries evaporated. She could tell with that look her fear was unjustified and Seven's feelings were strong, and there, just like hers. The furrow in her brow disappeared and her frown turned slowly into a bashful smile.

They stared at each other for what seemed an eternity before Seven closed the distance between them. "I am at your mercy, Jenny."

A loud knock on the door stopped her progress just short of her goal.

"Room service," came the muffled yell through the door. Seven stared at the irksome disruption and growled.

She looked back at Jenny who appeared to be a little dazed. Seven leaned in close to her ear and whispered a promise. "As soon as he's gone, I'm going to kiss you. For real."

She stood and walked to the bathroom, quietly closing the door to hide her presence in the room. It wouldn't do to have anyone see her, just in case anybody was asking around. Jenny remained motionless and somewhat nervous looking for a moment, staring blankly into space, taking small breaths through slightly parted lips. At the second knock, she walked in a daze to answer the door.

A young man in a white jacket rolled a large cart into the room and pulled the tableside up, locking it into position. He began setting the table as the petite blonde stood nearby, patiently waiting for him to leave.

He got the distinct impression she didn't want to talk, so he made quick work of removing and storing the plate covers, getting the bill signed, and getting out of there. He glanced down at the check on his way out and gasped at the massive tip. *American.*

As soon as the door was closed and latched, Seven came out from her hiding place. Jenny was lost completely in deep thought, not having moved one inch since bolting the door. Seven walked over to her and stood looking down as Jenny came out of her daze and met her eyes once more. Seven led her to the edge of the bed, sat, and with no further words between them took Jenny's face in her hands and brought their lips together.

There was no pressure or demand in the kiss. Their mouths moved in a gentle dance as they glided together slowly, testing the feel of the other's lips, tasting the softness of the other's mouth. Their motion was in perfect synchronicity as they breathed deeply the comforting scent of warm skin, temporarily lost to all else in the world.

The sensation was immeasurable. Maybe it was because there was so much more feeling behind this kiss, but Seven fell deeply into the warmth and softness of Jenny's beautiful, full lips.

She pulled her tighter and let her guard fully down, allowing the emotion of the moment to wash over her. She had to admit, this awareness was a first for her too.

Her body came alive as if charged, but she forced herself to pull back and look at Jenny's face. The worry creases and wrinkles were no longer there. Her eyes were closed and a tiny smile appeared at the edge of her mouth. If Seven didn't know better, she could have sworn the girl was asleep.

When she finally opened her eyes, a tremendous smile grew across her face as she blushed and held Seven's gaze with hers. "Wow," she exhaled heavily. "I'd like to order another one of those, please."

Seven complied with her request.

Chapter Twenty-one

Raul Argulla stood expressionless in the sub-basement of the Reyes Hacienda. This was the first time he had ever been invited into the stately home, so it seemed somewhat fitting that it was mostly his own doing that finally got him there. He moved aside the collar of Maria's shirt with the toe of his shoe, eyeing the bruises made by large hands around her neck. He had wondered why she never called.

Manny stood behind him, twisting the hem of his sweater nervously in his hands. Without turning around, Raul pointed behind himself toward the sniper rifle leaning in the shadows against the wall. "Do you see that?"

"Yeah," Manny said, throwing a glance over his shoulder.

"Do you know what it is?"

"It's a really big gun."

"It's a sniper rifle. Undoubtedly the one used to kill your father. Now why don't you level with me about this person you and your father asked us to hunt. She wasn't a thief, was she?" Raul already knew the answer, but wanted to finally get the details from young Reyes. Manny called him for help and he arrived as a testament to their friendship. He felt certain that without Armando Sr.'s bullying presence, Manny would tell everything.

Without hesitation, Manny divulged his father's

private information. "She was an assassin sent from the United States. I think dad said she was from the Department of Homeland Security. She was here for him."

"That much is obvious. What I want to know is why?"

"They must have found out about his middle eastern connections. He invested money for the organization that funds Al-Qaeda. He was connected to the 9/11 bombings somehow. Financial transfers, investments, something of that nature. His connection in Washington that sold him the information said by killing him, they could effectively disrupt the finances of at least six different terrorist organizations."

Raul was shocked at this information, but remained calm. *No wonder that prick was so freaked out the night he came to see me.* "Why didn't he just run? Disappear. Surely he was connected well enough to do that if he wanted."

"He was more afraid of his cover being blown with his terrorist backers than he was of the Americans. He didn't want them to find out the U.S. had targeted him. That was why he desired so much to wipe out the American team with no trace."

Argulla turned back to face Maria's body, a smile flashing briefly across his face. *The American saved me the trouble.* Argulla would get what he wanted without the sniper after all, with just a minor adjustment to his story. If they picked up the sniper, she would be able to tell the truth about what happened here. But without her...only he knew, now that Maria was dead. He would make sure the sniper wasn't pursued. Raul turned back to Manny. "So there are six of my men dead down here, plus Maria. Your father, and did you say ten others upstairs?"

"Eight upstairs and two in the outbuildings. Security guys."

Raul wondered where the rest of Reyes' security was, but then realized Maria must have figured out a way to remove them from the picture. The older man removed the smile from his face before turning around to face young Manny once more. "I'm concerned for your welfare, my friend."

"Me? Why? Do you think I'm in danger?"

It's like taking candy from a baby. "Yes. I certainly do. Now listen to me. When we alert the authorities, they are going to ask all the questions I just asked and then some. They are not discrete, no matter what they say. If they go after this sniper who must have done all this killing and left the scene, the same thing your father feared for himself will happen to you. The people he was dealing with won't just drop this because he's dead."

Manny stared wide-eyed, and nodded in gullible agreement. Raul couldn't believe how easy this was.

"So we have to come up with a credible story about what happened here, that will give the authorities what they need. If you're not careful, this could all come back on you."

"Me?" Manny spluttered. "I didn't do anything!"

"Doesn't matter." Raul turned away, barely able to contain a smile. He plastered his serious face on once more. "The fact is, you're Armando's sole heir. I'm guessing he's worth a couple hundred million easy. That gives you one hell of a motive. It would take them all of a heartbeat to write your name on the suspect list, even if you told them about the sniper."

"But...but..." Manny looked like he was about

to cry.

"Come on, son. Let's go back upstairs and get out of this hole. Don't you worry. We're going to come up with a plan that'll end this right. I promise. That's what friends do for each other, right? Help each other out of binds?"

Manny nodded and let Raul put his arm around his shoulder and lead him up the stairs. He guided the young man to his father's study and poured them both a stiff drink. Handing the drink over, and taking a long swallow himself, he continued. "Okay, so the way I see it, if you sic the police on the sniper, the Arabs will get you. If you don't, the cops will pin this on you. I can only think of one solution to save you."

"Please, Raul. You have to help me."

"We pin this whole thing on Maria. It'll be easy to put her prints on the rifle. We just have to fabricate a motive for her. She is a well-known murderer. It won't be much of a stretch for the authorities to believe she went on a killing spree. We'll set it up to look like one of my guys downstairs strangled her as she was trying to kill him."

"I can't let you do that, Raul. She worked for you. That would bring the suspicion in your direction. It wouldn't be fair to you."

"It'll work, Manny. I'll grease the authorities generously to make sure she takes the blame. Not only that, but you're the old man's only family. If you're not complaining, they'll close the case as quickly as they can. We just have to make it believable."

"Weren't you close with her?"

"She was a killer, Manny. An assassin. Perfect to take the blame. I hired her because she was a good fuck. That's all. In her death she will continue to be useful by helping you out of this dangerous situation."

"You'd do this for me?"

"Of course, my friend. Anything."

"What are we going to tell them was her reason?"

"Easy. We'll tell them your old man was fucking her. He dumped her and she came over in a rage. You came to me for help. I sent my men over to get her. She killed everybody. We put her prints on the rifle. We set her body up with one of the others downstairs so it looks like he killed her before he bled to death. A hundred grand in the right hands will convince them to close the case quickly, saving the family embarrassment, and it's over. Your father's Arab friends will never be the wiser."

Manny downed the rest of his drink as he considered the plan.

Raul gently placed the cherry on top of the chocolate fudge sundae. "It will take a while for an estate of this size to be settled. I would be happy to float you a couple million to live off while you get used to being the man of the house. I can send over my estate manager to help you run the properties and such, if you need him. It's a big responsibility, running an operation of this size."

"I guess I should call the police then."

"Be strong, my friend. You can do this. Your life depends on it. You call them, and I'll go back to the cellar to set up Maria's body. Don't forget to sound upset."

Manny nodded numbly and reached for the phone.

Raul headed for the cellar, chuckling to himself. *Must remember to get the knives off the men before I leave. Wouldn't want my young friend to find out they were the ones actually doing the killing.*

ℳℒℳℒ

A lethargic voice muffled by a squashed up pillow complained about the hour, stating in unintelligible words something about refusal, ungodly, and hungry. Seven pulled the pillow from under her head and whapped her with it. One green eye popped open and stared threateningly at her attacker.

"Come on, crabby. Get up. We gotta go. I really don't have any desire to become a political prisoner today."

"Oh god," Jenny whined. "What the hell is in that Chicha stuff, anyway? I could sleep for a week." She lurched off the bed and stumbled ungracefully into the bathroom as Seven flipped through the pages of the visitor's guide, looking for a nearby rental car company.

Jenny stepped into the shower before the water had fully warmed up. Running her head under the cool stream helped to clear out the cobwebs, eradicating her sleepy fog better than coffee ever could. As the water warmed, she placed a dollop of shampoo in her hand and began to scrub her head. Thoughts of the previous night raced through her brain, each vying for position as the top contender. The kiss, or kisses as the case may be, finally won. A close second was the embarrassment she felt at rambling on and on like a juvenile ass. In third place, was their plan for exiting the country today.

The kiss: I can't believe I just blurted out I had a crush on her like that. I thought she might just laugh at me, or something. She didn't! She feels the same about me I do about her. God! How great is that? And her kiss! If I didn't know better, I'd say smoke was coming out my ears. I guess I'm a lot more inexperienced than I thought, because that kiss blew me away. I swear my insides turned inside out. When she moaned into that second kiss, sweet Jesus. It felt like there was a live bass flopping around in my stomach.

A burst of happiness forced itself from her mouth in the form of a laugh.

"Did you say something?" Seven yelled through the door.

"No, you must be hearing things," Jenny yelled back, her voice sounded extremely loud to her own ears.

Now about my rambling...she seemed to take it all in stride. Actually, now that I think about it, I'm sure there's about a million things I wish I'd said that I forgot. Oh well, that's the beauty of a long car ride... plenty of time to assault her with irritating questions and personal concerns. She laughed again, but quieter this time.

Jenny avoided thinking about the day ahead. She was nervous about it, so preferred to think about pleasant things, like the woman waiting for her in the next room. Last night after a few really nice, long, leisurely kisses, Seven directed her to their table for dinner. Jenny's head was a little scrambled, so she let Seven do the talking. Uncle Nick had come up with what they both hoped was a fast and safe plan to get them out of Bolivia. It wasn't without risk, however. Sneaking from one country to another never was. The unknown factor was whether they were still being hunted or not.

The first step of the plan seemed simple. They

would rent a car, for cash if possible. Then, they would drive to a small village on the shores of Lake Titicaca called Huatajata. Unfortunately, they would have to drive right through La Paz. There would be a substantial military and police presence in that area, which presented their greatest risk for being spotted.

Last night when Seven relayed this information, she must have thought Jenny had a screw loose. There probably wasn't an English-speaking human alive that didn't think Titicaca a hilarious name, but when Jenny heard they were going there, she burst into a fit of schoolgirl giggles that eventually became contagious. It was unexplainable, but for some reason the two women set off on a tear-streaked laugh-fest that ended with Jenny falling off her chair clutching her stomach, and wheezing in an attempt to catch her breath. For the rest of the evening, all Seven had to do to entertain herself was say the words Huatajata or Titicaca and Jenny would start laughing all over again.

Even now, in the shower, just thinking about her bizarre outburst made her chuckle.

Seven watched under her brow as Jenny padded across the room wrapped tightly in a hotel towel and liberated of a bottle of water from the minibar. She chugged half without stopping for breath. Seven grinned and shook her head, returning to her task.

"You're all pink," she said.

Jenny chuckled. "Nothing like a cold shower followed by a scorching one to wake a person up. Whatcha doin?"

"Trying to make an ankle holster out of this belt for my gun. You gonna be ready to go soon? It's gonna be light in a little while."

"Yep. Fifteen minutes." Jenny brushed past,

leaving the scent of citrus soap drifting behind her on the air. Seven breathed deeply and smiled. "Did you know you hum while you're brushing your teeth?" She asked. "It's adorable."

Jenny just laughed and continued to dress.

❧ ❧ ❧ ❧

The rental car the two women acquired was, to say the least, lacking. They were well out of the city now, having decided Seven would drive and Jenny would navigate. "Ew. It smells funny in here, and the dashboard is actually sticky," Jenny said, crinkling her nose in disgust.

"As long as it gets us there."

"I need a bucket of hand sanitizer."

Seven chuckled. "You've been kind of quiet this morning. Everything okay? I mean...last night...I... well...are you having second thoughts or anything?"

Jenny was amazed how quickly Seven's facial expression could go from stoic soldier to unsure woman. She may be supremely confident in her professional abilities, but when it came to relationships, she was just like everybody else. Vulnerable.

Jenny unlatched her safety belt and kneeled on the seat, leaning across the center console until her lips were a hair's distance from Seven's ear. She kissed her lightly on the neck just below her ear and whispered seductively, "I doubt anybody's *ever* had second thoughts about you."

"Oh dear lord," Seven expelled a lungful of air as a flush crept up her face. "Je...Jenny. It's probably best if you don't do that while I'm driving."

"Am I *driving* you to distraction?" She teased,

still whispering in her ear.

"You're gonna distract me right off a cliff if you don't stop."

"But what a way to go." Jenny chuckled, leaving a row of feather light kisses along her ear.

"P...Please put your safety belt back on."

Jenny plopped back down in her seat with a satisfied grin on her face. She glanced over at her friend's glazed eyes and flushed cheeks, incredibly amused with herself for having affected her in such a way. "To answer your earlier question, no. I'm not having second thoughts. In fact, I can't stop thinking about you. You're an unbelievable kisser, you know that? With you...it's like a sensual dance...a work of art....a..."

"Jen!"

"What?" She looked over at her friend, still grinning from ear to ear.

"You better change the subject, or I'm going to have to pull over." Seven's frustration was obvious in the crease between her eyebrows.

"Promises, promises."

"God, I've created a monster. You're such a flirt! Have you forgotten we're in serious danger, here? I need to stay alert."

"Trying to change the subject. Clever. Won't work though. I have a captive audience, and lucky for me, it's you. Actually, if you must know the truth, the reason I've been quiet is because I'm pretty nervous about all this."

"About us?"

"No, but we'll get back to that. About this trip we're on. I'm sorry about the teasing. I'm feeling a little jittery and having some fun helps ease it a bit.

I think I've got some post-traumatic stress going on from my abduction by Maria." Suddenly serious, Jenny continued. "There was a moment, Sev, when she cut my shirt open and my bra. She poked that skinny knife of hers into my skin over my heart, and I was saying my goodbyes to the world. I may have appeared calm on the outside, but inside I was crying for all the things in life I would never have a chance to know. It was very harsh. I'm only twenty-four and I've worked so hard to get where I am. I haven't really had much fun, or a life at all for that matter, and I realized how much I regretted that."

Seven reached over and took Jenny's hand in hers, bringing it up, and pressing her lips to the young woman's knuckles.

"It's like what you said about not wanting to look back on your life not having done something you really wanted, for whatever reason. In that instant, I looked back on my life and had regrets. I'm too damn young to have regrets. I don't want to encounter that feeling again. I want to be brave. Take chances. Live."

"You are brave, and in case you haven't noticed, you're running for your life from an obsessed drug lord and god only knows who else, doing your best to save a government assassin. Call me crazy, but I'd say that's taking a pretty big chance."

The women drove in silence for a short while. Jenny seemed deeply lost in thought. "Is that what you're doing with me, Jen? Taking a chance? Do you think I'm a risk?"

Jenny answered thoughtfully. "No. I don't consider you a risk. You've been nothing but extremely wonderful to me. Taking a chance? Yes, I think so. I'm definitely stepping out of my comfort zone here, but the more I do, the more right it feels. If anybody's at risk, it's you, from me. I don't have a lot of confidence in my ability to stick with a relationship. It's not that I don't want to. It seems more like I just have bad luck choosing partners."

"Maybe you've just never had one worth sticking with."

"Do you think there could be something more between us, Seven? Or am I gonna end up screwing you over too?"

"If people could see into the future, there would be a lot less broken hearts. If you're looking for relationship advice, you're certainly asking the wrong person. You've got more experience in that area than I do. But if you ask me...'something more' is worth the risk. I've never met anyone like you, Jen." *In for a penny, in for a pound.* "Do you remember when you asked me what I was looking for in a partner?"

"Mmhm."

"I avoided answering because at the time I didn't know where your head was at, and I didn't want to influence you at all. Dan told me a little about your emotional turmoil, and that you were beginning to think you might be gay. If I was the reason for that, I felt you needed to come to terms with it on your own. Not because of anything I said or did. I feel like you have, now. At least, since last night you seem to be dealing with it okay. You didn't run screaming from the room when we kissed, anyway." Jenny chuckled.

Seven continued, "So back to the question I never answered...what I've been looking for, what I've always hoped to find...is someone just like you."

Oh my god, she said it. Jenny was a little stunned, but happy. She couldn't believe someone as together as Seven would ever be interested in her.

Seven glanced over to the passenger seat. She wasn't used to leaving herself open like this. Deep down she felt, hoped, and prayed the woman sitting next to her would not be the kind to treat what she was giving lightly. "Yes, I think there could be something more between us. If you want there to be, that is. I want you to take it slow, Jen. There's no hurry. Think about what you want, who you are, what feels right to you. Remember, you can't plan the rest of your life in one day. You can only plan the direction of your life. I'll be here for you regardless of what you decide."

Jenny reached over and brushed a stray hair behind Seven's ear, letting her fingertips linger for a moment on soft skin. "You're too good to be true."

"If you decide you want this…want me…I don't want you to worry about damaging our friendship. We have a strong bond, Jen, and now that I have it again, I don't intend to let go. We're friends first, and always, no matter what, okay?"

"Okay, friend." Jenny reached over and took Seven's hand in hers, entwining their fingers, and holding the offered hand to her heart.

☙❧☙❧

"What's up, navigator? You seem really nervous all of a sudden," Seven asked Jenny as the young woman bit a thumbnail and stared pensively out the car window.

"I just wish we could go around La Paz. I don't like having to drive right through the middle to get on the road to Huatajata. I'm sure the news about Reyes has gotten out by now. Even if we're not stopping here, the police and military presence is high and they could be looking for us."

"Barring any serious traffic, we should get through it in less than an hour. I just have to be careful not to get a ticket or drive erratically or anything. So no more groping me," she said with a laugh, trying to lighten the stress a little.

"Speaking of traffic, looks like it's building up ahead."

Seven slowed the rental car to a crawl, quickly finding herself blocked in a traffic jam. A half-mile ahead they could both see the flashing lights of a police barricade. She immediately started looking every which way for possible escape routes. Jenny's eyes grew round and her heart quickened.

"What do you think is happening here, Sev? Do you think this is for us?" Jenny said in a whispered voice tinged with panic.

"Just play it cool, Jenny. Don't panic. It could be nothing more than a coincidence."

"I can be cool. I was born cool," she said with a nervous laugh. "All right. Deep breath. Let's come up with a plan, just in case. My old roommate at school and I used to make crank calls for fun sometimes. It's just a little bit of light acting. No problem. So, if they ask you for I.D., pretend like you don't speak English or Spanish, only Greek. Okay? And I'll take it from there. I'll talk us out of it."

Seven raised an inquiring eyebrow. "Crank calls, how deliciously juvenile," she said with a 'do tell more' inflection in her voice.

A policeman walked slowly down the line of stopped cars, leaning into the driver's window for a moment at each of the trapped vehicles. His pace seemed casual, which gave Seven cause to relax her posture a bit. Her heart rate quickened as he reached their car and leaned in, looking closely at the two good-looking women in the front seat. He decided to pause here a little longer than at the other cars so he could enjoy the view.

"Hola," he said to the driver, a gorgeous brunette. Seven smiled and nodded at him without speaking.

"Hi!" Jenny barked, a little overenthusiastically. "No habla español. Speak English?"

"Sí. Yes," he replied, captivated by lovely green eyes and a bubbly personality.

"My friend is Greek. She doesn't speak either language." Jenny laughed for effect, rolling her eyes and feigning frustration. "Hey, what's going on? Is there an accident up there or something? We're supposed to be meeting some other students in La Paz in a little while." She smiled broadly at the policeman, her apparent enthusiasm at being a tourist spilled out like a burst dam.

Touristas. "No ma'am, just a security blockade. We should have it opened back up in a short time."

"Ohhhh. Somebody rob a bank or something?" Her inquisitiveness was charming. Seven could barely keep a straight face.

"No, nothing so exciting I'm afraid." He smiled at the cute blonde. "The presidential motorcade is coming through at any moment. As soon as he's past, we will remove the barricades. Where are you ladies headed?"

"We're meeting some friends at the University and then probably heading over to Jorge's for a drink. Do you know it?" Jenny mentioned the only bar she knew. One often frequented by her Peace Corps friends.

"Sí, sí. Haven't been there in a long time."

"Well, maybe we'll see you there. Have a nice day." Jenny pulled a fast one in dismissing the man. He didn't know if he was ready to leave, but found himself saying goodbye and walking away without realizing it had been done.

Jenny exhaled and slumped smiling into her seat. She looked over at her friend who sat grinning behind the wheel.

"This may very well be the first time this ever worked."

"What ever worked?"

Seven pulled her hand from under her leg where she was hiding it out of sight, and revealed to Jenny her fingers had been crossed. "I'm normally not much for superstition, but in this instance I was willing to make an exception." They laughed together, the relief evident in both their expressions.

"You were great, Jen. You even had me convinced, and I *know* where we're headed." She smiled over at her friend. "You're such a cute little tourista, that guy would've eaten right out of your hand. Why did you want me to only speak Greek?"

"I thought if he was looking for an American, it would be more convincing if you appeared to not be one. And, I thought if he asked for I.D., I would come with a story about how you got mugged in Cochabamba, with a knife wound in your arm to prove it."

"I don't care what anybody says about you, Jenny. You're a clever girl."

"Tch." A playful swat on the arm emphasized she got the joke and was faking her displeasure.

A short while later the barricades were removed, and traffic began to crawl forward at an agonizingly slow pace. Even though the policeman had alleviated their fears to a certain degree, neither could completely shake the feeling they needed to get as far away from this city as soon as possible. Both visibly relaxed as they got further and further away from La Paz, and closer to Huatajata, and their ride to Peru.

"Tell me again, what are we looking for?" Jenny asked, as they drove slowly down the main road through Huatajata.

"I'm looking for a trustworthy looking fellow to pay to take our rental back to La Paz. Maybe I should cruise by the local church. What do you think?"

"Why not try the bus station? Maybe there's someone there who is looking to head that way already?"

"Good idea. Once we ditch the car, we'll walk back to the lake marina and look for our guy. My uncle said he'd be wearing a baseball cap with the Peruvian flag on it. He'll give us a ride across the lake and drop us a couple miles outside of Puno. Nick says the border patrol is very lax around there, so as long as our driver is on the level we should be okay. If he's a Peruvian, he would probably know the best place to drop us so we're not spotted. Then we hike a short distance into Puno, grab a room, and relax because we'll be almost home free."

❧ ❧ ❧ ❧

The journey across Lake Titicaca made it possible for Jenny to enjoy herself and briefly forget she was on the run. The further she got from Bolivia, the lighter her mood until she was swept up in the feeling of being on vacation. The lake was a stunning sight; massive dark waters surrounded by the towering snowcapped peaks of the Andes Mountains proved an exceptional target for her Nikon as she snapped image after image.

Almost half the size of Lake Ontario, Titicaca sat over 12,000 feet above sea level, making it the highest commercially navigable lake in the world. The vistas alone made it worth her camera lens' greedy eye, but the local people made it truly fascinating. Indigenous, pre-Incan Uro Indians lived off the lake, puttering around in hand made totora reed boats, and floating reed islands wearing their brightly woven sweaters and tall brown bowler hats. These beautiful and friendly people were what Jenny would take with her in memory as she looked back on this time.

At one point, the young woman trained her lens toward Seven sitting relaxed in the bow of the boat, her silky locks whipping loosely behind her as she leaned into the cool wind. Her cerulean eyes sparkled in the late afternoon sun. On her face was a relaxed look Jenny was witnessing for the first time since they were reunited. As the miles passed, so did the strain that had etched itself in her features. Jenny found she was holding her breath as she watched the woman through her lens. She was stunning. *Focus. Click.*

As if sensing eyes upon her, Seven turned to notice the camera pointed her way and favored the photographer with a brilliant white smile. *Focus. Click.* She stood and made her way to where Jenny was sitting. "Cold?" She asked, smiling down at her friend, doing her best to hold the blowing hair off her face.

"As a matter of fact, I am a little chilly. How

much longer do you think it will take to get across?"

Seven removed her leather jacket and wrapped it around Jenny's shoulders. The toasty interior immediately warmed Jenny. She pulled the jacket closed tightly around her neck, the warm scent of leather and Seven giving her a sense of contentment and security she found supremely comforting. "Probably about another hour."

The rest of their boat ride passed quickly as they relaxed shoulder-to-shoulder enjoying the scenery. As promised, their escort dropped them with a friendly smile on the shore and pointed them in the direction of Puno, Peru, then pushed the boat back out and headed south along the coast. Heading toward the city, they debated potential cuisines they might choose to enjoy for dinner. They stuck close to the shore, walking casually along a road still in sight of the water, and eventually ended up at the lakeside hotel their escort had recommended. Jenny checked them in and returned to Seven with a smile. "I got us the Suite. It sounds pretty swanky, so it should be nice. The lady said it had two balconies overlooking the lake and a wood burning stove. Wanna go up and check it out?"

"Absolutely," Seven said, following Jenny through the lobby. No sooner had the door clicked shut, Jenny found herself pulled into a hug. Soft lips found hers for a kiss filled with passion, not demanding, but definitely more than the almost chaste kisses from the previous evening. She parted her lips, wordlessly inviting Seven to explore further, and in a matter of moments her heart was pounding and her knees were growing weak.

It was all Seven could do to pull herself away, wanting nothing more than to sweep this beautiful girl from her feet and carry her to the bedroom. She felt to her very core that loving Jenny would be an experience the likes of which she had never known.

Seven held Jenny at arms' length, looking for any sign of indecision or regret. She saw nothing but adoration and passion looking back at her, cheeks flushed pink, a charming, somewhat bashful smile slowly growing across her face. The smile was contagious as they looked breathlessly at one another. Both women sensed that what was happening between them was something big. The anticipation of what they could become together made life seem so much more beautiful.

"Hungry?" Seven finally asked, breaking the silence between them.

"Starved!" They laughed and backed out the door. "So what did we decide on? Italian or local cuisine?"

"I think local. Why don't we ask the desk clerk for a suggestion?"

"Excellent idea. I think a celebration is in order. I could definitely use a tall, cold drink of an alcoholic variety."

"I would like to raise a glass to you, my beautiful young friend. I owe you my life, and don't know how I will ever repay my debt."

"Uh…I believe I owe you mine as well, so let's call it even. Deal?"

"Deal. But I'm still picking up the check."

"Oh yeah? With what? Last time I checked you were cashless." Jenny laughed at the exchange, wrapping her hand around Seven's forearm and squeezing playfully.

"No, I'm loaded. I still have some left from what

you gave me the other day."

"Ah. I thought you spent it all on souvenir snakes."

"Surprisingly they're not all that expensive. I know...it appeared to be worth a fortune, especially the reaction it drew, but alas, it only cost a few Bolivianos." Seven snickered again, remembering the blood-curdling scream caused by her serpentine prank.

Dinner ended up being at an open-air, lakeside bistro with live local music and a wonderful selection of fresh food and cocktails. "The atmosphere here is just what the doctor ordered." Jenny smirked at her own pun, commenting on the comfortable setting overlooking the water. After two Brazilian caipirinha cocktails apiece, the pair were well into bold tales of mischievous adventures from their pasts, and debates on what would make up the ultimate dreamscapes for their futures. Seven idealized a solid home-life with a career that could make her proud and happy to go to work each day. Jenny dreamed of love and happiness, with a healthy dose of working for the betterment of others to give her satisfaction in her career. Jenny dreamt of someday having a baby, but laughingly committed to just a dog for now. Seven dreamt of a horse ranch in the mountains somewhere, made of stone and wood and glass with a gigantic stone fireplace.

As they celebrated their successful escape, both women shared their innermost thoughts about their pasts and their dreams for the future. They shared their disappointments and successes in life, gaining knowledge of each other that brought them closer. Seven admitted this trip to Bolivia had been her greatest personal failure and her greatest success all in one. Tears welled in her eyes as she reminisced about Marcus, knowing how much he and Jenny would have taken to each other. Jenny felt her failures lay in her intimidation by her family and her successes lay in her tenacity to see the right thing done, be it in life or as a medical professional.

"You're an amazing woman, Jenny. So beautiful, talented, funny…I can't imagine what you see in me, but I'm sure glad you see something."

"I see a lot. I see strength and loyalty. Beauty, and not just physical but inside too. Wit. I see a woman I admire. Someone who would sacrifice everything for what was right. You're the definition of an honorable person, Sev. They were right to give you that medal. What you did was brave, but who you are is honorable."

"Wow. You make it sound like I should be canonized or something. Trust me, Jen. I'm far from perfect."

"So am I, so how about we try being imperfect together."

"Deal. Of course, if you're the picture of imperfection, I can take that kind of flaw all day long." Seven leaned over and gave Jenny a quick kiss on the cheek just as their dinner arrived. A server placed two large orders of ceviche on the table as they happily inspected the whole, lime-marinated fish. The fish was served cold, never having been touched by heat, though the acidity of being completely submerged in lime juice cooked it through to tender perfection. Jenny's eyes matched her smile as she dove into the delicacy, not stopping for air until half the fish was gone.

Seven wasn't sure which she enjoyed more, her incredible meal, or watching the beautiful girl at her side dive into her feast with such enthusiasm it bordered on reckless abandon.

"I've never had this before, it's fantastic!" Jenny exclaimed. She glanced up to see her friend watching her eat and smiling. Pink crept up her neck as she realized how her manners had gone right out the window as she wolfed the entrée down. "Um, I guess I'll have to add 'how to eat like a Marine' onto the list of things you've taught me this trip, huh?"

Seven laughed deeply, her rich, melodic voice drawing stares from nearby tables as patrons stole glances at her stunning smile. She couldn't remember ever being with anybody that made her feel so completely at ease. "Jenny, I want to thank you. I truly missed not having you in my life. I'd forgotten what it's like to feel so good, to laugh so hard. I think I've laughed more in the short time we've been together than I have in years. As a friend, I absolutely adore you, and as potentially more than a friend, I want you to know I will never take you for granted. I've been around enough to know someone special when I meet one...and you're it."

Seven's heartfelt words momentarily took Jenny aback. Her intense gaze gave Jenny butterflies, a feeling she couldn't recall ever experiencing with another. She looked into her beautiful eyes, now the color of a deep blue lake, and was lost in their depths. Her breathing deepened as she fought to control her own desire.

"I will never take you for granted either, Seven. You make me feel things I was beginning to believe I wasn't capable of. When I look into your eyes, I see truth. I'm not sure how to explain it, really, but even though this time we've had has been terrifying, strangely I've never been happier. I want this." Jenny paused. "I want us. I think I'm a little nervous though. There are so many factors in my life to consider. I appreciate you're being patient with me."

They gazed over the candlelight; the romantic atmosphere held nothing compared to the sparks flying at their particular table. "I want this too, Jen. I want you. Take your time and think things through. I want you to be sure. Is it the thought of your family that has you doubting yourself?"

"Yes. I wish it weren't the case, but it's like a black cloud between me and happiness."

"Just be sure, Jen. That's all I ask. I'll be here for you no matter what, okay?"

Jenny nodded her assent and picked up her fork, attacking the fish once more. "Mmm. Maybe we should get dessert, too. What do you think?"

❧❧❧❧

Their suite had an open-ended divider wall separating the master bedroom from a small kitchenette and comfortably furnished living room. The thickly cushioned, wood frame furniture gave it a warm feeling of home. It was a corner room surrounded by windows with a narrow balcony overlooking the water. The view was breathtaking. Even at night, the play of moonlight on the water framed by snow-capped peaks standing sentinel was a testament to the romance of this small Peruvian city. Seven thought it would make an excellent honeymoon destination. She wondered if that frame of mind had anything to do with the heated necking she and Jenny had engaged in upon returning from their romantic dinner.

Jenny ambled out of the bathroom wearing a new t-shirt and a fluffy white hotel robe. She was deep in thought and looking freshly scrubbed as she headed toward the living room, where Seven had graciously volunteered to sleep on the couch. The light in the room was low, only the moon and flickering city lights reflecting off the white washed walls of their suite. Seven was lying on the couch, having already brushed her teeth and gotten ready for bed. She had one long bare leg flung out from under her blanket, and one arm resting behind her head on a pillow. Somewhere in the distance, the faint strains of local charango music wafted in on the cool mountain breeze.

Seven watched Jenny walk toward her, thinking about how cute she looked in that robe, and admiring the slight swagger in her gait. Jenny knelt in front of the couch and reached up to touch Seven's cheek, leaning down for a tender kiss. "Thank you," Jenny said.

"For what?" Seven asked with a gentle smile. She lazily ran the backs of two fingers down Jenny's jaw to her chin.

Jenny leaned into the touch, purring her contentment. "For listening. For getting me through that mess. For saving my life. For everything. For understanding. For having fun tonight. Just thank you."

"You're welcome," Seven said, and closed the distance for one more lingering kiss. "Sleep tight."

"You too." Jenny stood and headed toward the partition wall separating the bedroom. With one last glace over her shoulder, she said, "goodnight."

࿇࿇࿇࿇

Two hours later both women were sleepless and still staring at the play of light on the ceiling of their respective rooms. Seven gave up on sleep and got up to pace the living room, finally giving way to the tortured thoughts racing through her mind for hours. She stared at the damnable wall separating her from her desire, pacing back and forth wishing just this once she could put her honor aside, charge into the next room, and take what she wanted.

She wanted Jenny.

She wanted her so badly she couldn't remember ever feeling this intense level of desire for anybody before. She stared at the wall under hooded eyes, willing it to disappear, pacing from side to side with the quiet grace of a caged panther. Seven was sure she would go mad if she didn't have her. Erotic thoughts swirled with images in her mind of Jenny's tender lips and soft, warm skin, the rise and fall of her breasts. What it would be like to touch her, to hold her, to taste her, to crush her with kisses so deep she would surely drown in them. She whimpered quietly at the thought and closed her eyes.

Stop it! Stop it. She admonished herself. *Get a damn grip on yourself, Marine. This is too important. She is too important. You cannot afford to blow it with her. God, I feel like a hormone-crazed teenager! Maybe I could just sneak around the wall and watch her sleep for a little while. Yeah, right, you creepy stalker. Just leave her alone. She's got to find her own way, be it with or without you. Now calm-the-fuck-down.*

Seven paced over to the balcony door and leaned her forehead on the cool, night-darkened glass, slumping her shoulders and putting her face in her hands. She rolled her forehead from side to side, appreciating the refreshing chill. *Maybe I should just tell her how I feel. Maybe I should just go in there, and say 'You make me insane. I want you so badly I can't see straight. I want to tear your clothes off and make you scream my name.' Oh yeah, that's romantic. Well, maybe I wouldn't say it exactly like that. But maybe if I did, it would at least clear the air and help her decide if she wants me too. Yeah. And even if she doesn't, at least I'd know for sure. That would have to be better than sitting out here wondering. Okay. Come on, Seven. You're a woman of action. A decision maker. Let's do this.*

In the bedroom, Jenny's thoughts were also racing. She rolled over onto her side and stared out the dark window. *What are you afraid of? Your family's opinion of you? Dad is as conservative as hell. He's not going to take this well. Society's opinion? That she's not right for you, and you'll hurt her in the process of finding out? That you'll hurt her, period? That you'll hurt yourself? What if you sleep with her and it just feels wrong? Oh don't be stupid, Jen. I think you can be pretty sure that's not going to happen. She turns you on and you know it. God, she is too sexy for her own damn good. I cannot believe I am having these thoughts about a woman.*

She tossed once more, rolling back over to her other side. *It's just so strange feeling. It's as if she's the first person I've ever known that I'm totally comfortable with. I can just be myself, completely, and she likes me as is. Jesus, Jenny, you think too damn much. You want her. She's not going to wait around forever while you make up your mind. Why don't you just act? Just act. Do it. Go. Have some fun. What the hell. Do like*

Dan says. If it doesn't work out, chalk it up as a life experience and move on. No. She is too important. This feels too important. I don't want to blow it. What was that? Jenny raised her head from the pillow and sat up as she heard a faint noise coming from the living room.

Seven lifted her face from her hands, intent on continuing her pacing around the room, or acting on Plan A. She hadn't decided for sure which route she would take. As she raised her head, she caught a subtle movement reflected in the glass. For a moment, she considered it a figment of her overactive imagination. Seven turned slowly toward the demon wall that had been the focus of so much of her recent attention to see her lovely friend standing quietly in the shadows. She was not dreaming.

Jenny leaned against the wall with her hands behind her back to hide the slight tremor she knew was there. She stared silently for several minutes at the figure by the patio door. *Her hair is so beautiful, it's almost blue in the moonlight. And those long, toned legs, my god. She could crush me to death with those things and I would die a happy woman.* It was chilly in the room. Seven didn't appear to be cold, even though she only wore a black sleeveless tank and matching cotton briefs. She stood with one leg locked and the other bent in a sort of cowboy hitch kind of way. Jenny stopped breathing as Seven looked up and noticed her.

Their eyes met in silent understanding across the moonlit suite. The shadow play caused by moonlight reflecting off the lake made the room seem like a dreamscape. Jenny dropped her hands to her sides, blushed slightly, took a deep breath, and hesitantly stepped toward the watching woman. "I don't know what to do." She blushed again and looked at the floor. "I mean...with a woman. I'm not sure..."

Feet don't fail me now! Seven thought as she watched what she hoped was her dream about to come true.

Her feet didn't fail as she strode across the room and engulfed the young woman in her arms. She took Jenny's upturned face into her warm hands and brought her lips down for a soul-searing kiss so intense in no time both women could hardly breathe. She backed Jenny against the previously damnable wall and pressed the full length of her body into her willing captive, lengthening and deepening the next kiss to a level and intent that left no room for doubt as to what would follow.

Jenny moaned softly as she reveled in the feel of Seven's lips and hands on her face, her ears, her neck. "I want you, Seven," she breathed heavily into the taller woman's ear. "I realized my reservations couldn't compare to how much I want to be with you." She wrapped her arms around Seven's waist, letting her hands roam over the powerful muscles on her back. Suddenly Jenny could think of nothing more important than feeling those muscles without the hindrance of fabric. Her fingertips found and lifted the edge of Seven's black tank top and she pushed her curious hands underneath the taught material. She was not disappointed as the words *so strong* floated through her mind on a euphoric cloud. The warmth and softness of skin further fueled her desire.

Seven's hands left Jenny's face and made their way in an electrically charged trail down her arms, to her waist, and finally stopped on her behind, kneading and pulling her forward into a muscular thigh. Jenny sighed audibly as Seven's traveling hand found its way across her t-shirt and palmed her breast, a thumb making lazy circles around the sensitive center. The pleasurable sensation shot straight through to her groin. For Jenny, the need to be horizontal, naked, and completely wrapped around this woman was now unbearable.

Jenny pressed her body forward, never breaking the kiss, tugging Seven's shirt in a backward motion. She shuffled them carefully around the wall toward the comfortable bed until Seven's knees were at the edge. A tiny push had Seven sitting with Jenny straddling her lap. Both calmed slightly from their labored breathing as they looked smiling into each other's eyes. "You are so beautiful, Seven. I can't believe how lucky I was to find you again after all these years."

"And I can't believe how lucky I am to have the sexiest woman I've ever seen straddled half naked on my lap," Seven added with a rakish grin.

"Play your cards right, Marine, and she'll be fully naked and on your lap in a couple minutes," Jenny came back with some cheek of her own, blushing at her own forthright behavior.

"Jen, are you sure about this?" Seven asked seriously. "I don't want to pressure you into something you're not ready for." *Oh yes I do. Stop that.*

Jenny took a quivering breath and briefly dropped her head. She cleared her mind then looked into Seven's eyes. "I've never been more sure of anything in my life," she whispered earnestly. "I want you so badly Sev, I'm just sorry it took me so long to figure it out. Nothing on earth is more important to me, than this. Than us."

"You have no idea how happy I am you figured

it out in my favor." She flashed a sexy, crooked smile under hooded eyes intent on her target.

Seven eased her strong hands from their resting place on Jenny's behind to her hips and under her t-shirt, roving up and down her waist, over her taught, quivering belly, and finally coming to rest on the soft curves of her full breasts. Her thumbs worked magic over sensitive nipples. Jenny breathed deeply, closing her eyes and leaning her head back to speed the passage of air to her lungs. Her heart pounded as this latest stimulation sent the gut above her sex into butterfly spasms. She reached down to Seven's side and began to inch the black tank top up with her fingertips. "Off. Must have this off. Now," Jenny whispered, her voice ragged and desperate as she pulled on the fabric. Seven disengaged her hands and raised them over her head, laughing. Jenny reached over her own shoulder and grabbed a hand full of t-shirt from behind, pulling it over her head and tossing both to the side without ever breaking eye contact with the focus of her desire.

"What's so funny?" She smiled into another kiss.

"You're so enthusiastic, Jenny. You're fearless. Once you decide your direction, you attack without doubt or question. I love that about you."

Seven leaned back and pressed the flat of her palms on Jenny's abdomen. She forced herself to breathe as she worshiped the beauty before her. With infinite care, she slid both palms up, taking perfection in her trembling hands, in awe of the strength and softness of Jenny's body. Seven ducked her head, eager to taste what she so admired, eliciting a gasp from her partner. A purely sexual spark traveled like raging wild fire to her core.

Jenny's hands found Seven's breasts as she

explored her body, feeling alive in a way she had never experienced before. Jenny gently pushed her dark haired beauty back and stretched languidly over her body, thrilling at the first sensation of skin-to-skin contact as her breasts and belly found their counterparts on her partner. Their lips and tongues came together again as they wrapped themselves completely around each other. Jenny moved slightly forward and back with feline grace, creating a heady friction between them, moaning into the thought that this feeling was surely one of the most exquisite sensations known to lovers the world over.

Time passed slowly in focused mutual exploration of each other's bodies. "My god, Seven," Jenny panted on ragged breath. "The feel of your hands on me, I swear my heart is going to beat right out of my chest and fly across the floor." She laughed breathlessly. "I can actually feel my pulse pounding between my legs."

"I'm going for an aneurism, personally," Seven replied with a throaty laugh. "Feels like my brain is about to pop. I can't believe what you're doing to me." She breathed heavily, her desire evident in her eyes, her flush body. "You're making me absolutely crazy, Jenny. I've never felt anything this extreme before. I feel so connected to you somehow. I can't explain it."

Their verbal banter broke the intensity of the moment, giving each woman a chance to catch their breath as they lay face to face, noses almost touching, their arms and legs entwined. Seven paused to just look at and appreciate the peacefulness of Jenny's innocent young face. The flush tone of her skin, swollen lips, mussed hair, the physical signs of their coupling making her the most exquisitely beautiful creature she had ever seen. *She is everything I dreamed of and so much more.*

"Hey. You wanna share that bottle of champagne the hotel left us? I stuck it in the fridge a few hours ago," Jenny said, untangling herself from arms and legs and padding across the floor toward the fridge. "You've made me work up quite a thirst."

"Hurry back, I'm not done with you yet," Seven intoned with a gleam in her eyes, then sat up, already missing Jenny's presence though she only disappeared seconds ago. Her breathing slowed and she pondered her good fortune and the strange, almost obsessive need she had to be touching her every second.

Jenny swaggered back seductively, a loud pop from the champagne bottle ringing through the quite room. The foam erupted from the bottle. Jenny tried to catch the overflow in her mouth, missing most of it as it ran down her arm. She drank directly from the bottle, chuckling as she sauntered toward the bed. Choking on her mirth, Jenny said, "God, there's nothing worse than laughing champagne out your nose." She laughed harder at her totally blown attempt at seduction. "Sorry, couldn't find the glasses. Guess we'll have to rough it."

It crossed Seven's mind for the zillionth time how adorable this woman was. She pulled Jenny forward until she stood between her legs, wrapped one long arm around her waist and accepted the bottle with her other hand. She took a long, refreshing swig, then filled her mouth again and sucked a perfectly positioned nipple in with it. She used the tip of her tongue to mix warm, sensitive skin with cold, fizzing champagne. "Mmmm." She reveled in her lover's quick intake of breath. Seven followed a couple get-away drops down Jenny's body with her lips, leaving a trail of hummingbird kisses in their wake. She reached the edge of her bikini briefs and ran her tongue along Jenny's belly where fabric met skin, pulling occasionally at the garment with her teeth.

Champagne forgotten, Jenny stared in awe at the graceful beauty before her as she slowly kissed a path down her body. She glanced to the ceiling and wondered what good deed she'd done to deserve this. Her hand moved lovingly over thick black hair as Seven's long fingers wandered under fabric and pulled down, relieving the panting young woman of her final piece of clothing. "Better put that bottle down before you drop it," Seven said, smiling into fluttering skin. Her strong hands kneaded their way up the backs of Jenny's muscular thighs.

Jenny was suddenly nervous and very excited. Her body shook with adrenaline. She barely got the bottle on the bedside table as Seven pulled her down onto the bed.

With immense tenderness, Seven traced her fingertips down Jenny's cheek and leaned in for a deep, unhurried kiss, rolling the young woman onto her back and positioning herself over her. Jenny's breath caught at the desire evident in Seven's smoky blue eyes.

Seven reached behind Jenny's knee, pulling her leg up and wrapping it around her as she moved against her in a natural rhythmic motion as instinctual as breathing. Seven locked her elbows, arched her back, and pushed against her lover's center, holding her breath, staring intently into Jenny's lovely face so as not to miss one expression of pleasure shown there. Every breath, every moan, every sigh, the scent and softness of her skin, Seven wanted every detail seared into her memory for all time. Finally, not able to hold out any longer, the desire to touch her quivering partner overwhelmed her. She slid a hand between their bodies, seeking out warm, wet flesh.

"Oh god." Jenny could think of nothing more creative to say. In fact, she couldn't think about anything at all except the exquisite sensation she felt. Every nerve ending in her body came alive as though screaming for release. Seven's efforts quickly brought her to new heights, her muscles clenching, her breath coming in short gasps, her fingers digging into her captor's back. "Oh dear god, Seven…" Jenny's body seized as Seven swallowed her scream in a smiling kiss and held on for dear life as her partner suddenly displayed a fit of super human strength.

Seven held Jenny in her arms, rocking her gently as she caught her breath. "Hold on to me tight, baby. I won't let go." She covered her face and eyelids with kisses. "You are so amazing Jenny, you feel so good. Are you okay?" *I've been waiting for you all my life.*

"Ungh…" She smiled, intelligible conversation impossible.

Seven reached for the champagne bottle and brought it to her lover's lips. They drank deeply. As she leaned to return the bottle to the nightstand, she felt her shoulder being pushed gently back to the bed. Jenny suddenly appeared fully alert as she lowered her mouth to a ready nipple. She reached up and placed Seven's larger hand over her own, guiding both down the taller woman's now quivering belly. "Show me," she whispered in her lover's ear.

"Oh…oh my."

꿽꿽꿽꿽꿽

The sunrise over Lake Titicaca illuminated two sleepy lovers wrapped together on the cushioned loveseat they had moved from the suite onto the balcony overlooking the water. The morning air in the Andes Mountains was cold, and they were naked, so the thick blanket from the bed cocooned them both warmly from head to foot. The sky began to glow with the rose color of the coming dawn. The flush of pink resembled the skin tone covering sated and fatigued expressions, a remnant of their night's exertions.

Seven sat with one knee raised, the other and her arms firmly wrapped around her lover, whose back was pressed to her front. Jenny's arms were wrapped around Seven's raised leg with her head resting on the tall woman's knee. Seven trailed slow, undemanding kisses up and down Jenny's neck in a lazy way as both women were deep within themselves, her long black hair spilling over them. *I am so in love with you, Jenny.* Seven thought to herself, but didn't speak the words. *Don't scare her off, Sev. It's too soon.*

The phone in the room rang. "Guess that's our wake up call." Seven chuckled and they looked at each other and smiled. "We didn't need it after all."

Seven untangled herself from her cozy perch and answered the phone. Returning to Jenny's side, she pulled the young woman into her arms and held her tight against the chill of the cool mountain air. "I guess we should think about getting out of here, huh?"

"Uhuh. Wanna stay here forever," Jenny mumbled into the chest of her warm body blanket.

Seven scooped the blonde up in her arms, blanket and all, and walked into the suite, placing her gently on the bed. She kneeled in front of her. "Are you okay about everything, Jen? Last night? I feel like maybe I could have shown a little more restraint."

"I'm more than okay, Seven. You didn't show restraint because I didn't want you to. I've never been happier about staying up all night in my life. You're the most wonderful lover I could have ever hoped for."

"Jen, did you feel anything...more? I mean, maybe it was all in my head but I felt a connection with you unlike anything I've ever known." Seven hesitated, afraid she was sounding like a lunatic.

"It was like my soul was humming," Jenny said after a moment's thought. "We've always had a strong bond that was hard to figure out, but last night it was like a tuning fork ringing true. I felt it all right. I feel it still. It feels like something that was meant to be since the day we met all those years ago."

"Good. Then I'm not crazy." Seven pressed her lips into soft blonde hair. "How 'bout we try out that monster Jacuzzi in the bathroom?"

"Mmm. That's the best offer I've had in"—Jenny glanced over at the clock—"at least thirty minutes."

Chapter Twenty-two

The rental car the two sleep deprived women picked up in Puno was a vast improvement from the one they had the day before. Comfortable leather seats, a working radio, and nothing sticky on the dash went a long way to impress the young doctor. "You could eat off this thing," she commented, referring to the tidy vehicle.

"Thanks, I'll pass. I could use some lunch though. You interested in finding a place to eat with a nice ocean view?" They were driving north on the pacific coast heading toward Trujillo, a town in the la Libertad province of Peru. Seven's uncle Nick had arranged for them to meet the Captain of a US Navy vessel who was willing to fly the pair back home under cover on a supply transport. They would meet at the ship, which was temporarily stationed in Peru as part of a humanitarian effort to help victims of a recent flood. The captain was an old college buddy of Nick's, and promised to deliver them safely back home for the price of Nick forgetting the thirty-five-year-old poker debt he still owed him from their university days.

"That's sounds great. I could eat a house. I think I burned a week's worth of calories last night." Jenny smirked at her new lover.

"You're telling me." Seven raised a cheeky eyebrow. "Are you sure you never did that before? Because everything on me was screaming you were a pro."

"Well," Jenny said with an air of superiority, "I did get an "A" in anatomy." She ran a suggestive fingertip up Seven's bicep.

"Don't tease me now, or I just may pull the car over and go for a repeat performance."

"In a car? How romantic." Jenny laughed, now getting into the game she had started by striking a seductive pose.

"Well, you were the one that said the car was clean enough to eat off of."

"Ahh ha-ha!" Jenny swatted her friend on the arm, laughing sarcastically. Her cheeks turned an adorable rosy color.

"I win. You blushed first," Seven deadpanned.

Jenny unfastened her seatbelt and leaned over to the driver's ear.

"No fair taking your seatbelt off!" Seven complained, but not too strenuously.

Jenny nipped her earlobe and whispered a few choice words in her ear, kissing her neck in the place she liked it most. She could feel the heat rising under her lips just before she sat back with a self-satisfied smirk on her face. "Who's blushing now?" She whispered.

"Okay, that does it. I'm pulling over."

"For lunch, I hope." Both women laughed as Seven eased the car slower and turned west onto a road that would take them to the sea. A bit of driving brought them to a small fishing village where they found a thatched roof cantina with a wood deck built out over the sand. The five tables on the deck were all empty, but a young woman behind the bar greeted them and bid them to sit wherever they liked.

"Well, this could go one of two ways," Seven said, eyeing the establishment with a suspicious grin. "Either we'll get food poisoning, or end up having the best meal of our lives."

"I vote for best meal," Jenny said.

The server approached them with two icy looking Pilsen Callao cervezas. Jenny took a long pull on the cold beverage. "Mmm. Looking good so far."

Seven asked the woman in Spanish if there was a menu, and she said no, explaining they just served whatever fresh catch was coming in off the boats that day. She placed an order for two of the fish du jour. The woman smiled and left them to enjoy the scenery.

They put their heads together, laughing and teasing one another while they enjoyed their drinks and grew closer without the strain of being hunted. They took turns spouting off random music lyrics, challenging the other to remember the singer and song title. The tally had Seven way ahead, and she always managed to come up with a lyric that was suggestive in nature, doing her best to make her young lover blush.

"Why do you always do that?" Jenny laughed and pinkened up at her latest lyric.

"Because when you blush, I think it's absolutely adorable. You are so damn cute, Jen, I just can't get enough. I could stare at your expressions for the rest of my life." Seven suddenly did a little blushing herself at her unplanned admission. "Okay...how 'bout this one?" She voiced a lyric she thought most closely expressed what she felt whenever Jenny was in her arms.

"I know that one. The Cure. 'Love Song.'" Jenny looked down at her hands and smiled. When she looked up, the love in her eyes was quite visible to the older woman. It took Seven's breath away. As Jenny opened her mouth to sing the lyric, a sound across the small cantina drew their attention.

An extremely old woman dressed in a brightly colored and tattered poncho commonly worn by the local Quechuan tribe stood unabashedly staring at them and cackling. She laughed and smiled, pointing at them and speaking in a language neither could understand. Her wrinkled brown skin spoke of decades spent in the seaside sun, but her eyes were bright and full of mischief. She pointed a gnarled brown hand in their direction and cackled, mumbling incoherently.

"Is she laughing at us?" Jenny asked, the toothless smile of the old woman becoming infectious.

"I have no idea. Sure looks like it though. Maybe she's nuts." Seven started to chuckle as the old woman continued to chatter away.

At that moment, the server showed up with two large plates with whole grilled sea bass, fresh lime, white rice with black beans, mango salsa, and a pile of fried plantains. The aroma of spices coming off the plate made Jenny hum in anticipation. "Toldja."

Seven looked up at the server and smiled. She indicated the old lady with a head nod and asked, "Do we get a discount for being the entertainment?"

The server laughed and looked over to where the old woman was still pointing and seemingly talking to herself. "That's my great-grandmother. I'm sorry if she's bothering you. Usually she keeps to herself, but she seems to have taken a liking to you."

"What is she saying? I can't understand the dialect she's speaking," Jenny asked, smiling back at the toothless old woman.

"She's Quechua. She doesn't speak Spanish like

most of us. She says what you have is a gift. I'm not really sure what she means by that, she can be kind of mystical at times."

The server called over to her great-grandmother and asked her something in the old woman's language. "She asks if she may meet you."

Seven and Jenny both nodded their agreement and the old woman approached.

The great-grandmother took Jenny's hand in hers and petted the back of it, her eyes twinkling all the while. She reached up and brushed gnarled knuckles down her rosy cheek saying what sounded like terms of endearment. She then approached Seven and took one large hand in both of her tiny brown ones. To the taller woman, she laughed, said a few more things neither understood, then with one last toothless smile, she turned and shuffled away.

"She said it was an honor to meet you, and no circumstance will divide what is one. She also said old souls sharing happiness and harmony was magical. Thank you for agreeing to see her. I can tell it meant a lot. Please enjoy your meal."

They did. Jenny dove into her lunch with fervor while Seven watched, amused. After a moment, she joined in, and both ate in silence while pondering the strange encounter.

"Well?"

"Well, what?"

"Come on, Jen. I know you're dying to comment on the old lady."

"And I know you probably thought she was going to tell our fortune and ask for money afterward." Both women laughed at each other. It was still surprising for Seven to be with anyone that knew her at all, let alone so well.

"Well, it's a little unsettling to think we're so transparent, but you have to admit when she mentioned our harmony, that struck a chord...no pun intended."

Seven chuckled at her friend and nodded. "Yep, okay. I know what we talked about this morning was strange, but I felt it to. We do have something special, Jen."

"The closer I am to you physically, the better I feel. It's a powerful feeling, and when we're together like last night, I felt in tune with myself."

"Do you believe in the 'old soul' thing like your grandmother used to tell you?" Seven asked.

"I'm skeptical, but yes. I think I do. Maybe we're both old souls. Maybe we recognize that in each other on some level. Don't you think there's something special with how we've always bonded?"

"Yeah, but when you told me your grandma used to call you that, I always thought she just meant you were mature for your age."

"Maybe it means more. Sometimes, not often, but from time to time I've felt like I knew things I had no business knowing. I have no idea where I learned these things, but it was as if I knew them from birth. That sounds dorky, doesn't it?"

Seven thought about it for a minute and smiled at her new lover. "Yes, it does sound dorky." Jenny slapped her playfully and laughed. "But, I have to admit, that kind of thing has happened to me too."

"What do you think it all means?"

"For us? I think it means we keep an open mind."

⚜⚜⚜⚜

Two young men in crisp, starched, and pressed Navy blues stood sentinel in front of a chain link fence guarding the entrance to the USS McFarlan, a Wasp-class amphibious assault ship. The vessel was part of a small group of ships stationed in Peru on a humanitarian mission. In previous years, tight security would not have been necessary while offering assistance in a peaceful country, but after 9/11 and the attack on the USS Cole, it became apparent any vessel with US on the side had potential to be a target for terrorists. Every man and woman serving in any capacity was in a constant state of alert.

One young man who appeared no more than eighteen years old eyed the two attractive civilians as they approached, and whispered "hot chicks at twelve o'clock," under his breath to his guard duty partner.

"Look sharp, seaman," the older of the two said to the young man. "These could be the VIPs the Captain is waiting for."

"No chance, Suarez. Capt'n said he was expecting some badass super commando or some shit. Not a couple of models from *Outside Magazine*."

"Don't be a tool, Rossi. Capt'n said to give 'em white glove treatment, and I quote 'Medal of Honor recipient and genuine American hero.' He didn't say anything about a super-commando."

"Whatever."

"It's your funeral."

The two women approached, led by a tall, gorgeous brunette with dazzling eyes. The woman behind was definitely the kind you could take home to mama. She stared back at him with an amused gaze. Both were a breath of fresh air to the cocky Midwestern boy.

Rossi couldn't help himself. "Sorry, ladies. I'm working now, but I'll be free for that drink Friday night. Pick you up at eight?" He smiled charmingly.

Seven had explained to Jenny before they arrived at the vessel she would probably not recognize the person she would become in front of other military personnel they would meet. She asked respectfully that Jenny hang back and watch, but not to interfere and definitely no teasing. Nothing could ruin a tough reputation faster than being ribbed by a cute, petite blonde.

Jenny happily stood back and enjoyed watching her lover go to work.

To the young seaman, Rossi, Seven slowly arched an eyebrow up to her hairline as she stepped up and stood to her full height, eclipsing him by a good five inches. She let a scowl form on her face and flared her nostrils, never once breaking eye contact with the suddenly nervous young man. Her ramrod posture, no-nonsense demeanor, and a sub-vocal growl alerted both men immediately that even though she was dressed as a civilian, this woman was not to be messed with. Her bearing screamed military.

Seven said nothing. Menace radiated from her every pore. Jenny had to hide a smile as poor Rossi's face turned pale under the potent inspection of the formidable woman towering over him. She shifted her menacing gaze to the older boy and he stood to attention and puffed his chest out slightly.

After several painful minutes of being silently chastised, and completely intimidated, the older boy bravely spoke up. "May I help you, ma'am?"

In a whisper barely audible above the light sea breeze but brimming with aggravated intensity, Seven said, "Captain Michelis and Dr. MacKenzie to see Captain Devitt. He's expecting us."

Rossi quickly joined his partner at attention, both men acknowledging Seven's rank. "Yes, Ma'am. Please wait here while I call it in. An escort will be here shortly to take you to the captain."

Seven nodded her understanding, still staring intently at the now sweating Rossi, who remained standing at attention. Seven was a civilian now, but these kids didn't know that. Might as well have a little fun. She stepped over to the older boy. "Suarez, is it?"

"Yes, Ma'am."

"The people on board this vessel are depending on you to keep them safe. This is a very important job, not to be taken lightly. Do you take this job seriously, Suarez?"

"Yes, Ma'am."

"More seriously than your friend here?"

"Yes, Ma'am."

"That's good. Because when I'm on this ship, I want to know men who take their jobs seriously and not a couple of fuck ups are watching my back. Understand?"

"Yes, Ma'am."

Seven turned and winked at Jenny, a tiny smile tugging at the edge of her mouth.

A short while later, a female officer arrived and led the pair up the gangplank. As they were walking away from the two guards, Seven smirked as she overheard Rossi say to his buddy, "Dude. I'm sorry I got you in trouble, but that was awesome! That chick ripped me a new asshole and she never even said word one to me. How the hell did she do that?"

The older replied, "Rossi, for once in your life

could you please just shut the fuck up?"

Jenny leaned over to Seven, speaking low for her ears only. "That growly thing you did was hot," she whispered, as the taller woman blushed and gave her the evil eye.

The officer stuck a hand toward Seven and introduced herself as Commander Wahlston. "It's an honor to meet you, Captain Michelis. I've heard some stories about you." Seven rolled her eyes, unseen by the older officer. "I have to say, I think Captain Devitt is fairly excited to meet you as well." Jenny noticed how Seven said little but walked very tall. She showed no emotion on her face or in her demeanor, but her eyes never stopped moving. She took in everything. Along the passageways, they passed several people who acknowledged Seven and a few who stopped to shake her hand. Her manner to these people was gracious, soft-spoken and almost shy. She seemed embarrassed by the attention. She said to the officer, "I thought my uncle explained to the captain my need to be incognito here. It seems as if everybody knows me. What is going on?"

"Yes. Sorry about that. It was the General's doing. He's quite boisterous. He showed up and word got around. He and the Captain put us on communication lockdown until seventy-two hours after you've gotten safely home."

"General?" Seven asked, getting more wary with every step.

Commander Wahlston opened the door of the shipboard conference room to the sound of a booming voice carrying loudly across the enclosed space. Seven recognized the voice immediately. "I'm telling you, Devi, everything you heard is true. I was there.

Michelis!" The general boomed in his deep voice, welcoming the new arrivals.

Seven smiled broadly at the general and shook his hand. She had always liked this man. "Congratulations on your promotion, Brigadier General Lemsky."

"Damn good to see ya still on two sticks, Michelis," the general barked.

Seven hadn't seen the man since he was battalion commander in Kosovo, but she could tell he was still as wily as ever. "Thank you, sir. If you don't mind me asking...why are you here?"

"Was in Lima for a meetin'. I'm shipping out to the Middle East next week. Ol' Devitt here told me one of my favorite Marines was coming on board, so I thought I'd come see for myself. I guess I musta told your story once or twice over a whiskey or two, so the old salt gave me a call."

Seven turned to face the man standing next to the General. He was tall and thin with very white skin, and what was left of his hair was cropped very close to the scalp. He smiled at Seven as if they were old friends. "Captain Devitt. Thank you for your assistance. My uncle says terrible things about you. All of them true, I hope."

The two men boomed with laughter. "That old Devil Dog Nick is spreading rumors about my poker ability, isn't he?" Captain Devitt asked, chuckling.

"Well, let's just say, sir, practically every Marine in the 3rd Battalion is dying to sit at a table with you." The General started in on another round of laughter while the Navy man was looking a little like his feathers had been ruffled.

"Gentleman," Seven said, finally turning to her friend, "please allow me to introduce you to Dr. Jenny

MacKenzie."

Jenny stepped forward and exchanged pleasantries with the two men. "It's a pleasure to meet you, General. Thank you for your help, Captain. I have a tremendous amount of respect for the work you're doing here to help the Peruvians."

"Thank you, young lady. It's nice to see someone appreciates me around here." The three chuckled at his false hurt feelings.

"Jenny," Seven said, directing her attention back to the General, "Brigadier General Lemsky was the Battalion Commander in Kosovo when I was there with Marcus. He and Major Nichols are the officers that recommended me for the Medal of Honor."

"Ah yes. I had to beat it out of her, but she eventually told me the story," Jenny said, teasing her friend about her modesty.

"Young lady, do you know this rogue you're traveling with is one of the finest Marines I've ever had the pleasure to command? Her successes in the field and of those like her are the reason I'm wearing this star today. I have this old uniform of hers in my 'Hall of Fame' with four damn bullet holes in it, and she walks away without a scratch. That's my ideal of the perfect Marine. One who can wreak havoc when called for and walk away at the end of the day a better Marine."

Jenny's eyes grew wide as she looked at her friend. Seven obviously hadn't told her every detail of her heroic story. Jenny withdrew a small object from her shirt pocket and showed it to the General in the palm of her hand.

"Well, I'll be a pig in mud. Is that what I think it is?" All three leaned over to see what the young doctor was holding out. In her hand lay a bullet, its shape distorted from its impact with Seven's arm.

"You can add two more gun shots and a knife wound to the tally, General. Following Seven around has kept me quite busy."

"Damn woman has nine lives," the General stated happily.

"I didn't know you saved that," Seven said, a traumatic memory flashing briefly across her face.

"I thought you might want it as a souvenir. You know...I went to Bolivia and all I got was this damn bullet and a hole to go with it...etc. etc."

"Does your uncle know you were injured, Seven?" Captain Devitt asked, suddenly worried. "Do you need to see one of our shipboard physicians?"

"No thanks, Captain. Jenny saved my life. I assure you, I'm in the best of care." Seven looked over at her friend and flashed a beautiful smile.

The General piped in, "The U.S. of A. owes you a debt of gratitude, young lady. You must've gone through a half dozen scalpels just trying to cut through that thick hide of hers." They all laughed before the General continued, "So what the hell were you doing that got you shot in Bolivia?"

The Captain led them over to a large table where they all sat and helped themselves to coffee from a serving tray. Seven wasn't sure how much information to reveal. She trusted these men implicitly, but top secret was what it was. She knew she couldn't leave them with nothing, however. She couldn't expect these men to risk their lifelong careers without anything to base their judgment on.

"I'm part of an experimental branch of the Department of Homeland Security called the Black

Flag Company," Seven began to explain.

"Considering what you did for the Marines, and since Black Flag means 'take no prisoners,' I can guess what they're all about," the General said.

Seven nodded to the affirmative. "Yes, sir. On a discretionary basis." Seven went on to describe the BFC and how they worked. "Our target in Bolivia was a key member in a powerful network directly financing at least six terrorist organizations, including Al-Qaeda. It appears that one of our own sold us out. My crew was killed in an ambush, and I would've been too if it wasn't for Jenny. General, do you remember Marcus Johnson, my partner?"

"Yep. Good man. You two were quite a team."

"He was one of the men killed," Seven said sadly.

"That's a god damned shame!" The General barked, his anger at the loss of a good Marine was genuine.

"Now you can see why I need to get back without alerting anyone at the Department of Homeland Security that I'm alive. I need to flush out the man responsible, then I'm going to take care of it." Seven noticed Jenny make a negative movement with her head. She already knew Jenny wouldn't approve if she targeted Tak, but she couldn't let Marcus and Ty's death go unanswered.

Jenny was not an easily intimidated person, but she found herself sipping coffee at a large wooden table with two Captains and a Brigadier General and suddenly felt very, very young. She caught herself staring more than once at General Lemsky and thought he didn't look anything at all like Patton, Ike, or MacArthur, but he seemed to make up for in personality what he lacked in size. She felt like a fish out of water, but was seriously impressed with how smoothly her lover fit in. Even out of uniform and technically out of the service, people seemed to understand and respect a fellow Marine when they saw one. They could tell she was one of them without even knowing her. She had a commanding presence that was impossible to ignore.

Jenny watched her friend discuss the Captain's plans to get them home and smiled to herself. This woman was indeed different from the one she knew intimately, but she found she liked all sides of the complex personality she had seen so far. She had seen her fight. She had seen her laugh. She had seen her cry, kill, love, debate, and intimidate. It didn't seem to matter what Seven threw her way, she adored everything the woman had to offer. *It must be love, because even in my thoughts I sound like a lovesick fool.*

❧❧❧❧

General Lemsky said his goodbyes with promises to assist if called upon. Seven thanked him for his concern and assured him she had everything under control. It was just a tiny white lie, but she felt this was something that needed to be handled with a minimum of fanfare.

Captain Devitt led the women to an officer's stateroom where he indicated two navy uniforms hanging from a hook on the back of the door. "These should fit. My Executive Officer Wahlston, who you met earlier, pulled these together. We'll stuff all your packs and gear into Navy duffels and send them on to the supply plane. It will depart in about six hours, so why don't you rest for a bit, get changed, and when you're ready, meet me on the bridge. I'll have documentation collected for you by then."

"Thank you, Captain. We appreciate everything you're doing for us." Seven shook the man's hand and closed the door after he left. She sighed deeply. It had been a while since she had worn her warrior facade for so long. She had forgotten how tiring it could be to stay mean looking all the time.

She turned into the stateroom and was met with a huge smile, and eyes sparkling with pride.

"What?" Seven asked suspiciously.

"You're really amazing, you know that?"

"Why? What'd I do?" Jenny's grin was becoming contagious.

"You're just amazing, is all. I mean, you told me a little about your heroics and your career, but to see you here, like this, is quite impressive. You're like the military's version of a rock star. I would have thought that impossible for a woman. It's a hell of an accomplishment. From what I've seen, your reputation alone has probably gone a long way to help change people's attitude about women in combat."

Seven was somewhat mystified by Jenny's assessment. A blush crept slowly up her neck. "I...I wasn't trying to change anything, Jen. I was just doing my job."

"Be that as it may," Jenny said, walking slowly toward Seven wearing a predatory look, "I think it's sexy." She reached the stunned woman and ran her hands suggestively up her arms to her neck, pulling her down for a passionate kiss.

Seven backed up against the door like a kid unwittingly caught in her first kiss. She moaned and pulled away from Jenny, giggling nervously. "Je...

Jenny," she exhaled, "I can't do this. Not here. No way!"

Jenny laughed at the deer-in-the-headlights look on her partner's face. "Why ever not?" She asked innocently. "We're alone. We have a few hours to kill. You're sexy as hell, and we have two lovely uniforms in which to play dress up." She moved in for another kiss.

Seven ducked under an outstretched arm and bolted to the other side of the room. "I...I...no way, Jenny. I just can't. It's too close to home." Seven laughed nervously at her predicament. "It'd be like having sex in my mom's house while she's in the next room."

Jenny grinned. "We could try that, too." She kept up her predatory assault.

"This is somebody's berthing. Two somebody's."

"So."

"We could get caught."

"So."

"This place makes me feel the opposite of sexy."

Jenny chuckled under her breath as she backed Seven against the bunk and pushed her down to a sitting position. Seven leaned back on her hands as Jenny balanced her weight on a knee placed precariously between the taller woman's legs, and leaned in for a kiss. Jenny moved to nibble an ear and whispered a bit of bardish, "Methinks she doth protest too much." Teasing Seven was quickly becoming her favorite pastime, even more so because she begged her not to. Forbidden fruit was so much sweeter.

The stoic warrior gave in. Somewhere in her protesting mind, she thought *oh well, if you can't beat 'em, join 'em.* She wrapped her arms around Jenny's waist and pulled her close, kissing her soundly.

Jenny collapsed on top of her, pleased with her victory. In fact, she was enjoying their contact so much, she didn't register the sound of the metal on metal door latch being pulled until she felt Seven's lips pull away from her with a jerk. Seven sat up so quick she had to grab Jenny by the arms to keep from tossing her to the deck.

Several things happened at once.

Jenny was so startled at being busted she squeaked. Her body jerked and she slipped off Seven, thunking onto the deck. Her face landed embarrassingly in Seven's lap.

Seven cursed, "Shit!"

Commander Wahlston stood startled in the doorway, stuttering in embarrassment, "Uhh…umm…uhh…I…"

Jenny flew to her feet, turning beet red, and burying her face in her hands. "Oh my god," she lamented.

Seven found the entire situation hilarious. "I told you, Jen. But ohhhh no. You didn't care. You care now though, don'tcha? There's no such thing as privacy on a ship." Seven's shoulders shook with mirth. *Figures. An entire career in the military making it my mission to never stray, and the first time I do, I get busted.*

Seven stood as the officer was about to leave, "I take it this is your berthing, Commander Wahlston?"

Like Jenny, the older officer was turning pinker by the second. She swallowed her embarrassment and turned back toward Seven. Jenny's face was still buried in her hands, her shoulders now bouncing in silent laughter. "Yes, Captain Michelis. I apologize for barging in. I thought you were still in the conference room with the Commanding Officer. Did the uniforms I got for you fit all right?" She stepped all the way in and closed the door behind her.

"Haven't tried 'em on yet. We were about to when my friend here got distracted. Please don't apologize. We're sorry to intrude on your space and appreciate what you've done for us."

"I'm sorry, Commander Wahlston," Jenny squeaked from behind her hands.

The Executive Officer laughed and walked over to the blonde, placing a hand on her shoulder in a motherly way. "Don't be," she said to Jenny. "I've been at sea for a long time. I miss being around family sometimes. You're welcome to use my cabin as long as you like. I won't be back here 'till my shift is over in about six hours, and the officer I share this berthing with is ashore. Nobody else will bother you." She picked up a book from her desk then turned to Seven, "Captain Michelis, it's been a pleasure. Good luck on your journey."

"Call me Seven, and thank you."

"I'm Maggie. Nice to meet you both." With that, she left, latching the door securely behind her. Before the door was fully closed Seven heard the woman mumble, "Marines," and chuckle as the latch clicked shut.

"Sev, did she mean what I think she meant?" Jenny asked.

"Yep. She's gay."

Jenny chuckled and sidled back up to her tall partner, wrapping strong arms around her waist. "All the best ones are."

☙ ☙ ❧ ❧

The Chairman sat at the head of his dining room table as his wife served him a bowl of chocolate ice cream for dessert. He looked up at the woman, smiled his thanks, and wondered for the millionth time how a damaged man like him ever managed to find a woman to love him.

It had been just over forty-eight hours since last he heard from Team Alpha. He was beginning to wonder if perhaps Michelis got the better of them just as the phone in his study beeped. He palmed his bowl of ice cream, apologized to his wife, and left for his study.

"Yes," he said simply, picking up the desk phone.

"Chairman, this is Smith."

"Talk."

"The pair escaped into Peru. They had help, looked like a local. Spent the night in Puno like a couple of tourists. We have an idea why the doctor is involved now."

"And that would be?"

"They're lovers, sir."

"Ah." The Chairman chewed on that information for a minute. "Is the doctor being played, Smith?"

"I don't think so, sir. Vargas and I considered the possibility as well. That she might just be Michelis' ticket out. But after having observed them together, neither one of us think that's the case. It didn't look casual or contrived, if you know what I mean, sir."

"So, where are they now?"

"We followed them up the coast to Trujillo. They boarded the USS McFarlan which is in port on a humanitarian mission along with a few other US vessels."

"Hmm. Interesting." The Chairman reached over to his computer and typed a few letters. "The McFarlan. Captain Devitt. Don't know him. I wonder what our girl is doing there."

"Shortly after she boarded, General Lemsky was seen leaving the vessel."

"Sounds to me like Michelis is calling in backup. She's gone back to her roots. Why do you think that is, Smith?"

"Well, sir, if you want my honest opinion, I think it's because she doesn't know who, if anyone, she can trust at DHS. If she was dirty, she'd be running away. Not back into the fold of the military. She ran there because it's safe. That doesn't sound like the actions of someone dirty to me, but someone who is looking for protection, or help."

"If your theory is correct, that means she suspects me as well. If she is innocent of the accusations stated in Takashi's report, then she will target Takashi when she gets back in the country. Or me. If she didn't do what Takashi said, then she knows he did. Or I did."

"Sir, she and MacKenzie are undercover as Naval officers, and are about to board a C-130 back to the States. Once she gets on that plane, it'll be too late for us to eliminate her. If you want us to take the shot, it's now or never."

"No. I'm committed to riding this coaster to the end of the rail. As much as I would like to sweep this mess away, she is too valuable not to give her the benefit of the doubt. Takashi, on the other hand, isn't."

"Even if it means she might come after you, Chairman? She's unbelievable with a rifle, sir. I'd wear plenty of Kevlar if I were you."

"Thanks for the tip," the Chairman said

sarcastically. "Get on the first plane back. I'll have them tailed when they get off the plane and you can pick them up again stateside."

"Sir, if she is guilty of selling her team out, why do you think she would be following this course of action?"

"I have no goddamn idea." The Chairman hung up the phone and looked dejectedly at his melted bowl of ice cream. "Damn."

❧❧❧❧

The massive gray beast otherwise called the C-130 Hercules loomed ahead as the deep-throated cargo plane roared to life. The thrums of the four gigantic engines made everything in the vicinity, living or inanimate, hum with vibration. As the plane readied for takeoff, gray clouds were collecting in the late afternoon sky. The navy crews would once again be put to the test as more flooding rains were on the way. Local villagers and navy volunteers gathered to shore up the progress they'd made in an attempt to stave off further destruction.

Seven and Jenny made their way into the belly of the large aircraft, each woman a picture of polar opposites regarding their emotions. The older woman was grinning from ear to ear. The younger appeared as if she would soon throw up. "Why are you smiling?" Jenny finally asked. She thought maybe her friend was making fun of the virescent tinge of her skin.

"Because you look so cute dressed up as a Navy Medical Officer?" Seven yelled over the deafening noise.

"Ha ha, very funny," Jenny hollered back over

the din. "These clothes are not comfortable. How can you guys stand dressing like this all the time? Haven't you military types ever heard of natural fibers? Or Coolmax for that matter?"

"Well, there's not a lot of ironing in the field, and you know it's important we look freshly pressed at all times. So it's poly-blend or nuthin'."

Seven stuck out a supportive hand for her lover as they boarded the plane. The loadmaster escorted them to a couple of jump seats behind the cockpit. Jenny was definitely feeling wobbly on her feet, and she wondered for the umpteenth time if they had barf bags on board. "Dear lord, if I had gills they'd be green," she complained under her breath. The loadmaster reassured her she'd be fine. She wasn't so sure.

Jenny looked around at the cavernous interior, now empty of its load of humanitarian aid supplies the navy would put to use. It felt like being in the belly of a gigantic metal whale. Rolling tracks on the floor were enclosed on all sides by a network of metal tubing, cables, and other materials. There seemed to be something stuffed into every nook and cranny. "I hate flying! We're not even in the air yet and this thing feels like a boat with wings."

Seven laughed. "I love it. This is the same type of aircraft I dropped into Bolivia from. I guess it's appropriate I'm going home the same way I got here."

"You'd probably get off jumping right out the back, wouldn't you?"

"Oh hell yes. I love a good adrenaline rush as much as the next guy. Don't forget, you promised to let me teach you when we got home." Seven grinned the grin of the truly wicked.

"Funny. I don't recall making that promise." Jenny eyed her suspiciously.

Once the flight was underway, the doctor reviewed a few things they had discussed before disembarking the USS McFarlan. Seven mentioned Commander Wahlston had given her the uniform of a Lieutenant, which was a common rank for doctors in the medical corps. Seven, apparently, had been demoted. She only managed a Lieutenant Junior Grade ranking, but she supposed that had mostly to do with finding a uniform large enough to fit her six-foot frame. In order to keep up the disguises, she was to salute if saluted and follow Seven's lead if not. Once the plane landed in Norfolk, Virginia, they would take Captain Devitt's car, which had been left on the base, and head out. Seven would overnight the uniforms and identification documents back to Captain Devitt as soon as they were able.

Jenny's stomach settled somewhat as they flew well above the clouds and relatively turbulence free. Seven was sleeping soundly, for which the younger woman was supremely jealous. The aircraft's noise and bumpiness seemed to lull the tall brunette into a comatose-like slumber. There was no way in hell she could ever sleep on a plane, Jenny thought, especially a big lumbering beast like this one.

So much had happened to them in such a short time it seemed like a month since she'd gone hunting with Dan in the forest looking for the mysterious wounded 'man.' The news about Armando Reyes' death made the papers about the time they reached Peru, but no mention of Raul Argulla or Maria Velasquez was made. A shiver traveled up her spine as she flashed back to the look in Maria's eyes as she held the knife to her heart. She didn't think she'd ever be able to relieve herself of that terrifying visual.

Jenny closed her eyes, attempting to rest, but her mind continued to spin about things she'd seen and done. A part of her wanted nothing more than to get a hotel room with an ocean view and make like a vegetable for a week, but she knew their trial was not yet over. She was with Seven now, through thick and thin, and their Bolivian journey would not end until justice had been served in Seven's mind.

She looked over at Sleeping Beauty, who somehow managed to stay gorgeous even snoozing upright in the back of a cargo plane. *God, it must've driven the soldiers she worked with crazy to look but not touch. If I fell asleep like that, I'd probably end up with my mouth hanging open, drooling all over myself.*

Seven said when they landed, she needed to regroup and get some gear before returning to D.C., at which point she would determine if the Chairman could be trusted or not. Then she would figure out how to handle Takeo Takashi. The plan was to head to South Carolina and home. At the very least, she needed to reassure her mother she was alive and well. She could also pick up her father's kit. She may or may not use the rifle, but the scope would definitely come in handy.

The Loadmaster approached the two officers. Both appeared to be sleeping. "Lieutenant?" Strangely, the brunette stirred, but the blonde woman he was addressing didn't move. "Excuse me, Lieutenant Simms?" He said louder, reading the nametag on the blonde's uniform. Both women jumped but only the brunette answered.

"Yes," Seven said.

The Loadmaster looked between the two,

confused. "I'm sorry Jay-Gee," the young man said, using the abbreviated term for Junior Grade. "I didn't mean to wake you. I wanted to ask Lieutenant Simms something."

Seven looked a little embarrassed and gave Jenny a look that said, *he means you.* The taller woman promptly went back to sleep.

"Sorry," Jenny said. "Can I help you with something?"

The Loadmaster held up his hand, which was wrapped tightly in a clean white rag. Blood was beginning to soak through the nappy material. "I see that you're medical. I was trying to fix a stubborn buckle over there and managed to mangle my hand a little. Would you mind looking at it to see if I need stitches?"

"Oh. Sure." Jenny was pleased. Throwing herself into what she did best was a sure-fire way to take her mind off the swirling thoughts bouncing around in her skull. She unclipped her safety belt and leaned over to examine the bleeding hand. "I'm sorry, but that hand's gonna have to go." She only gave the Loadmaster an instant of wide-eyed shock before confessing to the joke.

"You're going to need a few sutures, but there doesn't appear to be any tendon damage, so you'll be fine. If you can grab a first-aid kit and my duffle bag, I can take care of it right now." The man re-wrapped his bleeding hand, and headed over to one of the many objects stuffed into a nook in the fuselage. Jenny stretched on a pair of green rubber gloves and set to work, happy to lose herself, even if just for a short while, in an activity that made her feel comfortable and in control.

Chapter Twenty-three

S even pulled slightly on the wheel of Captain
Devitt's car, steering the vehicle off Interstate
26 onto Meeting Street in the historic district of
Charleston, South Carolina. Jenny was sleeping
peacefully in the passenger seat, slowly coming awake
with the changing cadence of tires humming on
concrete and softly thumping over black-tarred seams.

"So this is Charleston," she said sleepily, her
eyes slowly creeping open. "I've never been."

"It's nice. This is the historic area. It's full of
great restaurants, beautiful old homes, and lots of
pesky tourists," Seven said as she swerved slightly
to avoid nicking a large bald man wearing Bermuda
shorts and a white Guayabera.

"How long has your mom lived here?" Jenny
asked, watching with amusement as a horse-drawn
carriage went clopping by, filled with late-night
revelers.

"A couple years, now. After she remarried, she
and her husband Joe moved out here to open up that
cheese shop I told you about. She wanted to put it in
a high traffic area, and she really liked this place."
Seven wound the car through some neighborhoods
while Jenny ooh'd and ahh'd at the various sights,
commenting on the cobblestone streets and towering
church steeples.

Seven considered the possibility that someone

looking for her might stake out her mother's house, so she circled the neighborhood several times looking for suspicious activity. Satisfied that the coast was clear, she eased the car onto a narrow brick driveway and got out to open an ornate wrought iron gate. Her passenger was breathless as she looked upon the stunning Georgian style home built of rough-hewn brown brick and wrapped in glossy white balconies. The black, slat-wood shutters on the home matched those of the carriage house, both dramatically accented with vibrant greenery and multi-colored hibiscus that seemed to bloom everywhere. Even in the darkness of the midnight hour, the lighting and landscaping made the home glow. The young woman couldn't wait to see it in the daylight.

"Sev, this house is absolutely beautiful!" Jenny gasped.

"Be sure to mention it to mom. She takes a lot of pride in this place. It was a wedding gift from Joe. He's a good guy."

As they extracted themselves from the vehicle, the front door swung open and Seven's mother verily flew down the steps and into her daughter's arms. Neither woman spoke for some time as Seven lifted her petite mother in the air and held her close.

"Hi mom. Sorry I scared you," she said, finally setting her mother back on the ground.

"Don't you ever do that again, young lady," Catherine said as she stepped back and wiped a few tears from her moistened cheeks.

When Seven called her Uncle Nick from Bolivia, he told her the DHS had notified Catherine that her daughter was missing in action and presumed dead that very morning. After Nick had broken the good news, Catherine swore she wouldn't believe it until she saw her daughter in person, whole and healthy.

Jenny thought the woman had aged extremely well, even dressed in pajamas and a dressing robe. She was still petite in size, just a little taller than Jenny and her hair was cut in a bob, which was light brown, now sprinkled with a bit of gray. Her smile was open and friendly, and her manner refined. She turned her attention to her daughter's guest and before Jenny knew it, she was engulfed in a gargantuan hug.

"Oh, Jenny. It's so good to see you again. I couldn't believe it when Nick told me you were bringing my daughter back to me. I couldn't believe it was the same little girl that used to sit on our front porch steps. But now I see it really is you. Thank you so much for rescuing my daughter. Nick told me what you did. I'll be forever in your debt."

Jenny blushed slightly at the unexpected rush of emotions coming her way. She found on some level she felt like a child again, standing in front of the woman who used to sneak her sugar cookies. "It was my pleasure, Mrs. Michelis. I…I mean…sorry. I'm not sure Sev told me your new name."

"Please call me Catherine, or Caty if you prefer."

Two freshly woken men and another woman came down the steps in their bathrobes and took turns hugging Seven, then introduced themselves to Jenny. Nick Michelis hugged Jenny then brought his wife Margaret over to meet the young woman. Margaret thanked her again for helping to return their beloved niece. Jenny thought Nick looked a lot like the man she remembered as Seven's father. Both had the same tall, dark looks with blue eyes that her lover inherited.

The last man to step up was shorter than Nick

by several inches with sandy blonde hair, receding at the temples, dusty gray eyes, and jovial rosy cheeks. In addition to his bathrobe, he also wore a pair of Mickey Mouse house slippers. He took Jenny's hand in his and introduced himself. "It's a pleasure to meet you, Jenny. I'm Joseph Garrett-Nelson, Catherine's husband. Please call me RJ. Welcome."

"Thank you, RJ. It's nice to meet you too. What does the 'R' stand for?" Jenny asked, curious about the initial that didn't appear to have a place in the man's name.

"Regular," Joe said with a wink. Jenny laughed and followed the group into the stately home for a quick tour and a few more opportunities to ooh and ahh at the architectural character of Charleston. RJ explained Regular Joe was a nickname he garnered in his college days, having taken it on as a campaign moniker while running for class president.

Catherine couldn't resist commenting on her husband's choice of footwear. "Oh Joe, why are you wearing those silly things? Where are the nice ones I got you for your birthday?"

"I like these," RJ replied. "Anyway, I wore them for Seven. I thought she'd think they were funny."

Seven laughed loud and long. It was good to be home. She didn't remember telling RJ she had a pair of those herself, but she'd add it to the list of things she liked about the older man her mother had chosen to marry.

"Come on, time for a midnight snack, everyone. The girls must be hungry." Catherine led the way into her kitchen and buried herself in the fridge, pulling plates, bowls, and saran-covered trays out from all directions. A veritable feast of leftovers soon covered the granite countertops and the small crew happily went to work devouring everything in sight with their bare hands.

Jenny munched cheerfully on a feta cheese stuffed kalamata olive as she observed her lover surrounded by people who adored her. The boisterous group chatted happily, full of smiles and laughter, overjoyed their beloved Seven had returned. Seven was in her element. It was so different from how conservative and staid Jenny's family was. She thought her mother would rather die than stand around the kitchen in her pajamas having an impromptu and somewhat raucous party in the wee hours of the morning. Jenny realized in a heartbeat, she felt more at home here than she ever did in her own home. With that thought and a smile, she snatched a cold grilled lamb chop off a platter and stuffed it in her mouth, moaning gratefully at the delicious explosion of flavor.

Jenny continued to sample the leftovers as she entertained herself watching Seven's family. Catherine, she noted, alternated between laughing with the others, and staring pensively at her daughter with the occasional tear in her eye. Uncle Nick had a personality as big as his height, and was full of opinions about everything under the sun. Nick's wife Margaret was quiet, but when she did choose to add to the conversation, her dry wit had everyone in the group falling over themselves laughing. RJ added the occasional anecdote, but mostly just seemed supremely content to be part of this boisterous family.

Jenny noticed Seven left most of the harrowing details out of their adventure, probably to spare Catherine the anguish of her near death. She played up Jenny saving her, and painted a picture making the young doctor look like the Lone Ranger riding to her rescue on a charging white steed. Everyone paused to stare over at Seven's petite hero. Jenny blushed, resembling a chipmunk with a cheek-full of nuts as she was caught chasing a chunk of pound cake down with a huge strawberry. An awkward moment of silence passed before the family burst into laughter, watching Jenny try to blush, smile, chew, and swallow simultaneously without choking.

Eventually the conversation turned serious as Catherine pleaded with Seven to give up her position at the DHS and pursue something less dangerous. Catherine made it very clear she didn't think she could survive the loss of her daughter, the way she had lost her first husband. She argued that she had never interfered with Seven's choices in the past, but this latest incident was just too much for her to take.

Seven promised to seriously consider her mother's wishes, but explained with a knowing look to her uncle that until the current situation was resolved, she needed to continue on her path. Catherine didn't understand that her daughter was still in great danger, which was how Seven wanted it to stay.

"Uncle Nick, can I have a word with you in the den for a minute?" Seven asked, wanting to discuss her strategy with a like-minded individual.

"That's my cue to hit the hay," RJ said to the group and turned to make for bed. "You coming, Caty?"

"Just gonna clean up here and get the girls settled, then I'll be up. 'Night sweetie." Catherine pecked her husband on the cheek and he toddled off, followed closely by Aunt Margaret. "Goodnight, everybody. See you in the morning...not too early, I hope."

Jenny and Catherine began cleaning up the

kitchen, chatting amiably about what the young woman had been doing since they'd last seen each other. When Jenny mentioned her meteoric success in medical school, the older woman smiled. "Seven always said you were brilliant. I asked her once why she hung around you all the time. It seemed unusual because of your age difference. She said you were intelligent, funny, and more mature than most of the fifteen-year-olds she knew at school."

Jenny laughed at this bit of information.

"Tell me, Jenny. I'm curious. All these years later…why did you hang around Seven all the time? She was so much older than you."

"Because she was intelligent, funny, and more mature than most of the eight-year-olds I knew at school." They laughed as Seven came back into the kitchen and started putting dishes away in the high cabinets. She nodded to Jenny, indicating she had spoken to Nick and would relay the information later, away from her mother's ears.

"Come on, girls. I'll show you to your rooms." Catherine led the way up a large curved staircase and down a long carpeted landing. "Sev, you're in your regular room, and Jen, I've put you down the hall here. RJ dropped your bags in there already."

The two younger women glanced at each other behind their hostesses back. Jenny was thinking it was going to be a long, lonely night. *Good lord, did she just wink at me? Wonder what that meant.*

Catherine opened the door to Jenny's room and ushered her inside. "Is there anything else I can get you girls before I toddle off to bed?"

"Actually mom, you and Jen are about the same size. Do you think she could borrow some clothes, maybe? She had to leave almost all of her stuff behind."

"Of course. I'll bring some things and some fresh towels around in the morning. Goodnight sweetheart. Goodnight Jenny. Sleep tight."

Seven waited for her mother's door to close before turning to her lover and smiling. Jenny whispered, "We haven't been in a bed since Puno, Sev, I don't think I can do it alone." She smiled seductively, running her hands up strong arms. "I don't know why but I thought you would tell your mom about us."

"I'm not keeping it a secret...it just never came up. Plus, we didn't really talk about it, and I didn't know how you felt. I thought I would discuss it with you before I started sending out the announcements, you know?" The taller woman bent over and planted soft lips on a willing throat.

Jenny moaned at the sensation. "It feels like forever since we've been alone together, Sev. I miss you." She lowered her voice to barely audible, "I want you."

Seven's knees grew weak at this last declaration. Her mind was already trying to find a work-around that would get her in bed with Jenny and out of her mother's house at the same time. "This is really strange for me, Jen. I've never brought anyone home before. It kinda makes me feel like a teenager again. Like my mom is gonna bust me makin' out in the basement and ground me or something. Kinda freaky. Aren't you wierded out at all?" She chuckled deep in her throat. After a long, heated kiss, she straightened up to leave. "By the way...the bathroom over there adjoins to my room. If you need anything in the night you know where to find me."

Jenny huffed in frustration, but decided to

respect her friend's stoic request. Jenny supposed she should be the one who felt awkward in this situation, but she was willing to forego a little mental comfort for another chance to be with her incredible new lover. She would wait. Patience was a virtue, after all.

❧❧❧❧

The man in the silk pajamas rubbed sleep from his eyes as he rolled over to answer the phone. "What!" He barked, not appreciating the middle of the night call.

The voice on the other end of the line said, "I thought you'd like to know your bird just showed up in Charleston."

The man sighed, seeing his own life pass briefly before his eyes. "Shit."

"How do you want me to handle it?"

"You know what I want. Wait for the first opportunity, then take care of her. Keep it clean unless she gets too close to me, then do what you have to do." He hung up the phone, rolled over, and buried his head deep under the pillow.

❧❧❧❧

Seven folded her arms across her chest and leaned against the doorframe separating Jenny's room from their adjoining bathroom. A faint light from her Mother's back yard seeped through the curtains illuminating the sleeping blonde in a mellow haze. Seven found she could barely breathe as she looked upon the slumbering beauty that had so thoroughly stolen her heart.

She had been sitting alone in her room listening to the house quiet and watching shadows on the wall, finally coming to terms with her silly fear of being caught in a compromising position by her mother. She couldn't have cared less if it was anybody else, but for some reason Mom was a different story. When she weighed her choices, she decided her desire to feel Jenny's touch far outweighed her childish fear of being embarrassed.

Seven thought perhaps that Jenny would sneak into her room at some point, taking the decision out of her hands. She knew she wouldn't be able to resist her if she had, but true to her word, Jenny had gone to sleep instead. Now she stood in the doorway watching her, the same feeling of animal lust she fought two nights prior taking control of her senses. She thought making love with Jenny all night in Peru would keep her beast at bay, but she found the opposite to be true. Now that she knew what was between them, she wanted the young woman more than ever.

She wanted to soar.

She wanted her soul to hum.

Righting herself from the doorframe, she glided into the room, letting her robe fall to the floor as she went. The garden lights faintly illuminated her nude form as she made her way to the four-poster bed. Sliding silently under the cool sheets, she gracefully moved her lengthy frame over until she was pressed against her lover's back.

A soft moan escaped the sleeping girl's lips. Ever so gently, Seven applied a trail of feather light kisses from her earlobe, to her jaw, down her neck, and back up again. She inched under her shirt and slid a warm palm over Jenny's waist, caressing her abdomen then moving up, brushing fingertips teasingly over the silky skin of her breasts.

The scent of Jenny's sleep-warmed skin was intoxicating to Seven. It was all she could do to keep herself calm, wanting nothing more than to ravage the sleeping girl.

Never opening her eyes, Jenny's voice whispered sleepily into the darkness, "God Sev, I hope that's you."

Seven chuckled as she eased Jenny onto her back, pushing up her shirt, and settling herself under the sheets and over her lover's body. Jenny remained dozing, a relaxed moan of pleasure occasionally escaping her lips. Three days with nothing but catnaps had finally caught up with her. If it wasn't for the waves of sensual ambrosia crashing languidly over her body, she had no doubt she would be in a comatose-like sleep.

Jenny thought she had died and gone to heaven as Seven's tongue and lips drew artistic patterns over her skin. She felt like a posable doll, her body a canvas for a master at work. Seven painted her with kisses as she moved ever lower, her leisurely pace ensuring Jenny's continued state of stimulated slumber. She wrapped powerful arms under and around the young woman's muscular thighs, anchoring her before she was sure to come fully awake.

Seven's abdomen spasmed in empathy as Jenny gasped and seized the moment her tongue found its intended destination. The combined assault of Jenny's scent, her taste, her throaty moans sent Seven's senses reeling. She was lost completely in the depths of Jenny's being. Nothing else in her world mattered except what was happening within the three-foot perimeter of her own body.

Emerald eyes finally eased open, only to snap shut soon after as her breathing went from rapid to gasping to briefly stopping all together as she struggled to swallow her own scream. Seven continued to hold her tightly, eventually bringing her head to rest on her young lover's abdomen. She listened contentedly as Jenny's heart rate slowed, the abating rhythm lulling both into a peaceful sleep.

❧❧❧❧

Seven's mother Catherine stood frozen in place outside the guestroom door. She had brought a pile of clothes for Jenny to choose from, intending to drop them in the girl's room, when she heard noises coming from inside. Initially she thought to enter, assuming she was having a nightmare. Her hand was about to turn the doorknob when she heard what was unmistakably her daughter's voice. Catherine's face flushed as it became obvious there was a seduction in play, and she was eavesdropping. *Walk away, Caty.* For some reason she was rooted to the spot.

She placed the pile of clothes outside the door, leaned her back on the wall, and sank to the floor. A million emotions seemed to overtake the petite brunette from every conceivable angle as she listened. Catherine placed her head in her hands and cried.

Just three days ago, Catherine thought her daughter was dead. Until she'd heard from Nick that the opposite was true, she was numb to the pain of it. The only thing she ever truly wanted for Seven was for the girl to find what she had known with Dean. Love. The kind of love books are written about. The kind of love that is all consuming. It was a blessing not easily found. The problems of the world seem small to a person who understands the depths of true love, because that person knows the meaning of what is important in life and what is not. She wanted her daughter to know what that felt like more than anything. When she thought her dead, Catherine's mind was consumed with the pain of knowing her only child never found what she wanted for her.

Now? She should have seen it the moment they got out of the car. It all made perfect sense. The looks between them, the way they stood near each other, the strength of the bond they'd shared since childhood, her daughter had found it. Finally. Her tears were tears of joy, the emotional roller coaster of the last few days catching up with her. The knowledge that Seven was alive, and had found someone to love made her want to ball her hands into white knuckled fists and scream with glee from the rooftops.

She had known Seven was gay since the girl was sixteen, and suspected much sooner. The child never was one for girlish pursuits, always seeming to be more interested in sports and outdoorsy endeavors than tea parties and princess costumes. By the time her daughter told her for sure at sixteen, she had already come to terms with it and decided she would never let something like that come between them. The only thing that mattered was Seven's happiness. She was a private person, however, so Caty never knew anything about her lifestyle. She had never brought anybody home until now.

Catherine quickly clamped a hand over her own mouth to keep from laughing aloud. Her tears of relief and joy quickly turned to mirth. The sounds coming from behind the door made her remember many enjoyable nights spent in a similar endeavor with the girl's father. She would enjoy bragging to her bridge club ladies that her daughter had brought home a doctor.

She finally stood and walked away, wiping the end of her tears from tired eyes. The last thing she heard before departing was Jenny telling her daughter that she loved her. Catherine couldn't remember the last time she felt so happy.

❧❧❦❦

Nine a.m. rolled around and the house was still quiet except for Catherine, who found herself surprisingly full of energy considering her night of very little sleep. She folded some towels fresh from the dryer and made her way up the stairs, entering Seven's room. She figured correctly that she wouldn't be there, and slipped into the adjoining bathroom to deposit the towels.

The door to Jenny's room was open, and the older woman couldn't resist a quick peek. She supposed her curiosity had something to do with wanting to see a side of her daughter she had never seen, something unguarded and real. The events of the previous night had gotten her thinking of Dean. She tried not to do this too regularly, as deep feelings of melancholy invariably followed. She loved RJ, but no one could ever replace the special kind of love she had with Dean.

A touch of jealousy brought a smile to her face. She remembered well the feeling of being wrapped protectively in the arms of your true love. There was a level of contentment in it that could only be found in that particular experience. She missed it.

Before she knew it, she was in the room. Her daughter slept on her side with Jenny tucked snugly into the curve of her body. One of her arms made a pillow for Jenny's head while the other wrapped protectively around her waist. Their legs were tangled together. Catherine sat next to her daughter and studied her features. It filled her to the brim seeing her like this. Happy. Relaxed. She hadn't seen Seven without the worry of the world since her father died. It made her heart sing. She reached over and brushed a tangle of hair from her face.

Seven stirred at the light contact. She rolled onto her back, the sheet dropping down to reveal two pairs of bare shoulders. Her azure eyes fluttered open and she smiled up at her...mother.

"Mother!" Her eyes shot wide open, a heated blush creeping rapidly up her neck to her cheeks. She glanced at Jenny who was still sound asleep. Seven pulled the sheet up over her head and whimpered, "Oh god, Mom. What are you doing in here?"

Catherine couldn't help herself and chuckled at her daughter's uncomfortable reaction. It was kinda funny, after all.

"Oh my *god*!"

She reached up and pulled the sheet off her daughters face. "It's okay, Sev. I'm sorry to have startled you. I know it's intrusive, me being in here, but I just couldn't help myself. I wanted to tell you how happy I am for you."

"You couldn't 'a told me at breakfast?" She muffled, her eyes wide, the sheet still clenched firmly just below her nose.

Catherine laughed. "Is she the one, Seven? Do you love her?"

Seven's eyes softened at the question. Catherine watched her daughter's face transform as a glowing smile and twinkling eyes took over her expression. It was all the answer she needed. "Yes, Mom. I love her."

"Well, you've never been one to do anything half-assed, my daughter. You chose well. I will be as proud to call her my daughter as I am you."

Catherine smiled warmly and looked over at Jenny. "Light sleeper, huh?" She said sarcastically. As if on cue, Jenny chose that exact moment to open her eyes. When her sleep-fogged mind registered Seven's mother sitting on their bed, her body jerked awake. "Oh god!" A strange noise resembling a squealing baby pig left her mouth as she buried her entire body in a fetal position under the sheet. "Oh god...oh god... oh my god," her muffled voice said from beneath the linen.

Catherine laughed again. Seven now joined her mother appreciating the ridiculousness of the situation. "I don't think I've ever seen that exact shade of pink anywhere, Jenny," the older woman said. Jenny was trying to make herself as small as humanly possible. Her lover's mother reached over and tapped her on the shoulder. "Come up for air, please, young lady. I have something to say to you."

"Oh god," she squeaked in a tiny voice. After a very long moment, a ruffled blonde head with wide eyes poked out from under the sheet, the linen grasped firmly and held just below her nose.

Catherine laughed again at the pair. "You two look like a couple of Kilroys."

"Sorry Mom," Seven said, her blush finally beginning to fade. "We didn't exactly plan to have you find out about us this way."

Catherine leaned over and kissed her daughter on the forehead. "It's okay, love. I'm very, very happy for you." She got up and walked around to Jenny, leaning over and placing a heartfelt kiss on the young woman's forehead as well. "You chose well, young lady. In my opinion, you got the finest human being to ever walk the earth. Please take good care of her."

Catherine walked from the room, leaving two speechless women staring at each other in amazement. In perfect unison, as if choreographed by Ester Williams herself, the lovers dove back under the sheets and giggled in a simultaneous chorus, "Oh my god!"

❧❧❧❧

Breakfast, much like their midnight snack, was a riotous affair. Catherine prepared heaps of French toast and homemade waffles cut in strips for dipping in vats of warmed Canadian maple syrup, crème caramel, and strawberry rhubarb sauces. Strong French roast, crispy bacon, and a mountain of fresh fruit salad and cheeses accompanied the feast. No one bothered to sit, but stood around the bar gabbing happily and stuffing their faces.

Jenny leaned into Seven and fed her a chunk of pineapple. "Dan says hi. Oh, and he said to say 'told ya.' Don't know what he meant by that, but I assume you do."

Seven grinned, chewing with a silly smile on her face. "So he's okay? They all made it away from Argulla's people all right?"

"Yep. He almost peed his pants when he heard my voice on the phone. Said they've been worried sick about me since the news about the Reyes massacre got out. Looks like Maria Velasquez is taking the fall for all the killings, post mortem. I'm sure that's Argulla's doing. I didn't tell him what really happened, though I promised I'd fill him in someday over a keg of margaritas."

Seven turned to her mother. "Mom, did Uncle Nick explain to you I needed to borrow Dad's kit? I'll return it as soon as I can." Seven hoped she wouldn't have to use it, but she needed to do some recon and surveillance on the Chairman, and she wanted the security blanket of a rifle to do it. Her plan was to stalk the man as if he were a target, and find out everything about him she could. Uncle Nick would assist by pulling a few strings to see if the guy had a history of dirty tricks.

"Yes," Catherine said, worry evident in her frown. "Why don't you keep it, Sev. Your father would've wanted you to have it anyway. I can't let you leave in good conscience, however, without saying I don't want you to do whatever it is you're going to do."

"I know, Mom." She kissed the older woman on the forehead. "I have to finish this. I can't leave this man to do the same thing to others he did to me, and my team. It just wouldn't be right."

"Seven, have you given any more thought to what we discussed last night?" Uncle Nick said, swallowing a mouthful of waffle.

The tall brunette looked at her lover and smiled. "You're welcome to ask her, Nick, but I wouldn't hold out hope for the response you're looking for. She's about the most determined person I've ever met."

Jenny realized the conversation had turned to her. She looked between the two Marines. "Determined is a kind way to say stubborn. So might I assume you plan to ask me something I won't want to do?" She squinted suspiciously at the two conspirators.

Nick decided to wade in and test the waters. "Jenny, I think it would be a good idea if you stayed here while…"

"No."

"You didn't even let me finish my sentence."

"It doesn't matter. The answer is no."

"Toldja," Seven said, never looking up from her concentrated mission to fork a slippery grape.

"This could be incredibly dangerous, and you're a civilian. Are you prepared to risk your life and Seven's? Because if the bullets start flying, she's going to be more concerned about you than about saving herself."

Jenny lowered her voice to a dangerous whisper, while the others in the kitchen chatted away on a completely different topic. "Nick, I may not be some kind of cock-swinging commando like the two of you, but I guarantee, I will not be a liability to Seven."

Seven choked on her grape.

"She cannot go into this alone, and I plan to be there to watch her back. I will not be separated from her while she's in danger. I can't be. Regardless of the concessions we'll both have to make to stay together, it's the only option."

Seven's shoulders shook in silent laughter as Nick got his first taste of Jenny's stubborn side. She reached over and took the girl in her arms, giving her a reassuring hug, and kissing her on the head. She wanted to send the message to Nick there was more going on here than just a stubborn streak. His wide-eyed grin showed her he'd gotten the message.

"Do you agree with Nick on this, Sev?"

"I would prefer it if you were out of harm's way, Jen, but a deal is a deal. We promised to see this through to the end, and that's what we'll do. I'd be lie'n though, if I didn't say I was worried about the Chairman. He's the unknown factor in all of this, and the guy didn't get where he is by being bad at what he does."

"So you think he's behind Takashi?"

"God, I hope not, but it's possible. The whole Bolivian situation was a screw up from the get go. To me, that says Takashi acted alone. The guy is damn good at computers, but he's green and definitely not a player. I want to believe if the Chairman was involved, the ambush would have been handled efficiently and I'd be dead. He's not the kind of guy that would send a rag-tag bunch of locals to handle a professional team. That was a huge mistake. The Chairman never struck me as a man to make mistakes, let alone one as basic as that."

"So if nothing pans out with the Chairman?"

Seven nodded toward her uncle. "Between us we should be able to determine his position. Nick is going to call me as soon as he finds out what we need to know. After we deal with him, we'll make a move on Tak. We've been playing defense since this game started, Jen. It's time for us to go on offense."

Jenny looked pensive. She knew damn-well Seven was harboring a deadly grudge against the computer tech. She didn't think anything she could say would divert her from extreme action, but she would try anyway. "Okay, when do we leave?"

"After breakfast. Got another long drive ahead of us, then we'll stalk the target." Seven accepted a set of car keys and a cell phone from her uncle.

"I'll take care of getting Devi's car back to him. You take mine."

"Thanks, Uncle Nick. For everything." She hugged the man who was a substitute father to her for so many years. Before letting go, he whispered in her ear. "She's a feisty one, Marine. Think you got the right stuff?"

She chucked him in the ribs. "Semper Fi." With a wink, she turned to say goodbye to her other family.

❧ ❧ ❧ ❧ ❧

"Damn it, Janice, where are those requisition forms?" General Lemsky bellowed from behind his office door. He barged into his secretary's office, looking somewhat flustered. "You know I have a million details to attend to before I ship out. Can you please get them for me?"

"They're in the basket where you asked me to put them, General," Janice said good-naturedly. Her boss had the roar of a lion, but the heart of a teddy bear.

"Oh." The General sheepishly wandered back into his office, never noticing the man in the dark suit who stood patiently near his secretary's desk.

Janice looked up and noticed the weathered looking stranger with the hawk-like eyes. "May I help you, sir?"

"Good afternoon, Janice. I desire an audience with the General, if you please." The Chairman handed the secretary his card.

She didn't look at it. "The General sees people by appointment only, Mr...."

The Chairman didn't bother to end Janice's

sentence, but stood patiently until the woman looked at his card. She looked up and scrutinized the man in the dark suit more closely. Satisfied he looked legitimate, she placed his card in a special barcode reader tucked under her desk. She watched her computer monitor for the result, her eyes widening slightly when the information she required came to the screen. Without any further hesitation, she picked up the phone.

"General, there's a gentleman here to see you."

"I don't have time for any unscheduled meetings, Janice," the General barked over the phone, but could be clearly heard through the door.

"He said go right in, sir," Janice said, completely unaffected by the General's outburst.

A smile twitched at the corners of the serious man's face as he entered the General's office.

Lemsky heard the door to his office open and close, so he took a moment to rearrange and straighten his commanding presence for the benefit of his audience. He turned and took the measure of the man before him.

"Thank you for seeing me without an appointment, General."

"Thank my secretary," he growled.

The Chairman, like most people in Washington, knew Lemsky's dark side was really false bravado. He was one of the most liked men to hold his rank. A consummate professional, the General wasn't afraid to give credit where credit was due. In fact, he was often seen yelling it from the rooftops.

The General examined the stranger's card. *Department of Homeland Security. No name.* "You gotta name, son?"

"They call me the Chairman. I was dealt the

moniker a couple decades ago, long before I actually was the head of anything. It stuck."

The General already suspected what this was about, but wasn't going to give this man an inch. He sat and indicated his guest should do the same. "So you're a spook. Ex C.I.A.?"

"Very astute, General. How'd you know?"

"It's the way you take everything in without appearing to. And, it's the eyes. They always tell a tale. Yours have seen a lot."

"Indeed they have. They're seeing things still. Things I'd rather not see."

"Like?"

"Like two exceptional men under my command who are now dead, killed by a traitor. Like another I don't wish to see suffer the same fate. Like my department, my brainchild, which I believe will be instrumental in eliminating terrorism in our lifetime, being in jeopardy."

Lemsky considered the man before him. Michelis was wary of him, but didn't know if he was involved in the treachery or not. He seemed a straightforward, shoot-from-the-hip type, which the General liked. He was a good judge of character, and his senses told him this man was clever and cunning, but straight as an arrow.

"What does the DHS want with me, Mr.... Chairman?"

"I'm going to talk to you, General, based on the assumption your former Captain Michelis told you about my department, the Black Flag Company. She would have had to make informational concessions in order to gain your trust, so without going into too much detail, let's assume you know whom I am, and where she is. Feel free to break in with any questions. I'll answer if I can. What you probably don't know, is my information says Michelis turned for profit and that is why my men are dead."

"Funny. That's the same thing she said about you."

"I figured as much. That's why I'm wearing Kevlar." The General couldn't help but smirk a little at the comment. He knew better than anybody that if Michelis wanted somebody dead, there was a pretty good chance they were going to get that way.

"I know who Michelis is, Mr. Chairman, and I guaran-god-damned-tee-ya I'll take one 'a her over a hundred 'a you any day 'a the week. Your information is wrong, and you haven't given me one single reason to believe you're not to blame for this fiasco."

"Oh, I am to blame, General. You see, I designed and handpicked every one of my ops teams. That this team ended in disaster is no one's fault but my own. It means one of the two people left alive was a bad choice. The only thing I can do is get to the bottom of the situation. If I can't come to a definite conclusion regarding who is at fault, then I have no choice but to clear the slate of the remaining team members. You can understand my reluctance to do this. I want to believe Michelis is innocent. She is one of the most valuable recruits I have, and to lose her would be devastating to me. But I must do what I must do."

The General's voice lowered to a dangerous whisper. "If you think for one minute I would feed you information that would condemn a Marine who has bled and killed for the sake of this country, you are sorely mistaken, Mr. Chairman." He emphasized the word mister as if it had left a bad taste in his mouth.

"I've known people with character the likes of Michelis my entire career. She would die before she would ever sell out the flag."

"I'm not looking to condemn her, General. I'm looking to save her. From me. Help me, please."

Lemsky stood and paced around the room, huffing and puffing about various items he needed to attend to before departing for the Middle East. In reality, he was merely stalling for time while he considered his stand on the matter. His gut told him this guy from the DHS was on the level, but what if he was wrong? It was a gamble to trust him, and in the pot was the life of a decorated Marine. It was time to raise or fold. "All right, Chairman. In the immortal words of Papa Hemingway, 'the best way to find out if you can trust somebody, is to trust them.' What do you want to know?"

"Anything you can tell me. What happened down there?"

"She said her team was sold out by a man named Takashi. She thought you might be involved as well, but wasn't sure. She intended to find out and deal with it on her own when she got home. She was shot twice in the ambush that killed her teammates but escaped, and was later stabbed by some psychotic woman who was actually responsible for the death of the man she was targeting. The young doctor she was with saved her life, and helped her to escape the country."

"Did she have any proof on Takashi?"

"She said he was the only one, except for maybe you, who knew exactly where they'd be down to the longitude, latitude, and minute. Plus, she said the doctor gave him an impromptu psych test over the phone and he failed miserably. Every red flag flew right to the top of the pole."

"What was her involvement with this Raul Argulla character?"

"He had an ulterior motive to do with Reyes, not Michelis. That, and apparently his attack dog had a grudge against the doctor for some reason. Michelis killed her to save the young woman. She said she didn't have anything to do with the deaths at the Reyes place, except for Argulla's people, who were holding MacKenzie hostage."

"You might be interested to know, General, the woman Michelis killed was considered one of the most successful hitters in Latin America. Interpol had also suspected her for years as being a possible serial murderer. If it were true, they say she would be the most prolific female serial ever recorded in the world."

The Chairman figured at this point, he pretty much had all the information he was going to get from General Lemsky. It was pointless to ask his opinion because it was obvious he admired Michelis a great deal. The man with the hawk-like eyes thought he would test the General with one more piece of information, a small test to determine if he really did admire her as much as he claimed to.

"General, would you be interested to know Michelis and Dr. MacKenzie are sleeping together? Would that information change your take on what they told you aboard the McFarlan in any way?"

The General's eyelids closed to dangerous slits as he tried to reassess the motives of the man sitting across from him. He thought perhaps he'd misjudged him completely. Lemsky couldn't think of a single good reason for this Chairman bastard to say something like that unless he had an ulterior motive, or was just being spiteful. It didn't pertain to their conversation or Michelis' situation at all. Maybe the man was hoping to flush out something personal about the Marine he could use against her.

The General's voice lowered to a dangerous whisper, which grew in volume as he spoke. "Now you listen here, Mr. Whateverthehellyournameis. Courageous people like Michelis defending this country is what keeps me sleepin' at night. I don't give a good goddamn if she's fuckin' the First Lady. You better not even be thinkin' of spreadin' her personal dealings around like it had somethin' to do with your fucked mission. So help me god, if you try pinning this on Michelis with some bullshit story about her being a traitor because she's a deviant, I will make it my personal mission in life to squash you and your department like a horse turd under my boot heel. Am I makin' myself perfectly clear?"

For the first time since he arrived, the Chairman saw the proud and bullheaded man that had achieved the position of Brigadier General. *Hmm. Threats. Threats are good.* The Chairman stood and extended a hand to the angry man. "Thank you for your time, General. I appreciate your candor." The man in black turned and headed for the door, a small smile playing at the corner of his mouth.

His decision was made.

Chapter Twenty-four

I t's Smith, sir."

"Talk."

"We're on the move, Mr. Chairman, heading your way and we've got company."

"So. That idiot lucked into someone that knew what they were doing."

"Looks like it, sir. He's a pro for sure. We only managed to spot him ourselves after the Virginia state line."

"Has he spotted you?"

"Don't think so, sir. We marked Michelis' vehicle at their first stop and have been keeping a good distance."

"Shit! This could get messy," the Chairman's voice was pitched slightly higher than it normally was.

In all the time Smith had been on Team Alpha, he had never once heard the Chairman curse or appear nervous in anyway. The man was a machine of efficiency. He had to admit it unnerved him a little. "Sir?"

After a long pause, and a deep sigh over the phone the man replied. "What?"

"You sound a little edgy, sir. Anything else we can be doing for you?"

The Chairman chuckled. It was definitely the first time Smith had ever heard that sound leaving the man's mouth. "Tell you what, Smith. How 'bout I sic a sniper with Michelis' track record on you and see how you like it?"

"No thanks, sir. I think I'll pass."

"That's what I thought. When you get within a hundred and fifty miles of my house, put the rest of your Delegates on alert and get them into position."

"Sir, if you don't mind me asking, why don't we just hit the guy and deal with Michelis now? Why let her get close to you at all?"

The Chairman thought about that question but decided not to answer. There was a small percentage of doubt in his plan still nagging at him, and he just couldn't let it go. He wanted to keep his options open, and to tell Smith the details of his plan would cut off his possibilities for improvisation. "Just call me when you're in position."

"Will do. I won't contact you again until we're ready to go."

The Chairman hung up the phone. He pinched the bridge of his nose between his thumb and middle finger in an attempt to relieve the pressure building in his head. Dealing with Michelis would be nothing compared to the grief his wife would give him when he told her she had to leave town.

♔ ♔ ♔ ♔

"It's me."

"It's about damned time. Is it done?"

"No, but it's about to be."

"What the hell are you waiting for? This is too fucking close for comfort."

"You said you wanted it clean, and for her to disappear. Can't exactly accomplish that in the middle of D.C. now can I? They brought me to the perfect place, some woods outside the city, but it got dark and I lost them. I had to wait for daybreak to find 'em again. She's dug in and watching some guy in Maryland. Gotta sniper rifle by the looks of it. I'm guessing the guy she's watching is toast."

"You're right. He is, and I'm next if you don't succeed."

"She's with somebody. A blonde woman. What do you want done with her? I can't leave witnesses."

"Kill her. I don't give a shit."

"That'll cost you double."

"No way. I'm not paying for two. That guy Reyes who was going to be footing the bill for this little adventure is dead. So this is on my dime and I'm not paying for two. If you can't leave witnesses, then you gotta do what you gotta do, but don't look to me for payment." Tak was kind of hoping at this point his hit man would make it a messy kill. At least then, he wouldn't have to pay the bonus money.

The man with no name hated working for tight ass pricks like this weasel. Who the hell ever heard of bargaining for a murder? He would kill the blonde too, to protect himself, but would find another way to take it out of his client's ass. "Fine. I'm moving in now. She'll be dead in ten minutes. I want you to meet me in the same park, same bench as last time exactly twenty-four hours from now and bring the rest of the money. A hundred K. Don't be late and don't even think about trying to rip me off, or what this chick would'a done to you ain't nothin' compared to what I'll do. Got me?"

"I hear ya, I hear ya. I'll be there."

The slight man with the goatee hung up his cell

and turned the ringer off, sliding the device into his shirt pocket. He removed a silencer from a leather bag in the car seat next to him and screwed it onto his pistol. Checking the clip was full, he got quietly out of his vehicle and looked through his binoculars. His prey was exactly where he'd left them. They were positioned about a hundred yards downhill from him, dug in behind a fallen tree. Their focus was on the house below, so they never suspected he was doing to them what they were doing to the man down the hill.

He plotted a silent course toward them and began his decent. Killing them in this place was easy money. Hell, he wouldn't even have to dispose of the bodies. He'd just toss a few leaves and branches over them and he'd be back in the city before lunch. A headshot to the brunette first, then while the blonde was spluttering and gasping in shock, he'd pop her a couple times and be done with it. Easy money.

⁂

"Thanks, Uncle Nick." Seven snapped her uncle's cell phone closed and turned to her friend. "It's looking like the Chairman is clean. Not only that, but apparently the guy is really, really connected. Like practically related to the president connected."

"Does that sound like a guy who would sell out countrymen for money?"

"No. Plus he's got money. Family money. Nick says they guy was deep undercover CIA for a long time. Was considered one of the men instrumental in ending the Cold War, and has been decorated more times than he can count. He also designed and created a few of the more unusual departments in the CIA, all of which have been successful producers. In spook circles, he's considered a real bad-ass."

"I guess that explains how he came to his job at the DHS."

"Yeah. His profile just doesn't fit. Being connected doesn't matter all that much. I mean, just 'cause you're a Morgan or a Rockefeller doesn't mean you can't be a sneaky, corrupt bastard, you know? But the other stuff? A guy choosing to spend a career in the line of fire? Doesn't make sense."

"And look at his place." Jenny scanned the area. It was a lovely piece of property with well-groomed lawns, modern architecture, but not flashy, clean. The stylish one-story home was blanketed on all sides by wooded hills, creating a private oasis in the Maryland side of the D.C. suburbs. If you were in the house, it would feel as if you lived in the country. The structure was wrapped in floor to ceiling glass and plank decking designed to make the most of its natural, wooded surroundings. There were no Ferraris or anything ostentatious to be seen. "It's very tasteful and respectable. A guy with that kind of money could be doing the manor home thing, but it's like he's trying to show himself as a regular guy."

"The question is…is that contrived or for real?"

The two women had been surveilling the Chairman's house since late last night. The drive north from Charleston had been uneventful, and when they'd arrived in D.C. had proceeded directly to the DHS offices where they picked up the Chairman's trail. Seven thought she'd done a pretty good job of it, considering her previous stalking experience was limited to crawling on all fours through the dirt.

They had followed the man home, staked out the

surrounding area, and come up with a plan. Parking a mile away, the women hiked through the woods and found a good spot to dig in with a clear line of sight available. Their hide was about a hundred yards from the Chairman's back yard, the surrounding hills providing Seven with an advantageous angle for which to spy on the older man.

If her Uncle's connections turned up anything dirty, and the evidence was solid, she would hit him from the hilltop. If not, she would break in and confront him face to face. It was risky, but she had to know. Her life and future depended on it.

She and Jenny had fashioned a pretty decent hide out of a collection of branches cut from nearby trees and scavenged from the forest floor. They could sit fairly comfortably in an upright position, shielded from sight by a large moss-covered tree trunk, long dead, lying sedentary on the leaf strewn earth.

Their discussion about the Chairman's guilt or innocence had reached a lull, as both women pondered the significance of the information they had received from Nick.

Unseen by either some distance away, a sharpshooter chambered a high-caliber round into his rifle, pressed his eye to his scope and made minor adjustments to small dials on his weapon, calculating for distance and wind-speed. His breathing was slow and even as he prepared to fire on his kill-worthy target. He had made much more difficult shots than this before, but none quite so personally important to him. It was critical he hit this target. To miss would be devastating.

Jenny flipped around and faced the house once more. Propping her elbows on the tree trunk, she pressed the binoculars to her eyes and looked again at the house containing the man she never met, but who had become so very important in her life. She hoped beyond reason this man was a good man. Even in the middle of all this craziness, Jenny knew her life was finally on track. She couldn't bear the thought of losing it so quickly.

If the Chairman wanted Seven dead, they were in much more serious trouble than either was willing to admit. They were in a fight for survival. Together. Though she had the utmost confidence in her lover's abilities, there seemed little either could do against the might of the U.S. government. If this man was dirty, rich and as connected as Nick said, he had the power to turn Seven into a monster in the eyes of the public, and have her hunted everywhere she went until she was dead.

"Sev," Jenny spoke low, never taking her eyes off the glass house.

"Hm?" Seven was looking through the scope of her father's rifle, checking out every square inch of the man's property.

"Just in case this turns out badly, I want you to know something."

"Hm?"

"I love you."

There was silence between them for a moment as the older woman moved her eyes away from the scope and trained them on the profile of her lover instead. The blonde was still focused intently on the house. "And not the 'You're my best buddy, and I'm so glad to have you back' kind of love...but the I'm *in* love with you. That kind of love."

Seven reached out and brushed her knuckles

softly down the girl's rosy cheek. She opened her mouth to respond as Jenny pulled her face back from the binoculars. As she turned her head away from the lenses and made eye contact with hypnotic blue orbs, her face went instantly pale, the smile fell quickly from her face, and her head immediately snapped back to the binoculars.

Seven's declaration of love never made it from her mouth as she watched Jenny become suddenly terrified. "Jen! What's wrong? What happened?" Seven put her eye back to the scope and looked in the same general direction as her friend.

"I...I saw something, Sev. Just a flash. I...I don't know what. Just as I was pulling my head away, something caught my eye. Not even sure what it was...but it wasn't right. I'm almost positive it was something we need to see. Over there. That side. To the left of the house somewhere." She pointed over the tree trunk.

Seven trained her scope in the direction Jenny indicated and looked intently at every tiny detail. Trees, shrubs, lawn furniture...anything that wasn't wide-open space garnered her attention.

"There!" Jenny whispered a bark. "Look at the first clump of flowering bushes to the left of the second oak. The small one, do you see it?"

"Yep."

"Look on the ground to the left of the flowering bushes."

Seven focused on every leaf of the bush Jenny pointed out, and then she saw it...another sniper in a ghillie suit hiding behind the bush. She could just make out the slightly blue coloration of the glass on his scope. His rifle was trained on her. In the time it takes a hummingbird to flap its wings, Seven realized she was the kill-worthy target. Her heart leapt into her throat as the sniper's weapon kicked, a small bit of smoke following the speeding bullet from its barrel.

Seven tackled Jenny to the ground behind their tree, the sound of the rifle report just then reaching her ears. An instant rush of adrenaline pounded in her head like an oncoming train. "Stay here," she whispered to Jenny as she crouched low and ran to the other end of the fallen tree, removing the 9mm from her belt as she ran. She didn't know how everything got so fucked so fast, but she sure as hell wasn't going to go down without a fight. She'd change her position quick as she could, and come at them fast and hard from an angle they weren't expecting.

That was her plan, anyway. Then she peeked around the tree to see if there were any others and saw the sniper. *What the hell is this shit?* Out in the open, he walked at a slow and steady pace toward her, holding his rifle overhead in surrender. He called out, "Clear!" His voice was easily audible over the space between them.

A voice some distance to Seven's left answered. "Clear!" Then another yelled the same not far from her right. She saw the closest man through the trees closing in slowly. He had an automatic rifle hanging loosely from a shoulder strap, his arms over his head in clear view. It appeared her only avenue of retreat was back up the hill.

Seven took a deep breath, willing herself to remain calm. The closest guy could cut her to pieces with that weapon if he wanted to, but he didn't. Why? She kept her gun trained on the man who was slowly closing in and backtracked toward Jenny. Something strange was going on here and she didn't know what, but she wasn't planning on sticking around to find out. That sniper tried to take her out. Why were they coming at her now like a bunch of zombies from *Night of the Living Dead*? Why didn't they fire on her? At least then, she could fight back. At least then, she would know where she stood.

As she reached Jenny's position, the blonde ran to her and wrapped her arms around her waist, fear in her eyes. A quick glance told Seven the gunman from her left was near enough for Jenny to have seen, and the three of them were steadily closing in on her position. Jenny had seen him and was scared. With her gun still trained on the nearest man, she put her free arm around her lover's shoulder and gently repositioned her so she was between the gunmen and Jenny. She bent to retrieve her rifle and balanced it on her hip, pointing in the direction of the man coming up on their left. She shifted her gaze from left to right, making sure the men stayed in her sights. "Back up, Jen. Up the hill. No sudden movements. We'll get to the road and then make a run for it."

As they started to walk away from the closing men, the one to her right called out. "Wait! Michelis, wait. Don't go that way."

Seven paused, still confused about what the hell was going on when the sniper that shot at her came up the hill. He was still carrying his rifle overhead, and it was obvious he had been running by the fine sheen of sweat on his handsome face. Seven thought he looked familiar. The man propped his rifle against a tree and pulled his ghillie suit off, so the woman could get a good look at him. As he walked closer, one of his hands dropped into a salute, "Captain Michelis. It's a pleasure to see you again, Ma'am. I'm relieved to see you alive and well."

Seven was still wary, but she expelled a relieved breath at seeing a friendly face. "Son of a bitch. Vargas! Darnell Vargas. Jenny, this guy was one of the rookies I was with that day in Kosovo I told you about, like four years ago." Seven's weapons were still trained on the men to her left and right.

"I thought you were a better shot, Vargas. Damn, you weren't more than two hundred yards away and you missed me. Did you get soft since you left the Corps?" She couldn't resist ribbing the guy.

Darnell chuckled. He couldn't help puffing out his chest a little with pride at being in the presence of his hero again. "Oh, I didn't miss, Captain." He signaled to the man on Seven's left and the guy trotted up the hill toward the road. Two minutes later he yelled down, "All clear, T.L."

Seven looked back toward Vargas. "T.L. So you're a Team Leader with the BFC?"

"Not me. Him." Darnell pointed a thumb toward the man on Seven's right who stepped forward and dropped his weapon to the ground. He nodded a silent greeting toward his counterpart. Jenny was still pressed protectively against Seven's back. "Tim Smith, T.L. of the Alpha squad. Nice to meet'cha Michelis. Can we dispense with the weaponry now?" He indicated the 9mm still pointing at his heart.

Seven lowered her weapons. "What did you mean, you didn't miss?" She asked Vargas.

"See for yourself." T.L. Smith led the way uphill to their third Delegate who was standing over a dead man with a large caliber bullet hole in his forehead. He was a smallish man with a goatee, and had a large pistol with a silencer grasped loosely in one hand.

"His name is Lou Conti. His buddies called him the Mouse, though most people didn't know him long enough to learn his name. He's a hired gun on the East Coast, works for whoever's paying. This is who Takashi paid to kill you when he found out you escaped the initial assault. He figured with your skill, you might find a way to make it out of Bolivia alive, and he couldn't have that."

Jenny covered her eyes and stifled a sob. Seven pulled the young woman close and gave her a supportive squeeze. She wasn't sure if Jenny's distress was from seeing yet another violent death, or from how close they had come to being killed. She had to admit, she never saw this guy coming. She expected killers around every corner when she was in Bolivia, but realized she was ignorant to believe her arrival home wouldn't be noticed.

"So you guys were here to protect us?" Seven asked Vargas.

"Yeah. The Chairman said not to move on you unless you shot at him. Otherwise, we were to watch your back. He took a chance you'd take the time to figure out he was clean, and not come in firing."

"Speaking of the Chairman," the Team Leader said, "he's waiting to see you, Michelis. Come with me, and one of the guys will hump your gear down to the house when they've finished here."

Seven hugged Jenny tightly, "Come on, sweetie. Let's go. This will all be over soon." The couple held hands as they picked their way down the hill toward the man who could have easily ended their lives, but chose to save them instead.

The interior of the Chairman's house was as tasteful and comfortable as the exterior. Beautiful dark hardwood floors ran everywhere, accented by white and light earth tones with modern furniture in a mixture of leather, wood, and geometric patterned fabrics. An amazing collection of eclectic art and sculpture added color to the rooms and the fantastic light from walls of seamless windows gave it the feeling of being open to the outside.

Team Leader Smith led the pair into the Chairman's office, which was similarly decorated, and nodded to the man seated behind the desk. "Special delivery, Chairman," Smith said, and left the room.

The older man walked around his desk to stand face to face with this formidable woman. He grasped her shoulders with both hands in a friendly gesture and smiled, something Seven had never seen before in the year she'd known the man. "Glad to see you're not dead, Michelis. I'm glad I'm not dead, too. Thanks for not shooting me."

"Not much chance of that happening, sir. I never got an opportunity to sight-in my father's rifle."

The man chuckled and patted her on the back in a fatherly way. "I knew him, you know. Your father. He was a good man. We CIA types didn't really rub shoulders much with the military guys, but once in a while our paths would cross. He was intelligent and respectful. From what I heard, damn good at what he did. You obviously got your nerve and resourcefulness from him."

Seven's eyes widened slightly and she smiled. She hadn't known that bit of information, but always liked hearing about how her Dad was from other professionals. It gave her a closer connection to him somehow.

The Chairman moved over to stand in front of Jenny. He took her hand in his, "Dr. MacKenzie. It's an honor to meet such a brave and talented young woman. Thank you for coming to the rescue of my Team Leader. Tell me…how big of a jolt was it to find your childhood friend running for her life through the Bolivian jungle?"

Both women appeared slightly shocked that he knew of their childhood friendship. "Gargantuan. But a very happy surprise, none the less."

"Thank God you were there to save her. You did your friend and your country a great service on that day, Doctor."

"And she repaid it in kind."

"Yes. Maria Velasquez. A nasty piece of work to be sure. Interpol was thrilled when they found out she was dead. I took the kill credit for my department, of course. Thank you, Seven." He nodded in the tall woman's direction. "In hindsight, you both were probably in more danger from her than you even realize, or ever were from Reyes. His men were hired local thugs, no real talent, but Velasquez was much more than just a hitter. She had a passion for blood. A suspected serial murderer."

"I knew that," Jenny said, thinking back to the knife blade so close to her heart. "I could see it in her eyes. She carried a long thin knife, and she held it over my heart. It was all she could do to keep from plunging it in. Her hand was shaking with the need for it."

The Chairman's eyes narrowed and he reevaluated the young woman. "Thank you, Dr.

MacKenzie. That information will be extremely helpful for Interpol to know. What you've said matches the M.O. on a large number of unsolved homicides in South America and other parts of the world. Interpol suspected her, but couldn't prove it. This knowledge will close many cases for them." He paused to reflect on what might have been. "You may very well be the only person to have seen that blade who lived to tell the tale."

The Chairman walked back around his desk and put his hand on the phone. "Now…please have a seat. Welcome to my home. If you'll excuse me a minute, I need to call my wife and let her know it's safe to return. Then, I'll put on some coffee and throw together some lunch for us while we discuss what to do about our mutual problem, Mr. Takashi."

Jenny and Seven sat quietly while the Chairman spoke to his wife. His manner toward the unseen woman was amusing to the pair, because they both read him as a different kind of man than the obviously infatuated one speaking to his wife. "Yes dear. Okay. Mmhm. All right. I did. I know, I'm sorry. I will. I love you too, honey. Hurry home. Me too. Bye. You first. Hang up. No you first. Okay, bye."

He hung up and looked at them somewhat sheepishly. "That conversation never makes it to the office, Michelis. Understand?"

"Sir," Seven confirmed. Jenny snickered as they headed for the kitchen.

"My wife says there's a crab salad in the fridge and some fresh croissants in the breadbox. Sound okay to you guys?"

"Sounds delicious," Jenny said as they were directed to the kitchen table. The Chairman busied himself with the coffeepot. "You have a beautiful home, Mr. Chairman."

"Thank you, Doctor. My wife's doing. She has a passion for beautiful things. Why she ever chose to be with a crusty old brute like me I'll never know. If it weren't for her, I'd probably be living in an efficiency apartment with mismatching sheets and foil duct taped over the windows."

The pair laughed at the visual. Seven had never bothered to imagine a personal side to the Chairman. She discovered she liked the man. Jenny suggested he call her by her first name.

"Tell me, Jenny. Have you ever considered a position with the government? My department could use someone like you. Brave, intelligent, talented. You pretty much fit my requirements for employment."

"Uhh...um...gosh. Well, I never considered it. I'm really more into saving lives than taking them, Mr. Chairman. No offense intended. It seems as though your group is into the opposite."

"You'd be surprised. Many teams of all kinds make up Black Flag. All designed and created to specialize in different things. Only a couple of them concentrate on the dark arts like Michelis' team. No two configurations are alike. They all operate independently and without knowledge of each other. Their assignments are basically follow ups to work I've already done."

The Chairman put a tray full of sandwiches on the table, along with cream and sugar for the coffee. "For example, I had already determined Armando Reyes was a key player in the 9/11 attacks, even if not directly. I assigned him to Seven's team, so they could confirm or deny what I already thought, and decide on an appropriate course of action. I give them nothing but a name to start with, so everything they found out was original information, not colored by what I already knew. If I didn't already consider him a kill-worthy target, I would've assigned him to a team more suited to deal with his level of threat to our country."

Seven found this conversation very interesting. The Chairman was revealing more than he ever had about the inner workings of the department.

"The ultimate goal of the BFC is to eliminate the power terrorism has in the world. Some of the other team's sole focus is on humanitarian efforts, education, any number of fields that can provide a positive force to balance the negative. We might determine that a man like Reyes being eliminated would greatly weaken the financial structure of the largest terrorist groups. We might also determine that financing, training, and encouraging positive anti-terrorist locals goes a long way to help deter support for the jihadist groups. Even a single respected individual, if properly trained and financed, can sway support of thousands toward the greater good and away from the bullies and zealots."

"And how would a medical professional fit into a group like that?" Jenny asked, curiosity getting the better of her. It was obvious the Chairman could be charismatically persuasive when he wanted to be.

"Any number of ways. I currently only have one medical team, but there's always room for another. They cross reference areas of unrest with those in dire need of medical assistance, then travel there to help as many as they can, plugging our message if the opportunity arises. People are a lot less likely to fight against the people who saved their children's lives. It's a drop in the bucket, but every friend gained is one less enemy. Every step we take is designed to weaken their infrastructure, and strengthen ours."

"That's all very interesting, Chairman. I promise to think about it," Jenny said graciously, not sure if she would be willing to consider a position like that. Then again, it really wasn't all that different than the Peace Corps, except she'd be getting paid.

The Chairman smiled at the young woman then turned to Seven, "Shall we discuss the remaining member of Team Epsilon, Michelis?"

"Not much to discuss. He's a dead man walking." Her demeanor grew very serious as she visualized the punishment she would personally mete out on the traitor, the man responsible for the death of her friend and teammates.

"The day it became apparent your mission had failed, I assigned Team Alpha to find out your fate in Bolivia. I also assigned Team Lambda to follow and do a complete workup on Takeo Takashi. The team was already well into him by the time he filed the mission report the next day. In the report, he showed irrefutable evidence that you, Michelis, had sold out the team for money. He speculated you were dead, killed by a double-crossing Reyes, but that it was possible you had escaped. He suggested we send a team to track and kill you if you weren't already dead."

"Prick," Seven hissed through her teeth. "Did Alpha find me?"

"Yes. They caught up with you in Cochabamba. The other half of Alpha looked into the claim against you, and the information was solid. Bank records, phone records, a number of things proving your guilt, the initial plan was to hit you there. But Lambda was starting to report suspicious activity by Takashi, so I instructed Alpha to hold off on the kill until we could get better data."

"Thanks," Seven said. Jenny looked a little stunned.

"Also, there was the unknown factor of Dr. MacKenzie." The Chairman looked over at Jenny with a smile in his hawk-like eyes. "We thought maybe you were an accomplice, but your record was so clean I half expected to hear harps playing when you walked into the room." She still looked stunned. She had no idea how many close calls with death she's had in the last two weeks, but it was enough to last a lifetime.

"We were pretty sure at this point Tak somehow managed to hack into these facilities, place the records in there, and cover his tracks. A pretty amazing feat, if you think about it. Not just anybody could hack into something as securely guarded as a bank. Makes him a dangerous man on a whole other level."

"How did a smarmy dirtbag like that get into DHS? You put me through the ringer with all the interviewing and security checks, and I was career. How did this guy, with so little character he sold us out first chance he got, get into the BFC?"

Gone was the fatherly look of pride he showed while describing his brainchild. Seven briefly glimpsed a flash of the man who was renowned as a force to be reckoned with in the shadowy world of undercover. It was the look of a dangerous man. "It was my fault. He was my choice." The Chairman looked supremely upset at himself more than anything. "I'm usually a very good judge of character, but with him I totally blew it. His record was clean. He didn't develop a gambling problem until several months after he started at BFC."

"Gambling problem? Are you telling me my team is dead because that *motherfucker* had a bad night at the craps table?" Seven seethed. Jenny thought she looked like she was going to come right out of her skin. Her eyes flared to near black in extreme anger. She reached over and placed a calming hand on her lover's forearm.

"Team Lambda's report is in my office. You're welcome to review it when we're done here. Apparently over the course of about four months he became mob indebted to the tune of a quarter million dollars."

"Jesus," the women said in unison.

"It was enough to warrant a death threat by the local family. Word is, they sent a couple guys to abduct him, then took him to a warehouse and forced him to watch them murder another guy who didn't pay. Takashi knew there was no way he could pay, so he contacted Reyes and sold him the information for a million. He must have done a good job scaring Reyes, because the guy coughed up the exorbitant fee without a struggle."

The Chairman reached over and refilled their coffee cups, pausing for a moment to spoon sugar and cream into his. "Takashi has been deemed a kill-worthy target by Team Lambda."

"I want the kill," Seven commanded, leaving no room for debate.

"Sev."

"No, Jen. I need to do this for Marcus. For me."

"Please. Can we at least talk about it?" She squeezed her friend's arm to get her attention back where it belonged. Seven sighed.

The Chairman watched the interaction and thought the couple an interesting contrast to each other. It was obvious the young doctor had a problem with Seven's black and white method of problem solving, the ease with which she would end a life. This was one of the things he admired about Michelis the most. He wondered how they would manage a compromise on something this cut and dry. The man was curious to see who would win the argument.

"I will leave it to you to determine a course of action, Michelis. I will inform Lambda they are off."

"Thank you, sir."

Jenny looked forlornly at her coffee cup.

"Now," the Chairman stood and began clearing plates from the table, "when do you think you'll be back in the office, Michelis? I need to design a new team for you. Maybe something different this time, 'eh?" He thought it best to encourage her to get back on the horse.

"I'm not sure I'm coming back, sir." She and Jenny had only touched on the subject. Last they'd spoken of it, Seven hadn't made up her mind.

The Chairman had been afraid of this. He knew Marcus Johnson was more to Michelis than just a teammate. "Do what you have to do to finish this mission, Seven, then let's talk. I'm in no hurry. I know you suffered a great trauma, and I don't want you to feel pressured into a rash decision. You need time to process what's happened and heal. Take what you need, and when you're ready, we'll talk. I'm leaving you on the payroll in the meantime."

Hm. Not so subtle. Seven smiled and acknowledged the man with a nod. "I'll give it my full consideration, Chairman, but first things first. I need to put Takashi to rest. Now."

❦❦❦❦

"Okay…all right already. Enough with the puppy dog eyes. I'll talk about it, but I'm not promising anything. You know who I am, what I do, and what he did to me, to us, to Marcus and Ty. I don't understand why you won't just let me put a bullet in his head and be done with it. No messy trial. No lawyers getting rich. No embarrassment for the department. It's clean, it's done with, end of story." Seven was exasperated Jenny would not let the Takashi thing go.

The couple had checked themselves into a hotel about twenty miles from the Chairman's house. After yesterday's car trip and a long night huddling in the woods, both were in dire need of a shower, a nap, and a change of clothes.

"Sev, I've seen thirteen people die violent deaths since I found you in the woods. You might be immune to that level of violence in your life, but I'm not. The fact that I seem to actually be getting there myself scares the shit out of me. That's why I was crying today when Vargas killed that guy behind us. Because I was *glad* it was him and not us. I didn't care he was dead. Even if he was a bad guy, I don't want to be that person."

"Takashi is a criminal. A traitor. I will not let him go unpunished."

"I didn't say that. Let the bastard rot in jail for the next twenty years for all I care. Just don't kill him. This would not be like the hits you made when you were a Marine. You had no power to punish those men any other way. To kill one of those targets you were stopping them from doing further damage to innocent people in their paths. Tak is not one of those guys. Killing him wouldn't be about the greater good.

With time, it would taste a little less like justice, and a little more like revenge…possibly even homicide. It's not really him I'm worried about, as much as you."

Seven walked to the window and drew the curtains closed, enveloping them in total darkness. She punched a few buttons on her watch, setting an alarm to go off in two hours, long enough for a solid nap. She found she really couldn't argue Jenny's point anymore, so instead pulled back the comforter on the king size bed and fell bonelessly into a heap, not bothering to remove her clothes. Jenny slid in beside her, planting a kiss on the crown of her head, and rolled over, falling fast asleep.

Seven always found the alarm on this particular watch annoying, which was why she made a point to turn it off before it sounded. She thought it would be much nicer to wake Jenny up with a whisper, rather than a screaming buzzer. She never managed to find sleep herself, having spent the entire two hours trying to figure out a way to satisfy her need to see Tak dead, and accomplish her lover's wishes as well. She had come up with a plan, and though there were no guarantees, she knew Jenny wouldn't argue with it.

"Hey, Sleeping Beauty. Time to get up." Seven leaned over and kissed her lover's sleep-warmed cheek.

"Uhhh," Jenny complained groggily. "I could sleep for a hundred years," she moaned, the pillow muffling her voice.

Seven opened the drapes to late afternoon sun and plopped back on the bed, nudging her lover once more. Jenny continued to moan complaints into her pillow as she kicked her uncooperative legs over the edge of the bed and let gravity drag her out from under warm sheets. She stumbled blindly into the bathroom and turned on the shower as Seven pulled Tak's file under the light and opened it.

She picked up the phone and dialed a number listed on page two of the report. After three rings, a man's deep voice answered the phone, "Konnichiwa."

"Konnichiwa, Takashi-sama. Eigo o hanasemasu ka?" Seven asked, struggling through a mostly unfamiliar language.

"Yes, I speak English," the man answered politely.

"Takashi-sama, my name is Seven Michelis. I am a business associate of your son Takeo. My apologies for disturbing your evening. I wonder if it would be possible for you to meet me for a short time, perhaps a restaurant of your choosing? I have a matter of some importance to discuss with you regarding your son."

"Yes, Miss Michelis. My son Takeo has mentioned you. I believe he referred to you as a modern-day samurai."

"He honors me. May we meet?"

"Of course. A restaurant will not be necessary. Please. You are welcome in my home."

"That is very gracious of you, Takashi-sama. I can be there in one hour." Seven hung up and banged on the bathroom door. "Come on, Sleeping Beauty. We gotta go!"

Jenny poked a wet head out the door. "Whazzup?"

"I've got a plan that could solve both our problems. Come on. We're going to meet Tak's father."

"We're wha...Hey!" Seven snatched the wet towel off her lover and spun it into a rattail, threatening the blonde with a welt if she didn't get a move on. Jenny squealed and scooted over to her bag, grabbing a pair of jeans and a t-shirt off the top.

They drove to the Virginia side of D.C. while

Seven explained her plan to Jenny. As predicted, the young woman did not argue. Seven didn't promise Tak wouldn't die, or that she wouldn't kill him, but at least she was willing to explore a possible alternative. They reached the Takashi residence just as the hour was about to be up, and Seven sighed in relief. Being late was rude, and rude was not acceptable in Japanese culture. Jenny volunteered to watch the back of her eyelids in the car while her friend visited Takashi senior.

Seven surveyed the typical Virginia suburban house. From the outside, it looked like every other house in the neighborhood. She remembered Tak saying his parents had decorated the interior in traditional Japanese style with polished hardwood floors, sliding rice-paper doors, and peaceful green atriums. She took off her jacket before knocking, hung it on a peg, and undid her shoelaces.

Takashi senior answered the knock and Seven bowed low, a formal bow, one meant to show respect for the elder. She was careful not to hold the bow too long; custom dictated that as bad form. "Konnichiwa Takashi-sama, it is an honor to be invited to your home. Thank you for seeing me on such short notice."

"You are welcome, Miss Michelis. Please come in." The man was at least a head shorter than Seven, with ramrod posture and stern features. His eyes were dark and framed by gold-rimmed glasses, and they gleamed with curiosity at meeting his son's boss.

Seven removed her shoes and stepped into the house, sliding her socked feet into one of the many pairs of slippers sitting neatly by the door.

"I must say, Miss Michelis, you are very polite for an American. No offense, it's just that most don't know our culture, so to us they appear rude."

Seven laughed good-naturedly. "Takeo told me you were very traditional people. I have a great deal of respect for the many cultures of the world. Much knowledge can be gained by studying the way others live, what they believe and hold dear. You have a beautiful home."

"Thank you. Your words are wise for one so young."

"Ah. Not as young as I look, Takashi-sama. I have seen many things."

"So Takeo said. Please, join me for a drink." The older man led the way to the dining room. Seven removed her slippers outside the room and followed him in her socked feet. He invited her to sit in a place of honor at the head of the table, and she sank down onto the red cushioned floor. The tall brunette waited in silence while he retrieved and poured rice wine into small china cups and served her. "Kanpai!" They lifted their cups and drank deeply of the strong beverage.

Seven's focus was drawn to the daisho hanging proudly on the wall. Tak had told her once upon a time that he was descended from Samurai. The long sword, called a katana, and the short sword, called a wakizashi, made up the daisho, the elegant weapons of men who took their warring very seriously. She could tell by the wear and craftsmanship that the blades hanging on the wall were authentic and very old.

Tak's father watched the woman intently as she evaluated the daisho from afar. He was pleased that not only did she seem to know what they were, but how exquisite as well. "Beautiful," she whispered in awe.

"I see you recognize quality when you see it,

Miss Michelis. They belonged to my great-great grandfather. One of the last of the Samurai class. They were handed down to him for untold generations."

"I've studied ancient weapons and war a great deal, Takashi-sama. I've always been drawn to swords more than any other weapon. Sword fighting required skill, grace, and a certain amount of style. True warriors lost something of themselves when they went to guns. Winning became more about luck, numbers, and brawling, than about skill. Battle was taken from the skillful few and given to the rumbling masses. It is an impressive daisho. I have seen many, and these may be the finest I've laid eyes on."

"You are gracious to say so, Miss Michelis. Now, what did you wish to see me about? If it is as urgent as you say, I would have to assume Takeo is in some sort of trouble."

"Yes, sir. I'm sorry to be the bearer of bad news." Seven slid the folder containing the Lambda Team's assessment of Takeo's activities over to his father. "Please read this report. When you're through, I'll tell you what I know from personal account, and what I'm planning to do about it."

As the older man read, his posture became less rigid and his stern appearance seemed to sag with the weight of information he was digesting. When he was through, he closed the folder and slid it across the table toward his guest. Removing his glasses, he sat quietly for several minutes with his face in his hands, the color having drained long ago.

"My son never became the man I'd hoped for." He looked much older as shame and sadness set in.

"I'm not sure how much Tak told you about what he does for the DHS. Our team's assignments were generally kept under very tight wraps."

"He didn't tell me details, but he told me enough about your team's professional experience to speculate."

"On our last mission, my team was killed in an ambush. I, myself, was shot twice while escaping. This happened because Takeo sold the information of our mission and our whereabouts to cover his gambling debts."

On the surface, the older man took the news stoically.

"One of the men killed was my best friend. As I'm sure you can imagine, I won't rest until Tak has paid for his crime, not only to me personally, but for being a traitor to our country. If he could do this to us, his friends and immediate co-workers, I'm sure it wouldn't be too much of a stretch for him to take the next step, selling state secrets, hacking government or financial institutions for personal gain, etc. With his talent there is no limit to the types of crimes he could commit if motivated."

Mr. Takashi downed the rest of his saki, and poured them each another. "Why are you here, Miss Michelis?"

"I am here because I am willing to offer Tak a chance to redeem himself. At least, in your eyes. I'm sorry to say, in my eyes, he has no chance of ever doing that. I promised a friend I would attempt an alternate course of action, instead of killing him outright. Though it is what I do, she felt the element of revenge would taint me. So for that reason, I am willing to offer him the choice of seppuku."

The man glanced over at the smaller wakizashi sword on the wall. In the time of Samurai, a warrior who was dishonored could redeem himself with his superiors by committing suicide, or seppuku as it is called in Japanese culture. A warrior would disembowel himself using his wakizashi. The Samurai would require permission from his superior to commit such an act. Tak's father knew if he gave the blade to this woman he would, in effect, be giving his son permission to commit suicide. He would be telling his son, that in order to save face he must die by his own hand. "That is very decent of you, Miss Michelis. I'm not sure my son deserves such consideration. He has brought great shame to our proud family."

"I will give him this option, though admittedly it was not my first choice. His only other option will be prison. Whether he will choose seppuku, I do not know, but considering your family's tradition and history, I consider it better for him than being branded a traitor, tried, and sent to prison for a very long time. If he chooses not to accept, the FBI will pick him up before the end of tomorrow. One way or the other, Tak's life as he knows it is over."

"What if he runs?"

"Then I will do what I do best."

Seven drank the rest of her rice wine, collected the folder, and stood. She bowed once more to the older man and headed for the door, padding quietly across the tatami floor. She didn't actually have to verbalize what she wanted. She knew the man understood she was there for the heirloom. "Please take your time to think about what I said. I will await your decision in the foyer, Takashi-sama."

The man remained silent, staring blankly at his quivering hands, which were folded neatly on the table.

⚚⚚⚚⚚

Takeo Takashi was pissed.

Pissed off and piss drunk.

He couldn't believe with all the money he'd given that bastard bookie Sal over the last six months, the prick couldn't at least serve him a decent scotch. He had just been asked to leave the poker table at Sal's because the more in the hole he got, the louder and more obnoxious he was to Sal's other guests.

Tak justifiably explained if the prick served him decent scotch, he wouldn't be so edgy. Nothing made the computer tech more wound up than bad booze and bad cards. When Sal was kicking him out, he tried to appease his temper by telling Tak it was for his own good. Apparently, one of the other high rollers at the table was a highly ranked mob boss, and not one to suffer fools.

"Down another thirty fuckin' grand and probably end up with a goddamn hangover from that shitty scotch, too," Tak said aloud to no one in particular.

He stumbled up the stairs outside his building and fumbled in his pocket for the keys to the door. "Shitty ass condo," he mumbled, as if it was somehow the building's fault he couldn't find his keys. "Time for me to get outta this 'hood anyway and move uptown. Why not? I deserve it." He continued to grouse as he rode the elevator up to his floor.

Tak dropped his keys in the hallway and swayed dangerously as he bent to pick them up. He noticed the carpet was a little threadbare in this area and began his cursing anew. Unlocking his door, the young man stumbled in and made way straight for the kitchen where he'd left the light over the oven on. Reaching into the fridge, he grabbed a bottle of water and chugged half before stopping for air.

A short distance away a shadowy figure sat motionless in the dark, watching as the drunken man rifled through his refrigerator, illuminated by the dim appliance light. With satisfactory snack obtained, Tak walked into his living room with a half drunk bottle of water in one hand, and a floppy slice of cold pizza dangling from his mouth.

He hit the light switch on the way in. Tak's attention was immediately drawn to a shape caught at the edge of his vision that wasn't a normal part of his living room landscape.

Seven said nothing, but sat watching his entry with a stony expression on her chiseled face. Her legs were crossed and her posture easy, feigning relaxation, but the woman was anything but. To see this bastard happily traipsing through life as though nothing was out of sorts, while her friend's corpse lay burnt to dust in a muddy hole, seared her brain behind stormy eyes.

Tak's alcohol-induced haze evaporated instantly as his eyes flew open in horrified recognition. His body jerked in abject terror, jaws seizing shut on his late night snack, sending the soggy triangle to the floor with a wet flop. His water bottle flew through the air, sending a curving water snake sailing overhead in a graceful arc before gravity brought it splashing to the ground.

Tak's panicked eyes darted around the room, searching for an avenue of escape. He snatched the cell phone from his belt clip and frantically tried to dial nine-one-one. Seven stood, and in three powerful strides slapped the phone from his hand. Tak spun and launched himself toward the door, deciding to make a run for it.

Seven hammered a powerful hand against the door as he vainly attempted to turn the knob with shaking hands. She pressed the warm steel barrel of her 9mm behind his ear and whispered dangerously, "Not gonna happen, dirtbag."

Tak stopped shaking and started mewling pathetically as urine wet an uninvited trail down his pant leg. Seven cringed and took a step back to keep her boots from getting splashed. With the gun still pressed firmly behind his ear, she threw all the deadbolts into place and grabbed the whimpering man by the collar, shoving him none too gently into the kitchen. "Come on, you pathetic piece of shit. Let's get you sobered up so we can have a conversation you'll remember in the morning."

She shoved him into a kitchen chair and told him if he twitched, she'd throw him out the window. He briefly considered trying to feign innocence, but could tell by the look in her eyes the time for that was way past. She made a pot of coffee, putting twice as many scoops in the filter as she normally would. When it was ready, she filled four cups and added generous amounts of sugar and cream. She put them all in front of Tak, along with what was left of his cold pizza and watched as he drank and ate everything she put down.

Seven spun a kitchen chair around with her foot and straddled it, resting her arms on the back and her chin on her arms. She watched as the paunchy little traitor slowly came back to himself, his clarity returning. He wasn't shaking from fear as much now, but the terror was still there in his eyes. *Good. At least he has the decency and intelligence to be afraid for what he's done.*

"Why didn't you just shoot me from half a mile away like you do everyone else? You're gonna torture me or something, aren't you? At least then, I wouldn't've known it was coming. You're a cruel bitch, boss." Tak finally found his voice.

Seven remained silent, her cold, piercing gaze further unnerving the twitchy man.

"Aren't you going to ask me why I did it, or something profound before you kill me?"

"No. I know why you did it. Everybody at Black Flag knows why you did it."

Tak looked sharply at her with this news.

"That's right, Takashi. The Chairman had a team on you less than twenty-four hours after we went missing. You've been deemed a kill-worthy target."

Tak knew it could come to this, but somewhere in the back of his mind, he never thought it would happen. He thought the Chairman was just another bureaucratic suit. Turns out, the guy was smarter than he gave him credit for. His fear returned in the form of more shaking as the implications sank in. He looked into the icy stare boring into him and saw no sympathy, only cool, clear detachment.

Seven watched as Tak's features shifted from fear to denial to defiance to anger and back to fear. "I want you to see something, Tak." The sniper reached into her shirt pocket and removed a small ring, which she held out for the computer tech to see. "Marcus had this with him when we went down there. It's an engagement ring. He was planning to propose to Alicia when we got back. You remember Alicia? You met her that night we all went to Bennigan's and drank a couple gallons of beer."

Tak said nothing, but stared fixedly at the ring.

"I want you to feel the reality of what you've done before we discuss your next step."

"Fuck you, boss."

"Aww. What's wrong, Tak? Can't face it? You don't want to feel responsible for the pain and loss Marcus' fiancé must be feeling right now? His mother and sisters? Ty's parents? You don't want to put yourself in their shoes? You don't want to admit to yourself you caused so much grief for so many people just to line your pockets? That's pretty pathetic, Tak. No wonder your father is ashamed of you."

Tak's head snapped up, his puffy red eyes boring into his tormentor. "Leave my father out of this, you damn bitch."

Seven retrieved the bag she had sitting nearby. She unzipped the case and removed the Takashi's priceless family heirloom. She slid the wakizashi slowly across the kitchen table, the intricately carved wooden scabbard generating a low scraping sound on the linoleum.

Tak's eyes bulged out of his head and what color was left in his face drained completely away. "Where did you get that?" He demanded with a shaking voice.

"After I told your father what you did, he gave it to me." Seven paused to let the words sink deeply in. "It's for you."

The only sound that could be heard was the low hum of the nearby refrigerator, and the far off thrum of late night city traffic. Tak stared at the ancient weapon without speaking, tears running unhindered down his face.

"Consider it a parting gift, as we will no longer be requiring your services at the DHS."

"What did he say? My father?" The woman barely heard his words.

"He said you brought great shame to your family and your ancestors."

Tears turned to wracking sobs as the depth of what he'd done finally sank in on a personal level. He could live with almost anything, but not his father's shame. He tried so hard his whole life to make the old man proud. He asked himself, *when did it all turn around for me?*

Seven waited for his crying to subside, spending the minutes thinking of Jenny. She had wanted to come here, but the older woman pleaded with her to stay, not sure if Tak would turn violent when cornered. She was glad the stubborn young woman had agreed to wait in the car. This intense emotional upheaval would be difficult for anyone to witness.

"Seppuku is your choice. You should be grateful I'm giving you one. You have a chance to redeem yourself in the eyes of your father. If you decide you can't do it, the FBI will be here to pick you up before end of day tomorrow. Long, embarrassing trial, the end result being they'll throw away the key. Black Flag will make sure of it." Seven checked her watch. It was just a little after 11:30 pm.

"Don't bother trying to run. You're a priority one target for the BFC. You wouldn't make it out of the city."

"Why...why didn't you just kill me?" He asked, dragging the back of his hand across his nose. It would have been so much easier to have had the choice taken from him.

Seven didn't give Tak the satisfaction of an answer. Instead, she picked up the engagement ring, slipped it back in her pocket, and stood to leave. "I hope you make the right decision. Be a shame to drag your parents through that." It was cold, she knew, but she couldn't resist one last nudge in the direction she wanted this to go. A trial would suck for everybody, and the only reason she agreed to it as an option was that Jenny insisted. *Dear lord, Seven, love has made you soft.*

She left the condo. The last she saw of her former computer tech was him resting his folded arms on the kitchen table, with his head slung low between them, weeping.

Chapter Twenty-five

The drive south on George Washington Memorial Parkway toward Alexandria, Virginia was a quiet affair. It was a little after one a.m., just under two weeks since her HALO drop into Bolivia. Seven couldn't believe how much she was looking forward to sleeping in her own bed and scrubbing the last vestiges of this disastrous mission off in her own shower.

She glanced over at her sleeping lover. When she had gotten back in the car after her meeting with Tak, Jenny had inquired about the details, satisfying herself that everything had gone according to plan. Then she said, in a voice thick with exhaustion, "Take me home, baby." She leaned her head against the passenger side window and fell asleep.

Seven smiled to herself, happy beyond words this beautiful woman sleeping next to her had assumed, in an innocent and honest way that 'home' was with her, no matter where she happened to be.

An abrupt end to the craziness of the last two weeks left Jenny back in the States without a home or a job, and Seven without a team and unsure of her future. It was a little nerve-wracking if she thought too much about it, but she felt good about where she was with Jenny, and nothing else could come close in terms of importance. They had a lot of details to discuss, a lot of dark doors to close, and a few exciting new ones to open.

Somewhere in the back of her mind, Seven briefly entertained a bit of nagging doubt that Jenny's feelings for her might change now that the excitement was over. Since they'd been reunited, their time together had been one big adventure, always on the run, under fire. They needed each other to survive. Now that things would be settling down, would it still be what the young woman wanted?

Seven's thoughts turned to her confrontation with Takeo, wondering if she did the right thing in leaving the computer tech to decide his own fate. She hoped so. She was so very ready to be over and done with this, and stalking Tak if he made a run for it was the last thing she wanted to do. All she was interested in now was putting this disaster behind her, and making a future with this amazing girl at her side.

She pulled Uncle Nick's car to the curb in front of her place and turned off the engine. Jenny was so out of it she didn't even open an eyelid. Seven hefted her out of the car, holding her in her arms like a child as she mumbled something unintelligible and wrapped her arms loosely around Seven's neck.

❧ ❧ ❧ ❧

The sunrise had come and gone as Takeo sat at his kitchen table. His tears long dried, he stared motionless at the wakizashi sitting mere inches from his right hand. He lazily moved his arm so he could brush his fingertips along the surface of the wooden sheath, carved with such skill and pride centuries earlier. He had spent countless hours in his father's home staring at the weapons of his ancestors while his father filled him with tales of honor and glory.

He wondered what it must have been like to be a Samurai, back in the days when the fierce warriors were the elite in their society. What must it have felt like for a Samurai to have shamed their master. Were they proud to perform seppuku? Were they frightened? Had any samurai ever chosen to run away instead of facing their duty?

Takeo Takashi may have been descended from their proud class, but he sure as shit didn't feel like it.

He had no more tears to give.

He was numb, his mind blank to every detail of his existence, save one. He couldn't stomach the eyes with which his father would look upon him if he were ever to see him again. He thought many times he would rather be dead than to see that 'look' trained in his direction. Well, here it was. Put up, or shut up time. Life as he knew it was over, so it may as well be literal.

He had one last opportunity to make his father proud. What was it to be? Do it? Or say 'Fuck the family, I'll take my chances in prison.' Prison. Shit. He always assumed Michelis would just kill him. He never even considered the laugh-riot that would be prison. Beatings. Rapes. Years of endless suffering and stolen freedom. He wasn't cut out for that shit.

His butt was numb from sitting in the same position for hours. Finally, tired of thinking, he said aloud for no one's sake but his own, "You wrote this program, Tak. Be a man and execute it."

Tak snatched the ancient weapon from the table and pulled the gleaming blade from its sheath. He walked into the living room, removing a kitchen towel from where it hung on the oven door, and wrapped it around the sharp steel a few inches from the hilt. Without any further thought or ado, he kicked off his shoes, pulled his shirt overhead, and kneeled on the floor in front of his family portrait that hung in a place of honor. The young man sat cross-legged as he stared into the eyes of his father. Grabbing the hilt with his left hand, and the towel wrapped blade with his right, he positioned the tip of the short sword a couple inches below his belly button and plunged it home. He continued to stare at the photo as he dragged the razor-sharp steel from left to right across his abdomen.

God it hurt...but it would be over soon. He closed his eyes and waited for death to visit him.

❧❧❧❧

Upon waking, the first thought that skittered through Jenny's mind was of being submersed in ultimate comfort. She wasn't fully awake, but her senses told her she had somehow achieved the rare feeling of being perfectly positioned on a soft, fluffy cloud. Not too warm, not too cold, she was surrounded by goose down and Seven's comforting scent. She sighed contentedly, feeling if she moved even an inch her perfect comfort would be ruined.

Through the fog of sleep, Jenny realized she didn't even know where she was. She decided to open an eyelid and peek around the sunlit room. She was immediately rewarded with the sight of her lover coming in the door, a loving smile decorating her stunning face.

Seven looked adorable. Bare feet and long muscular legs met an old pair of baggy gray USMC shorts that looked like they'd been through the wash a million times, and a soft heather gray tank top that hugged her shape nicely. She carried a tray laden with goodies, setting it on the unoccupied side of her fluffy king size bed. She sat next to Jenny and drew her into powerful arms.

"You feel so good, Jenny." Their lips met in a leisurely kiss. "Did you sleep well?"

"Mmmm." Jenny soaked in the warmth and strength of her partner. "I must've been totally out of it, Sev. I don't even remember getting here." She buried her face in Seven's warm neck. "Where is here, anyway?"

"My brownstone in Old Town Alexandria. I mean...um...well...*our* brownstone. If you want it to be, that is. I know we haven't really discussed it, but...oof." The rest of her sentence was pressed into nonexistence by a pair of insistent lips.

"I can't remember ever wanting anything more," Jenny whispered, as the two lost themselves in each other's eyes. Seven took the young woman's smiling face in her hand and brushed a thumb lightly over the soft skin of her cheek.

"I love you, Jenny. I didn't get a chance to say it yesterday before everything went crazy, but I want you to know I feel the same way. I'm in love with you. I've never felt this way before, and it's unbelievably scary, and wonderful, and so many other things. What I feel when I'm with you is what I hoped I'd find for as long as I can remember. I want to make a life with you."

Tears gathered in the corners of the young woman's eyes. The smile left Jenny's face and for a moment, Seven thought maybe she'd gone too far in her admission. Then in a total reversal, Jenny laughed and cried simultaneously. "Wow. You don't say much, Sev, but when you do, look out! I've been obsessing over thoughts that maybe I'd scared you off. We've come so far so fast. I was afraid…"

"Shh," Seven pressed a finger to Jenny's lips, then removed the finger and replaced it with lips of her own. Both moaned into the contact as Jenny pulled Seven down on top of her, their breakfast tray forgotten. The lovers spent untold minutes tangled together, exploring each other's mouths, each kiss in itself an unhurried declaration of love.

It felt so good to be together, focusing completely on the other without threat of death or disaster looming ever-present overhead. After a good hour of nothing more pressing than two pairs of lips getting more familiar, Jenny's stomach growled loudly and their kisses turned to chuckles. "You want some coffee?" Seven asked. "It's probably cold by now."

"Bathroom first, then coffee," Jenny stated as she darted away. Once the bathroom door was closed, she yelled through the wood. "Then a tour! I wanna see our house!" Seven could hear her giggling through the wall.

How did this bizarre thing happen? How did I go to South America, watch my best friend die, and find the love of my life all in the span of two weeks?

The phone rang and Seven rolled over on her side and picked it up. She listened intently as Jenny came padding out and helped herself to a cold breakfast of scrambled eggs, toast, and lukewarm coffee from the tray. When Seven hung up, she turned to Jenny and simply said, "It's over."

"So he did it, then?" Jenny asked, referring to

Takeo's suggested suicide.

"Yeah. That was the T.L. of Team Lambda. I asked they keep an eye on him in case he decided to run. He didn't. He said he'd let the Chairman know. I should probably go in at some point and pick up my IDs, and file a mission report. You wanna come?"

"Yes. I'm not letting you out of my sight. It's my job to watch you at all times."

"Ha! And I thought I was the stalker." They grinned at each other and Seven stood. "Come on. I'll give you the quick tour and we'll get cleaned up and go. If you want to check in with your Peace Corps people, I can put you in an office while I'm writing my report. What do you think of the place so far?"

"You have the most heavenly bed I've ever slept in, and I can't believe you have a fireplace right in the bedroom. That's so romantic."

"It is now."

"I think I could be perfectly happy just staying in this room for the rest of the week."

"That can totally be arranged." Seven waggled an eyebrow and stole another kiss.

Jenny was impressed with the colonial townhouse, admiring Seven's taste in decorating, stating more than once she thought it a perfect reflection of the older woman. Polished hard wood floors anchored its classic style, clean, uncluttered lines, beautiful like the woman who lived there. "It looks like a catalog spread for Pottery Barn. I really love it, Sev. It's extremely comfortable."

"Yeah. Those Pottery Barn guys can do wonders with a credit card."

"Come on," Jenny said, taking the smiling woman by the hand. "Take a shower with me, then we can get moving. The sooner we get all our stuff done, the sooner we can get back here and you can show me how you do that thing with your tongue."

Seven wondered which 'thing' Jenny was referring to. When it occurred to her, a blush rose quickly up her cheeks and she took the stairs two at a time. She had the shower running and was out of her clothes by the time Jenny reached the landing. "C'mon, c'mon! Get a move on," Jenny heard coming from the bathroom.

Jenny finally managed to stump Seven with a lyric in the shower. It was a popular Howard Jones song in the '80s, which led to a loud rendition of 'Like to Get to Know You Well,' one woman singing in tune, the other out, while scrubbing copious amounts of chamomile and rosemary scented shampoo into each other's hair.

On the way to Seven's office, Jenny talked incessantly about everything from shopping for new clothes to D.C. area medical facilities. The couple agreed to take a month and do absolutely nothing before they even began to speak about their career options. The brunette made sure the blonde understood "absolutely nothing" did in no way include plenteous amounts of training in 'target acquisition,' preferably to be executed in every room of the house, and on every surface.

When talk turned to serious matters, Seven expressed her desire to attend Ty and Marcus' memorial services. Ty's family lived in Manhattan, and Marcus' mother and sisters all still lived in South Carolina. She reasoned they could drive back south and return Uncle Nick's car at the same time.

Alicia, Marcus' would-have-been fiancé lived in Georgetown. Seven wanted to visit the young woman as soon as possible to express her condolences in person. She'd only known her for a few months, having recently relocated to the area to be with Marcus, but it didn't take long for the two to become friends. They had their adoration for the short, unhandsome, and completely loveable man in common.

She wanted Alicia to have the engagement ring Marcus intended to give her. She and Jenny had discussed whether or not this was a good idea, thinking it might only make matters worse for the young woman, but in the end they decided she would probably like to know how much he truly loved her.

Also, for some reason, she really wanted to introduce Alicia to Jenny and vice versa. Via Marcus, Seven figured Alicia probably knew her better than most people, and since she couldn't share her happiness and good fortune with Marcus, she felt Alicia would like to be a part of it. Alicia, more than anyone, would understand the significance of Seven having found someone to love. She wanted to stay close to Alicia, and help to watch out for her if she could. Marcus would've wanted it that way.

Seven pulled the car into a parking space outside her office building and took a couple deep breaths as she looked upon the place she associated with so many bad memories. She took Jenny upstairs, through multiple layers of security, and stuck her in an office to make phone calls while she set to work on her reports.

After some time, she steeled herself, and began cleaning out her team's offices of their personal items, placing everything in boxes to be shipped to their families. She found her mood sinking lower and lower as the reality of losing three people she'd come to care and feel responsible for sank deeper into her psyche.

By the time she packed Ty's Nolan Ryan autographed baseball and Mario Lemieux hockey puck into a box, tears were tracking freely down her face.

"Don't you dare start thinking any of this was your fault," the Chairman spoke softly from the doorway.

Seven quickly brushed the moisture from her cheeks and turned, trying to cover her temporary emotional setback. She pretended to be busy with something else. "My team. My responsibility."

"My team. My responsibility," the Chairman said with emphasis.

It didn't help to lighten her mood, but Seven appreciated her boss was trying to make her feel better.

"Brilliant how you handled Takashi, by the way. I was wondering which of the two of you" —he nodded toward the doctor sitting in a glass walled office a few yards away—"was going to win that argument."

"Argument?"

"About whether or not you would kill him."

"Oh." Seven chuckled. "I guess we both won."

"She's...um...tenacious."

Seven chuckled again. "You have no idea."

"I'm happy to see you didn't empty out your desk with all the others. Does that mean you'll be returning to work?"

"I haven't decided anything new since yesterday, sir. All I know for sure right now is I need some time away. Jen and I have agreed to revisit our professional ventures in a month or so."

"You're one of the most valuable people I have, Seven," the Chairman said. The rare use of her first name denoted the depth of meaning behind his words. "I don't want to lose you. If you decide you're done with being a sharpshooter, I'll find something else for you to do. I'll design a new team, one that will capitalize on your best abilities."

She met his eyes. "Shooting is all I know, Chairman. Not much else I could contribute to an organization like this."

"Bullshit." He startled Seven with his blunt response. "You have many skills. I've watched you very closely, Michelis. You're the most gifted strategist I've seen. Careful. Intelligent. Loyal. Diligent. Creative. Resourceful. I've seen a conference room full of pros strategize for a week and not come up with a plan as good as what you whip off the top of your head. The reason you've always been successful is because you have the ability to see all the angles in a realistic light."

"Not this time."

"No. We were all fooled this time. After Takashi, I'm thinking I need a new team whose job will be to monitor the other teams."

"I wouldn't tell anybody else that if I were you, sir. There'd probably be a mass exodus."

"Good thinkin'. Thanks for coming in today. I would've taken your report later."

"I needed to get this all behind me. Plus, Ty's memorial service is in a few days, so I wanted to pick up his things to take with me. I'll be seeing Marcus' girlfriend later."

The Chairman nodded. "I'll take care of getting Takashi's personals back to his father."

"Thanks."

They shook hands and Seven watched as the Chairman departed, stopping to say hello and goodbye to Jenny on his way out the door.

The young woman stretched and ambled over to

her lover, inserting herself into strong, waiting arms and resting her head on a tall shoulder. "Can we go soon, baby?"

"Yeah. Sorry it took me so long. You okay with stopping by Alicia's on the way home?"

"Of course. I'd like to meet her."

"Then maybe a quick stop at the grocery to lay in supplies for a couple days."

Jenny gave her a questioning look.

"Well you said you wanted to spend the rest of the week in bed. I just thought if we had the right consumables I could feed you in bed every day, and we would never have to leave the house. We'll turn the A.C. really cold and light a fire in the bedroom fireplace. It'll be like we're snowed in with nowhere to go."

The implication was not lost on Jenny, as a villainous smile took shape on her face. She pushed away from her hug, and was bouncing on the balls of her feet with excitement at the prospect of two whole days in bed with Seven. This would be a marathon of the most delightful variety. "Well, what are we waiting for? Let's go!"

Seven was glad to be laughing after the strain of the last couple of hours. She handed her friend a box to carry, grabbed another for herself, and led the way out.

Hours later and on her second glass of chardonnay, Jenny stood in the entryway of their kitchen, mesmerized by her lover as she moved about the cooking space, preparing something for dinner. The tall brunette was so graceful, she looked more like a dancer than a combat trained lethal weapon.

Jenny let her gaze wander from head to toe,

appreciating every inch of her poetry in motion. She wore a shredded pair of button fly Levi cutoffs, the butt so worn they were threadbare under the back left pocket. On top, she wore a boy's v-neck undershirt with no bra. Jenny's mouth dropped open at the sight of Seven's muscular legs when she knelt to retrieve a cookie sheet from under the oven.

Seven had to call Jenny's name twice before the young woman realized she was being spoken to. Jenny jerked her attention back to earth. "Sorry. What did you say?"

"I said your cheeks are all flush. Maybe the wine is making you warm."

Jenny was momentarily embarrassed because she knew the real reason her cheeks were flush. Then it occurred to her she didn't need to be embarrassed anymore. They were lovers now. She could take action if she wanted to. "You're right," she said and placed her glass on the counter. She took Seven's hand in hers and towed her into the living room. A slow spin and a little shove later the older woman found herself lying on the couch, held in place by the weight of a focused blonde.

"What...about...dinner?" Seven managed to get out during the assault on her lips.

"Anything out there that's gonna burn the house down?"

"No...oof." Jenny couldn't get naked fast enough.

The couch turned out to be quite comfortable. Then there was the thick wool rug in front of the living room fireplace. After that, the second floor landing. Then, the third floor landing. Eventually they made it to the master bedroom where they spent the rest of the darkest hours on a feather cloud lost in the most pleasurable of endeavors.

At sunrise, Seven returned to the kitchen and finished making dinner. She brought the tray into bed, laden with a heaping bowl of Carbonara and a plate of hot garlic bread. They teased each other as they took turns sharing the same fork until no more room or energy to lift the utensil remained.

As they settled in, Seven teased, "If you were a rock band, you'd be Joy Division." She punctuated the remark by nipping at the division that had recently given her so much joy.

Jenny laughed and replied, "If you were a rock band, you'd be the Sex Pistols."

They were enjoying their new game. Seven's turn. "If you were a rock band, you'd be Concrete Blonde."

Jenny's turn. "If you were a rock band, you'd be the Violent Femmes." They fell into laughter.

With the empty tray deposited nearby, Seven rolled over and drew Jenny into the protective safety of her arms. The front of her body pressed snugly against the smaller woman's back, her knees tucked under her, creating the feeling of being fully wrapped in tall, warm, beautiful blue-eyed security blanket.

Just as the spent couple was about to drift off to sleep, Seven's low voice asked, "Jen, do you remember how my father used to always quote classic rock lyrics and ancient Greek philosophers?"

"Mmhm."

"He told me once Aristotle said a true friend is one soul in two bodies. Do you believe that's true?"

"Now more than ever," Jenny whispered, and drifted off to sleep. Seven soon followed, a smile of contentment on her face.

Epilogue

ONE MONTH LATER

"Sev," Jenny said, nervously.

"Mmhm?" The taller woman pressed herself against the shorter one's back and spoke closely into her ear. The friction on her breasts sent a thrill to her gut. "What is it, baby?"

Jenny shivered at the contact, the sensation of a warm breath on her neck sending tingles up her spine. "I...I don't know if I can do this."

Seven looked down over her lover's shoulder and slowly slid her strong hands around the girl's waist, coming to rest on a strap that hugged the young woman's thighs. "Sure you can, Pumpkin Head. You're fearless, remember?"

"I mean...I...I...I mean I haven't really had long to think about it, and now that we're doing it, I'm not sure I'm ready." Jenny was beginning to breathe faster as the hands tugged and pulled on the harness surrounding her body. One of Seven's hands slid over her abdomen, just above where the butterflies were rapidly multiplying. She rubbed the flat of her palm in slow, calming circles over the nervous woman's belly.

"It's gonna be great, lover. You'll see. I bet after the first time you'll want me to take you there again and again."

"Really?" She asked doubtfully as her heavy breathing graduated to full out hyperventilation.

"Of course." Seven kissed her on the neck and nibbled an earlobe as she ran her fingers under the straps once more to make sure they were snug, but not too tight.

"I think you're getting some sort of kinky thrill out of this, Sev. You are, aren't you?" Jenny's voice elevated a notch as she felt Seven's knees press into hers, urging her forward slightly.

"Abso-freakin'-lutely."

"Oh god." Jenny started to whine a little as the combination of adrenaline, and the feel of her lover's body pressed against her urged her senses to spin out of control.

Seven wrapped her strong arms around the young woman's waist and pulled her closer. Jenny leaned her head back to rest on the shoulder behind her. She closed her eyes for a moment and took several deep, calming breaths.

Seven's heart rate began to climb as well, as she leaned into her lover's ear and whispered, "Do you trust me, Jenny?" There was a smile in her voice.

"Yes...Yes! You know I do." The sensation grew bolder. Jenny felt her heart beat pounding in her neck, through her chest, between her legs.

The pressure behind her increased and she was forced to take another shuffling step forward. "Oh god," she exhaled heavily.

Through the fog of her rapid breathing, she heard a wicked chuckle in her ear. Seven snaked a hand up to her breast and squeezed, pinching a nipple between her fingers to get her lover's attention off what lay ahead. Jenny gasped and flashed a 'don't you dare' look over her shoulder. Her lips were caught and held in a powerful kiss.

"Technically it's not too late to say no." Seven gave her one last out.

"You...you want this, don't you?"

"You know I do."

"Okay. Then let's do it. Now, before I lose my nerve." Seven applied a little more pressure and they inched forward once again.

Blue eyes locked onto green as one face sprouted a tremendous smile and the other a nervous twitch. They inched forward.

"Jenny?" Another tender kiss on the neck. The woman in front could feel her lover's heart pounding into her back.

"Yeah?" Panting now. *God I'm thirsty.*

"There's one more little thing I need to say before I push us both over the edge."

"O...Okay, baby. I'm all ears. Do....do I need to pull something, or..."

"No. Just listen." One last small push and it would be too late to turn back.

"Okay," Jenny panted. She swallowed several times to prepare her throat for the scream she knew was coming.

Seven reached around to her lover's front and took hold of Jenny's left hand, pulling it behind her. She slipped an elegantly engraved, platinum Tiffany band from her pocket and slid it over the girl's ring finger.

The feeling of cool metal gliding over her skin caught Jenny by surprise. For a moment, she forgot the position she was in, and stared numbly at the gorgeous band on her finger.

"Will you marry me?" A deep and vibrant voice said into her ear.

Then the final tiny shove and she was falling.

Her feet left solid material, the howling wind stealing her voice as the earth rose to meet them. She screamed so loud, she would surely have broken glass if she'd been near any. Her adrenaline induced yell of ahhh morphed into a prolonged yes, which turned to screaming laughter as she fell toward the earth at a hundred and twenty miles per hour.

"Woohoohoo!" Jenny heard Seven shriek from four inches behind her left ear. "Isn't this fantastic?"

"Oh my gaaahd! Did you just ask me to marry you?" Jenny screamed over the deafening wind.

"Yes! Did you just accept?"

"Yes! Oh my gaaa ha ha haaaaa! Wooo!" Jenny's hooting and laughter was not lost to the howling noise.

Seven pulled the ripcord, deploying the parachute and slowing their fall to a reasonable rate of descent. The lovers turned to face each other as best they could while strapped in the tandem harness. Smiling lips met as they glided safely toward the earth.

About the Author

Leslie is originally from Michigan, spent her high school and college years in Texas, and now lives in sunny South Florida with her partner of 25 years and Biscuit the crazy Westie. A degree in journalism led to a career as a copywriter and creative director in the advertising and marketing industry. She includes completing the New York City Marathon (slowly) and climbing Mt. Kilimanjaro (also slowly) amongst her greatest accomplishments. Leslie wrote her first short story at the age of ten and received her first A++ in any subject outside of gym or band, so setting forth a love of storytelling. Personal interests include reading, scuba diving, and visiting Canada and Key West as often as possible.